TIME TURNS

Out of Time, Book Four

C.B. Lewis

A NineStar Press Publication

Published by NineStar Press
P.O. Box 91792,
Albuquerque, New Mexico, 87199 USA.
www.ninestarpress.com

Time Turns

Copyright © 2019 by C.B. Lewis
Cover Art by Natasha Snow Copyright © 2019
Edited by Elizabetta McKay

Printed in the USA
First Edition
September, 2019

Print ISBN: 978-1-951057-46-6

Also available in eBook, ISBN: 978-1-951057-43-5

As a consultant analyst for the most technologically advanced firms in the country, Danny Ferguson knows he's seen a lot of crazy stuff, but nothing comes close to his newest position at the Temporal Research Institute, the world's foremost time travel organisation.

The corrupted piece of code Ferguson found on the TRI's closed network is a serious concern for Lysander O'Donohue, the director of the TRI. Unable to trust his own people—any one of whom might be the source—he's forced to put all his trust in Danny to solve the mystery of the corrupt code and find the identity of the enemy within.

But when an unexpected temporal gate opens, a straightforward code analysis becomes something a lot more complicated.

To Gus, for much hand-holding through the first three books.

Chapter One

THEY SAID THE veins of Danny Ferguson ran with coffee.

He told them to sod off as he downed his second espresso.

Cassandra snickered as she poured some milk into her own cup of tea. "Well, when you over-caffeinate and give yourself a heart attack and die, don't come crying to me."

"Ha!" Danny struck a dramatic pose, gazing into the distance. "I'm immortal!"

"You're a knob," Shiv said with a snort.

Danny ran his finger around the inside of his cup, catching the dregs, and licked them off. "Jealousy doesn't suit you, Shiv." He rinsed out the cup and set it down to dry. "Catch you at lunch."

"One day," Cassandra called after him as he headed towards the canteen door, "you'll take your full tea break like a normal human being."

Danny spun around. "And one day, you'll beat my stats and get my bonus!" he called back and then widened his eyes in mock shock. "And one day, pigs'll fly!"

"Knob!" Shiv repeated.

Danny grinned as he headed out into the hall.

The caffeine had kicked in already, giving him a nice buzz. He didn't need it, but sometimes, a jump-start didn't hurt when he was stuck on monitoring all day. It was the dullest part of the job, but he could hardly be on coding every day. It was only fair to give everyone else a chance to catch up.

He'd been working with IDD—International Digital Development— for nearly a decade, straight out of his PhD. They needed people with a good eye for coding and anomalies and had gotten his attention with a stupidly high salary that had exceeded all expectations.

Still, they couldn't say he wasn't amazing at his job.

He stopped at the door and waited for the scan to sweep his face, then held his fingertips over the sensor, tapping the pattern for the week. The door slid open, and he wandered into the sprawling office he shared with three other coders.

"What'd I miss?"

Ravi glanced up through the projection in front of him, raising his eyebrows. "In the ten minutes you were gone?"

"Rav farted," Ekaterina said, pausing her own screen. "So much excitement."

Ravi rolled his eyes at her. "Nothing. You missed nothing."

Danny wasn't surprised.

Monitoring could be bloody tedious. His quad had the week's rotation on monitoring: a full day's shift of sitting and auditing code for external clients, assessing for glitches and anomalies overlooked by the computers. Sometimes, there could be minor problems. Once in a while, it was a bug that could—if left alone—start a chain reaction and break everything. Mostly, it meant sitting on your arse all day, admiring the amazingly complex codes some of their clients had come up with.

He settled in his seat, reclining the chair back as far as he could.

The chair had been one of his greatest triumphs.

When he started working at IDD, he had one of the usual workstations with a standard ergonomic monstrosity of a seat—the 'in' thing for any office. Maybe they were scientifically good for you, but Danny hated it. He'd end up on his feet all day, pacing as he scanned the code, and, apparently, distracting people.

He had to sit, his manager had insisted because everyone else needed to concentrate too. Danny had agreed, and he'd ordered a better chair, paid for by himself. The fact that he chose the biggest, comfiest reclining armchair in the building was a minor technicality.

His boss had hit the roof about it, but Danny cheerfully argued the semantics. It ensured he worked his best; his numbers had shot up since he'd gotten it; no one was being distracted; and he'd paid for it out of his own pocket, so no harm done. He ended up winning the right to keep the chair.

Thus began a long and glorious rivalry with his line manager.

He pulled the projection of his latest project up in front of him, wrapped it around the front of the chair, and set it scrolling. This particular vast batch came from some anonymous external client. He'd worked with their stuff before. Once you were familiar with a particular style of code, you didn't easily forget it.

Sometimes, they were told who the clients were.

Most of the time, they were left in the dark.

They could make guesses, but it was anyone's money because unless some big news story broke as a result of something they'd uncovered, the likelihood of finding out the client's identity fell somewhere between slim and nil.

Danny put on some Rachmaninoff in his headphones and settled back to focus on the code whirling around him. Beautiful, complex, and intricate with layer upon layer folded into it, whoever had written it had to be doing some incredibly hi-tech stuff.

Some time later, someone yanked his foot.

Through the screen, he could see Ravi.

Danny paused the scrolling screen and lifted his headphones. "Aye?"

"Lunch?"

Danny checked how much he had left on the file in front of him. "I'll finish this off first. Half an hour, give or take."

Ravi glanced at the clock. "Sorry, mate. I'm too hungry. I'll catch you after."

Danny waved him off, setting the file in motion again.

Fifteen minutes later, he realised his lunch might have to be delayed. Thirty minutes later, he was sure of it. An hour later, he was swearing the air blue as he picked apart the code and tried to work out where the anomaly had started.

Whoever had messed with it had gone in deep and hidden it well, layered in so neatly he'd almost missed it.

Four and a half hours later, his stomach growling, he sat in front of his boss as Carrigan scrutinised the file and the cascades of red-marked issues Danny had managed to find. He wasn't certain he'd caught everything, but whatever was going on with the data, someone had manipulated the client's system.

"This is all one issue?"

"Looks like it." Danny confirmed. "Whoever did it wanted to hide in plain sight—made dozens of little adjustments, easy to overlook because they didn't stand out individually. But put them all together, and that's what we've got."

Carrigan shook her head in disbelief. "They're not going to be happy about this." She glanced up at Danny. "You've worked with this company's files before. I'm guessing you figured out that much."

"I spotted it," Danny agreed. "Three months back, aye?"

"Is it possible you overlooked anything like this in those files? Something you missed?"

Danny gave Carrigan a look. "*Really*? You have to ask?"

Carrigan snorted. "So, that's a no?"

"If there was anything to be found, I would have found it." Danny's stomach growled. He pressed his hand to it. "Mind if I bugger off to the canteen while you're catching up? I'm starving."

Carrigan waved towards the door. "I'll contact the client and let them know. Be back here in half an hour."

Danny gratefully headed out of the office. First stop was the loo, then the canteen, which was deserted since the evening staff were on their way in and the morning staff were leaving. Most people didn't hang about for dinner.

He stacked a tray and claimed one of the seats by the window. The three chocolate mousses—a private reward for a shitload of work—were balanced out by the chicken salad and fruit juice. He'd started with the mousses, and if anyone judged him for it...well, sod them.

Outside, the sunset cast stretching shadows over the London skyline, pale beams of light breaking through the heavy grey clouds that said it'd be pissing down soon.

He pensively licked chocolate off the spoon. At least he'd be heading home soon. Carrigan could talk to the client and give Danny an update before he left, but it wasn't as if there was any more he could do tonight.

He'd get back to the flat, nip down the gym for a bit, and then do anything but stare at a screen all night.

When he got back to Carrigan's office, the woman had a call open. Audio only, but Danny wasn't surprised. The poor old bat already had a dozen screens projected over her desk, and from the sound of it, she'd sent them on to their client to spread the shit around.

"Right." Carrigan frowned, her grey-salted brows pulling together. "That's...unorthodox."

"Given the circumstances, I consider it necessary." A man with a soft-spoken American-accented voice said. "Discuss the matter with your colleague, and if he's amenable, I'll make the arrangements."

Carrigan terminated the call and glanced across the desk at Danny. "Well, you're either going to love me or hate me for this."

"That's...ominous."

"The client wants you to go up there and work in-house for a few days. Weeks if necessary."

Danny gaped at her. "Eh?"

"My thoughts exactly." Carrigan pushed her fingers through her sandy hair. "If there's a security issue, they want to clear it up in-house. The CO believes that if you can access all their coding data, you may be able to pinpoint a source."

"But we don't go in-house," Danny said, and then a horrible sneaking suspicion crept up on him. "Have you got me working on government stuff?"

Carrigan looked shifty. "Not exactly, but it's...complicated."

Danny scratched his cheek. "And this would be monitoring for as long as I'm there?"

"As far as I know," Carrigan said with a sigh. "Look, I know it's a terrible assignment, but you're the one who spotted the anomaly, and you're the one they want there."

Danny leaned back in the chair. "They really want me, eh?" He folded his arms over his chest. "So what do I get?"

Carrigan gave him a look. "If this is about the bloody chair again, do you want me to promise I won't touch it?"

Danny inclined his head. "It's a start. What about travel? Will I have a commute? Is it far? Do I get compensated for any extra travel? Do I get put up somewhere if it's not nearby?"

"Ah." Carrigan frowned. "I can't tell you exactly where but..."

Danny groaned. "So it's in the backside of nowhere then?"

"Just a minute." Carrigan's fingers flew across one of the screens, and she sent off a message. "Can't hurt to ask."

"Do I even get to know who I'd be working for?"

"Not until you get there."

"Sounds like I'm joining spies." He made his accent stronger as he said, "The name's Fergushon, Danny Fergushon. Shaken not shtirred."

"This isn't a laughing matter, Danny." The screen blinked with an incoming message. Carrigan flicked it open, and Danny read it—backwards—through the transparent projection.

"Manchester?" He swung forward to study it more closely. "Not a chance in hell! If I wanted to stay up north, I would have stayed in Paisley!"

"Danny—"

"Look, tell him he can take anyone else. I'm not going all the way back up there."

"Danny—"

"No! He can't expect me to—"

"Danny!" Carrigan rotated the projection and scaled up the bottom half of the message and the lump sum he would receive if he could temporarily relocate and identify the problem in-house.

Danny stared at it. There were a lot of zeros. "Fuck me..."

"Does it change things?"

"Aye..." Danny counted the zeroes again and then met Carrigan's eyes through the projection. "What the hell have you got me into?"

Chapter Two

WHEN IT FELT like the world wasn't going to plan, Lysander followed the example of one of his role models and indulged in a cup of Earl Grey tea, hot.

He'd always found something soothing about it, the warmth and the flavour. As he drank, it gave him time to consider the current problem laid at his feet and to remember he had dug himself a hole and chosen to step into it.

Once, he'd have had someone to refer it up to. Now, he perched at the top of the tree as Director of the Temporal Research Institution.

Around two decades earlier, the news broke that the TRI did far more than research history: they used time travel to verify historical events in person. When the public learned about it, they went justifiably nuts that a small group had been secretly using such incredible technology for whatever they wanted.

An international team formed the Supervisory Board, letting Lysander get a foot in the door. The Board was there to maintain neutral oversight of the TRI, to ensure no one could tamper with historical events as the world knew them, while also managing assigned historical research time-jumps.

Tampering had been attempted once, before the TRI was forced to go public. An agent had taken it upon himself to stop a World War. Instead, by ignoring the bigger picture, he ended up caught up in the plot he'd tried to stop and blamed for the part he'd played. The guilt had destroyed him.

And now...

Lysander sipped his tea.

The TRI facilities were in a closed compound. All the systems were run on private networks. Any coding had to be accessed internally. If someone had messed with the code, it could only be a member of staff. Maybe more than one, which was an unexpected concern.

He turned the delicate china cup, balanced against his fingertips, warm and smooth to the touch.

After successfully ousting the former director, he'd worked carefully for years to bring the Supervisory Board and the TRI into a more harmonious relationship. Someone trying to undermine it all—and him—was...irritating.

The IDD coder who had identified the corrupt code would be arriving in three days.

Bringing an outsider in-house was risky, but if there was someone working against them, it felt wiser to deal with it internally. In any other situation, the coding staff would liaise with security to fix any errors, but when any one of them could be responsible, it was impossible to know who to trust.

Lysander had considered putting out a call to Mariam Ashraf, the former director. She'd been with the TRI since its inception, and if a situation like this had ever arisen before, she'd have known about it. Unfortunately, with her retirement, she'd signed a dozen waivers to be sure she would never discuss TRI business outside the facilities. If Lysander was seen calling her in, it would raise a lot more questions among the staff.

His monitor pinged, and he turned his chair around.

"Fana?"

"Sir," his assistant's voice rang through the link, "the AM team is ready for departure."

The teams had two jumps scheduled per day. Occasionally, he went and watched. Even if he was responsible for all global time travel, it never stopped being a thrill to see it happen right in front of him.

He sometimes wondered what it would be like to go back and see where his family had come from before decades of war had destroyed so much of it. Maybe visit the ruins he'd hiked through when they were thriving cities. He couldn't, though, as much as he wanted to. The rules and regulations about who could go back were strict. He would be disqualified at the first hurdle.

"I'll sit this one out, thanks, Fana."

He set his teacup down, staring into middle distance.

Plans needed to be put in place. The IDD operative would need to be accommodated and briefed. It would be easy enough to find someone to supervise him, but the issue arose in knowing whom to trust with the information about the corrupted code.

As far as Lysander knew, staff satisfaction was at a record high. He delegated tasks but always kept one hand on the reins. If problems of any kind showed up, whether reported officially or through the gossip network, he kept eyes on them.

Either no one had any idea about their code-hacker or the people who did had shifted their loyalties.

It had the potential to be a serious problem.

Lysander tapped his fingers in an erratic beat on the edge of the desk.

It would just take one person talking, and the culprit could go to ground. It could be anyone as well. Better to play all his cards close to his chest and keep the situation between him and the IDD agent. It would stop things getting complicated and suspicious across the agency. That meant a cover.

The staff knew about the IDD and the external monitors checking the coding for irregularities. It had only started in the last year when there'd been glitches between TRI coding and some of the external technology they'd imported. Neutral eyes spotted those problems better than people who used TRI coding on a daily basis.

Technically, the IDD monitor needed to be familiar with the code.

Lysander smiled. Well, it was an option.

He touched a glowing light on his desk. "Fana, find out if Ben Sanders is available. I need a word."

An hour later, the man appeared in his doorway.

Lysander brushed aside the personnel file he'd been reading. "I hope I'm not dragging you away from anything vital."

Ben sat down opposite Lysander. "Reconfiguring the new gate design. I think we may be able to decrease the energy input if I've got the calculations right, and I might've solved the problem I had with the timer programming as well."

Those developments were both good news, though they were going to be put on hold for the time being. The code issue needed to be dealt with first.

"For now, I'll need to take you off the R and D," Lysander said. "I hate to do it at this point, but I have someone I need you to train."

Ben raised his eyebrows in surprise, and Lysander couldn't blame him. Of all the people who worked in the TRI, Ben Sanders knew the system better than anyone. His late father created it, and Ben had grown up tinkering with it since childhood. Using him to train someone was on a par with asking a rocket scientist to teach someone how to turn on an engine, but there was no one better in Lysander's opinion. If anyone could get the IDD operative up to speed and fast, it'd be Ben.

"It's not the new kid, is it?"

It took Lysander a moment to recall the young man who had been brought in on Jacob Ofori's request. Mackenzie Robertson. It didn't happen often, but, once in a while, someone got headhunted by senior TRI staff for their skills.

"No," he confirmed. "Not him." He couldn't help noticing the relief on Ben's face. "Is there a problem I should know about?"

"Not really. It's just—" Ben tugged his earlobe with a frown. "I don't know. Normally when we pick up someone so young, it's because they have a skill we need. From what I've seen of the kid—" He laughed ruefully. "I'm probably too used to being surrounded by insane geniuses. This one seems kind of ordinary."

Lysander chuckled. "You're spoiled for choice with smart people here," he pointed out with a half-smile. "You know the requisition requirements. He wouldn't have been headhunted if there wasn't something there."

"Mm." Ben cocked his head. "So who am I playing teacher to?"

"You know the IDD have been monitoring our code."

"Of course," Ben said. "I don't know how they can be expected to do that when they don't know—" He eyed Lysander suspiciously. "What does training have to do with the IDD?"

Lysander had expected Ben to make the jump. It made things easier to let him make his own assumptions and work from there. "The IDD executive feels the same way. They've requested to have one of their operatives trained in-house so they can familiarise themselves with our coding system."

Ben groaned, leaning back in his chair. "You know I don't think the IDD are necessary."

"I know, but with those glitches last year, we need to be sure." Lysander transferred the personnel file across to Ben, who leafed through it. "This is the one they're sending."

"Sending? Not asking if they can send?" Ben peered through the projection.

"Too late for that, I'm afraid," Lysander said smoothly. "They only had a narrow window available. They'll have him up here in a few days."

"Ugh." Ben flicked through the file. "Well, at least they're sending someone with half a brain. That's a start."

"Half a brain? The man has a PhD."

Ben snickered. "Like that's hard." He shut down the file. "Sounds like he's going to be an interesting addition."

"Mm. I need him up to speed as soon as possible. The sooner we get him trained, the sooner we can get rid of him and get on with our work."

"Which is why I'm the poor bugger who gets to train him?" Ben guessed. "Your generosity never fails to stun me."

Lysander laughed. "If you want a job done well, then you pick the right *tool* for the task." He unfurled a hand in Ben's direction. "Case in point."

Ben pushed himself back to his feet. "Sometimes I wonder why I like you."

Lysander looked up at him with all the grave innocence he could manage. "Because I'm a kind and generous manager who listens to your every concern?"

Ben snorted. "I think it's because you're so full of bullshit," he said, grinning. "Can't help admiring that." He braced one hand on the back of the chair. "D'you need anything else, or can I get back to my gate?"

Lysander shook his head. "That's all. I'll let you know when your new project arrives."

Ben clutched one hand to his heart. "I'll be waiting with bated breath."

Lysander smiled as the younger man left. Having Ben to deal with the problem would definitely make things a lot easier.

Chapter Three

IT WAS RAINING as Danny's train pulled into the central station in Manchester.

Of course it bloody was.

The city was steeped in grey cloud but, thankfully, he didn't have far to go. A message on his Leaf indicated a pod would be waiting for him, and as he walked down the lines of passenger pods waiting outside the station, a beacon illuminated on one of them, and the door opened.

As soon as he stacked his case and backpack and sat down, the door closed. The pod slid out of the parking bay and shuttled off into the lunchtime traffic.

Danny watched the city glide by. He'd been to Manchester in the past, and he'd enjoyed himself there. Plenty to do, if you had the time for it. He had hoped he'd have a place somewhere near the city centre, but as the shuttle headed east and away, he had a sinking feeling it would be out in the sticks.

Carrigan hadn't been able to tell him anything about who he would be working for. It had gotten her all red-faced and sweating, which made Danny think it had to be government. Definitely something more confidential than a run-of-the-mill business.

As the city gave way to the suburbs and the suburbs gave way to fields, Danny slouched down in the seat. Backside of nowhere felt like an accurate description. He put his earphones on, muffling the hum of the pod, and settled back to listen to some Handel.

Half an hour later, the pod pulled into a huge building that turned out to be nothing so much as a giant parking lot. The door slid open, and Danny warily climbed out, peering around. Dozens of personal pods hung in rows along the ceiling, suspended from the orderly lines of grav bays. Maybe hundreds.

The place was massive.

His pod started beeping, and a metallic voice advised, "Please remove all luggage and personal items."

Danny hesitated, frowning. There were only two doors in the place—the main entrance and a closed double door about five metres away. There was nowhere else to go, and, as far as he could see, no one around.

To his relief, the double doors opened.

"Mr. Ferguson." A slight blonde woman in a sleek suit stood on the other side. "I apologise for the delay. Please come with me."

Danny grabbed his case and backpack. "So this isn't the end of the line?"

She gave him an amused look. "Not quite."

Danny followed her through the double doors into a concourse of what appeared to be a subway station. Clean and shiny, it had two single-lined tracks. Magna-tracks. Not electric. Very unusual. Magna-transports were moved entirely by magnetic force. Not something that could be hacked or easily interfered with.

"This way," his guide said, leading him to a waiting train. Four streamlined carriages stood alongside the platform, each one with enough seats to fit at least forty people, which meant they were going somewhere with a train that could carry at least 160? Combined with the number of pods in the docking bay, it gave the impression of a very big organisation indeed.

Danny sat and propped his rucksack on his case. "I'm guessing you won't tell me anything either?" She gave him a bright smile. "What about your name? Or do I call you Agent Double-Oh-Something?"

It earned him a laugh. "Sabine," she replied. "I'm Sabine Hausmann."

He offered a hand. "You already know, but Danny Ferguson."

She smiled and shook his hand. "A pleasure, Mr. Ferguson." She sat opposite him. "I've been instructed to take you to your accommodation to allow you to get settled, and then you will meet your employer."

Danny's heart sank. "So this isn't a commuting gig, then?"

"For your convenience and for the sake of security, this is the better option," Sabine said.

Danny sighed gloomily. Definitely no chance of going out to the clubs in the city, then. He gazed out the windows as they shuttled along. The tracks were contained within transparent tunnels, which let him see the rolling landscape. All very...rural. Nice, if you liked that kind of thing.

There was still no indication of where he was going when the train drew into a station fifteen minutes later. It was as bright and sterile as the other end of the line.

Sabine didn't wait to see if he was following as she led him up a ramp and out into the bleak grey daylight.

Turned out he'd guessed right about the scale of the place. They were in the middle of a vast compound. In one direction, a massive, industrial-sized warehouse jutted up with at least four levels. In another, a tower block with glass frontage. A huge building with at least a dozen storeys and two wings lay directly ahead, beyond a courtyard with a fountain.

The final building seemed to be their destination.

H-block, Sabine explained, was the residential area of the facility. Within ten minutes, he'd received his security pass, the digital key to his suite—not room, he noted—and ascended up to the ninth floor in a pristine high-speed elevator.

"We'll give you an hour to get your bearings and have something to eat," Sabine said as she led him down a long, airy corridor. "I'll come back to take you across to meet Mr. O'Donohue then."

He glanced around distractedly, taking in his surroundings. The name of the building suddenly made sense. Based on the layout, it had to look like a giant *H* from above. The place felt like a high-end apartment complex. There were maybe a dozen doors, and from the space between them, each set of rooms had to be pretty spacious. He tried to school his reaction when they reached his door and he opened it.

The place turned out to be better than he'd expected—not a suite, but a full-blown, fully furnished flat. The wide, brightly lit living room with kitchenette had views overlooking the courtyard. Off to one side, he could see the bedroom through an open door and to the other, a generously sized bathroom. He could've fit his flat in London inside it with room to spare.

He left his case by the door as he walked into the living room.

"We hope this will be sufficient." From the tone of Sabine's voice, she knew exactly how good it was.

Danny rocked on the balls of his feet. He couldn't let them think he'd been won over so easily, not when he'd been thrown into the deep end and, as far as he knew, the deep end might be made of lava. "It'll do." He turned to face her. "Anything else I should know?"

"The in-house Leaf will provide you with details of the available facilities. There's a canteen downstairs, but if you prefer to order in to cook for yourself, it can be arranged." Sabine glanced at her watch. "I'll be back to pick you up in an hour."

He waited until the door closed before running through to explore the rest of the flat. It could have been a show home in one of those fancy flats down in the Docklands. The bedroom had enough storage space for the biggest clothes hoarder, despite the massive king-size bed in the middle of the floor.

The in-house Leaf was on the table in the dining area of the living room, and he opened it up, unsurprised they already had his fingerprint and retinal scan on record.

Apparently, they had a pool in the basement and high-end gym facilities fancy enough to make his gym-mates in London weep with envy. He also had access to a massive digital archive of books, television shows, and films. And there were options for every TV channel available, up to and including porn.

For a fancy and so far unnamed prison, it had everything a man could want, except the ability to get out and about.

He scratched at his beard thoughtfully.

They'd provided all the comforts of home, but they had still pressed him to move halfway up the country and stashed him inside a locked compound. On the one hand, he couldn't help being a wee bit impressed. They didn't do things by halves. On the other hand, he didn't have a clue where he was or what he was actually meant to be doing. It always got his back up when he didn't have control in a situation.

Carrigan had told him to go up, be on his best behaviour, and get the job done.

Well, two out of three counted, didn't it? As if he ever made things simple for the management at home anyway.

He just needed to put his foot down, making it clear he wasn't some corporate drone who'd jump on command. If they wanted his best work, they would have to understand he'd want to lay some ground rules too.

First things first, though...

He took his pass and the Leaf and headed down to the canteen.

It matched the scale of the outside of the building and, like the rest of the building, seemed to have been abandoned. There were long rows of tables for dozens of people as well as smaller individual ones, but not a soul in sight.

Danny wandered over to the ordering station and examined the options. From the look of it, they had a pretty diverse staff with options for vegetarians, vegans, lactose-free, gluten-free, Halal, and Kosher. He picked out a Thai curry and, while he waited at the pickup area, skimmed through more information on his Leaf.

Nothing gave away his whereabouts, and he wondered if maybe the canteen had been cleared so he wouldn't have anyone to poke for answers. There was no reason for the secrecy now, not when he'd let them lock him inside their closed compound.

By the time Sabine showed up to collect him, he still had no idea.

"If you'll come with me."

She led him back across the wide courtyard to the towering building looming over the arrival station. There were a few people in the foyer and halls, but none of them paid any attention to him, which seemed a bit rude. But then, to be fair, he only noticed them because he'd been scanning the walls for any clue about where on earth he was. He hated going in blind.

The elevator swept them up to the top level of the building. Tinted glass walls ran the length of the corridor, only broken by pale columns and the occasional door. Several of the offices were obviously occupied, but some were empty and open. Danny spotted a rooftop garden as they headed along the central corridor.

Sabine led him into a waiting area and smiled at the tall black woman behind the desk. She was striking with her hair braided in an ornate coronet around her head. "Mr. Ferguson from the IDD to see Mr. O'Donohue."

"Mr. O'Donohue is on a call." The other woman glanced at Danny. "If you'll take a seat, Mr. Ferguson, Mr. O'Donohue will be available in a moment."

Sabine gave him a quick smile. "I expect I'll see you soon," she said before slipping away.

Danny sat on one of the elegant armchairs. The whole office made a statement: we're successful and wealthy, and you wish you could be like this. There were paintings—originals, not prints—on the walls, and ambient music played so softly it was barely noticeable. *Purcell. Interesting choice.*

He was still sitting there five minutes later, hands folded, thumbs tapping against each other, when the secretary's comm link chirped. She offered him a slight smile.

"Mr. O'Donohue will see you now."

Danny rose and entered the office.

Whatever he'd been expecting, it definitely wasn't Mr. O'Donohue.

O'Donohue stood by a cabinet, pouring a tumbler of water from a glass jug, and turned with a half-smile. It took everything Danny had not to stare at him. It was daft. He'd seen good-looking men before. Shagged a few of them as well, but he'd never seen anyone on O'Donohue's level.

Blue-black hair, streaking silver at the temples, was drawn back from a face that looked as if it had been sculpted by Michelangelo. Everything about him seemed pretty much bloody symmetrical, from his features and his neat little beard to the ornate hairsticks holding his hair up and the suit tailored to fit him like a fancy glove. Smooth light-brown skin made him appear almost ageless, if not for the fine lines webbed around his dark eyes.

Somehow, he also managed to give the impression of height, but when Danny got close enough, he realised he had at least four inches on the man.

"Mr. Ferguson." Danny recognised the voice and accent as the one on Carrigan's phone. He offered a manicured hand. "A pleasure to finally put a face to the name."

Danny shook his hand, surprised at how cool O'Donohue's skin was. He tried to gather his scattered wits. Right. Time to take back some of the control here. "You too." He followed O'Donohue's lead as his potential new boss sat down in one of the two armchairs near the window. Casual. Informal. He could deal with that. "I was surprised to get the invitation."

O'Donohue's smile altered slightly. "Yes. We rarely issue them, it's true." He ran an index finger around the rim of his glass. "How do you find your accommodation? We try to cater to all possible needs."

Danny shifted on the seat. He wanted to be asking the questions, specifically about the kind of work he'd been caught up in, but the accommodation seemed like a good place to start. "I wasn't told I'd be stuck in a compound in the middle of nowhere," he replied. "The flat's nice, but I can't guarantee my best work if I can't get out and let off steam once in a while."

Mr. O'Donohue inclined his head. "You understand there are... security issues which must be taken into consideration."

"I get that." Danny leaned forward, propping his forearms on his thighs and folding his hands together. "Here's the thing, though. You've pulled me out of my life, got me all the way up here, and now I'm finding out I'm pretty much your prisoner."

Mr. O'Donohue's expression gave nothing away. "A well-paid prisoner." He balanced his glass on the arm of the chair, gazing at it as he held it there with the tips of his index finger and thumb on the rim. "Let me be clear. For the sake of your social life, you would risk your opportunity to work here?" His gaze returned to Danny's. "Am I correct?"

Danny sat back a little. Okay. Not quite as easy to play with as Carrigan. "I didn't say that."

The enigmatic smile returned. "I see." O'Donohue picked up his glass and took a sip. "You will accept the accommodation provided, then?"

If it meant accepting it or losing the job, it wasn't as if Danny had a choice. Still, better to go down fighting. "Do I get to know where 'here' is before I make the decision?"

O'Donohue studied him for what felt like an uncomfortably long time.

Across the room, the comm chimed on his desk.

"Mr. O'Donohue, the PM team are ready."

O'Donohue rose from the chair. "Come with me."

Danny rose, frowning. "You didn't answer my question."

O'Donohue slanted a sidelong glance at him. "Do you want my answer?" He set down his glass and walked towards the door.

Danny hesitated for a second, furious at himself for wanting—needing—to know the answer, then strode after him. "I'm not someone who likes cryptic bullsh—stuff."

"I'm astonished," O'Donohue said mildly, leading him back along the corridor to the elevator.

Danny snorted as they stepped into the elevator. He settled back against one of the handrails, fighting the desire to cross his arms over his chest. O'Donohue seemed to be trying to wind him up. The best he could do was pretend he didn't mind.

O'Donohue rested one hand against the rail and gazed out over the compound. "I'd consider it a favour if you could be discreet when we get to our destination."

"And tell them what exactly?" Danny inquired. "Everything I don't know?"

O'Donohue looked back at him. "You underestimate how much you *do* know." He pushed off from the rail as the elevator came to a halt. "This way."

This corridor wasn't as brightly lit as the top floor. Less visible windows in the hall and more offices and rooms in use. Definitely no garden this time around.

O'Donohue lightly brushed his fingers over a console by one of the dozens of doors and led Danny into a hive of activity. Seven people were positioned in front of projection screens around the room, some with panels hanging in front of them thick with coding that Danny recognised at once.

"Mr. O'Donohue!" One of the women hurried over. "The team is ready."

O'Donohue smiled. "We won't get in your way, Malia. Do what you need to. Pretend we're not here."

The woman returned to her station.

Danny scanned the screens, but his eyes kept coming back to the main projection in the middle of the room. It seemed out of place—a video link to what appeared to be a bunker or a warehouse or some kind of metal-plated room with something like a heavy metal doorframe in the middle of the floor.

"What's going on here?" he asked in an undertone, loath to interrupt fellow coders at work.

O'Donohue had his left arm folded over his middle, his left hand cupping his right elbow as he stroked at his goatee. "Wait a moment."

Danny frowned at him, then looked back at the main screen.

"Opening the connection in five," Malia called out.

On the edge of the screen, a countdown descended.

The coding on the screens went wild, far more complex and intricate than anything Danny had accessed, and when the count hit one, the empty doorway in the bunker flooded with light.

Danny's mouth dropped open.

"Area is clear. Team Delta, go!"

Two people ran into the frame in the bunker and stepped straight through the gateway of light. When the light winked out, they were gone. Gone. Jumped through a gate, and he'd heard rumours and stories, and now, he'd seen...

"Fuck me..." Danny breathed. "Holy fucking shit." He turned to stare at O'Donohue. "This...is this the TRI?"

O'Donohue smiled slightly. "Now, have you made your decision?"

Chapter Four

THE COCKY, OVERCONFIDENT man who had stepped into Lysander's office had vanished.

Instead, a six-foot-tall, bearded kid stood, as if in a candy store, eyes wide, staring at all the screens as they waited for the pickup. Ferguson had one fist pressed to his mouth, and he was practically bouncing on the spot.

Lesson 101 on handling a computer genius.

Lysander had been given plenty of time and warning from Carrigan about the kind of person he'd hired.

Ferguson's personnel report had made interesting reading. A certified genius, brilliant at his job, but he knew it and made sure everyone around him knew it too. Stubborn, determined to do things his way or not at all, Carrigan had advised Danny would be a handful.

Those kinds of people could be a nightmare if you didn't know to expect it. Especially, if you didn't know how to play to their ego, their confidence, and above all else, their intellect.

"Primary rendezvous in five..."

Lysander watched him from the corner of his eye. Ferguson looked like he might start hyperventilating, his eyes wide as soup bowls. Lysander saw the tiny jerk of his fist, a mini air punch, when the gate connected.

"Team Delta accounted for." Both agents were visible on the screen.

Lysander turned to face Ferguson, who didn't even notice, still staring at the screens. "Shall we return to my office?"

Ferguson blinked at him. "Oh. Right. Yes." He fell into step beside Lysander, but as they left the room, he glanced back.

Lysander hid a smile, waiting until they were in the elevator before speaking. "If you plan to return to London, I can arrange for transport to the station immediately."

"What? I never said—" Ferguson seemed to realise how he sounded and cleared his throat self-consciously. He leaned back against the handrail again, trying to appear casual. "I mean, I'm here. I might as well do the job."

Lysander kept his eyes on the view. "And the accommodation?"

A long silence fell, and he glanced at Ferguson, who had been so indignant about the 'prison.' Ferguson exhaled noisily. *A little too dramatically for good measure*, Lysander thought, amused.

"It'll be fine. I'll manage."

Lysander inclined his head. "Very good."

Ferguson wouldn't have left even if he were given a cardboard box to live in, not if his expression in the communication room was anything to go by. You could always find a way to change peoples' minds when you gave them a glimpse of something to pique their interest and offered them a chance to play with it.

Once they were back in his office, Lysander sat behind his desk and motioned for Ferguson to take the seat on the other side.

"As you can imagine, we have some very strict nondisclosure agreements in place."

Ferguson winced. "I bet."

Lysander paused for a moment, considering how to proceed. The success of the operation depended on Ferguson's discretion. "As far as the staff are aware, the IDD have sent you for in-house training on our systems, to ensure you're monitoring accurately."

Ferguson frowned. "They don't know about the problems with the code?"

"No, and until we find the culprit, I plan on keeping it that way." Lysander met Ferguson's eyes. "I need you to be as discreet as possible, which means you'll have to sit through some in-house training so no one questions it."

Ferguson sank back in the chair, a pensive expression on his face. "Do you have any idea who could be behind it?"

It was a fair question, but there were some cards he didn't need to show. "I have a few suspicions, but no one I'd put money on yet." Lysander propped his elbows on the arms of his chair and laced his fingers in front of his chest. "I know you are an intelligent man, Mr. Ferguson. I need you to use your skills to resolve this problem for me. Quickly and thoroughly."

Ferguson stroked one hand down his beard, frowning. "Well, which do you want?"

"Excuse me?"

"Quick or thorough. I can't guarantee both, so it's up to you which is more important."

"Thorough," Lysander said at once. "But if it can be done quickly, too, I would appreciate it."

For several seconds, Ferguson said nothing; then he got up from the chair and went to pour himself a glass of water. This, Lysander knew, was another of the tipping points. Ferguson liked to get his own way, according to all reports. He liked to push back against authority figures, regardless of rank.

Lysander took a moment to study him.

He had a bit more colour than some of their internal technicians. A fading tan, from the look of things. Not maintained, so probably from a vacation. He was in good shape as well. Gym, Lysander guessed. Especially from the size of his upper arms.

Otherwise, he clearly took care of himself, his beard thick but well managed, and his hair styled to give a casually effortless look. Proud of himself and his appearance, and more than a little bit cocky. It fit with everything Lysander had read about him.

"I'll need my own space," Ferguson said abruptly. "If I'm to keep this under wraps and get it done quickly, I'll need somewhere no one can bother me."

"It can be arranged," Lysander agreed. A room had already been set aside for the purpose. "We'll call it assigned study."

Ferguson sipped the water, then looked down at it. He didn't seem happy when he spoke. "I'm going to warn you now—there's a chance I won't be able to find the person behind this."

Lysander inclined his head. He'd anticipated that risk. "Can you guarantee you're going to do the best you can to find them?"

Ferguson's mouth curled up at one side. "Do I seem like someone who would work half-arsed?"

"No." Lysander smiled slightly. "But it doesn't hurt to check." A light illuminated on his desk, an incoming message. He flicked it open. "Your tutor has arrived." He motioned to the seat opposite him. "He'll give you the tour and get you started."

Ferguson returned to the seat. "He doesn't know why I'm here either?"

Lysander shook his head.

It had been a tough decision, but Ben had a bad habit of talking too much at the wrong time. Only a few months earlier at the shareholders meetings, he'd accidentally let it slip about the new gate developments. It put some people on edge and there'd been meetings with some high-ranking politicians a week later.

This time, it would be safer to keep everything on a need-to-know basis. "As far as he knows, you're here to learn. He'll be demonstrating the system and giving you the basic background in the coding we use."

"Right." Ferguson set the glass down on Lysander's desk. "So, keep the chat limited to personal stuff, surface work stuff, life and that?"

"Anything but your real reason for being here." Lysander touched the light on his desk. "Fana, let Ben know to come through."

As soon as Ben walked in, Ferguson got up and held out a hand, though Lysander recognised a bit of posing when he saw it. "All right?"

Ben grinned, shaking his hand. "All right. Ben Sanders."

Ferguson's eyes went as wide as they had in the gate room, and he didn't seem to realise he still had Ben's hand gripped in his when he turned to stare at Lysander. "Is—" He turned back to Ben, a dazed, awed expression on his face. "You're Tom Sanders's son, aren't you?"

Ben snorted in amusement. "What gave me away?"

"Ah." Lysander couldn't help laughing as Ferguson realised he hadn't let go of Ben's hand and hastily yanked his own back. "Sorry. I forgot to mention you'd be working with him."

Ferguson threw a half-hearted glare his way. "I swear to God, you're trying to see how much of a tit you can make me look by close of play."

Ben laughed aloud. "Don't worry about it," he said, patting Ferguson sympathetically on the shoulder. "He does that." He leaned a little closer. "Don't trust him just because he seems all angelic."

Lysander schooled his expression into one of innocence. "You're giving Mr. Ferguson a bad impression of me, Ben."

"Like you need the help," Ben said with a chuckle. "You need to fill me in on anything or can I steal our new boy?"

"You know all the background, I think." He raised an eyebrow at Ferguson. "Any questions?"

"Only one." Lysander made a sound of inquiry. "Are you going to call me Mr. Ferguson the whole time I'm here? Because it makes me sound like my dad and not a dashing young computer genius."

Ben snorted again. Lysander suspected it was because of the look on his own face. It took effort not to laugh at Ferguson's wide-eyed, mournful expression.

"Do you have a preference?" he asked. "You don't really strike me as a Daniel."

Ferguson blinked in horror. "God, no! Danny is fine."

"Very well." Lysander agreed. "Danny." He gestured towards him. "He's all yours, Ben."

Chapter Five

DANNY HAD NO sodding clue what to say.

It wasn't every day you met the son of the inventor of time travel.

Hell, how often did you meet a ridiculously hot man who took you into a mysterious room to reveal that, actually, he ran the only time travel agency in the world, and, by the way, if you look over there, you'll see people travelling in time? Never! That was how often!

It was all a bit much.

"Bit of a shock?"

He glanced at Ben freaking Sanders walking along beside him. He looked a little younger than Danny, a couple of inches shorter, and skinny, with a cheerful, open face and dark brown eyes under a frizz of sandy hair. Not the most intimidating person in the world. "What gave it away?"

Ben grinned. "We've been walking for two minutes, and you've been staring ahead, all googly-eyed."

Danny laughed self-consciously. "Well, aye. It's— They didn't tell me where I'd be working."

"And Ly's bloody good at dropping a bombshell," Ben said, swiping his hand over the control of the lift. "What stunt did he pull this time? Sliding the contract over the desk and letting you read the company name?"

Danny made a face as they stepped into the lift. "Took me into a room with a gate and people time travelling."

Ben burst out laughing, then hastily tried to stifle it, a hand to his mouth. "Oh Christ. He really wanted to surprise you."

On one hand, Danny wanted to be annoyed. It was a bit of a bastard thing to do to someone, to throw them off guard like that. On the other hand, O'Donohue—Ly?—didn't normally do it to new people, which meant he really wanted to get Danny's interest and keep him there.

"Is he always like that?" he inquired.

Ben chuckled. "Ly's good with people."

"Ha!"

"Oh, I don't mean nice and polite and makes you feel at home." Ben's grin widened. "He knows how people tick. He's the reason this place runs as well as it does. He knows how to get people to work. If you have a button, he'll find it and push it to get the best out of you."

Like showing someone the most high-end and inaccessible technology available with the chance to get up-close and personal with it.

"Right."

"He already found one of yours, didn't he?" Ben guessed as the lift slid to a stop.

He wasn't wrong. "I didn't fancy staying on the compound. I think he thought a demonstration would change my mind."

"Did it?"

Danny shot a crooked smile at him. "Well, I'm still here, so I'd say so." He followed Ben out into another glass-walled corridor. He glanced at the man. "No offence, but I don't know why he's got you babysitting me. I mean, it's a bit below your pay grade, isn't it?"

Ben laughed as he led Danny by door after door. "If you're going to learn about our coding and systems, he knows I'm the best teacher. I've been playing with it since I was five years old."

And the intimidation came crashing back again.

Christ, he'd barely worked out the basics to get to his favourite games by the time he turned seven, and Ben Sanders had been playing with time travel for years.

"Did your—" He hesitated.

"Yes, my dad taught me." Ben shrugged. "Don't be afraid to ask. He died more than twenty years ago. It's not as if you're poking an open wound." He pressed his hand to a console by one of the doors, which slid open.

The room on the other side was a computer tech's wet dream come true.

"Jesus..." Danny breathed, walking in.

On the left side of the room, a time gate connected to a gantry linking pieces of computers and other unfamiliar machines. If he hadn't been walked in through the door, he could easily believe he'd stumbled onto the set of a science-fiction film.

"It's a bit of a mess," Ben said, wandering over to the right side and opening up half a dozen screens across the wall. He must have noticed

Danny wasn't paying him any attention because he came back to Danny's side. "If you want to have a peek, feel free."

Danny walked forward, staring at the gateway. "It won't connect or anything, will it?"

Ben laughed. "Nah. We never give it enough juice to form a connection. It's the testing bay—to make sure we haven't made changes that'll crash the system."

Danny couldn't help himself; he reached out and ran a hand down the frame. He'd read about them. Anyone with an ounce of curiosity would have read about them. People tried to build their own and everything, but no one had pulled it off. He'd seen pictures of what happened when gates were built wrong, but this one...this was the genuine article.

"Probably expected something a bit more streamlined, eh?"

He glanced at Ben. "What?"

Ben gestured at the gate. "It's so clunky. People expect something more modern."

Danny studied the gate. The frame was a good eight inches thick, not including the casing, solid and sturdy. "With the amount of power you're putting through it, you wouldn't want something flimsy, would you?"

"Ah, a true geek," Ben said happily. "Historians always seem disappointed."

Danny rolled his eyes, running his hand reverently down the casing. "What do they expect? Holopads or some bullshit?"

"I swear I caught a seventy-something from Oxford trying to find a flux capacitor."

Danny studied the gate. A panel loosely fixed to one side with glowing numbers. He frowned, studying it. True he'd only seen a live gate for a couple of minutes via a video feed, but he couldn't remember seeing a panel like that. "Is this a new bit? I didn't see it on the gate in the jump."

"Good call." Ben sounded surprised. "All our gates have a manual control. I've been working on developing an automated timer to guarantee digital precision." He shrugged. "It might not go anywhere, since jumps don't always go smoothly, but it could be useful." He nudged Danny's shoulder with his own. "Come on. Got something a lot more interesting than an empty gate and a dodgy timer for you."

Danny turned doubtfully, wondering what could outweigh a time gate. The screens were lit up like the Blackpool illuminations, and his mouth dropped open. The gate might be impressive, but the code running across the screens was the beating heart of time travel.

"This," Ben said proudly, "is my baby brother."

The rest of the afternoon went by in a blur.

By the time Danny stumbled into his room, a stupid grin plastered all over his face, he felt like he'd ascended to cloud nine and beyond. Time travel! The coding behind it! The son of the creator behind the coding behind it!

He tipped himself over the arm of the couch and lay there, beaming at the ceiling.

To think he'd been pissed off about coming all the way up.

Now, he knew he'd have done the job without any financial incentive if they'd asked.

He hadn't moved fifteen minutes later when the door buzzed. Danny grumbled half-heartedly as he rolled off the couch and onto his feet then headed over to the door. He couldn't hide his surprise at finding Ben on the other side. "Uh..."

"You had dinner yet?" Ben inquired. "A bunch of the other coders are having a meal downstairs if you want to join us."

Danny glanced back into the room and to the Leaf he had for company. Yeah, technically he had research to do, but a man needed to eat, and it wouldn't hurt if he knew the kind of people who might be involved with the coding issue.

"You twisted my arm."

This time around, there was hardly a seat free in the canteen.

There were people of all ages and backgrounds, and at least three different languages were being spoken as he and Ben collected their food. Then Ben wove his way through the mass of people to one of the long tables.

"Fresh meat!" Ben declared as he sat and motioned to Danny to sit beside him.

Danny raised a hand in greeting to the others sitting there. They were eyeing him with interest. "All right?"

Ben waved a fork. "Danny, meet Mel, Leon, Tamara, Guy, and Janos."

"Just so you know," Danny said apologetically, "I'm never going to remember."

Guy gazed at him. "None of us remember anymore." A gawky skinhead, he looked like he might be of Chinese descent. "This place, it leaves you nothing but a shell."

Tamara smacked him on the arm with a grin. She seemed older than him, maybe mid-forties, with shocking-pink hair and tattoos peeping out from her collar and sleeves. "Don't scare the fresh meat."

Guy made a face at her. "You always ruin my fun."

"So you come from the IDD?" The man opposite Danny was watching him curiously. "We have never had someone from your department to visit before."

Danny pulled on his best cheeky chappie grin. "I go where I'm told," he said, digging in to his casserole.

The man—Janos?—glanced at Ben. "This is a new development."

Someone immediately getting suspicious? Interesting.

Danny gave Janos a quick glance over. Maybe fifty-something with grey scattered in his blond hair. Big and buff, which said he had to be a regular at a gym somewhere. Bit of an accent as well. Something European. "You been here a while, then?"

Green eyes met his. "Twenty years and we have managed fine."

Ben chuckled. "It's nothing personal, Danny. We've had problems when external staff have been involved before." He patted Danny's shoulder. "He's all right, Jan. He won't be sticking around long; he's getting his training, then heading back to London."

"And he's here what? A few weeks?" Leon inquired. He had a strong Liverpool accent and the most impressive dreadlocks Danny had seen in his life. "Will it be enough? It's not an easy code, like."

"I can hold my own," Danny said.

Danny couldn't help feeling Ben was poking fun at him when he said in a hushed voice, "He's a *doctor*."

"Well, that changes everything," Mel exclaimed, clasping her hands to her heart. A curvy woman with a mass of tumbling blonde curls, she had the deepest dimples Danny had ever seen. "A real doctor! I don't think I've seen one of them around here before! Except maybe Guy...and Leon...and Tamara...and wait, me!"

Danny snorted.

Ben gave him an amused look. "Only person here who can't match your qualifications is Jan, and that's because he's self-taught."

Danny turned his attention back to Janos. For someone to be good enough to work in the systems *and* be self-taught, he had to be some level of genius. "Seriously?"

Janos shrugged placidly. "I like machines."

"So everyone in here's a coder?"

Ben glanced around. "Agents, cleaners, techs, historians…"

"Agents?" Danny's grin strained his cheeks.

"Oh God," Tamara groaned. "They sent us a timer."

Leon propped his forearms on the table. "Are you full or part?"

"Eh?" Danny inquired, his fork in his mouth.

"Time travel fan," Guy said. He made rings with his fingers around his eyes. "Your eyes are so big. It means you're a fan."

Danny always hated being off balance. Best way to power through it was to smile and act like he didn't mind. "Half, then. I mean, it's not like I have pyjamas with clocks on them or any bullshit."

Ben seemed to be struggling not to laugh. "It happens a lot. Two days, maybe three, and it's not as shiny and exciting." He paused, searching the room. "Actually, let's get it out your system…" He rose from the chair and waved. "Qas! Qas, come here!"

"What're you doing?" Danny demanded warily as a man a few tables over got up and approached. "Did I volunteer to get hazed?"

Janos chuckled. "If it means to be handed a small and friendly puppy?"

Qas—an Arab-looking man with unruly black hair and a sunny smile on his face—probably only a couple of years older than Danny himself. "What's up?"

Ben beamed up at him. "Danny, meet Qasim. Qasim, Danny. Our new adopted IDD agent, in for training." There was mischief in his expression when he grinned at Danny. "Qasim is our best trainer and former time agent. He did—how many? Seventeen missions?"

Danny blinked at the man.

"Fifteen, not counting the last one," Qasim said, holding out a hand to Danny. "Nice to meet you."

"You're a time traveller…"

Qasim gave Ben a look. "Ben…"

Ben snickered again. "What? He was going to meet one eventually. Better to make it someone who wouldn't get pissy about it."

Danny belatedly remembered to shake Qasim's hand, still staring. But all things considered, it was justified. "Sorry," he managed to say. "Today's been a whole mess of surprises."

Qasim's smile widened, his eyes dancing. "Let me guess. Lysander O'Donohue?"

Danny laughed helplessly. "A bit."

"I helped," Ben put in.

Qasim smiled reassuringly. "Word of advice, from me to you." He beckoned Danny closer and confided, "They're both clowns, and you shouldn't trust them as far as you can throw them."

Danny liked him at once. "I'll remember that."

As Qasim returned to his own table, Ben pulled his chair in and nudged Danny. "See? Human like the rest of us."

Danny nodded, but it didn't change that he'd actually spoken to a real live time traveller. Well, another thing off the bucket list. He picked up his fork again. "So," he said, "tell me about here."

Chapter Six

"IT'S GOING WELL?"

"Yeah." Danny was sitting on the opposite side of Lysander's desk and more at ease than the last time Lysander had seen him, when he'd passed him on to Ben Sanders for tutoring.

In the four days since then, Lysander's various eyes and ears reported that Danny had mingled well with the members of the coding team, and, from the sound of things, everyone had accepted his reason for being there at face value.

"There's a lot to take in," Danny said. "Ben definitely knows what he's on about."

Lysander couldn't help smiling at that. "You could say that," he agreed. "I hear he introduced you to some of the coders."

Danny grinned. "Aye. They're a good bunch."

Lysander settled back in his seat. He tapped a knuckle to his lips. "Did any give the impression of being unhappy?"

Danny scratched thoughtfully at his beard. "I know some of them think it's a waste of time for me to be here, but most of them don't seem fussed. Janos grumbles like a bear with a sore head, but I think he likes being left to get on with stuff."

It earned a chuckle.

"He has his ways," Lysander agreed. He hadn't spent much time around Janos Nagy, but had seen him at work, and the man knew what he was doing. He also had no patience for idiots, and it showed.

"So, he's not on your list of potentials?" Danny rightly guessed.

Lysander inclined his head. It worried him that he didn't even *have* a list. Or a single suspect. It had to be someone with access and who knew the in-house coding. The TRI staff base was vast, and it didn't help that so many of their staff had the know-how to mess around with the code.

"Ben let me know you've been picking up the code pretty quickly," he said.

Danny's face broke into a delighted grin. "Aye? He never tells me if I am or not."

"All the better to keep you motivated," Lysander guessed with a small smile. "He's been impressed with your progress, but don't tell him I told you."

Danny laughed and his eyes glinted. "Right. Another of our dirty little secrets, eh? One—don't tell him I'm a secret agent. Two—don't let him know I know he's been complimenting me behind my back."

Lysander smiled, caught off guard by how disarming Danny's laugh was. "Something like that, Double-Oh-Seven."

"Are you my *M*, then?" Danny asked, bracing an arm on the desk between them. "Handling me and all that?"

The wording made Lysander raise his eyebrows, and he couldn't help being surprised and amused when he saw Danny's lips twitch. He must have realised what he'd said, and he straightened up awkwardly in the chair.

Lysander tried to be a good, restrained person, but sometimes, he couldn't help himself. He propped one elbow on the arm of his chair and rested his chin on the back of his fingers.

"I didn't know you wanted to be...handled, Mr. Ferguson."

Danny flashed a rueful grin. "Well...set myself up nicely for you, didn't I?" He self-consciously rubbed the back of his neck. "You know what I meant."

It was pretty obvious Danny really didn't like being laughed at, and Lysander had been on the receiving end often enough to know how to change the subject rather than make things worse.

"A slip of the tongue, that's all." He waved his hand dismissively as he sat up. "It can happen to anyone." He rose from his chair. "If you'll come with me, I want to show you where you'll be doing your... homework."

Danny nodded gratefully, getting up.

The room was one of the unused offices, a level down from the executive suites, not quite below Lysander's own office. A coding base and monitoring unit had been installed in the days since Danny had arrived.

"It's basic," Lysander said as they walked into the room, "but it should have everything you need."

Digital desks were inclined against one wall, and they'd installed the most up-to-date monitoring units on the market. It looked like a reclining armchair with control scanners installed in the arms.

"Is it ready to go?"

Lysander motioned towards it. "Registered to your prints and facial geometry. No one else should be able to access it."

Danny sat on the chair and pressed his hand to the scanners on the arm. Screens illuminated in front of him immediately, and he whistled under his breath as he spread out the panels to wrap around him.

"You don't do things by halves, do you?"

"The higher the quality, the smaller the risk of things going wrong," Lysander said, sitting against the edge of one of the desks and watching as Danny started skimming through the screens, sifting through the drives and files. "We've given you direct access to the coding mainframe, but, for security reasons, there's a limit to what software and systems you can activate."

Danny brushed aside the projections. "So, on my best behaviour, eh?"

Lysander smiled. "I wouldn't expect anything less."

A hint of mischief glinted in Danny's eyes. "No opening gates or that? Bugger. I wanted to sneak off for a wee nosy around in history."

"Definitely not that much access," Lysander amended with a chuckle.

Danny settled back in the chair, opened different screens up again, and ran his fingers along the projections. Ben wasn't kidding when he described Danny as a fast learner. The speed with which he went through the files and folders matched some of their experts.

"Do I just monitor things from here?" Danny suddenly inquired. "Or do you want me to try and undo some of the corrupted code if I can?"

Lysander blinked in surprise. "Do you think you'd be able to do that?"

Danny shrugged. "Ben showed me the foundations of how it's all built. If I have access to the base code and can work back through it, I could probably unravel the stuff that's been added."

It was definitely one way to deal with the problem.

"No," Lysander said after a few seconds of thought. "Prioritise finding the source. We need to know what's behind it before we try and undo it all. It could be part of some bigger plan, and if you start taking pieces away, the culprit might get spooked."

Danny studied the screens, his face lit in pale blues. "Right." He peered up at Lysander through the projections. "Do I come in here on my own when I'm done with Ben? Or would it be better for me to wait until most people have gone home?"

Lysander had to smile. "I appreciate your paranoia, but you can say you want to take what you've learned with Ben during the day and put it into practise to make sure you're picking up everything."

"And people might think I'm a bit too keen if I'm staying up all night doing homework," Danny agreed. "Don't want anyone thinking that."

Lysander gazed at him gravely, schooling his expression. "People might think you're...hard-working."

Danny burst out laughing and closed up the screens. "God forbid." He pressed his hand to the scanner on the arm of the chair again and powered it down. "Speaking of being a lazy arse, I'm about to go for some lunch." He cocked his head. "Fancy coming down for a bite?"

For the first time in God only knew how long, Lysander was blindsided. "Excuse me?"

"Lunch," Danny repeated. He wrinkled his nose. "Unless the rumours are true."

Lysander couldn't help snorting. "Which rumour this time?"

"Cyborg," Danny said cheerfully. "Or robot. Y'know. Doesn't need to eat and looks so perfect all the time, he could have been made in a factory."

Lysander pressed his knuckle to his lips to keep from laughing. "That one again?" He wrinkled his nose. "Flesh and blood, Mr. Ferguson, and crazily busy." He inclined his head towards the door. "Don't let me get between you and a good meal."

Danny pushed himself to his feet. "If you're sure?"

"As tempting as it is, I have a meeting in fifteen minutes and some calls to make." He walked Danny to the door of the room. "The trials and tribulations of being in charge."

"Bit of a bugger, really."

"You're not wrong." Lysander paused by the door and touched the console. "Before you go, I should warn you— We couldn't restrict access to the room without raising questions, since you're not meant to be doing anything unusual. People will be able to come in at will."

"Make sure they don't see anything they shouldn't?"

"Exactly." Lysander led him towards the elevators. "If they catch a glimpse, it's no big deal. They know you're learning coding, so no questions should be asked."

Danny rocked on his heels, his hands shoved in his pockets, as they waited for the elevators. "What happens if I find out who's behind it?"

Lysander watched the numbers rising on the panels beside the door. "I'll deal with it when the time comes."

"Thought you might say that." Danny shot a wry smile at him. "Trials and tribulations of being in charge, eh?"

"Mm." Lysander stepped to the side as the first elevator doors opened. "Enjoy your lunch, Mr. Ferguson."

After Danny's elevator descended, his own arrived, and he returned to his office, straight into a collection of messages and memos from Fana and then a teleconference with representatives from three different governments regarding claims made in a TRI report regarding their shared history. Apparently, they believed there were inaccuracies in the report.

It happened with frustrating regularity.

Lysander had long since learned the careful dance of diplomacy, tact, and providing the historical evidence without causing a political firestorm.

Two hours—and no resolution—later, the call ended. He had another scheduled in three days, once each country's relevant experts had been able to study the evidence. Sometimes, they accepted it. Sometimes, they didn't. Either way, he'd done what he could, and the report was based on valid and accurate information.

Lysander rubbed at his eyes with both hands. His head ached, and there were still hours to go before he could take a break.

Still, it was his hole. He'd dug it for himself, and he couldn't blame anyone else for that.

A ping from his monitor made him lower his hands.

"Yes, Fana?"

His aide sounded amused. "There's a delivery for you, sir."

In the name of stretching his legs, he got up from the desk and went through to the reception room. "Is it the Burley file?"

Fana tried to fight a smile as she handed him a shoebox-sized plastic carton. "Mr. Ferguson dropped this in for you ten minutes ago."

Danny?

"Did he say what it was?"

From the look on her face, Danny had, but she shook her head. "He said you might need it. That's all."

Frowning, Lysander retreated back into his office and closed the door before he opened the box. A handwritten paper note lay on top of the contents: *If the mountain won't come to lunch, then let lunch come to the mountain. Hope the mountain enjoys it.*

Lysander stared at the message and then lifted the note away.

The box contained four varieties of sandwiches including lactose-free and gluten-free, a tub of spiced couscous with roast vegetables, a pot of mixed fruit salad, some savoury rice bites, and a richly iced piece of cake.

Lysander touched a knuckle to his lips, trying to keep the smile from his face.

Danny Ferguson had an unexpected skill for surprising him.

Chapter Seven

THE WORKROOM WAS ten paces wide and eight paces deep.

Danny knew this, because he'd been circling the bloody floor for nearly an hour, staring at the code in front of him. Sitting in the chair suited him better for basic monitoring, but he'd found another knot in the code, and this one...

It hadn't been there before, but it had been woven in with the other pieces so naturally he'd nearly overlooked it. Trying to find the point where it had been introduced was turning into a bitch of an exercise.

Walking sometimes helped. A change of perspective, shaking himself up a bit. Of course, he'd walked into the walls a few times too. The eternal problem of pacing with a digi-lens on one eye.

He had pieces of the code projected on the desks as well, scattered with four or five generations of scribbled-down notes.

This new addition didn't provide a solution either, just another strand in an ever-growing tapestry far more complicated than he or O'Donohue had anticipated.

It made him suspicious how smoothly new pieces of code were slipping in. As far as he knew, his cover had been accepted across the board, but if someone continued to mess around with the code, maybe they'd guessed and were adding more to keep him on his toes.

Alternatively, maybe the culprit had no idea and had their own timetable and plans.

Either way, Danny was starting to see why there'd been so many zeroes offered in the paycheque.

He paused mid-step, one foot inches above the floor, staring at the code.

Something...

Something hooking in to it from...from...

He blinked, scrolling back.

"Aha!"

Danny ran back to the desk, dragged up a file, and examined the screeds of code. The culprit had gone back further. The series of layers were so fine, like a delicately constructed web. He tracked the latest thread through, marking each new point.

Thank Christ O'Donohue had given him all the space and tools he needed.

The file spread around him in a spectrum of colours. He'd picked a different colour for every new strand of code he identified to keep track of the dates and patterns. The different tints helped when something new showed up in the middle of the rainbow.

And still, he hadn't found his way back to the source.

O'Donohue had to be frustrated as fuck. They were on a closed system. They had a limited number of staff. Machines had been checked—by Danny in the wee small hours of a Sunday with O'Donohue's authorisation and company—and cleared.

It was a pain in the arse, like a riddle without an answer.

Every time he thought he was getting closer, it turned into one step forward, two steps back.

Danny reached up to remove the digi-lens from his eye. There were always problems with using them, especially if you forgot to blink enough to keep the bloody thing moist. His eyeball felt like he'd rolled it in sand. He rubbed his eyelid gingerly. Eyes, he was pretty sure, weren't meant to feel crunchy.

He was groping for the box for the lens in his back pocket when the door opened behind him. "I don't think you've met Danny yet..."

Danny swore under his breath and yanked his hand out of his pocket to shut down the projections on the desk. He turned with a quick—and hopefully convincing—smile. "All right, Ben?"

Ben gave him a strained smile. He wasn't alone. A skinny dark-haired teenager with a wide grin stood just behind him and raised a hand in greeting. "You didn't show up for your session today," Ben said. "Want to jump in with Mackenzie for this afternoon?"

"Mack," the boy put in.

Danny didn't miss the way Ben's lips tightened briefly, which didn't seem like him. Ben was the most laid-back person he'd met in the agency. "Mack," Ben corrected himself and stared imploringly at Danny. "We're about to get started if you want to come too."

"Might as well," Danny agreed, grinning. "It's this or more homework." He glanced at the boy as he headed across the room. "I'm Danny."

The boy beamed at him. "Mack Robertson. I'm new. You too?"

"Temporarily," Danny confirmed. "Enjoying it?"

"Fuck yes!" Mack went pink. "I mean, yeah. It's amazing. I mean, it's time travel, and I never knew I'd be able to do it and…"

He continued to babble excitedly as they headed towards the lifts. He seemed to be channelling Danny's inner monologue from the day when he'd found out the TRI had hired him, and Danny couldn't help grinning, thanking Christ he'd at least managed to stop himself word-vomiting all over everyone.

Over Mack's head, Ben rolled his eyes as they stepped into the lift.

"And Jacob sent me over here today," Mack finished, when he finally ran out of air. "And I'm to do some studying with Ben." He paused for a breath, squinted up at Danny, and inquired, "So what do you do?"

Danny had to fight to hide his amusement. Christ, it could have been him from twenty years back, if he'd been skinny and a bit more androgynous.

"Computer stuff," he said. "Coding and auditing."

Mack made a sympathetic face. "Not as good as going back in time, eh?" Danny raised his eyebrows, and the young man's face went scarlet. "I mean, I bet it's really useful and everything and you need the coding to do the gates and—"

"And breathe?" Danny suggested, chuckling.

Mack ducked his head sheepishly. "Sorry. I just—it's—I mean, no one else—"

"No one else gets how exciting it is?" Danny laughed and patted the kid on the shoulder. "Yeah."

Mack looked relieved, rocking on the balls of his feet. "Yeah."

"He joined us a couple of months ago," Ben put in. "Headhunted."

Ben's attitude suddenly made a lot more sense. The long-term TRI staff had to be numb to the thrill by now, seeing it all day in and day out. Seeing someone new getting excited and giddy was probably a novelty for the first few days, but he could imagine it would get wearing after a while. Especially for someone as excitable as Mack Robertson.

"This your first day on coding?"

Mack scuffed the toe of his boot. "Yeah. Jacob said it would be useful for me."

Danny shot a glance at Ben, who looked like he'd bitten into a lemon.

Thankfully, Mack could be quiet while Ben trained them, but it quickly became clear to Danny that coding was never going to be his strong suit. His hand shot up every five minutes, and after the fifth time, Ben sat down beside him and told Danny to work through the exercises while he explained them again to Mack.

It took another hour before Ben managed to get Mack onto one of the training hubs to do a basic exercise, his headset on and screen wrapped around him.

"Friendly little bugger, isn't he?" Danny murmured as Ben slouched at the table beside him at the other end of the room. Danny's own exercises had been finished for forty minutes. "Not a coder, I think."

"Mm."

"And they headhunted him?"

Ben made a face as he sat down. He pulled up his legs to sit cross-legged on the chair. "Apparently."

"So that's how people end up in here?"

"Mm. We skim the cream from the top before anyone else can get them."

Danny glanced over at the boy. "What does he do? Shit gold nuggets?"

Ben snorted. "God knows. Sometimes, they keep it under wraps in case it turns out to be false advertising." He tugged at his earlobe, frowning. "Don't know what's so special about this one. It's not often I'm kept out of the loop."

Danny glanced towards the boy who had skills enough to be headhunted and conveniently joined the TRI shortly before corrupted coding had appeared. Coincidences were like Santa Claus: they didn't exist.

Still, he didn't need to make Ben suspicious.

"Is it the whole hereditary-master-of-the-company thing?" he inquired. "I mean, why you're kept in the loop."

Ben rolled his eyes. "Hardly master of the company. Yeah, Dad started it, but when the rest of the world found out..." He shrugged. "I have a stake in it, and I'm never going to go without, but it's not mine. Dad never mentioned it in his will. Couldn't, I s'pose. I'm lucky I had people who grabbed some for me when we went public."

Danny eyed him. So many questions were kept out of the public sphere about Tom Sanders and especially about his death. Most rumours said an accident. Others said he'd blown himself up.

Ben noticed his expression. "What?"

"Do you mind if I ask something about your dad?"

Ben hesitated and then shrugged. "All right."

"What—when—" Danny pushed his fingers through his hair, trying to find a good way to ask an impossible question. "No one outside knows what happened to him."

"Ah." Ben smiled sadly. "No. I don't know all the details. What we do know is someone attacked him, and he tried to escape through a temporal gate. His attacker smashed it. Short-circuited the gate." He looked away. "It's... Based on what we know of the system, we—everyone believed it—" His breath hitched. "Fatal. Broke the connection. Killed him."

"Jesus Christ..."

Ben smiled wanly. "He didn't help." He shrugged. "I hoped dad might've survived. There were letters I thought might have been from him. We had a team in here searching for him a few years ago. Trouble is when some bastard steals all connected tech from his gate, it's very hard to find any trace of where he might have ended up."

"Did they ever catch the people who attacked him?"

Ben stared blankly ahead for a moment. "Sort of. I heard two of them died, but I—" He glanced at Danny. "It's not the kind of thing you can really tell a kid, and then the TRI went public and so much was locked down. Nondisclosures and all that." He smiled sadly. "I just wanted to find him, you know? To show him what I've been able to do with everything he taught me."

Danny could only nod. What a bastard of a way to lose a parent. His own parents still lived on the same street they had his whole life, puttering along, safe in the knowledge their son had made a name for himself in his field and their daughter had given them three grandkids.

Ben rubbed at his forehead. "Shit. Sorry. Dropped the mood a bit there."

Danny knocked his shoulder. "My fault. I asked." He hesitated. "You all right?"

Ben glanced at him. "Yeah. Yeah, I'm okay. It's just—it—you think you're used to it, and then you remember you're not." He slid forward in his chair. "I should check on our new boy. Can you look busy? I want him to think I've been working you hard, instead of giving you my life story."

Danny obliged, opening out several projections and spreading them in front of him. He watched from the corner of his eye as Ben approached Mack. The boy glanced up, and Danny squinted. Maybe he'd been staring at screens too long, but he could swear a blue light flashed from Mack's right eye.

Weird.

He didn't mention it to Ben, but when they dropped Mack off with his supervisor, Danny paid close attention to everything Ben said. If something seemed off about the boy, O'Donohue would want to know about it.

Okay, Ben mostly complained about babysitting a useless kid, but it had to be suspicious too, didn't it? Mack had been brought in for a reason. He had to have some special skill.

Ben was still going when Leon and Tamara joined them in the canteen.

"What's he on about now?" Leon inquired.

"New kid," Danny put in when Ben paused mid-complaint to shove some food into his mouth. "Turns out he might not know how to do basic coding." Ben uttered a muffled string of nonsense, which Danny attempted to translate, "Or switch a console on?"

Ben made an indignant sound, glowering.

"Not everyone is as smart as you, Ben," Tamara said, laughing. "He might not be able to code, but I'm pretty sure there were plenty of things you couldn't do at his age."

"I did it without being a surly brat," Ben said indignantly.

"Did you?" Tamara raised her pierced eyebrows. "Did you really?"

Ben opened his mouth and snapped it shut again.

Danny glanced between them and then inquiringly at Leon, who shrugged. "Don't look at me. I don't know what she's on about."

"Don't," Ben said, pointing his fork her way.

"Don't what?" She grinned widely, showing the gap between her front teeth. "Don't tell them about the time you pretty much raised a barricade and demanded justice for all and staged a revolution for the good of all mankind?"

Danny stared at her and then over at Ben, who had buried his face in his hand. "What the hell...?"

"I was eighteen," Ben mumbled, "and accidentally helped Ly to oust the previous director."

"Mm. Staged a coup and everything." Tamara snickered and nudged Leon. "You should have seen him. He stood on tables and yelled and everything. I'm amazed he didn't start waving a flag."

Leon shot a look at Danny. "I think we need to see evidence, like."

"Yeah," Danny agreed, eyeing Ben in disbelief. "Pictures or it didn't happen."

Ben lowered his hand with a rueful smile. "We got nondisclosured again." He made a face at Tamara. "I think you're trying to get me into trouble."

She smiled sweetly. "Just saying. Don't underestimate someone because he doesn't seem like much."

That, Danny thought, sounded like bloody good advice.

Chapter Eight

LYSANDER FROWNED, TAPPING his index finger on his desk. "So what are you saying? You think he's a spy?"

"I don't know." Ben paced back and forth on the opposite side of the desk. He'd been waiting for Lysander to arrive in his office, and Lysander hadn't even taken his coat off when Ben had demanded access. "I know he's technically meant to be working on coding samples, but the stuff he had in the study room didn't seem like any coding I gave him."

Lysander sighed inwardly.

It was a risk he'd been forced to take, not being able to keep people out of Danny's workspace.

"I wanted to give him a challenge, so I gave him some random data," he said, as if he hadn't planned for such an eventuality. "It's nothing to worry about; I can promise you that. I wanted to see if he's as good as you think he is."

Ben sank into the chair as he pushed his fingers through his hair, leaving it standing on end. "You're sure? I mean, you said the IDD sent him? How do we know they haven't sent someone in to steal information?"

Lysander rubbed at the hollow of his cheek with his thumb. "When I said they sent him, it was a mutual arrangement," he finally said. "They wanted to provide the best work possible, and I agreed it would help if they had someone brought up to speed on the intricacies of our coding."

Ben pulled his legs up onto the seat and pressed his hands to his crossed ankles. "You're sure? You know how much people want our tech."

"They can continue to want," Lysander assured him. "Mr. Ferguson is on the same closed system as the rest of us, with set facilities at his disposal. He has no means to take any data out with him, and the access he has is still restricted to coding, even if he did want to try and rob us blind."

Ben sat silently for a moment and then puffed out a breath. "You must think I'm such a paranoid nutcase."

"Not at all," Lysander murmured. "You know what happened to your father. I can't blame you for being watchful when it comes to his technology."

Ben untangled his fingers and pressed his face into his hands. "Christ," he mumbled, muffled. He rubbed at his eyes then lowered his hands. "Sorry. I should have known you would have checked all the details."

"It *is* my job."

Ben laughed tiredly. "Yeah, and I'm taking up what spare time you have." He pushed himself up from the chair and rolled his shoulders. "You should've told me you'd approved him. I wouldn't have come in and made a spectacular arse of myself."

Lysander smiled warmly. "Hardly a spectacular ass," he said. "A mediocre ass."

"You have a way of making a man feel special." Ben made a face at him. He hesitated. "You're sure he's really only here to learn about the coding?"

For a moment, Lysander considered explaining everything, but Ben had a bad habit of running his mouth when he knew something.

Years ago, it had been useful, when Lysander needed to set plans in motion without anyone being aware of his influence. Ben had been his mouthpiece then, though he hadn't been aware of it at the time. Say the right words to the right person and apply the right pressure to get the desired result.

Now, the last thing he needed was his very vocal mouthpiece.

"Only about coding," he replied, and it wasn't a total lie. "The sooner he's done, the sooner he leaves."

Ben looked relieved. "Okay. I'll keep him on track."

It turned out Ben's unexpected invasion of his office was a sign of things to come. Less than three hours later, Lysander had barely finished another conference call with Mumbai when Fana sent through a notification of someone to see him.

Danny Ferguson had turned up in reception, a grim look on his face.

Lysander met his eyes. "Something up?"

"If you have a minute?"

Lysander stepped back and motioned for Ferguson to join him in the office.

Unlike Ben, Danny didn't pace about or rumple up his hair. It looked like he had already been doing it on his own time.

"What do you know about Mack Robertson?"

Lysander circled back behind his desk and sat, indicating to the other chair. "In what context?"

Danny sat on the edge. "Do you know why they headhunted him? What's so special about him? Why did he get picked up for special training in here? Where did he come from? Do we know whether he's an asset or a liability? Is..." Danny trailed off when Lysander started to laugh. "What?"

"I had exactly the same conversation not three hours ago."

"About Mack?"

Lysander smiled, amused. "About you."

Danny sat up straighter, indignation all over his face. "You what?"

Lysander held up a hand. "Someone expressing concern, that's all. Newcomers tend to make long-term staff a little nervous."

"Who?"

"It doesn't matter," Lysander replied. It would only make Danny skittish around Ben if he knew, which would make Ben suspicious again. "What matters is that they're no longer concerned."

Danny didn't seem convinced, but he sat back in the chair. "Right. What about the kid? Any chance he's the one behind the code?"

"I'm assuming there's a reason for you to ask?"

"I ran into him yesterday when Ben came to get me for my coding session. Something felt...off about it all." Danny frowned. "Maybe he's just being a teenager, but some things Ben said didn't feel right."

Lysander had to admit he had never considered Mackenzie Robertson before. "In what way?"

"Seems a bit coincidental he came in just before the coding anomalies showed up," Danny pointed out. "Ben says people are headhunted for specialised skills, but he doesn't know what this one's in for."

"Usually, any information would be available to the relevant department," Lysander said, puzzled.

"Which means Ben, when it comes to coding, doesn't it? But Ben doesn't know and says the little bugger's not any good at it anyway." Danny sighed. "Maybe I'm getting caught up in your spy games and seeing suspects where there aren't any or some bullshit, but I thought I should let you know."

It was a good call.

The boy's personnel file didn't give much away. Twenty-one, from Preston, a little farther north. He had an average set of grades and had been registered at one of the local colleges. Some basic skill with a computer but more interested in history than technology.

Off the back of that information, Lysander would have expected him to be installed with the historical department if anything, but the line manager was listed as Jacob Ofori. Ofori had been the senior supervisor for the agents and the data assessment teams for years, which—again— didn't explain why Mack had been assigned to learn coding.

The file had come across his desk for approval four months ago, and, back then, he hadn't asked why. Headhunting happened occasionally, and if it came from someone as high up as Jacob Ofori, then he generally signed the paperwork with no questions asked.

"There's something off, isn't there?" Danny broke into his train of thought.

Lysander glanced at him. "Excuse me?"

"You frowned. I mean properly." Danny motioned to his own face. "You had lines and wrinkles and the lot."

Lysander glanced back at the file, drumming his thumbnail thoughtfully against his lower lip. "Nothing serious. Only a few questions for his supervisor."

"There's something else."

Lysander raised his eyebrows. "More?"

Danny touched the skin below his right eye. "I think the kid might have an eye implant or something. I'd swear I saw a light coming from his eye, but it wasn't the reflection of the screen. Could be copying data with it."

Another glance at the personnel file provided the answer.

"He has a medical aid," Lysander said with a small smile. "The boy has a false eye due to a birth defect."

Danny didn't appear so much embarrassed as flustered. "Oh. Aye. That'd be it."

"Not many people would've noticed," Lysander offered, because even a misplaced catch could be something. "It may be worth checking out as a precaution. Thanks for bringing it to my attention."

"Well." Danny shrugged and rubbed the back of his neck self-consciously. "It's not like I've got you anywhere with the code. Whoever's writing it is a cunning bugger."

"Even cunning buggers make mistakes." Danny snorted. "What?"

"You, saying that with your accent," Danny replied with his contagious grin. "You sound ridiculous."

Lysander chuckled. "I guess I do." He glanced at his watch. "I hate to kick you out, but I've got another meeting in five minutes. I'll check on Robertson, and you focus on the code."

"On it." Danny got up and then paused. "Are you about to miss your lunch again?"

Lysander gave him a look. "I don't need a waiter."

"Ha. No wonder you're a skinny wee skelf." Danny pulled out his Leaf and opened up the menu options, then flipped the projection for Lysander to see it. "What do you fancy?"

Lysander inclined his head. "You're not going to leave until I pick something, are you?"

"Nope."

Lysander studied the menu. More often than not, he snacked on soup and some crackers or a sandwich between calls, but he wasn't about to refuse a better option. "The chilli with rice." He glanced up at Danny through the screen. "If you're determined to get it to me, I'll be in the meeting for an hour, Mr. Ferguson."

"Danny," Danny corrected. "And it'll be brought up then."

The man was as good as his word.

Lysander had just seen the HR department heads out when Fana buzzed and then came into the office. She seemed amused as she set a savoury-scented box on his desk.

"Delivery, sir."

"Something funny, Fana?"

Her lips were twitching. "Not at all. Do you need anything else?"

He considered turning over some excess filing to keep her distracted and not entertained at his expense, and then a thought occurred to him. The reason for Danny's visit. "Actually, yes. Get me Jacob Ofori as soon as he's available."

With both of the temporal jumps already out of the way, Jacob showed up five minutes later when Lysander had barely finished wolfing down his lunch. Ofori had been a member of the TRI staff before Lysander had ever heard of the place. More significantly, he was the former police detective who had investigated the disappearance of Tom Sanders and discovered time travel existed. The investigation had forced the TRI into the public sphere. Lysander had never uncovered the twist of politics that led Ofori to head the investigative side of the agency, but there could be no mistake he was damned good at his job.

Everyone liked him throughout the agency, but Lysander couldn't shake the feeling Jacob always stayed on guard around him, despite maintaining a civil façade. It was, he supposed, only fair when Jacob had been a witness to the fall of Elwin at Lysander's hand. Who wouldn't be a little suspicious of his boss's motives, after that?

"The jumps both went cleanly," he said as soon as he sat. "Primary pickup for the first, tertiary for the second."

"Tertiary?" Lysander tilted his head inquiringly. "No major problems?"

"Ying said they were caught up in the festivities and couldn't get away without raising suspicions. Given Hui's hangover, I'm not sure how true the excuse is."

Lysander smothered a chuckle. "I suppose it happens." He opened up the Robertson file. "I called you up because there have been some questions raised about this young man." He turned the file for Jacob to see it. "You headhunted him."

Close to a dozen years of working together and Ofori was still almost unreadable. Almost. His lips tightened slightly as he gazed at the projection, which provided enough validation for Lysander's growing suspicions.

"I did," Jacob replied. "You signed off on it. What's the problem?"

"There's no record of why."

Jacob snorted. "You never ask. Why start with this one?" The fine lines around his dark eyes deepened, and he studied Lysander. "Something's happened."

It wasn't a question, but the statement of a detective spotting the outline of a crime.

Lysander forced himself to relax back in his chair. He'd played this particular game for a long time. "Some questions have been raised about Mr. Robertson," he said placidly. "I would appreciate an answer. Why did this man get a position here?"

Jacob matched his posture. Whatever he knew, he didn't want to talk about it and was falling back into his old policing habits. "We believe he has a role to play."

"I need more of an answer."

"And you didn't tell me why you need to know."

There were so many options with how to handle people. Lysander knew he could play the director card and force Jacob's hand, but Jacob's guarded demeanour said there was something more to the boy than simple nepotism. Jacob could be opaque when he wanted, but more often than not, he tended to be direct and—to Lysander in particular—borderline blunt. For him to be hiding something, it had to be significant.

Trust for trust, then.

"Someone has hacked the coding on our systems." Lysander recognised the surprise—shock—on Jacob's face. "I have a member of the IDD working to identify the source, under the guise of getting in-house training." He inclined his head. "Your boy has raised suspicions because he arrived only weeks before the coding first appeared."

Jacob eyed him, frowning. "Why are you telling me now?"

Lysander met his eyes. "I know I can't shake your doubts about me, but you can't deny we both do what we need to in order to safeguard the TRI and its people." He gave Jacob a moment to let it sink in and then quietly repeated, "Why did Robertson get a position here?"

Jacob rubbed at his salt-and-pepper beard with one hand. "What I tell you can't leave this room," he finally said. He didn't sound happy about it.

"Likewise," Lysander agreed.

"You read the Sanders report?"

Lysander frowned. The hard copy document had been given to him on the day he became director. It contained a summary of the police investigation into the disappearance and/or murder of Thomas Sanders. The report confirmed Sanders's assailants had been sent from a point in the future, but with little clarification as to how they were identified and why. At the time, Lysander had noticed the gaps, but had been told those questions would be answered in due course.

"Sanders was attacked by two people," Ofori said. "It appeared to be a home invasion gone wrong. One of them died on the scene, struck in self-defence. The same day saw a baby born with identical DNA. Within three hours, to be exact."

Lysander stared at him. "Robertson?"

"We've had eyes on him since then as a precaution," Jacob explained. "Around thirty people know all the details altogether. The people involved in the original investigation, several TRI staff members—

present and former—who assisted the police, and some of the senior ranking officers. To prevent any...incidents, we sealed the information.”

“The timeline,” Lysander murmured. “I can see why it’s restricted. Why bring him in now?”

Jacob said nothing for a moment, then explained, “We believe at some point in the near future, he’ll make contact with the person who sent him back.”

“Do we know who this person is?”

“Yes. And we also believe he still has Sanders’s stolen computer drives, which means he will have access to the blueprints for the original temporal gates.”

Lysander glanced away, hoping he didn’t look as shaken as he felt. “I heard some data had been taken, but I’d assumed since no one has been using the technology, they weren’t able to understand what they had.” He glanced at Jacob. “Is there a reason?”

“Twenty-five years to life,” Jacob replied. When Lysander shook his head, confused, he explained. “Patrick Harper—at some point in the future—tries to get the tech for his past self. Harper’s younger self lacked any foresight and had no qualms about illegal activity. He ended up getting convicted for a series of crimes tied to the stolen drives. Conspiracy to murder, abduction, handling stolen data, perverting the course of justice. There was a long list. He had—and as far as we know has—no idea he was responsible for the initial robbery and assault.”

“God...” Lysander shook his head again, dazed. “So let me get this straight. Some time in the future, this guy will use the gates to send Mackenzie Robertson to steal Sanders’s blueprints? Using Sanders’s blueprints? If he already has the technology, why does he need to steal it?”

Jacob grimaced. “That’s what we don’t know. We do know their gate didn’t work as planned, and it dropped them about ten years later than they intended. We have no idea what he wanted them to get. We only know he sent them to Sanders’s house.”

“I’m guessing Ben doesn’t know?”

“To the best of our knowledge, no,” Jacob said. “We don’t know how it’s going to happen, and you saw Ben when he thought his dad might be alive. He would get obsessed with it. He might do something...” He hesitated.

"Unpredictable?" Lysander remembered Ben's erratic behaviour in his teens. At best, he was vocally rebellious. At worst, he'd helped two men perform an unauthorised temporal jump because he felt it was the right thing to do.

A few years earlier, he had retreated from the TRI completely. No one knew what he'd been up to apart from some travelling. Most people thought he'd spent some time coming to terms with everything that had happened to him.

By the time Lysander persuaded Ben to return to the TRI, he was calmer and no longer fixating on his father's death. Age and knowledge had eased his temper, but Lysander didn't doubt it could be stirred up again, especially if it involved his late parents.

Jacob nodded. "He's a good kid, but he doesn't need something to trigger him again. If we're careful, we can contain Robertson. Ben doesn't need to know."

Lysander touched the edge of the desk. "Contain? Wouldn't that be altering the timeline?"

Jacob gazed at him, his expression opaque. "We don't know if our actions now will affect the past. All we're doing is trying to prevent a criminal from using illegal tech."

"Which we both know is bullshit."

Jacob shrugged. "I don't know about you, but I don't feel comfortable watching a kid—no matter who he is—walk blindly into his death. We're not stopping him. We're just...protecting him."

Lysander's lips twitched. "Protecting. I see. And of the others who know about Mr. Robertson, how many know about this...protection?"

Jacob considered it. "Four. The less people who know, the better." He gazed evenly at Lysander. "I know you're heading the Board now, but if you tell me to let the future go the way it's meant to and let this boy die, we're going to have words."

Technically, it went against the rules of the institution, yes, but Jacob had made a valid point: they couldn't know what would make the boy choose to become a temporal thief. No matter what they did, it might have no bearing on the future, and, either way, the boy was in the TRI now.

"We don't have any idea what will set him on his path," Lysander said finally. "The future is...unpredictable." He shrugged expressively. "We keep eyes on him and see what happens." Jacob looked relieved, but

Lysander had to say, "I don't get why you thought bringing Robertson in-house would be a good idea, though."

Jacob gave him a wry smile. "Friends close, enemies closer. We've been trying him out in different departments so we have somewhere to keep him and keep an eye on him, especially with our mastermind coming up for parole."

Lysander massaged at his temples. "I can see why the information was withheld, but this...complicates matters." He met Jacob's eyes. "Is there any possibility this boy has the technical proficiency to access and corrupt the code?"

For the first time since they'd started working together, Jacob seemed uncertain. "I don't know. I don't think so. He seems like an average kid. As far as we can tell, he doesn't have any special skills, but he could be good at hiding them."

Lysander rubbed at his forehead. He could feel a headache building. What had started as a calm year seemed to rapidly be going in a different direction. "Great."

Chapter Nine

"YOU LOOK AWFUL."

Danny squinted up as several people sat down at the table around him. It'd been a long weekend. With a lot of the staff off and the buildings deserted, he'd put all his focus on working on the code. Since no one had been around to boot him out of the room to get some rest, he couldn't be sure if he'd actually remembered to sleep or eat.

"Got caught up in work."

"Someone's keen," Ben said, settling in the seat opposite.

Danny shrugged. "Home's waiting. Sooner I get good enough, the sooner I'm back in civilisation."

"This place isn't exactly great for socialising," Mel agreed, nudging Danny as she sat down. "Is it true they're making you stay on site until your training is done?"

Danny stabbed his gnocchi with his fork. "Yeah."

"A precaution?" Guy asked as he sat down beside Ben.

Danny wrinkled his nose. "'Parently someone thinks I could be a spy."

Mel burst out laughing, and Ben choked on his drink, but Guy frowned. "Someone told you this?"

Danny glanced at him. "I heard. Maybe Janos? He thought I shouldn't be here."

Ben wiped at his spattered shirt with a paper napkin. "Could have been paranoia," he said, one side of his mouth tugging up. "It's not like we get many new people in here."

"But a spy?" Guy glanced between them. "Why would someone assume there's a spy?"

"Because we work in a top-secret international facility with limited access?" Mel suggested, laughing. "Because we time travel using technology no one else in the world has access to, and there's bound to be someone out there who wants it? Because we're *that* amazing?"

Guy frowned. "True." He turned to Ben, who seemed to be the font of all knowledge in the department. "Do you think it's true?"

Ben blinked at him. He had a mouthful of curry, the heat of it turning his face pink. "Mm?"

"About a spy? Do you think they'll find him—her—them—if there is?"

Ben gulped down the curry. "I think people get worried when someone new shows up," he said. "Janos *did* get antsy when Danny arrived." He flashed a quick grin at Danny. "Like I said, probably someone just being a bit paranoid."

Guy didn't seem convinced. "But what if there is someone?"

Danny eyed him. The man looked too uneasy. "If there is, I'm pretty sure O'Donohue would already know about it and have them out on their ear." He held up both hands on either side of his head. "He who knows all and sees all and hears all..."

Ben and Mel both burst out laughing.

"You're not wrong," Ben agreed. "Ly's a shifty bugger. You'd have to be four steps ahead to pull one over on him."

Danny picked up his fork again and skewered several pieces of gnocchi in one go. "Maybe don't tell him I said that about him?"

Mel sniggered. "He probably already knows." She leaned closer, widening her eyes in mock horror. "What if he bugged you?"

Danny made a face. "He bugs me all the time." Mel cackled, and he grinned at her. "What if you're the spy?"

"Me? Nah! I'm not bright enough."

"Doctor Carver?" Ben said, amused. "Not bright enough? Firsts in two fields?"

She batted her eyes at him. "I'm but a simple woman."

"That's it," Danny declared. "I'm calling it. Mel's the spy."

"This isn't funny," Guy said, shaking his head.

"Lighten up, Guy." Ben nudged him. "Ly would know about any problems."

Danny concentrated on his food for a couple of minutes, hoping his face didn't give him away. O'Donohue really didn't need people realising something was wrong.

He'd hoped the weekend would give him enough time to unravel all the knots, but it had been a forlorn hope. He'd made a breakthrough at last, though, and from what he could tell, there hadn't been any new additions to the code since he'd last spoken to O'Donohue. Or at least there hadn't been any additions that he'd *found*. Still, best not to get complacent about.

He had just skewered the last lumps of lukewarm gnocchi when Mel poked him in the ribs.

"Are you sure you shouldn't be sleeping?"

"I'm all right." He put his fork down then glanced over at the counter. "This is a daft question, but do any of you know if O'Donohue likes fish?"

A careful silence fell, and his three companions exchanged glances.

"Why?" Ben inquired. "If it's in the name of pranking him..."

Danny shrugged. "I'm going to grab him some lunch."

The next silence seemed even deeper.

"You're taking O'Donohue lunch?" Mel peered at him. "Has he used special robot mind-control powers on you?"

Danny snorted, making a face at her. "The skinny bugger keeps on skipping his lunch. My mum's the one who used special mind-control powers to make me make sure people eat enough." Or too much, as the case had been back in the day.

"Mm. Right." Ben smiled at his plate as he mixed his peas in with his mashed potatoes.

"What do you mean 'right'?"

Ben glanced across the table at him, lips twitching. "Nothing."

"I think what Ben means," Mel confided out of the corner of her mouth, "is your boner for Ly is showing."

Danny was very glad it took a lot to make him blush. "What? Don't be daft!"

All right, yeah, O'Donohue was hot. Ridiculously fucking hot. And had a great wry sense of humour. And noticed when Danny wound himself in knots and helped him out. And so what if Danny wanted to make sure he ate properly? It didn't mean he was thinking about grabbing him by the tie and demanding a shag.

Well.

Not much.

Maybe a wee bit.

Aye, all right, there had been the one night when he needed to distract himself from code and all the bullshit and he'd had his hand down the front of his boxers and pictured someone else's hand there instead.

The other three were talking over him as he pulled himself back out of his own head.

"—and it's not like Ly has ever been out with people."

"There's a reason for the robot stories."

"Poor Danny," Mel sighed. "Doomed to a life of celibate pining."

"Hey!" Danny protested. "I never said I fancied the bastard."

Ben snickered, his eyes glinting. "Of course not." He swirled his fork in the mashed potato. "Don't worry. It's not like you have a chance there, if you did."

"Hey!" He glared around with indignation. "I'm a catch."

"So's a cold," Mel put in, then squealed when he poked her in the ribs. "Ben! Help!"

Ben was laughing openly now. "It's not you, Danny. It's Ly. Even if he's not a robot, I've never seen someone who lives and breathes work as much as he does. If you were going to get his attention, you'd have to distract him from work, and there's more chance of hell freezing over."

That sounded like a challenge. "If I fancied him, I bet I could get him to go out with me."

Ben rolled his eyes dramatically. "Yeah, right."

"I thought you didn't fancy him," Mel said, grinning.

Danny sniffed indignantly. "I don't. I'm just saying if I *did*, I know I'd be able to get him."

All three of them burst out laughing.

"Oh, please," Ben said with an eye-roll. "Pretty much everyone in the room has fancied Ly at some point. Even all the self-proclaimed straight men. Right up until the point he schools them in how badly they're doing their jobs and then the glamour wears off."

"It's true," Mel agreed with a sigh. "One time he had his hair loose..." She fanned herself with a hand and feigned a swoon.

Guy wrinkled his nose. "Speak for yourselves. I don't like men."

"Lies," Mel said cheerfully. "Lysander is everyone's exception."

"So, did you ever try?" Danny inquired, glancing at Ben, grateful for an excuse to redirect the attention.

"'Scuse me?"

"Try to distract him from work, since you seem to know *all* about it."

Ben gaped at him. "Me? Hit on Ly? Are you kidding?"

"Did you?" Mel seemed far too interested.

Ben waved a hand dismissively. "No! I met him when I was sixteen and, yeah, he's good-looking, but I'd never hit on him."

"Too busy staging a revolution?" Danny said, grinning.

Ben flicked a pea at him. "Piss off. Anyway, I have a type, and it's not him."

"You mean the non-existent type?" Mel inquired.

Ben gave a lofty sniff. "Shows what you know."

"Wait, what?" Mel gaped at him. "You're seeing someone? When did this happen?"

Ben's expression went blank. "I didn't say that."

"Oh, come *on*!" Mel reached over the table and clung to his arm. "I told you about every one of my conquests! Throw me a bone! Something! A name! A description! Where you met!"

A flare of emotions crossed Ben's face, and Danny recognised frustration when he saw it. Clearly, Ben didn't want anyone poking around in his private life. "I met someone when I was travelling. It isn't— I didn't— It's nothing serious. That's all you're getting." He pointed his fork at Danny. "Anyway, this isn't about me. This is about Danny and his hard-on for our boss."

Danny pushed his chair back. "And on that completely false note, I'm going to take my plate and go."

Mel leaned back in her chair, beaming up at him. "Go and get some lunch for your boyfriend. No!" She squealed, shielding her head when he tilted his half-full glass of water above her. "No, no, no! I don't have a drier with me!"

"Yeah, Danny," Ben said with an impressively straight face. "Don't get her wet."

"Ben!" Mel lobbed her napkin. "You filthy pervert!"

Danny couldn't help laughing along with Guy. "You're both idiots. Deluded idiots."

"I don't think we're the ones who're deluded." Ben waved. "Have fun being a feeder."

"Bugger off," Danny said cheerfully as he walked away.

Still, no matter what they'd said, he picked up a portion of rice and salmon for O'Donohue packaged up in a foil box to keep it warm. It wouldn't do any harm, and O'Donohue hadn't turned any of the boxes away. In fact, he'd picked out things himself a couple of times.

Danny frowned thoughtfully as he wandered across the courtyard towards the main building.

It would be completely inappropriate to fancy his boss. It had never been an issue before, not with Carrigan being a hatchet-faced old bird who didn't like his taste in chairs. It should have been high up the list of things a sensible man didn't do, but if O'Donohue hadn't punted Danny's offers of food and company, and he was only *temporarily* Danny's boss, that'd be all right, wouldn't it? Not like it'd be a long-term thing, not when he'd be heading back to London. A tumble with someone good-looking was never a hardship.

By the time he stepped out of the lift on the top floor, leaving it smelling faintly of fish, he'd come to a decision: Operation Distract O'Donohue had to happen.

Phase one would be finding out which direction O'Donohue swung. The others hadn't given Danny any useful information. It'd be bloody awkward to throw himself at the bugger only to find out he preferred the ladies or non-sexual relationships or, hell, if he did relationships at all. Life choices were all well and good, but a key thing for Danny as a shagger was to have a mutual shaggee.

There were already hopeful signs. The food thing, for one. And the way O'Donohue chatted with him. It came close to the level of flirting, so it just needed a little bit of a push. Sometimes, the way O'Donohue smiled as well, when it actually reached his eyes, was encouraging.

Danny shifted the box in his hand as he approached the reception room outside O'Donohue's office. Fana didn't pretend to act surprised anymore. The first day, she'd informed him in no uncertain terms that 'Mr. O'Donohue doesn't take meals from anyone.' By the fourth time, she smiled when he showed up. Seemed like he had a co-conspirator who also worried about the silly bastard starving himself for work.

"What's on the menu today?"

Danny held up the box. "Salmon and rice with a side of vegetables."

"You're upgrading," she said, smiling. Her teeth were incredibly white. She touched the intercom on her desk. "Sir, lunch delivery. Do you want me to send him in?"

O'Donohue agreed, and Danny straightened up before he walked through the door. He stopped dead as soon as he crossed the threshold, staring.

For the first time in the ten days since he'd arrived, O'Donohue had let his hair down. The front parts were drawn back from his face and clipped at the back of his head, but the rest fell around his shoulders and halfway down his back. Mel's reaction to it suddenly seemed completely reasonable.

"What's the occasion?" Danny inquired, trying not to think how it would feel to twist his hand into those long dark waves.

O'Donohue glanced up from the document in front of him. "Excuse me?"

Danny waved vaguely to his own hair. "Yours. It's down."

O'Donohue's lips twitched, and, for a second, he looked self-conscious. "No reason."

Danny laughed, holding out the box as he crossed the room. "Aye, right. Come on." He yanked the box back when O'Donohue reached for it. "I'll trade you your lunch for it."

O'Donohue raised his eyebrows, but there were creases of amusement around his eyes. "Is that really necessary?" He reached for the box again, and Danny pulled it farther back, trying not to grin.

"Definitely necessary." He gave the box a quick shake. "And it's a nice lunch and all."

O'Donohue met his eyes. "My ears were cold this morning." He held out his hand. "Satisfied?"

Well, if that didn't turn imposing businessman into adorably precious little shit, nothing would.

Operation Distract O'Donohue was definitely on.

Danny slid his empty hand under O'Donohue's and placed the box in his upturned hand. He didn't miss the surprise crossing O'Donohue's face or the way his hand jolted against Danny's palm. "That wasn't so hard, was it?" He winked, withdrew his hand, and turned and strode out the room, leaving O'Donohue staring in his wake.

Chapter Ten

"WE'RE SETTING UP the sim of sixteenth-century Kabul for three o'clock."

Lysander studied the reports into the new pair of agents. They'd been headhunted six months earlier and had gone through the rigorous courses of training: languages, history, culture, etiquette. They were two new operatives for the West Asia and North Africa unit. "They've come through their training quickly."

Qasim El-Fahkri smiled. "What can I say? I'm ruthlessly efficient."

Lysander laughed. "And modest as always." He shut down the files. "Do you think they're ready for this?"

"They've passed all the written and verbal examinations in Persian and Arabic so far, so, technically, they should be ready for standard missions in compatible regions." Qasim shrugged. "They seem good under pressure, but you know we can't be sure how they'll react once they get through the gate."

"Of course," Lysander agreed. "No one can tell how the unexpected will affect them."

Qasim always swept in like a breath of fresh air, one of the few people in the TRI who had never been intimidated by Lysander.

Nine years earlier, he had been one of their best agents, and now, he was the top trainer in the TRI. Getting stranded in the past for a month had given him a degree of experience no other agent could match. If he spotted any issues, he had no problem with coming to Lysander directly.

Lysander knew he could trust him and vice versa. After all, Lysander had managed to arrange matters and get a gate open to bring Qasim back from the past, when he'd been stranded in the fifteenth century.

"Do they know it's a sim?"

Qasim widened his eyes innocently. "I might have forgotten to mention that."

Lysander hid a smile with a finger. "Limit it to two hours, unless they have to be pulled out early."

"Do you want to sit in?"

"Not today," Lysander demurred. "I have a concall with the IDD this afternoon, and I need to get an update on Ferguson's progress."

Despite being a great agent, Qasim had a terrible poker face in every other capacity. His lips twitched.

"Is something funny?"

"Ferguson," Qasim said. "He's a funny man. Ben threw me at him to stop him being so star-struck around agents." He cocked his head. "I heard he's been bringing you lunch packages."

Lysander hoped to hell the heat in his cheeks didn't show too much. He had no reason to be embarrassed about the fact, even if it felt kind of domestic. If Qasim had heard about the lunch boxes, it meant the news had to be doing the rounds of the whole facility.

"What of it?" he asked as casually as he could.

Qasim's face broke into a sunny smile. "I think it's sweet, especially from a Londoner."

"A Scottish Londoner," Lysander corrected. "He's a good man but stubborn as an ass. I figured I could humour him." He leaned back in his chair. "Is there anything else I should know about the sim or the trainees?"

Qasim shook his head. "We're all set." He jerked his thumb over his shoulder, towards the door. "Shall I...?"

"Sure."

Qasim paused at the door. "Do you want me to shut down the chat? About Danny's lunch service? I know it can be annoying."

Lysander considered it. If anything, it would only make the rumours worse. "It's fine. There are worse things for them to speculate about than where I get my meals."

Qasim smiled. "Let me know if you change your mind."

"I will. And pass my regards on to Riza."

Qasim's face lit up. Years of marriage and two kids hadn't dampened his affection for his husband. "You know it always leads to dinner invitations."

Lysander laughed. "Part of a cunning plan for more free meals." He waved Qasim out.

He'd never expected to end up socialising with the El-Fahkris. Riza— once Rhys Griffiths and a former supervisor in the TRI—had never forgotten that the combined efforts of Lysander and Ben had saved

Qasim from the past, and he insisted on celebrating every year. Ben and Lysander had ended up as unlikely friends after one too many of those dinners.

Lysander sighed, stroking his small beard pensively.

It wasn't unusual for him to be the subject of gossip. He always had been, long before he joined the TRI. Back then, it had been worse because people were assholes. Here, it was because everyone had an opinion about their boss.

If people weren't speculating about his ethnicity—he'd heard at least eight suggestions—then they were talking about his love life or his mannerisms or whether he was a robot. Power-crazed megalomaniac sociopath had made it into his top ten weird suggestions.

Years of experience dealing with that kind of bullshit helped, but Danny didn't have to deal with it too.

The wind had picked up outside, the rain pelting—icy and grey— against the windows. He watched several drops roll down the glass, trying to figure out how to deal with the issue. If he asked Danny to stop bringing food, whether he did or he didn't, people would speculate about why. It was harmless gossip, but harmless gossip could easily turn harmful.

The trouble was...

The trouble was it felt...nice. It had been a long while since anyone did anything thoughtful and generous for him, and Danny had no reason to do it. He didn't get anything out of it. He didn't ask for anything from it. He only did it because he wanted to make sure Lysander had a decent meal.

At least he could warn Danny and let him know about the whispers in the hope it wouldn't cause any problems.

He glanced at his watch.

Danny was scheduled to be in the study suite, and Lysander *did* need to go for an update anyway, so he slipped out of his office and headed to the level below.

The moment he opened the door of the suite, all the screens blinked off.

Danny stood in the middle of the floor, squinting. "Oh! All right?" He rubbed at one eye with a finger. "Didn't realise you'd be popping in."

Lysander winced as he shut the door. "Sorry. I should have let you know."

"I'm quick on the draw." Danny waved the tiny remote in his hand. "'Course, I'm going to be blinking spots of light off my vision for the next ten minutes." He cocked his head. "What's up? You look worried."

It had been a long while since anyone had spotted it. Lysander wondered what part of his expression gave him away. He'd spent so many years cultivating a neutral mask that it disconcerted him to know someone could see beyond it.

"I wanted to warn you people are talking about your one-man dinner service."

"Ah." Danny scratched at his nose with his thumbnail. "That might be on me."

Lysander stopped short. "You told them?"

"Not...exactly." Danny gave him a lopsided smile. "I don't think when I'm half-asleep, and I asked them if you liked fish." He laughed ruefully. "They weren't much help anyway, the wankers. Sorry. Should have been thinking."

Lysander had to smile at that. "It's an easy mistake to make. I wanted to be sure you knew about it in case anyone starts on you."

Danny seemed both surprised and pleased. "Aye? You didn't need to worry. I'm a big lad, y'know."

Lysander shrugged with a quiet laugh. "You don't need to bring me food, but you do anyway. Let's call us even."

Danny laughed. "All right, then."

Lysander glanced around the now dark room. "How's it all going anyway?" he asked, motioning around.

Danny touched the remote, and the screens lit up again. "It's getting there," he said, meandering in a circle. He'd projected codes all over the walls, on every screen, on the desks. He beckoned Lysander over to the most colourfully lit desk. "Take a wee peek at this."

Lysander approached to stand beside him. The whole surface glowed with coding and notes and patterns in all colours of the rainbow.

It could have been in Mandarin for all Lysander knew.

"What is it?"

"The date it all started."

Lysander glanced sharply at him. "You're sure?"

Danny grunted in confirmation, and close up and by the harsh light from the screens, Lysander could see the shadows under his bloodshot eyes. "I've been back further, but can't find any trace of tampering." Danny tapped the desk. "Twenty-first of September."

"September..." Lysander stared down at the desk.

Mackenzie Robertson had been brought in on the twelfth of September. Whether or not the boy had some involvement in the coding, it couldn't be a coincidence. He'd been reassigned from the coding team after Lysander's meeting with Jacob, restricting his access to the system.

Lysander glanced at Danny. "Have there been any changes since you started working on it?"

Danny pressed his hand to the middle of Lysander's back to steer him around to face one of the walls. The heat of it and the firm gentle pressure made his breath hitch. Danny had touched him before, more than once or twice as well, but for the first time, Lysander had no desire to move away from it.

Lysander made himself focus on the wall.

"Whoever did it added bits and pieces here and there," Danny said. "I don't know if they did it deliberately, but it wasn't so hard to find. It might be because I know to look for it, but it didn't feel as complicated."

Lysander glanced at the wall. "And this is...?"

"The last time anything changed." Danny's voice sounded rougher than usual. No wonder if he'd been spending all his time closed up and going through the code. "You remember when I came to see you about Mack? Same date."

Coincidence on top of coincidence.

And Danny's hand still pressed against his back, a warm solid weight. His thumb kept moving, brushing up and down slowly. All Lysander had to do was step away from the contact, but, somehow, he couldn't.

"Do we know what the code did?" He kept his eyes focussed on the code that meant nothing to him.

"Not yet." Danny kept stroking his thumb idly up and down. "But now I know the date it all started, it gives me a fixed time frame to work in." He turned to Lysander, triumph in every exhausted line of his face. "Like I said, getting there."

Lysander met his eyes. The man had been working himself to the bone all week. "I think you need to take a break."

Danny blinked slowly, as if he didn't understand. "But I'm getting there."

Lysander smiled crookedly. "If I work you until you drop dead of exhaustion, I don't think Miss Carrigan would be happy." He glanced back at the walls. "You've been on this for more than a fortnight straight. You need a day off."

Danny stepped away to sit against the edge of the desk. "It's not like there's much to do in here. Working keeps me entertained."

While there was some staff in on the weekends, they were usually in lockdown for mission prep or working in the prop warehouse. There were no jumps scheduled for weekends, which did restrict anyone on site to entertaining themselves with the gym or media facilities of H-block.

"You've shown you're capable of discretion," Lysander said. "I'm sure I can arrange a weekend pass and a hotel for you in the city."

Danny stared at him for so long Lysander started to wonder if he'd fallen asleep with his eyes open.

"Would it be okay?" he prompted.

"Isn't that a security risk?" Danny finally said. "Me, I mean."

"Like I said, you've been discreet."

Danny folded his arms, frowning in thought. "What if I get hammered?"

"What?"

"If I get hammered?" Danny gazed back at him. By the glow of the screens, Lysander could see the flecks of gold in his hazel eyes. "What if I'm pished and I started spouting off about time travel and the TRI and the traitor?"

Lysander frowned, puzzled. "Are you saying you don't want to go out?"

Danny pushed himself up off the desk. "I'm saying I might need a chaperone."

It was Lysander's turn to stare. "Excuse me?"

"A chaperone. Someone to knock me on the head if I start running my mouth." One side of his mouth turned up. "And since you're the only one who knows why I'm here and knows what I know..."

"Me?" Lysander felt blindsided. "You're joking, right? I mean I'm— it's—" He shook his head, dazed. "I don't think you want me chaperoning."

The smirk widened into a smile. "Why not? It might be fun."

"I don't—" Lysander broke off and ran a hand over his face. Danny was right. There weren't any other options. And technically, yeah, he did go out. He just...didn't go out with a handsome contractor who brought him lunches, even in a chaperone capacity. "I'm not sure I'd be good company."

"You don't have to go," Danny said, his smile softening. "I can go without a bevy or two. The dancing won't be as magical, but I'll manage." He shifted one foot to knock the toe of his boot against Lysander's shoe. "I'd like it if you did come, though." He winked impishly. "I'd like to see you let your hair down."

Lysander gave him a stern glare. "If I do agree to come, I'm only there as your chaperone."

Danny grinned at him. "Chaperones can have a drink and a dance."

Lysander couldn't help laughing. "I think you're trying to be a bad influence on me, Mr. Ferguson."

Danny visibly relaxed, unfolding his arms and tucking his thumbs into his pockets. "I don't know what gave you that idea." He cocked his head, somehow seeming much younger and more nervous. "Are you coming, then?"

In what Lysander would later consider a spectacular lapse of judgement, he agreed. "Only as your chaperone," he repeated. "For the security of the TRI."

Which would make no difference if the rumour mill downstairs got hold of it. The lunches were bad enough, but if anyone saw him out with Danny, word would spread like wildfire. Still, he'd agreed now, and if he was being completely honest with himself, the idea of a night out with Danny sounded far too good.

Danny's eyes danced. "Keep telling yourself that," he said happily. He glanced at his watch. "You coming down for lunch today?"

Lysander tried to glare sternly at him. "Don't try your luck."

Danny just laughed.

Chapter Eleven

O'DONOHUE LIKED TO keep him on his toes.

Danny groaned aloud when his Leaf shrilled at eight o'clock on Saturday morning. He groped for it, squinting at the message, which notified him that a pod would be waiting for him at the transport hub within half an hour. He couldn't remember the last time he'd moved so fast in his life as he shoved a change of clothes and some essentials in his holdall and dashed for the door.

Two minutes later, he ran back into the flat to actually put on something more than a pair of boxer shorts.

He couldn't help thinking O'Donohue had done it on purpose, and he imagined the man hiding a grin behind one curled finger as he sent the bloody message with the bloody time limit at eight o'clock in the bloody morning.

By the time Danny had dressed and downed a hasty mug of coffee, his brain had twitched to life and reminded him just how long it took to get to the city. A stop in at the canteen provided a bacon buttie, and then he headed on his way.

It was a brighter day, at least—cold and crisp, but with the sun bright in a clear blue sky. Danny poked through his holdall as the pod shuttled towards the city, considering the clothes he had with him. They were all right for going out on the tiles, but Operation Distract O'Donohue would need something better than all right.

The pod dropped him off at a fancy hotel in the centre of the city. Once he'd checked in, Danny wandered out in search of a better class of distraction-wear.

The streets were chock-a-block with people getting ahead of the Christmas rush. To avoid the worst of it, he found a couple of more high-end shops and simultaneously upped the level of his distraction-wear and spent a crazy amount of money.

By mid-afternoon, he'd retreated to the first art gallery he could find and spent a couple of hours wandering through the galleries and their small Impressionist exhibit. He'd parked in front of a Renoir when the Leaf in his pocket chirped. Danny flicked open the screen and grinned.

Chaperone, checking in. Are you staying out of trouble?

Danny considered his reply, then turned around and took a picture of himself with the painting and sent it back. *Get me. I'm being all cultured and shit.*

And nothing's on fire. I'm impressed.

Danny snickered and picked out a tiny rude emoticon. He frowned and then sent another message. *When are we meeting?*

Do you have plans for dinner?

Danny blinked in surprise. All things considered, he hadn't expected Operation Distract O'Donohue to be reversed on him. Dinner could be a lot of things, but when he'd touched O'Donohue's back, he hadn't moved away, and he'd agreed to come out and drink and maybe dance. Which meant, hypothetically, dinner could possibly, technically, be called a date. He had a funny feeling he was grinning like a bellend.

Nothing set in stone.

O'Donohue didn't reply for another fifteen minutes, by which time Danny was pretty much done with the exhibition. He'd had a chance to see a Degas up close, which he definitely counted as a highlight. At school, Danny had been crap at art, but he could appreciate it the same way he could appreciate a well-structured piece of code or a complicated piece of music.

Another chirp and another message, this one with an address and a time and a warning to come with an empty stomach.

Is this revenge for the lunch boxes?

O'Donohue didn't reply.

Two hours later, after a quick run to the nearest pharmacy—a man could live in hope—and a thorough shower and clean up, Danny climbed out of the taxi pod and glanced around with a frown. He glanced down one of the narrow side streets and checked the address again. It seemed to be right, even if a hole-in-the-wall place in a backstreet seemed like the last place O'Donohue would go for a meal.

"Good timing."

He turned, relieved, to see O'Donohue step out of a pod a few paces away. "This *is* the right place, isn't it?"

"It is." O'Donohue smiled as he approached. He looked good, Danny thought. As sharply dressed as usual, though this was clearly the smart-casual version of his wardrobe, with a long coat swirling around him and deep-blue scarf around his neck. His braided hair hung in a thick rope over one shoulder. "Come on. I'm hungry."

Danny paused to smooth his shirt under his jacket and then followed O'Donohue into the dimly lit street. There were several doors and a couple of nondescript windows revealing half-empty restaurants and dingy cafes.

"I forgot to ask if you like Middle Eastern food," O'Donohue said over his shoulder.

"Aye, well enough."

O'Donohue nodded as if satisfied and veered towards one of the restaurant fronts. The windows were latticed in this one, but through the gaps, Danny could see people, and when O'Donohue opened the door, the sound of chatter and laughter flooded out as well as the spicy, inviting scent of food.

Despite the exterior, inside looked like some kind of palace, white walls decorated with jewel-coloured highlights and lamps. There were lattices between the tables for privacy, and Danny couldn't see any empty seats anywhere.

"It looks a bit busy," he said.

O'Donohue laughed. "Don't worry about—"

"Lysander!" a male voice boomed out. Danny blinked in astonishment as a vast beaming man wove his way between the tables, arms outstretched as if he was welcoming his firstborn son. He exclaimed something in a language Danny didn't recognise, and O'Donohue embraced him, kissing him warmly on his cheeks.

Danny felt out of his depth all over again. O'Donohue really did have a knack for it. He could only stand and gape as O'Donohue spoke to the man in the same language, then motioned towards Danny. The man— clearly someone in charge—studied Danny and then beamed.

"Come! Come, I have a table for you." He led them through the assault course of the restaurant, chattering to O'Donohue all the while. Despite his size, their host wove between the tables and chairs as if he didn't notice them and ushered them to a booth on the far side of the restaurant, tucked beside the window. "Sit! I will bring menus and drinks for you both."

Danny sank into the chair, watching their host hurry off, and then turned a bewildered stare on O'Donohue. "What the fuck just happened?"

"Excuse me?" O'Donohue asked as he draped his jacket on the back of his chair.

"Private table, personal service, someone who knows you and speaking the language...?" Danny tried to glare at him. "Are you trying to make me look like a tit again?"

O'Donohue blinked owlishly at him. "Oh. Uh." He smiled a little nervously. "It's my favourite restaurant. I come here all the time." To Danny's astonishment, he self-consciously tucked a stray strand of hair behind his ear. "I figured you might like it."

Heat burned all the way up Danny's face. Shit. It only happened when he knew he had buggered up. "Oh." He scratched at his head, glaring at the table. "Right. Sorry." He managed to pull on a crooked grin. "It's not like you haven't yanked the rug out from under me before."

It got a smile out of O'Donohue. "I'll try my best not to restrain myself tonight." He pressed his hand to his heart. "Chaperone's honour."

Danny laughed ruefully. "Right." He slipped his jacket off and folded it beside him on the cushioned seat of the booth. "So...Farsi or Arabic?"

O'Donohue's smile was sticking around which was an exciting new development. "Farsi." He glanced up as the man bustled towards them, menus under one arm and a tray with a pot and glasses balanced on the other. "Omid makes sure I keep up with it."

"I only know 'please,' 'thank you,' and 'where's the toilet,'" Danny confessed. As much as he liked to travel, languages—like art and music— were always out of reach. To prove himself a little, he waited until Omid set down the tray of tea and thanked him.

He immediately realised his mistake. Omid started talking to him at once in rapid-fire Farsi.

Mercifully, O'Donohue saw the panic on Danny's face and interrupted in Farsi, laughing, and added in English, "We don't want to scare him away."

Omid gave a great boom of laughter and slapped Danny firmly on the shoulder. "English for you, then. Only English." He poured tea for both of them and then disappeared off with the tray, leaving them the menus. Danny picked one up, grateful for something to hide behind for a second to try to pull himself together.

"You've been to Iran?"

Danny peered over the top of the menu. "What?"

"If you know those words in Farsi, it usually means you've travelled." Lysander hadn't opened the menu. "I know 'where is the train station?' in at least seven languages." He gave Danny a wry smile. "Not sure what I'd do if I got a reply. I never learned the directions."

Danny set down the menu. "You travel?"

"Whenever and wherever I can," O'Donohue said. "You?"

"At least one big trip every year." Danny felt giddy, which was daft, but of all the hobbies to have in common with the man, he'd never expected it to be road-tripping. "Off-road if I can. I've got plans to finally get to Mongolia next year."

"The Steppe..." A distant look crossed O'Donohue's face. "God, it's beautiful."

"You've been?"

"Passed through part of it," O'Donohue replied. "Cross-continent train from Beijing to St. Petersburg." He pressed one curled finger to his mouth. "I tell people, and they figure the Orient Express. I never tell them there used to be an express freight service that let people hole up in one of the containers. Five days, pretty much non-stop. One hell of a journey. I almost got arrested when I got off in Russia."

Danny stared at him. "You're kidding."

O'Donohue grinned at him, boyish and full of mischief. "Pick out something to eat, then you're going to tell me the craziest trip you ever went on, arrests and all."

Danny eyed him suspiciously. "Are you fishing for blackmail material?"

"Does it matter?" His eyes glinted, and Danny couldn't help wondering how much more mischievous O'Donohue could get.

"No," he replied with a laugh and returned his attention to his menu.

Nearly three hours and more than a dozen plates of food later, they emerged into the street, fastening up their jackets against the winter chill. Danny couldn't believe how fast the time had flown in, comparing holiday destinations and experiences over far too much food. It surprised him how easy it was to speak to O'Donohue, now they were out of the office and O'Donohue no longer seemed as lofty or formal.

"I'm guessing Iranian food is your favourite if this is your local," Danny said as he pulled on his gloves.

O'Donohue reached up to draw his braid out of his collar. "It's never as good as Musa Joon's, but it's the closest I've found in the city."

Danny cocked his head. "Musa Joon? Is it a restaurant or a chef or something?"

O'Donohue chuckled as they walked out into the main street. "No. That's my grandfather."

"He's Iranian?" That certainly explained parts of O'Donohue's appearance.

"He's happy enough calling himself Canadian now."

Danny blinked. "Wait, you're not American?"

O'Donohue actually laughed out loud. "God, you know how to insult a man." He pressed a hand to his chest and shook his head mournfully. "All these years of being polite to people and you think I'm from south of the border?"

Danny laughed and knocked him on the arm. "Polite? After the stunts I've seen you pull?"

O'Donohue's shoulders were shaking with mirth. "Mostly polite," he corrected. "I've heard all kinds of speculation about where I come from, but this is new." He clicked his tongue in mock disapproval. "American..."

"Like you could tell where I come from in Scotland," Danny retorted with a huff.

O'Donohue's grin widened impishly. "You mean it isn't a fictional country?"

"Hey!" Danny tried to glare at him but failed miserably when O'Donohue raised his eyebrows, his lips twitching. Danny rolled his eyes instead and glanced away to keep from laughing. "So where do we go next? I need to burn off some calories, or I'll be rolling home."

O'Donohue thumbed opened his Leaf screen. "We have a few options. It depends what kind of music you want." He tilted the screen to let Danny see.

Danny studied the list of nearby venues and then stared at O'Donohue in delight. "They have a real ret-bar?"

"Oh God..." O'Donohue groaned, and, if anything, it only encouraged him.

"That's where we're heading!" Danny clapped his hands and rubbed them together gleefully. "Grab a pod. It's time for dancing!"

The club was exactly as tacky as Danny had hoped, the metallic walls in gaudy colours with framed pictures of album covers from different eras. They even had a bloody massive disco ball scattering light across the packed dance floor. And best of all, they were having a theme night!

All the best retro hits of the end of the twentieth century and beginning of the twenty-first.

"This. Is. Amazing."

O'Donohue gaped at him. "Are you serious?"

Danny beamed gleefully. "They did proper dance routines back then." He gazed around as he undid his jacket, searching out the music booth. "If they do requests, I'm going to be here all night!"

O'Donohue held out his hand. "Give me your coat. I'll be at the bar."

Danny tossed it to him. "Before we leave, I'm getting you out there for a dance," he warned, then threw himself onto the dance floor in time to join in with a rendition of the Steps version of "Tragedy."

He'd be the first to admit he wasn't the best dancer, but if a song had a dance routine, no one could stop him, and nothing ever reached the cheesy heights of the crap from the tail end of the century. Some steps and some instructions and he could tear up the dance floor until dawn.

After four songs and some serious regret about eating too much, Danny pushed his way towards the bar, where O'Donohue had perched on a stool, drinking a cocktail in a tall glass. It had stained his lips dark red.

"Done already?" he asked optimistically.

"Not even close," Danny replied, waving to the barman to catch his attention. A row of shots seemed like a good way to start, and he glanced at O'Donohue. "Think you can take me?"

He didn't expect O'Donohue to study him and then push aside his cocktail. "Bring it on."

It was probably the worst idea in the history of bad ideas—five glasses each, lined up on the bar in front of them, and O'Donohue's expression daring him to try. It didn't help when the bloody bastard reached out and ran his fingertip around the rim of one of the glasses.

"Ready?"

Danny glared at him. "Aye." He picked up the first glass. "Go."

Slam. Slam. Slam. Slam. Slam.

Five shots, all down.

He turned triumphantly to find O'Donohue still sipping the first one.

"What the fuck, O'Donohue?"

O'Donohue smiled placidly at him. "The sooner you fall over, the sooner we can leave." He drained the glass and put it down. "And it's Lysander."

Danny blinked, confusion vying with half-hearted admiration for the sneakiness of the bugger and annoyance at the foiled challenge. "What?"

"My name," O'Donohue said. "Lysander. I bought you dinner. I think we're on first name terms now." He slid one of his shots towards Danny. "Do you want another?"

Danny snorted, but he snatched the glass. "You're still going to dance with me before we leave, if it's the last thing I do."

"With?" Lysander asked with wide-eyed innocence. "Or against?"

Danny downed the shot and narrowed his eyes. "You're challenging me to a dance-off? Do you do them the same way you do your drinking contests?"

Another shot glass slid slowly towards Danny. "If you mean I win in my own way?"

Danny made a face at him. "You're right about being a chaperone. No fun at all." He downed the proffered glass, then turned and headed back out onto the dance floor.

The alcohol was catching up with him. He could tell because he didnae bother with the steps. That wisnae good 'cause he danced like his papa, and Papa's dancing like they did in a ceilidh, all whooing and having a wiggle to the music. S'the trouble—and the braw hing—about having a wee drinkie or two. Who gave a crap if he danced like his papa if he had a good time?

He got back tae Lysander by jiggling all the way. Some people yelled at him, but they were bastards, and he didnae gie a fuck, so they could all bugger aff. Lysander was supping his wee cocktail again. Hah. Cocktail. Cock.

"All right!"

Lysander gazed at him, eyes all glinty. "Having fun?"

Danny beamed at him. "Aye. You dancin'?"

"I think you're doing more than enough for the both of us."

Danny hooted with laughter. "Aye, right." He started a wee jig right up by Lysander's seat. "C'mon."

Lysander shook like he was about to pish himself laughing. "You're dancing like an idiot."

"Nah." Danny put his hands in the air, because it ay wis good. "Dancin' like a cert—cefert—proper genius. Got the papers an' a'."

Lysander laughed, and Jesus Christ, he was so fucking hot. "You could go back to the dance floor and dance with the people there."

Danny snorted dismissively. There wisnae anyone half as fucking hot. "Isnae the same." He flung his arm 'round Lysander's middle, leaning right in close. "I want tae dance with you."

Lysander looked at him all dark eyes and serious. "Why?"

Danny made a face at him. "Because." He squeezed Lysander's middle. "C'mon. Just yin."

Lysander didnae say a word. He knocked back his brew and got up and went doon the dance floor.

Danny jigged after him, happy as a pig in shite. "So you're dancin'?"

Lysander raised his eyebrows. "Think you can take me?"

Danny kent he could, and he gave it a good go, all kicks and whoops and arms in the air like a total fanny. He didnae ken the steps of this yin, but he watched Lysander and copied him right up until Lysander started spinning like a fucking top.

"Jesus fuck..."

Lysander kept spinning like one of they fancy ballet people with the tights, his hair wheeching 'round like the tail of a fucking comet.

Aebody was watching. Danny wanted to tell them to piss off 'cause Lysander didnae need anyyin but Danny watching, and, Christ, he'd never wanted to shag anybody so hard in his life. When Lysander stopped, Danny stottered over to him, pushing by all the clapping folk.

Lysander's cheeks were all red and he had a big smile. "I think I won."

"Aye," Danny said, staring at him. He grabbed Lysander's shirt and yanked him close and planted a kiss right on his gob.

Chapter Twelve

CHAPERONING WASN'T GOING to plan.

A good chaperone wouldn't be making out with the person he'd been invited to supervise. Especially not when said person was pretty wasted. Especially on the dance floor of a lame ret-bar.

He pulled away from Danny, who grinned at him. Drunk, he might be, but he definitely had some very clear thoughts going on in his big clever head.

"I think," Lysander said carefully as he withdrew his fingers from Danny's hair, "we should leave."

Danny's grin got wider, and he caught Lysander's hand and hauled him in the direction of the bar. It took Lysander a second to realise he'd been totally misinterpreted.

"Danny..."

"I'll get a pod," Danny said as he grabbed their coats and pulled Lysander onwards out the door.

"Danny!"

The other man paused, looking back at him. "Aye?"

"I didn't mean—" Lysander pulled his hand free and rubbed his forehead. "Damn it."

He flinched in surprise when Danny—with deliberate care—draped his coat around his shoulders.

"I get keen," Danny informed him solemnly as he pulled Lysander's coat snugly around him. "When I have a bevy, I get keen." He raised one hand from Lysander's coat, and his palm was warm against Lysander's cheek. "And you're fucking gorgeous, y'know."

Lysander smiled fondly at him. "And you're wasted."

"Disnae mean I'm wrong."

Danny's hand pressed gently against his cheek, and his thumb brushed along Lysander's cheekbone. The light from the street lamp turned his eyes to gold, and Lysander couldn't look away. It would have taken a hell of a lot of willpower—and maybe two fewer cocktails—to resist kissing him again.

Danny wrapped his arm around Lysander's waist and pulled them flush against each other, and Lysander sank his fingers back into Danny's hair as he darted his tongue against the other man's. Danny's hand spread on his back, and, God, it was tempting to indulge, only for a night.

Danny nuzzled the tip of his nose when they broke apart. "I've got a nice wee hotel room," he offered. "Big bed and everything."

Lysander pressed his other hand to Danny's chest, putting some space between them. "And you're drunk, and I'm not about to take advantage of you."

Hazel eyes squinted at him, and then Danny burst out laughing. "Take advantage? Fuck me, I found a gentleman!" He ran his hand up and down Lysander's back, but he didn't try to pull him closer again. "We've had a good night, though, eh?"

Lysander smiled. "Yes," he agreed.

It made a change, instead of spending time with either groups of ex-colleagues or his friends and their partners. He'd missed going out for dinner one-on-one with someone else, getting to know them and having a few laughs. Unfortunately, he couldn't do it often, not with his name tied to the TRI, especially when there were always people trying to find a way in the door.

Danny beamed at him again, then stepped away and groped in his own jacket pocket for his Leaf. After a couple of attempts, he managed to get it on and called for a pod. He paused and glanced at Lysander. "D'you want to share as far as my hotel? You can have it after." Lysander eyed him doubtfully, and Danny widened his eyes. "I'll be good. No hands or nothing."

For such a big man, Danny could make himself seem as innocent as a naughty schoolboy.

"A good chaperone would see you to your door," Lysander allowed with a smile.

It took all of two minutes in the pod before Danny patted his thigh. "Lysander."

Lysander kept his eyes on the overly friendly hand. He'd been on the receiving end of wanderers before. "Mm."

"Hm?"

"You said my name."

Danny peered at him. His hair stuck up in all directions over his bright red face, his expression unusually unguarded. "I did?"

"You did."

Danny squinted at him. "Oh. Lysander." He smiled. "It's a fancy name. Nice shape. All open." He slid a little closer and tilted sideways to rest his head on Lysander's shoulder. He yawned, warm and damp on Lysander's throat, and drew a circle on Lysander's knee with a fingertip. "S'not very Iranian, is it? Or Canadadian?"

Habit made Lysander cover Danny's hand with his own to keep it from drifting. "It's Greek," he murmured. "I got it from Shakespeare. My parents were English teachers."

"Mm." Danny nuzzled against his throat. "Can I kiss you again?"

God, he wanted to, but if they started again, it would be harder to stop.

"No."

Danny made a small, grumpy sound but settled his head more comfortably on Lysander's shoulder and yawned. "I danced lots," he murmured, still drawing circles on Lysander's knee. "Did you see?"

Lysander squeezed Danny's hand. "I did. And I kicked your ass."

Danny's breath chuffed against his throat. "You did all the..." Danny waved his free hand vaguely. "The twirly-twirly bullshit. Cheating."

"Twirly-twirly bullshit?" Lysander couldn't stop himself from laughing. "I did a pirouette."

Danny lifted his head and gazed at him gravely. "Twirly. Twirly. Bullshit." He poked Lysander in the middle of his chest. "Didnae tell me you could do that."

"You never asked."

Danny frowned indignantly at this very accurate argument, then huffed and rested his head back on Lysander's shoulder. "No one at work told me neither," he complained.

Lysander watched his hand where it lay over Danny's on his thigh. "They didn't ask either."

A down side of being the director meant the people who did talk to him wanted something, and the ones who didn't spent their time speculating. Very few people fell in between. His pre-teen ballet regime didn't really need to become common knowledge. Although if people knew he could still kick like a bad-tempered mule, they might be less inclined to gossip.

"I won't tell."

Lysander tilted his head to glance down at him. "Still being my secret agent?" he asked with a wry smile.

Danny peered up at him and smiled drowsily. "Nah." He gave Lysander's knee a squeeze. "Friend. Friends don't tell other people friends' secrets." He lifted his head to bring his face close and his eyes level with Lysander's and gave him a hopeful grin. "And friends sometimes shag each other."

Lysander laughed helplessly, wondering how the hell the man could make himself more endearing. He pressed his fingertip in the middle of Danny's forehead, pushing him back enough to resist the temptation to pull him closer. "And friends are sometimes drunk and optimistic and need a good night's sleep."

"Mm." Danny grunted with another yawn and peered out the window. "Don't think we'd have time for a quickie back here."

"Again," Lysander said, "optimistic." He glanced out the window, spotting Danny's hotel up ahead. He hesitated and leaned along the seat. "Danny." Danny turned to him, and Lysander pulled him close by the front of his shirt and kissed him once more. Danny blinked at him as Lysander drew away and smiled. "One for the road."

Danny scratched at his mussed up hair. "So that's...no to coming up?"

"That's no to tonight," Lysander confirmed. He pointed out the window. "This is your stop."

It took Danny a minute to get his legs in order and push himself to his feet as the pod door opened. He paused on the sidewalk, then bent and peered into the pod. "D'you wanna have a snog tomorrow?"

Lysander fought down a smile. "Go to bed, Danny."

As the pod pulled away, Lysander glanced back through the rear window to see Danny still standing on the sidewalk. He beamed when he saw Lysander and waved, thrashing his arm over his head.

Lysander sat back.

God, it had been a long time since he'd considered screwing around with anyone. He had a bad habit of being overcautious, but, with his position, there were some risks he couldn't take, no matter how much he might want to.

He sighed.

If he acknowledged the reality, it wasn't just about the job.

Technically, he could say the past didn't bother him. Most of it didn't, but the things that did...

He closed his eyes. Some people weren't worth remembering. Some people didn't even deserve the courtesy of acknowledgement, but once they were under your skin, they stayed there. No matter how much you tried to forget them sometimes, when you least wanted them to creep back, there they were. Every action tattooed across your history.

Danny was nothing like those people. He hadn't pushed, even with a drink or seven in him. He'd asked for permission before doing anything. For someone who had started out so demanding and obnoxious at their first meeting, it was a surprising turn of events.

When the pod pulled up outside his apartment block, Lysander forced himself back to the here and now, away from the more unpleasant thoughts. He lived in a quiet neighbourhood, and given the age of a lot of his neighbours, most of the windows were already dark as he made his way up the three flights of stairs to his apartment.

The lights came on as he opened the door. Once, it had been an apartment made up of several compact rooms, but he'd converted it into one large sprawling studio with an intricate mesh of metal supports woven across the ceiling like cobwebs. The only concession to modesty was the bathroom, tucked behind the back wall of the kitchen.

Lysander shed his coat, hung it on a hook by the door, and reached up to unbraid his hair. As he combed his fingers through his hair, he noticed the comm hub blinking for a message received and sighed. Only one person ever tried to contact him there, every weekend like clockwork. She was the only reason he kept the comm hub.

He hesitated and then brushed his finger over the message control.

"Hello, S—"

Lysander stopped the message. Not that. Not tonight. She didn't know any better, not anymore, but he didn't need to bring his good mood down. In the morning, he would listen and then make time during the day to call the care home and see how things were going.

He slipped his shoes off and padded across the floor to his unmade bed and sat on the end.

Tomorrow, he would see Danny again, and when he saw him, he had to make a decision. If he took the chance to have a relationship with Danny, however briefly, then there were things Danny needed to know, and he needed to know how Danny would react to them. Both of them needed to go in with their eyes open.

He fell back on the bed and stared at the ceiling.

Danny was a good man. A bit of an ass sometimes, but a good man and generous and surprisingly considerate. It would be all right. It would be better.

Lysander closed his eyes and tried to push back the memories crowding in. Meditating helped, so he lay there, focussing his thoughts on a ruined temple he had visited in Pakistan, breathing in steadily and out. In and out.

He must have fallen asleep where he lay, exhausted by his heavy duty of chaperoning and cocktails, because a repeating chirp from his Leaf in his breast pocket woke him. Lysander squinted at the clock on the bedside table, frowning.

It was barely eight o'clock.

He struggled up onto his elbow, groped in his pocket for his Leaf, and flicked up the screen.

A blinking message from Danny repeated over and over. Lysander's heart dropped.

Emergency! Come quick!

Chapter Thirteen

THE SHEET WAS all full up.

Danny crawled around the edges, staring at the tiny gaps, but he couldn't find enough room to write in them. He swore at it, because he could, and then carefully turned it over again. A good sheet. Thick. Didn't let the ink soak through. And it didn't have those bloody annoying stretchy corners to get in his way.

He was so close, nearly there, close as he could be without the code in front of him, even if his head kept banging like a drum and his eyes felt dry and scratchy as sand on toast.

He blinked carefully.

His head wasn't the only thing banging.

"Danny! Open the door!"

Danny grinned. Lysander! Finally!

He managed to get to his feet and wove across the room, kicking a few of those wee little tiny bottles out of the way. They rattled. Not enough in them to keep him properly pished but enough to help him relax and think in all the different ways. Shots of magic fizzy caffeine and all. Better than coffee, those.

It took him a couple of tries to shove the chest of drawers out of the way of the door. Extra security. Keep the spies out. Electric locks were all good and that, but no spy could get through a door blocked up with a chest of drawers.

He opened the door.

Lysander had him by the shoulders in a second, staring at him. "Are you okay? What happened?"

Danny squinted at him. "Eh?"

"You said it was an emergency!"

Danny remembered a message, when all the pieces started falling together. No wonder Lysander was all hair and wrinkles like he'd fallen out of bed and run all the way down. Still looked nice all messy and scruffy and stubbly cheeks. He didn't even have a tie on.

"Oh…" Danny rubbed at one eye. "Aye. I need you to take me back."

"What?" Lysander seemed confused.

Danny knew he had words, and he also knew the caffeine he'd dosed himself with was wearing off and the hangover would come soon. He pushed the door shut, then took Lysander by the wrist and pulled him through towards the bedroom of the suite.

"Danny! Danny, what the hell—" Lysander stopped when he saw the sheet all spread out nice on the floor. "Holy…" He pulled his wrist free and crouched down by the sheet. "What is this?"

Danny tried to crouch too, but everything went a bit whirly. He carefully went down on one knee, then the other. "Figured some stuff out." He tapped the sheet.

Lysander lifted the corner, studying the other side. "You had your Leaf with you." Danny thought he sounded awfy pissed off. "Why did you write all over the bed linen?"

Well, someone couldn't see the obvious, could they?

Danny shook his head. "Couldn't."

"Couldn't? Couldn't what? Use your Leaf?"

Danny sighed impatiently. "No. Bad Leaf. Public networks and shit." He waved to the sheet. "Didn't want anyone to be able to get at it." He managed a smile. "See? I'm good at secrets and shit."

Lysander looked at him funny; then one side of his mouth turned up. "So, this is your secure server right now? A bed sheet?"

"Can't hack a bed sheet," Danny said seriously. "But I ran out of space." He reached over to tug Lysander's arm. "Can you take me to m'room? I can work it out now."

"Danny, you're still drunk."

"A wee bittie." Danny nodded. "Not concentrating so hard. Realised some stuff I'd missed 'cause I stood too close to see all the bigness." He slid his hand down to pull on Lysander's. "Promise, it's all making sense. I have to get to it."

"Right now?"

"Mm." He sat on his heels. "Don't want to forget."

Lysander studied him, then pulled his Leaf out of his breast pocket. "You'll need to get dressed."

Danny blinked at him and squinted down at himself. He had his shorts on, and one sock. It explained why he had all the goosebumps and all. "I need trousers." He got unsteadily to his feet and headed for his bag.

Ten minutes later, Lysander helped him into a big pod. Danny kept a tight hold of the bag with the folded bed sheet until the pod was moving. Once they were on the way, he relaxed.

Lysander held out a bottle of water to him. "You need to drink."

Danny took the bottle gratefully. He'd taken a couple of paracetamol before they left the room. Lysander had insisted it would help, so Danny had done what he was told. The alcohol had come to get its revenge, and the thumping headache got worse every time the light shone in through the window.

Lysander must have noticed him squinting because he touched the control and the windows tinted to a darker shade.

"Did you sleep at all last night?" he finally asked quietly enough so it didn't clang inside Danny's head.

"Nah." Danny took another sip of the cold water. "Went to bed, then stuff..." He shrugged. He'd never been able to explain the moment when all the pieces shifted and suddenly fitted together, especially when, this time, a wrinkle on his pillow had given him the answer. "Wanted to write it all down."

Lysander gave him a smaller, softer smile. "And you remembered about the security risks. I'm impressed."

That smile, Danny decided, needed to show up more.

Then there was the rest of the night before as well...

"Do I get a snog for it?" he asked optimistically.

Lysander laughed. "Maybe once you're clean and sober again. Right now, you're...well, kind of fragrant."

Danny cupped a hand in front of his mouth and sniffed. "Christ! Aye, fair enough." He leaned back in the seat, closing his eyes. "Jesus, my head..."

He nearly shat himself when a cool hand pressed to his forehead. His eyes flew open to find Lysander crouched right in front of him.

"Drink all of the water and lie down," Lysander said. "You can sleep until we get there."

"You'll keep the sheet safe?"

Lysander smiled again. "I will."

Danny drained the bottle, then tipped sideways. The pod had plenty of space for him to stretch out on, and he must've gone out like a light, because next thing he knew, Lysander nudged his shoulder to wake him. His world swam as he sat up, and he groaned, clutching his head.

"Come on." Lysander offered his arm. "Lean on me if you have to."

The transport hub was deserted as they emerged from the pod. Most people didn't work weekends, so there were only a handful of personal pods in the grav bay. Danny couldn't see anyone else on the shuttle either. No people, but plenty of blinding sunlight. He whined pitifully, raising his arm to shield his eyes as the shuttle sped towards the main compound.

"I'm never drinking again," he vowed.

"I find that hard to believe." Lysander sounded amused but sympathetic. "Here." He pulled Danny's arm down and placed his slim cool hand over Danny's eyes like wearing one of those fancy eye masks. The ache in Danny's eyes subsided. "Better?"

"Aye." Danny touched Lysander's wrist. "You've got bloody cold hands."

Lysander chuckled. "Maybe I'm actually a robot after all."

Danny tilted his head enough to squint at him. "Nah."

"How can you be so sure?"

Danny couldn't stop the dirty grin spreading on his face. "Because no robot they've ever made could kiss like you did."

Lysander's eyes danced. "And you've kissed a lot of robots?"

Danny made a face and turned his head under Lysander's hand, closing his eyes. "Don't confuse me. My head hurts." He started in surprise when Lysander's other hand patted him on the head.

"Poor baby."

Danny snorted half-heartedly. "Now you're being a prat."

Lysander laughed.

By the time they reached the arrival hub, the hangover was definitely kicking in. The water and paracetamol had helped, but Danny could feel the world swimming as they made their way up the ramp to the courtyard. Lysander held one of his arms and carried Danny's holdall with the all-important sheet.

"Are you sure you don't want to rest for a little longer?" Lysander asked when they emerged into daylight. "You have your notes on the sheet."

Danny shook his head and immediately regretted it. "I'll start forgetting." He leaned on Lysander's arm as they walked through the doors of the main building, and almost collided with Ben.

Ben's eyes darted between them, and he frowned.

Lysander's arm tensed against Danny's. Danny knew this could raise all kinds of questions: Everyone knew Lysander hardly ever came in on weekends. People had talked about whether he spent them hanging upside down in his cave. He wasn't all dressed up and groomed, which would make people suspicious as well.

"S'the canteen open?" Danny blurted out. "I need a buttie."

"You sure?" Ben asked. "You look like hell."

"Mm." Danny forced himself to nod. "Mr. Bossy here says it'll make the hangover go away faster an' stop me talking bollocks to strangers."

He felt the change in pressure as Lysander relaxed. "This is what you get for going out drinking in public." He spoke to Ben. "Can you do a sweep and make sure there's no mention of the TRI in any of the news bulletins today? *Someone* thought it would be a good idea to get drunk and talk about work."

Ben winced. "Shit, Danny..."

"I didn't say *anything*!" Danny protested, hoping it sounded convincing enough. "You wouldn't let me talk about stuff." He swayed, pressing a hand to his head. "'N don't shout."

Lysander gave an exasperated snort. "You better hope no one heard you." He glanced at Ben again. "Working on the gate again?"

Ben shrugged. "Since no one needed any training on the weekend, I didn't see the harm." He waved towards the main doors of the building. "I was going over to H-block's canteen. Want to join me?"

Lysander's glare was pretty bloody real, and Danny did his best to act recalcitrant. "I don't think this one could make it over there." He pulled his arm against Danny's. "Come on. The sooner your head clears, the sooner we can have a talk about working practise."

Danny saw Ben wince in sympathy as they headed onwards into the building.

As soon as they were in the lift, Lysander sighed. "Thank you."

Danny leaned against the railing. "People'd ask questions about why you're in. Figured you being a pissed-off boss was a good cover." He tilted his head against the cool wall. "D'you think Ben suspected?"

Lysander sat back on the rail beside him. "I think we were both pretty convincing." He covered Danny's hand with his own. "You keep watching my back."

Danny looked sidelong at him. "Take my job seriously, don't I?" He closed his eyes again. "Christ, after I'm done, I'm sleeping the rest of the day."

"You've earned it."

He cracked open one eye. "Do I get that snog?"

Lysander offered his small, brilliant smile. "We'll see."

Chapter Fourteen

THE WEEKEND REALLY hadn't gone as planned.

Danny should have been enjoying a break from working his ass off. Saturday had gone great with a meal and plenty of good conversation at Omid's, then the club. Sunday...

Sunday morning completely blew a hole in Lysander's good intentions.

When he picked up the half-wrecked Danny from the hotel and got him back to the TRI facilities, he'd hoped the man would get some rest. It didn't work out as planned, so he'd stuck around to make sure Danny didn't get himself into a worse state.

Whatever he'd figured out, it was much more than the scribbles on the bed sheet.

Lysander watched him opening up projection after projection, layering them on the wall, skimming through them so fast they were a blur. Danny had spread the bed sheet on the floor, and he didn't seem to realise he wasn't alone.

Lysander had slipped away briefly, heading down to the canteen to pick up some food and water, because though Danny insisted he could work, there'd be a crash, and he'd need all the energy and fluids he could get.

Danny didn't notice him leave or return or notice the food and water until he paused to rub at his eyes and Lysander stepped right in front of him and told him to sit and eat. Even with a sandwich half-chewed in his mouth, his eyes were all over the walls, and one hand kept moving on the code.

Lysander knew there was no way he could stop him. The best he could do was sit and make sure they weren't interrupted. When he could, he pressed bottles of water or a snack into Danny's hand, although they were mostly ignored.

It took until mid-afternoon for Danny to finally sit back on his heels. He knelt on the floor, staring at a mess of code projected there, right beside the bed sheet. Lysander sat up on his chair and leaned forward.

"Danny?"

Danny squinted at him. His eyes were bloodshot. "I think I'm done." He tipped sideways, asleep before he hit the sheet.

It was another hour before Lysander roused him enough to get him to his room, and even then, Danny leaned heavily on his shoulder. No matter how physically fit Danny was, his dead weight pulled Lysander down.

"You need to eat something," Lysander said as he helped Danny into his apartment. "You'll feel worse if you don't."

"A piece?" Danny suggested groggily. "Wi' ham?"

"Piece?"

"Y'know. Bread wi' ham. A buttie."

He had enough food in his small refrigerator to make a sandwich at least. Danny only managed to eat half of it, which was better than nothing, even if he listed sideways with a bite half chewed in his mouth.

Lysander caught his plate before it could hit the floor, then crouched down and slapped him gently on the cheek. "Danny. Danny!"

Hazy eyes squinted at him. "Mm?"

"Swallow your sandwich." Lysander smoothed his hair back. "I don't think anyone would be happy if I left you to choke to death."

Danny managed to gulp down the mouthful and gave him an exhausted, beatific smile. "You're taking care of me."

Lysander smoothed his hair again. "I am." He couldn't help himself; he braced his hand on the arm of the couch and dipped his head to kiss Danny lightly on the lips. "Sleep well."

Danny's eyes were already half-closed, and he relaxed down against the couch. He didn't stir when Lysander pulled his boots off and hoisted his legs onto the couch as well. Lysander fetched the cover from his bed and draped it over him, then stepped back, gazing down at the other man.

Only three weeks ago, he'd taken pleasure in surprising Danny. Now, Danny had outdone him without trying. Lysander had never imagined he'd be so loyal or protective of Lysander's standing, but even when he was wasted, he remembered the importance of discretion and their cover.

Carrigan had said Danny was good at his job, but Lysander suspected everyone had been underestimating him. This definitely made some decisions easier, though the thought made Lysander's heart beat faster than it had in a long time.

He lingered for half an hour to make sure Danny was asleep and unlikely to surface for some time, and then he set out for home. On the way, he left a message on Danny's Leaf with a request to know he was all right when he woke.

When he got home, Lysander couldn't help checking his Leaf every ten minutes.

To distract himself, he put a vidlink through to the care home in Kamloops. If he didn't, his grandmother would panic and phone his mother, which would lead to the combined guilt trip from both. They were experts at it, and though he was a grown man in his forties, it wasn't about to stop them.

Bubbe was having a good day, thank God, which made things easier. Talking to her on a good day meant less stress, when she remembered the right name and didn't spend the call swinging wildly between lamentations at her failings as a grandmother and bitter anger at his 'foolishness.' She made noises about coming to visit, which he knew would never happen.

"How about I come and visit you this time around, Bubbe?"

She flashed the smile they had always shared. "I can show you my hothouse."

Lysander smiled too. "I'd like to see it."

Her expression turned stern. "You'd have to get rid of the beard, though. I can't show you to my friends looking like a drag act."

It was too much to hope for one phone call where she didn't criticise something. "It's my beard, Bubbe. I can do what I want with it." He recognised the gleam of battle in her eyes and quickly changed the subject. "Tell me about your hothouse. Did they let you put in the lilies?"

Her expression brightened. "Oh yes!"

And just like that, smooth sailing again.

Once finished with the call, he retreated to lie on the couch. It hadn't been a relaxing weekend, and talking to his grandmother was just the icing on the cake.

He didn't hear from Danny until 11:45 that night: *Had another sandwich and some water. Going back to bed. See you tomorrow.*

Lysander smiled. At least someone he cared about listened to him.

When he arrived at work the next morning, it came as no surprise to find Danny sitting in his reception room, waiting for him. The hangover had clearly been defeated because Danny looked fresh-faced and bright-eyed. He gave Lysander a quick grin and rose from the chair.

"You got a few minutes?"

Lysander glanced at Fana as she sipped her morning coffee. "When's the first meeting?"

"You've got an hour," she replied, "and the paperwork is all ready for you."

Lysander motioned for Danny to accompany him into the office. Half of him expected—maybe kind of hoped—Danny would pull him around and continue where they'd so nearly left off on Saturday, but Danny immediately went to the chair by the desk and sat.

Business first, then.

"Do you remember what you did yesterday?" Lysander asked, shedding his jacket and hanging it on the stand by the door.

Danny nodded. "Did I explain any of it? I can't remember."

Lysander shook his head as he sat. "I didn't get a word out of you for hours." He gestured with one hand. "Go ahead."

Danny propped his forearms on his knees, bracing himself on them. "Right." He frowned at his hands and raised his eyes to Lysander. "You know I've been finding random bits of new code threaded into the original." When Lysander inclined his head in acknowledgement, he continued. "I assumed there was a pattern to it, and I've been trying to find out what they were trying to do."

"I recall."

"There isn't one."

Lysander frowned. "What do you mean?"

"What I mean is the code is harmless." Danny rubbed at his forehead.

"I don't understand. You said yourself it's a corruption of the code."

"And it is, but it's the equivalent of putting a sticker on a famous painting—it's visible, but it doesn't do anything to change the painting." Danny sighed. "We've been trying to figure out its purpose, because you'd think with someone slipping it in there, hidden in so many layers, they were going to bring down the system or something. But no."

Lysander frowned, confused. "You mean it literally does nothing?"

"As far as I can tell." Danny gave him a rueful smile. "I mean, it's possible they've more still to add, which will change what they already have there. But, so far, everything they have seems to do jack shit."

That didn't make any sense. Why would someone go to so much trouble to plant so much hidden code if they weren't going to use it?

"What are the chances our suspect will come back and change things now? Is there any chance this is the ground work for something bigger?"

Danny shook his head. "Couldn't tell you. But based on what I've seen, if they wanted to make it damaging, they'd have to do a lot of work. If you want me to start stripping it out, I can get it out of there without too much trouble."

Lysander tilted in his chair, staring at a point beyond Danny. No. No, it felt too simple. It couldn't be so simple. Someone had still breached their systems and corrupted them. No matter how innocuous it appeared to be, it didn't change the fact that their system had been compromised, and they were no closer to identifying a culprit.

There had to be a reason for it. It didn't seem to be malice, but it couldn't just be mischief.

He drummed his fingers on the edge of the desk, lost in thought.

"What do you want me to do?" Danny prompted.

Lysander blinked and focussed on him. "Don't undo it yet. We still need to know who did it, even if it does turn out to be completely harmless. Whoever did it had a reason. Our security system has been compromised. We need to find out how and why."

"And keep tabs in case anything new gets added?"

"Exactly." Lysander rubbed at his right temple with his fingertips. "This is turning out to be stranger than I first thought."

"It could be someone is testing the system for weaknesses," Danny said, frowning thoughtfully. "Poking all the defences to see how far they can get unnoticed."

It seemed like the answer was pretty far.

"Keep working back to the source," Lysander said. "It has to be our priority. If we find the source, we find the answers."

Danny rose. He paused and braced one hand on the desk. "One more thing..."

Lysander met his eyes. "Yes?"

One side of Danny's mouth curled up impishly. "About the snog you owe me— Pecking me on the mouth and leaving doesn't really count."

Lysander ducked his head with a laugh. "You weren't meant to remember that."

Danny braced his other hand on the desk. "I was hung-over, not dead." He waited until Lysander met his eyes. "If you fancy it, I'm cooking for myself tonight. Don't feel like dealing with the peanut gallery asking about my weekend."

Well, there was an unexpected twist.

"You want me to come to dinner?"

"Call it an apology for buggering up your Sunday." Danny grinned at him, his eyes dancing. "We can see where it goes from there."

"You don't give up, do you?" Lysander smiled.

"Hey, I'm not the one who kissed you and legged it." Danny straightened up. "The invitation stands if you fancy it. I'm making a roast chicken with all the trimmings. It should let me dodge embarrassing questions for a few days."

Lysander gazed up at him. "And you don't think it'll cause gossip if I'm seen coming to your apartment?"

Danny winked at him. "You're a smart man. I'm sure you can find a reason." He headed for the door, then paused and glanced back. "Thanks, by the by. For getting me home and hydrated and all that."

"Purely selfish," Lysander demurred, shaking his head. "I wanted to take advantage of that big drunk brain of yours."

Danny snorted, then headed out of the office. After the door closed, Lysander heard him chatting to Fana, and he rubbed his cheek with his fingertips. He'd assumed the much more intensive flirtation had been because of the drinking, but apparently not.

An invitation.

Technically, if he let himself consider it realistically, it would be a second date.

He slid his fingers from his cheek to his temple.

The timing could not have been worse to get interested in someone, especially someone who would only be around briefly. It was just so rare for him to find someone from outside his limited social circle who he found attractive but also proved themselves trustworthy, and Danny was both of those things.

Thinking practically, though, Danny needed to focus on the job at hand, and distracting him from it wouldn't help either of them.

On the other hand, Danny didn't seem to get distracted easily. When he focussed, it seemed like nothing could break his concentration. Going to dinner meant they'd both be on downtime, which was good. They deserved a break, and if they took it together, who could blame them?

It amused and annoyed him in equal measure how many excuses and counter-excuses he managed to come up with through the course of the day. He was still thinking about it by the time he got to the end of the day, which confirmed how much he wanted to go.

What the hell.

One night wouldn't hurt anyone, and once he explained things to Danny, it might turn out to be a very short meal anyway.

After he finished the last of his meetings and dealt with all the paperwork, he showed up at Danny's door, as nervous as a kid on their first date. The anxiety faded away as soon as Danny opened the door. He hesitated for a split second, as if he couldn't believe Lysander had actually come; then his face broke into a grin.

"Good thing I put on enough tatties for two," he said happily, opening the door wider to let Lysander in. "D'you want a drink? Food'll be ready in about ten minutes."

"A drink?" Lysander couldn't help himself. "I thought you said you were quitting."

Danny shot an amused grin over his shoulder. "I don't remember saying any such thing." He waved to the table. "Make yourself at home and pour a glass if you fancy one."

The table had been laid for two.

"You knew I'd be coming?" Lysander picked up the bottle of wine on the table and poured for both of them.

"I hoped you would." Danny stirred one of the pots on the hob. "We had a good night on Saturday. I hoped you'd want to do it again."

Lysander couldn't help smiling. "Well, you weren't wrong." He swirled the wine in his glass and took a sip, the flavour crisp and sharp. He watched Danny working his way around the kitchen, setting out plates, stirring pots, and peering into the stove. "You look a lot better than you did yesterday."

Danny laughed. "Aye, it's amazing how shit you'll look when you stay up more than twenty-four hours and drink a whole mini-fridge and six cans of caffeine supps." He winced at the memory. "I won't be doing it again in a hurry." He glanced over at Lysander. "I hope I didn't get too friendly."

Lysander almost snorted wine through his nose.

Danny groaned. "Aye, I'm guessing?"

"You were...friendly," Lysander said, fighting down a grin, "but politely. Kept on asking for permission, and when you didn't get it, you were happy enough to cuddle."

Danny blinked at him, colour flushing across his cheekbones. "Ah, shit..."

Lysander smiled at him. "It made a pleasant change. Trust me, I'd prefer the cuddles to some of the drunks I've crossed paths with." Danny's cheeks still glowed red as he pulled the chicken out of the oven and set to work carving it. "Danny."

Danny glanced over at him. "Aye."

"I liked it," he said quietly.

Danny's expression brightened. He waved the knife at the chicken. "Which bit d'you fancy? Light? Dark? Leg? Breast?"

"Surprise me."

Danny turned out to be a solid cook, and Lysander wolfed down the plateful of food embarrassingly fast. It had been a long day, and when Danny made a narky comment, Lysander reminded him there'd been no lunchtime delivery today.

"Damn," Danny said, grinning as he mopped up gravy with a piece of potato. "You'll need to fire your waiter."

"If he wasn't stuffing me right now, I would," Lysander said with as much hauteur as he could muster.

From the expression on Danny's face, he wanted to say something, and from the colour rising on his cheeks, Lysander guessed it had something to do with 'stuffing.' He stared at his plate and then laid his cutlery down. Well, no better time to make things clear.

"Danny, before we—before this—"

He forced himself to take a breath. Danny was a decent man who had proven himself to be the master of discretion.

Past experience was a clingy bastard.

More than once, the men who had seemed decent were the ones who had really screw him over, spilling his private affairs to people who had no business knowing them. Every damn time, it whispered at the back of his mind. Working where he did, with the secrets he had to keep, the paranoid little worm of doubt had only grown over the years.

"What's wrong?"

He raised his eyes to Danny, who sounded worried and had put his cutlery down as well.

Lysander straightened his knife on the edge of the plate. "I'm trans," he said finally. "I wanted you to know in case—before—" He smiled self-consciously. "I thought you should know, in case you change your mind."

Danny frowned at him. "Eh?"

Lysander wasn't sure what to say. Of all people, he'd assumed Danny—from cosmopolitan London—would know. "It means—"

"I know what it means," Danny interrupted, waving a hand. "I'm not sure why you think I'd change my mind. I fancy you. Doesn't matter what you have in your keks."

Lysander felt like wires that had been holding him tense had snapped, and he laughed unsteadily with relief. The damned stupid fear wouldn't go away, no matter how many years went by. "Good. That's—you—" He managed a smile. "You fancy me, then?"

Danny held up a hand, chewing hurriedly on a mouthful of food, but when he swallowed, he said, "Aye. A lot. I thought kissing you gave me away." He reached for his glass of wine and considered it, then gazed across at Lysander. "Does everybody else around here know? About you, I mean. Not about me fancying you."

Lysander picked up his fork and prodded a piece of potato. "I don't see why they need to," he said. "They already speculate enough about whether I'm a robot or a First Nation Canadian or God knows what else." He shrugged. "You know what they would wonder, and it's none of their damned business."

"Fair enough." Danny's smile returned. "I'll add it to my secret agent file of stuff not to go blabbing about in the office."

Lysander wanted to hug the man. Personal or professional, he'd shown his worth over and over again. "I think I owe you that snog now."

"Ah, ah, ah!" Danny held up a finger reproachfully. "Dinner first. I cooked it. You're going to fini—" He paused, horrified. "Oh, shit. I sound like my mother."

Lysander couldn't stop himself from laughing.

Chapter Fifteen

FROM THE SPEED with which Lysander cleared his plate, he was either really enjoying Danny's cooking or equally keen to get to the snogging. Or both.

Danny had to hide his grin as he gathered up the dishes to carry them to the counter. "There's dessert if you want it," he said as he scraped the last dish clean to put it into the dishwasher. "If you're still—"

A hand pressed to his back, and he nearly dropped the plate in surprise.

Lysander could move like a cat.

"Leave it," he said.

Danny set the plate on the counter and turned to him. "D'you have something else in mind?"

Lysander grabbed him by the front of his T-shirt and pulled him down to kiss him.

Well, aye. Good diversion. Danny flung an arm around Lysander's waist, yanked him closer, and opened his mouth to Lysander's demanding kiss.

When Lysander's other hand grabbed his arse and squeezed, Danny broke the kiss, dunting the tip of his nose against Lysander's. "In the kitchen? That's not very hygienic."

Lysander laughed, his eyes gleaming. "Host's choice."

"Aye?" Danny glanced towards the couch, then beyond it to the bedroom. He returned his attention to Lysander. "How much are you up for?"

Lysander's dark eyes gleamed, and he pulled Danny flush against him. "I'm not here to waste any time."

Danny's mouth went dry, and his cock twitched. "Fuck me..." he breathed hoarsely.

"That's the idea."

Fantasies going from hypothetical to real were always a wee bit of a surprise, Danny thought, grinning like an arse again. The bedroom with that big fucker of a bed was calling out to him. He pulled Lysander's mouth to his and nudged him back a step, then another.

It turned into a dance, Lysander's grip on his arse steering him, twisting him about, pushing him up against the wall by the bedroom door, his thigh sliding up between Danny's legs, making him groan as his cock strained against his trousers.

"Missed the door," Lysander growled against his lips.

"Distracted," Danny retorted breathlessly. They were nose to nose, breathing hard, and shit, Lysander kept moving his thigh, rubbing against him, making it bloody hard to concentrate. Making a lot of things bloody hard. With effort, he caught Lysander around the waist again and twisted them around and staggered into the bedroom.

Lysander laughed, clenching his hand in Danny's hair. "That wasn't so difficult, was it?"

"Prat." Danny kissed him, and then drew away a wee bit, searching Lysander's face. He remembered how nervous Lysander had been when he came out to him. It told a story of a time when someone hadn't taken it well. God, he'd never want to make Lysander uncomfortable or push for something Lysander didn't want to or maybe couldn't do.

Lysander watched him carefully, the wariness there, below the surface.

"What is it?" Lysander asked, his hand sliding from Danny's arse to press against the base of his back.

"I was thinking," Danny said. "I'd like it if you told me what to do."

Lysander snorted in disbelief. "Danny, I know you. You hate being told what to do."

Danny ducked his head with a rueful grin. "Only when it comes to work or doing something I don't want to do." He met Lysander's gaze. "I think it's safe to say I want to do this."

Lysander's expression softened. "And you don't want to do anything wrong?"

"Maybe it's part of it," Danny agreed, running his hand the length of Lysander's spine. "But tell me you don't love the idea of having me do *exactly* what you want." He leaned closer to press a kiss to the corner of Lysander's jaw. "No questions." His earlobe. "No committees." He bit lightly on his throat. "No arguments."

He translated Lysander's fist clenching in his hair as an emphatic yes. "You'd be putting a lot of trust in me."

Danny shrugged. "You've never given me a reason to doubt you."

Lysander darted his tongue along his lower lip. He loosened his fingers in Danny's hair. "Kneel down."

Danny's heart thundered. Christ, he'd thought it would all be good for Lysander, but going to his knees, knowing he had the power to refuse, made his head spin. Give and take for both of them, and Lysander was watching him with a feverish hunger that made his cock ache.

He raised his head. "What n—"

Lysander brushed a cool fingertip across his lips. "Quiet," he murmured. He walked in a circle around Danny, not touching, not yet. Danny could tell he wanted to, though, in the twitch of his fingers and the heat of Lysander's gaze on him.

"Shirt off," Lysander finally said, stopping in front of him.

Danny kept his eyes on Lysander as he pulled his shirt loose from the waist of his trousers and peeled it up over his head. He tossed it by the dresser and let his arms fall back to his sides. Lysander's breath caught, and when he stepped closer and brushed his fingers down Danny's cheek, Lysander's hand shivered.

"I want you to take my shirt off," he murmured. "Carefully. I would be disappointed if you damaged it."

Danny rose up on his knee, pressing one hand to Lysander's hip. With the other, he reached up and twisted one button undone at a time. With each button, he trailed his fingers down to the next, tracing a path on the newly revealed bare skin. Lysander's heart pounded against his fingertips, but Danny kept his eyes on Lysander's face as he went.

When the buttons were all undone, he took each of Lysander's hands, undid the cufflinks, and tucked them into Lysander's pockets. Then, he knelt up and pushed the shirt from Lysander's shoulders. It slithered down his arms, landing in a crumpled pool at his feet.

Danny sat back on his heels, gazing up at Lysander as he folded the shirt. Lysander was lean, with a mat of dark hair running the length and breadth of his torso but didn't quite hide a spread of faded scar tissue down one side of his chest, rough-edged but faded and clearly long-healed. His hands were clenching and unclenching by his sides.

"Come here," he ordered, beckoning.

Danny rose at once, and Lysander pulled him close and kissed him again.

"Don't be quiet," he said between kisses. "The novelty wears off."

Danny burst out laughing. "Whatever you fancy," he agreed, running his hand the length of Lysander's back. Lysander's hands were at Danny's waist, and he didn't try to resist as Lysander steered him round. One cool hand pressed to the middle of his chest and pushed him. He fell onto the bed and braced himself on his elbows.

"Trousers off," Lysander growled, one hand at his own belt. "Now."

Danny couldn't remember the last time he'd stripped so fast in his life. It was a fucking relief, his cock hard and leaking, and he saw the flash of fire in Lysander's eyes. He sprawled back on the bed, legs spread, and raised his eyebrows.

"Like what you see?"

One side of Lysander's mouth quirked up. "I've seen worse."

"Hey!"

Lysander laughed, bright and warm, then bent down and wrapped his hand around Danny's cock.

"Jesus fucking Christ on a cracker! Cold!"

If anything, it made Lysander laugh even more. "Oh! Shit! Sorry!" He rubbed his hands together and made a show of blowing on them, then reached down and stroked his hand the length of Danny's cock. "Better?"

Danny huffed in mock indignation, undercut by the way he pressed himself against Lysander's hand. "Mm. Better." He wrapped his hand around the back of Lysander's head and pulled him down to kiss him again, his tongue darting against Lysander's in the same rhythm as Lysander was stroking him.

Lysander closed his fist around Danny's cock, then ran his thumb over the head. "Danny," he murmured between lazy kisses. "I want to fuck you."

Danny couldn't keep his hips from twitching. "I'm not stopping you."

Lysander leaned away enough to gaze at him. "You're sure?"

Danny met his eyes, then pointedly glanced down at his raging hard-on currently gripped in Lysander's hand. "I think you've got me convinced."

Lysander smiled and it lit up his face. He tightened his grip enough to make Danny catch his breath. "I want you on your knees," he said, his voice thickened with anticipation.

Danny covered Lysander's hand on his cock and lifted it away. He held Lysander's gaze as he lifted Lysander's hand to his mouth and kissed his palm, then licked a smear of his own precum from Lysander's fingers. Lysander hissed, baring his teeth.

"Knees," he growled. "Now."

The mattress shifted under Danny as he twisted over onto his knees, hands braced on the covers. Lysander ran his fingertips lightly from Danny's tailbone all the way up to the nape of his neck, sending a shiver the length of Danny's body. All but one fingertip lifted away, and it trailed lazily down to the middle of his spine.

"Lean forward," Lysander murmured with the gentlest of pressure from that single finger.

Danny swayed down, shifting from hands to forearms, his brow coming to rest on his fists. "Low enough?"

"Mm." Lysander teased his fingers along Danny's back. "You have no idea how good you look when you do what you're told." His voice sounded rougher than it had been. "Stay still."

Danny shuddered pleasantly as those cool fingertips meandered in patterns down his spine, then jolted when silky strands of hair swept down against his skin a split second before Lysander brushed his lips against the middle of Danny's back.

"Christ..."

Lysander's hands were at Danny's sides, and his mouth moved up to nip at Danny's nape. "I'm guessing you're prepared for all occasions," he murmured close to Danny's ear, his breath warm. His teeth caught Danny's lobe and tugged. "Where?"

"Bag on the floor." Danny groaned, breathing too hard, and moved his hands apart to twist his fingers into the covers. "Holdall. In case Saturday went well."

Lysander lifted his hands away. He barely made a sound as he crossed the floor and went through the bag. Suddenly, one hand brushed Danny's hip. "You have a choice," he murmured, sliding his hand under Danny's body and catching his cock again. Skin still cool, but shit, right now, Danny couldn't care less. "Hard or slow."

"Wh—what?"

A long slow pull of his hand, then a faster stroke, but firmer.

"Hard," Lysander repeated. "Or slow."

"Fuck a duck!" Danny yelped. "I don't care! Either! Both! Something!"

Lysander laughed and withdrew his hand. "Gentleman's choice." He sounded amused and playful, and Danny tilted his head for a glimpse of his flushed, delighted face. Lysander met his eyes. "Ah, ah. Eyes front."

Danny obeyed, shivering as cool fingers—slick now—played across his arse. "Got a face like yours and you make me stare at the pattern on the duvet?" he complained amiably, then caught a breath between his teeth as Lysander effortlessly slid two lubed fingers into him.

"I want to see how well-behaved you are," Lysander said, his voice laced with mischief. His other hand caught Danny's hip, holding him still, and he stroked his fingers as if he had all the time in the world, making Danny hiss, his hips jerking back against Lysander's hands. "Hard or slow?"

Danny tried to gather his thoughts, but everything was—ahahah—so much harder. And Lysander pressed and stroked and—oh holy shit!—right there, and soft, silky hair trailing all over his skin and lips brushing his shoulder.

"Danny," Lysander said, warm and damp at his ear. "I'm waiting. Answer me."

Shit shit shit shit...

"Hard," he blurted out, then caught his breath as Lysander caught his cock again. Hard. Aye. Hard was good. Slow...slow could come later.

Lysander nipped his earlobe again. "Good," he murmured, and then his hands were both gone and Danny had his arse in the air, bare and waiting, and it felt like for-fucking-ever. His fists were clenching into the covers, and behind him, there, the sound of a zip, of fabric moving, skin on skin—not his, not yet—and movement, the edge of the mattress dipping a little...

And hands were on his hips and the familiar pressure against his arse and...

"Jesus Christ, sometime today!" he exclaimed indignantly, his breath coming too quick.

Lysander's laughter rang out, and then he thrust home, hard enough to make Danny wrench at the covers.

"Fuck!"

Lysander held himself so still, but his breath came as fast as Danny's, and he laughed again, soft and sharp. "Correct." His hands tightened on Danny's hips, and Danny felt the fabric of Lysander's trousers against the back of his thighs as he started to move his hips.

Lysander was as good as his word. Christ, and then some. Lysander's hips pounded against Danny, hard and fast, and his hair swept down over Danny like a curtain, and his teeth and lips were at the back of Danny's neck, and one hand under him, catching his cock, catching the ripple of his own thrusts against Danny's arse in his hand, squeezing, growling Danny's name.

Danny's hips were moving urgently, trying to match Lysander's pace, but Christ, he was inexhaustible, and Danny's breath caught and his cock throbbed against Lysander's hand. "Jesus," he panted out, jerking at the covers. "Ly...fuck, Ly..."

Lysander's hand tightened on his cock, stroking faster. "Not my name, Danny," he growled. "Say my name."

Danny gulped in a breath. "Lysander!" He was coming and hard, and, shit, Lysander, still moving...

He pressed his head down between his hands on the covers, trying to keep meeting Lysander's thrusts, his pulse throbbing through every inch of him. Lysander was breathing harder now, low panting breaths, and his pace eased, but he kept moving, still moving, and grinding hard against Danny until he released a short, explosive breath. His weight pressed down against Danny's back as he braced on one shaking forearm.

Long hair trailed down against Danny's skin as Lysander draped over him, so close his every hot breath huffed between Danny's shoulders.

With effort, Danny tilted his head. "Not bad."

Another warm breath, a chuff of laughter. "Not bad?" Lysander braced his weight on his forearm and pushed himself up. He patted Danny's arse with his other hand as he withdrew. "I'll have to try harder next time."

Danny grinned into the bedding. Next time, eh? Definitely promising.

He heard the shifting of fabric again.

"Onto your back," Lysander said.

Danny obligingly rolled over. Lysander already had his trousers up and fastened again. No one would have thought he'd given anyone a good seeing too. His hair had all come undone, though, and his cheeks were a bit pinker than usual, and, Christ, he looked better than ever. Still, Danny wouldn't be him if he went all doe-eyed.

"You made me make a mess on my bed," he complained, gesturing to the spatter across the covers.

Lysander stepped closer to the edge of the bed and beckoned. Danny sat up, grinning as Lysander stood between his splayed knees and ran his fingers through Danny's hair. When he bent down and kissed Danny, he smiled.

"Your mess," he murmured against Danny's lips. "You can clean it up."

Danny drew back as much as Lysander's grip would allow. "Hey! That's not fair. Especially when I wanted to ask if you fancied staying and you'd have to sleep in it."

There was something satisfying about seeing Lysander surprised. Not the easiest expression to get on his face, but definitely worth the effort. Lysander blinked at him. "Excuse me?"

Danny wrapped his arms under Lysander's arse, holding him there. "You know me. I'm a cuddler. Kind of hard to cuddle someone when they bugger off as soon as the job's done." He tilted his head into Lysander's hand. "Anyway, you mentioned a next time."

Lysander had a collection of smiles. Danny had already seen amused, mischievous, delighted, and professionally satisfied. Now he was pretty sure he'd managed to get shy for the first time. Lysander glanced away, his lips curling, and he laughed quietly.

"I don't think it would be very sensible," he finally said.

Danny shrugged. "And downing six cans of energy drink and a liquor cabinet was? Doesn't mean you shouldn't do it once in a while." He squeezed his arms around Lysander's backside. "I don't hog the covers or anything."

Lysander brushed his finger down Danny's cheek. "How about a rain check?" When he pressed against Danny's arms, Danny didn't restrain him. He saw the immediate relief on Lysander's face, as if he'd expected to be held tighter.

"You know where I'll be," Danny said as he got up off the bed and crossed the floor to pick up Lysander's shirt for him. He shook it open and held it for Lysander to put on.

Lysander glanced at him, and the same shy smile crossed his lips as he slipped his arms into the sleeves. He watched as Danny did up each of the buttons and then covered Danny's hand on his chest. "Thank you."

Danny smiled. "I'm not sure what I'm being thanked for."

Lysander glanced down at their hands and then at Danny's face. "For letting me steer this time. I—it's not always easy finding someone who gets it."

Danny lifted Lysander's hand to his lips and kissed his palm. "Then they're twats." He kissed each fingertip and murmured, "And I liked it as well, y'know. Not having to think about what to do next or worry about buggering up."

Lysander smiled. "Is that so?"

"My bed sheets say aye."

Lysander rose on his toes to kiss him again. "You and your messy bed sheets." He sighed as he drew away. "What will we do with you?"

"Plastic sheeting," Danny said solemnly and beamed when Lysander burst out laughing.

Chapter Sixteen

PEOPLE ALWAYS GOT weirded out by Lysander's good moods.

He wasn't sure why, but he figured a lot of them had never seen him smiling. Maybe they thought a robot couldn't have emotions. More fool them. Still, he tried to rein it in when he headed to his office, even if the people who had seen him in the shuttle would probably spread it around.

"Morning, Fana."

She glanced up from her desk. "Someone's cheerful this morning."

"I said two words," he said wryly. "How could you tell?"

She grinned at him. "I know you, sir." She darted her fingers across the console, then transferred several files. "There are some reports for you to sign off on, the final approvals for a couple of the Medieval jumps, and an incoming briefing from the UN at eleven o'clock." She paused and skimmed the calendar. "There's only one concall scheduled for this afternoon as well."

"Quiet so far," he observed, unbuttoning his jacket.

"Well done. You jinxed us." She leaned back in her chair. "So are you going to tell me?"

"Tell you what?"

She gave him a glower his grandmother would have been proud of. "The cause for your good mood."

He couldn't stop the smile flashing across his face. "I had a good night. That's all you're getting."

She wrinkled her nose at him. "Not even a morsel for your poor, loyal assistant?"

"No." He laughed as he opened his office door. "How am I meant to retain my air of mystery if I tell everyone my secrets?"

She snorted and muttered something he suspected might be gently insulting in Somali.

"Charming as ever," he called as he walked into his office.

It was crazy how much the evening with Danny had raised his mood. The truth about the code hack had been a big relief itself, and then any doubts he'd had about pursuing any kind of physical relationship with Danny were brushed aside.

Luckily, when he'd headed home from Danny's afterwards, the shuttle had been deserted, with no one to see him grinning from ear to ear.

Of all the people to hand over control to him, he'd never expected it to be Danny.

Every bit of information in his personnel file made note of his stubbornness and his tendency to do things his way or not at all. And without hesitation, he'd given Lysander authority. It wasn't only for Lysander's sake either. He admitted it himself; he didn't want to worry about doing something wrong, and he trusted Lysander to make sure of it.

Lysander had played around with taking charge once or twice before, but it didn't seem the same this time. Before, it had never felt like anything more than role play. This time, it wasn't just playing, and it had been exhilarating in a way he'd never expected.

In the real world, getting anything done involved hoops to be jumped through and diplomacy and tact to be maintained. It was impossible to get straight to the point, to say what he wanted and get it without thinking himself in circles to avoid conflicts.

There, in that room, he had given a direct order, and it had been obeyed without hesitation or question.

He sat at his desk and ran his thumb along his lower lip, trying not to think of how readily Danny had gone down on his knees.

Enough.

Work had to be done. If he and Danny indulged themselves out of hours, no problem, but work had to come first.

By the time he finished the briefing with the team from the UN, it was rolling on to one o'clock in the afternoon. He wasn't surprised to see a light glowing on his desk, an incoming notification from Fana.

Lunch is waiting when you're ready.

Lysander fought back the smile, reassured to know he and Danny were both thinking about one another. He schooled his expression as he went through to get the box, though Fana's lips twitched as she handed it to him. If she had her suspicions—and she probably did—she wasn't about to spill them to the world.

A small note had been tucked in with the box of still-warm lamb pilaf and wedge of fruit tart: *To keep your energy up. You may need it.*

Lysander pressed his finger to his lips, heat blooming in his cheeks again at the implicit invitation and promise. As he dug into the food, he wondered if it would be presumptuous to show up at Danny's door at the end of the day.

He could technically grab a meal for them both from the canteen, but it might raise questions. Still, he had plenty of time to come up with some reasonable excuse.

He picked at the tart as he turned his attention back to one of the latest mission reports. The supervisor and team leader had already given it their general approval. All it required was his signature, and it would be ready to go.

Technically, he only needed to read the summary, trusting their historians and supervisors to do their jobs, but sometimes he couldn't help himself. In this case, the team had been—incredibly briefly—to Wallachia to get eyes on a certain warlord, who they could confirm was scary as hell, but definitely not a vampire.

Missions targeting dangerous historical periods or people were rare, but, once in a while, approval would be granted after a Sammy—the standard Samuels risk assessment, named for a lost agent—was carried out. All and any possible risks were taken into account. People were always interested in those dangerous times, so inevitably, at some point, someone would eventually have to go.

He'd read through half the report when an alarm shrilled out briefly.

Lysander glanced up, startled.

It wasn't the standard bell that notified the staff of a jump in progress, but the sound of lockdown, which meant something had happened.

"Fana. Get me security."

"Patching through, sir."

A video link opened up in front of him. Theo Nikolas, the head of the security division, appeared on the screen. He didn't look happy, which was a bad way to start a security meeting. "Mr. O'Donohue. We think we may have off-site gate activity."

Lysander stared at him blankly for a second. Impossible. But they were saying it had happened, so, somehow, it had become possible. "Where?"

"We're trying to pinpoint the power surge, but it's difficult." Theo glanced off-camera, then back. "So far, we have an area somewhere down south."

Lysander pushed aside his reports. "And you're sure it could only be a gate?"

"It matches the parameters of the energy surges Tom Sanders had recorded before Ben installed the energy dampeners in the gates," Theo replied. "It's possible it may have been something else, but it seems unlikely." He hesitated. "Sir, something about this has pinged an old record. I don't have the access or clearance to see what it is."

There were very few files closed to the head of the security team, and Lysander had a sinking feeling he knew which file it might be. "Give me the number. I'll look into it. You keep your team focussed on pinpointing the gate."

When the video winked out a few seconds later, Lysander ran his hand over his face.

Coincidences were never good, and before he opened the file, he knew what he was going to see.

He touched the control on his desk. "Fana, can you call up Ofori for me?"

Jacob arrived within five minutes, grim-faced. "Is this about the alarm?"

Lysander reopened the file. "We've recorded a power surge concurrent with the opening of a gate," he said. "Apparently, the energy spike matched this particular incident closely enough to flag the file."

Ofori sank into the seat opposite, staring at the Sanders file—the day when Mackenzie Robertson arrived in the past and ended up dead. "Shit..."

Lysander's hands were shivering. He dropped one to his lap and closed the other in a fist on his desk. "Does this mean what I think it means?"

"If you mean some bastard from the future might be running around?" Jacob frowned. "I don't know how that's possible. Last time I checked, Harper was still locked up."

"The man behind Tom Sanders's disappearance?"

"He's not due for release for a few years, so unless he's got someone else doing his dirty work for him, then..." He trailed off, staring into nothing. "It could be him again, further down the line after his first time fucked up."

"Shit."

Ofori made a sound of agreement, leaning back in his chair. He propped one elbow on the arm and pressed his fist to his mouth as he stared at the file. "Have they managed to locate the source? It would give us a starting point."

"They're working on it." Lysander got up and went to pour himself a glass of water. The pitcher rattled against the edge of the glass. Dealing with the past, he could do. Dealing with the future was a hell of a lot more complicated.

The silence felt unbearably tense until the security team patched back in.

"London," Theo said. "Somewhere on the south bank. We're tightening it in now."

"Fuck!" Jacob slammed his hand down on the arm of the chair.

Lysander couldn't blame him. If someone had come through the gate, London would make a perfect hiding place. If the jumper had arrived somewhere out of sight of the cameras, all they would have to do is blend into a crowd, and they'd disappear.

He touched the desk to mute the connection to the security team as they worked. "Do you still have contacts in the force?"

"A couple of my team from the Sanders case are high up there now."

Lysander blew out an unsteady breath. "Get on the line to them. See if they can liaise with the Met and get a team out to secure the arrival point."

Jacob rose from the chair at once. "We can't give the details until we know what's going on. Last time, we had to sit on so much information in case it caused a panic."

Lysander turned his glass in his hands. "Have them secure the scene now. We might be able to find out who we're dealing with." He managed a brittle smile. "Who knows? It's possible no one came through. It could have been a glitch."

Jacob didn't seem convinced. "And you believe that?"

"What do you think?" Lysander motioned to the door. "I'll send you the details as soon as the team gets them to me." It came as no surprise to see Ben standing on the other side of the door as Jacob walked out.

"What's going on?" Ben demanded, staring wildly between them.

Ofori glanced back at Lysander, and Lysander could see the warning in his expression. "O'Donohue'll fill you in."

Lysander beckoned Ben in and then went to the door. "Fana, all meetings and calls need to be put on hold for now. Make it happen."

Ben leaned on the back of one of the chairs when Lysander shut the door, his body rigid and tense. "Who triggered the lockdown alarm?"

"We're not sure exactly what's going on ourselves." Lysander perched on the edge of the desk. "The security team picked up an unusual high-energy spike somewhere in London. They're concerned because it resembled the energy spikes we used to get with the gates."

Ben frowned. "Someone's opened a gate in London? How?"

"I didn't say that." Lysander kept his expression as calm as possible. "We don't know anything beyond an energy surge right now. Jacob's using his old contacts to get a team from the Met to check out the site. It could be a factory or facility using high-energy equipment. Until we know for certain, the team wanted to err on the side of caution."

Ben stared at him. "But it could be a gate? A gate we didn't open?"

Lysander rubbed at his forehead. "Ben, I'm telling you what I know right now. Until the team gets to the site and sees what could have caused it, we're in a holding pattern."

"And the team is on the way there now? How long until we find out what they know?"

Lysander could hear the echoes of the frantic teenager who had demanded proof of his father's death and who screamed and swore and fought for the chance to save one agent. As cheerful and calm as Ben appeared to be, the fire and passion remained.

If it did turn out to be a gate, God only knew how Ben would react. He didn't know much about his father's death, but he knew technology had been stolen. Unless some other inventor had managed to build a gate, there could only be one source. If Ben started making assumptions—and he had a knack for extrapolating data—things could get messy real quick.

Right now, Ben was on edge, and they definitely didn't need him finding out what was really going on with the mysterious code, Robertson, and, now, this gate's possible connection to his father. The best option would be to provide a managed degree of transparency.

"How about you stay here until we find out?" Lysander suggested. "That way, you hear what I hear."

Ben eyed him guardedly, then sat on the chair. "I don't know how it would be possible."

Lysander wished he could provide some reassurance without giving anything away. "We work with time travel. We should have learned to believe the impossible years ago."

For a split second, Ben smiled, tight and sad. "Welcome to my life."

Chapter Seventeen

DANNY'S DAY HAD started pretty well.

He'd slept like a baby the night before—a good seeing to could do that for a man—and he'd woken up with a pleasant ache in his thighs and a stupid grin on his face. God, he wanted to send an invite over to Lysander for a second round, but Danny knew there was such a thing as being too keen.

Instead, his morning had been spent in Ben's company, doing an intensive course on the coding used for gate targeting.

While he could recognise the patterns of the code, there was something mesmerising about watching the way it was constructed. Ben had led him through it, stage by stage, explaining each step as they went.

Gate targeting was a fine art, Ben explained. In the early days, when the gates were being developed, connecting to a specific time and place had been one of the biggest problems. They could fix on a specific location, but there had been real problems with the temporal coordinates. If you did three consecutive jumps, you could end up at the same location in three different centuries.

"It's exact now, isn't it?"

Ben smiled proudly. "To the second. If you know exactly where and when your return gate is going to open, you just need to be close enough to walk through it."

"There's a thing..." Danny knew he was pressing his luck to ask any questions about time travel at all, but Ben never seemed to mind. "What if there's someone else about? Someone historical? What if they get between the agent and the gate? What if they come through instead?"

Ben laughed. "We have safeguards against that. Rendezvous sites tend to be isolated or out of the way. We've used warehouses before or dead-end side streets if it's in a city. And we always do a quick scan before the gate opens properly. Our agents have trackers so we can be sure who's there."

"It seems like a lot of luck when there are so many jumps and no one accidentally tripped through."

Ben chuckled. "There have been a few close calls, but if you saw a mysterious doorway made of light, would you go anywhere near it?"

Danny considered it. "I'd probably stare too long and it would close. Can you imagine being from, like, four hundred years back and seeing a crackling glowing floaty door, though?" He laughed. "You'd probably think you were seeing God's wrath or some bollocks and run away screaming."

"That's what we thought too." Ben agreed. "Now, let me show you how we incorporate the coordinates."

By the time it came to lunch, Danny's head felt oversaturated with information. Even concentrating on his food felt like an effort, and his spaghetti kept unravelling around the fork. After ten minutes, Ben took pity on him, letting him off the hook for the afternoon "to let you recover."

Danny made a face at him but had to admit relief at being able to retreat up to his study room to continue his own work. Compared to building the stuff from scratch, it was a walk in the park. Some of the stuff Ben had shown him turned out to be useful as well, which helped him as he started to tease apart the intricacies of the code.

The afternoon went by quietly enough, apart from a weird alarm ringing through the speakers. Since no one came to make sure he wasn't trapped or dead, he guessed it wasn't the fire alarm, turned up his music, and continued with his work.

A couple of hours later, he'd started a last circuit of the room, humming to himself as he juggled projections, when the door opened. Instinct closed his hand on his remote, and every projection winked out, leaving him squinting at the silhouette in the doorway.

"Mr. Ferguson."

Danny frowned. Not Lysander or Ben or any of the coding team. His vision came back into focus enough to see the visitor, a stern-faced older black man in a suit, who seemed very familiar. He seemed like the kind of person who could be terrifying when he wanted to be. "Aye?"

"My name is Jacob Ofori." He stepped into the room. "We need to get you back to your flat."

Ofori.

Danny blinked idiotically.

Jacob Ofori. *The* Jacob Ofori. Only the sodding police officer who had uncovered time travel and forced the TRI to go public. Christ on a cracker, he could still remember watching the interview with the man.

And now, the man waited there, looking at him expectantly.

"Er." Danny managed a sheepish smile. "What?"

Ofori raised his grey-peppered eyebrows. "Your flat," he said. "You need to return there. Immediately."

Danny had been nicked once—one too many brews and too few clothes on a night out—and right now, he remembered that tone of voice. It screamed police and a vibe of 'come quietly.' He took a wary step back. "What's going on?"

"It's nothing to be worried about." Which meant someone with more clearance had everything to be worried about. "We're carrying out some standard security checks this afternoon, and since you're an external member of staff, you don't need to be involved."

Danny frowned. "Well, that sounds like a load of bollocks." He almost bit his stupid tongue, but when Ofori lofted an eyebrow, he couldn't help explaining. "If anyone should be part of a security check, it's the people who don't work here full-time, and for a standard check, I'd've got more than ten seconds notice."

Ofori gave him a measured look, and Danny couldn't help feeling he'd managed to both annoy and impress the man at the same time. "I'll make a note of it," he said, "but right now, I've been asked to make sure you're back in your room."

Danny fingered the remote in his hand. "Did O'Donohue tell you to send me back?"

Ofori nodded. "This order comes from him."

Well, shit. Couldn't let the boss down.

"Lead on, then."

He couldn't help being both surprised and worried when the not-policeman accompanied him all the way to the door of his room, as if he expected Danny to leg it into the grounds and cause trouble. It got more unsettling by the second. The normally busy hallways were deserted, not a soul to be seen anywhere. Ofori didn't volunteer any information all the way over.

Danny paused before opening the door to his flat.

"This isn't a standard security check, is it? Is something going on?"

Ofori was bloody good. His face gave absolutely nothing away. "O'Donohue only told me to make sure you were back in your rooms."

Danny eyed him suspiciously, but acquiesced and walked into his flat.

As soon as the door closed behind him, he released an explosive breath. Rogue code and random security checks that had Lysander on edge enough to send Danny back to his flat, and left the halls of the massive buildings deserted?

A more paranoid person would be reaching for a roll of tinfoil to fashion a jaunty hat.

Danny considered dropping a line to Lysander because if things were going sideways, then Lysander would be at the heart of it and no one wanted to be left to deal with things on their own. Aye, he probably had people in the offices to support him, but Danny still felt useless not doing anything to help. He didn't send the message, though. Best not to be an extra distraction.

He tried to keep himself occupied, but in the limited confines of the flat, he didn't really have much to do. He tried watching a film and reading, but couldn't concentrate. Pacing didn't help. The last and most reliable option resulted in a massive pot of rich meaty stew, and he'd just dished up a bowl when someone buzzed at his door more than two hours later.

Danny hurried over to open it.

Lysander managed a thin smile, ashen-faced and drawn. "Can I come in?"

Danny opened it wider at once. God, he wanted to ask what was going on to drain the life from Lysander's face, but with all the security mess, he probably didn't have any place in that. At least he could provide comfort and support as much as possible. "Do you want something to eat? It's just ready."

A flicker of a smile crossed Lysander's face. "Please."

By the time Danny filled a second bowl with steaming stew, Lysander had taken a seat at the table, staring blankly at the wall.

"It's hot," Danny warned as he set the bowl down.

Lysander glanced at him. "I'm sorry."

"Eh?"

Lysander waved vaguely around the room. "The sending you to your room. The security checks. It— I guess it was kind of melodramatic."

Danny shrugged. "If there are checks, there are checks." He fetched two glasses of water and some cutlery, then sat at the table, studying Lysander. "Are you all right? You look like shit."

Lysander hesitated for a second too long. "We'll see."

Danny winced. "That bad?"

Lysander didn't answer, stirring his bowl of stew. He was silent for several minutes as he picked at the food, and Danny didn't know what to say to help.

"I can't tell you what's going on right now," Lysander said finally, gazing at him. "I know you want to ask, but I can't tell you."

"I thought you might say that." Danny tried to smile. "Security checks and everything told me something serious is going on." He jabbed a piece of beef and frowned. "Can you tell me if it's connected to the stuff I'm working on?"

Lysander shook his head. "No. I mean, it's not. Not as far as we know." He ate another mouthful and then managed a brittle smile. "I thought you deserved some explanation. Jacob told me you seemed shaken."

Danny snorted. "Well, aye. I felt like he wanted to slap some handcuffs on me."

Lysander's smiled brightened. "He *is* an ex-police detective." He propped his other arm on the table and stirred the stew again. "If there's any information I can give you, you know I will; you have my word."

He waved a hand. "You don't have to, not if it's TRI stuff. I'm just here to fix your coding problem. Anything beyond that isn't any of my business."

For a moment, a little of the weariness left Lysander's face. "You're a good man, Danny." He glanced down at his bowl. "And not a bad chef, either."

Danny shrugged with a small smile. "I like my food." He patted his belly, which had been getting a bit softer since he'd arrived. The coding puzzle kept luring him away from the gym. "Probably too much."

"You look fine to me," Lysander murmured with a smile.

Danny considered him. "How much time do you have?"

Lysander must have recognised his expression and laughed quietly. "Not enough for anything interesting. Technically, I'm only meant to be here to make sure you're not panicking, not to have something to eat or anything else."

"But if you weren't eating here, you'd probably skip dinner because of that-which-cannot-be-named?" Danny rose and went back to the kitchen and pulled out a loaf of bread. "That settles it. I'm feeding you up before you go back." He cut a thick slice. "Butter?"

"If you have it."

Danny returned to the table and sat and watched as Lysander ate. He took his time, tearing pieces of bread to dip in the sauce between bites from his fork. It looked like he needed the break, so whatever had happened had to be something big.

"You're not eating?" Lysander said a few minutes later.

Danny picked up his fork. "Waiting to be sure it didn't kill you first."

Lysander tore another strip from his bread and swirled it in the stew. "I think we'll both be fine."

They ate the rest of the meal in silence only broken by the clatter of forks on their bowls. Lysander finished first and laid down his fork with a satisfied sigh.

"Thanks."

Danny smiled at him. "Least I could do." He set aside his own bowl. "You heading back over now?"

Lysander grimaced. "I get the feeling it's going to be a long night." He rose from the chair, bracing his fingertips on the table, and Danny could see how much effort it took him to gather himself.

"Do I stay put?"

"For the time being, until we know how this is going to play out." Lysander hesitated. "I won't be able to come by again, not without raising questions."

Danny got up. "I'm patient."

Lysander snorted. "I've seen plenty of evidence to suggest otherwise."

Danny grinned ruefully. Well, he wasn't wrong. "Maybe a little." He circled around the table to stand in front of Lysander. "I'm open to bribery."

"I bet you are." Lysander carded his hand through Danny's hair. "I wonder what incentive I could give you..."

Danny tilted his head into Lysander's touch. "I'm easy pleased."

Lysander traced his thumb in a circle on Danny's temple and lifted his chin, bringing their lips close together. "Oh yeah?"

"Oh, aye..." Danny couldn't help himself, slipping an arm around Lysander's middle. "I even managed a shag with no cuddling once." He widened his eyes. "Oh, wait. That was you, you cruel bugger."

Lysander kissed him lightly, leaning back before Danny could deepen the kiss. "How about I guarantee a night? Cuddle-inclusive."

Danny tried not to grin. "Aye? You think you could manage that?"

Lysander stroked his fingers through Danny's hair, and, not for the first time, Danny knew he'd be purring like a bloody cat if he could. "It all depends on your good behaviour, doesn't it?" Lysander curled his fingers and tugged on Danny's hair. The sensation sent fire scorching in his veins, and he pulled Lysander closer. "Are you going to behave for me?"

"What do you think?" Danny hissed between his teeth as Lysander pulled on his hair again. It burned right through him, and, Christ, if Lysander couldn't feel his cock swelling, he'd have to be insensible. "Aye! I'll behave."

"Good." Lysander loosened his fingers and trailed them down the back of Danny's neck.

With him pressed so close, Danny felt some of the tension leeching out of Lysander's body. Good. He needed it. Get some food in the bugger and take away a little bit of the stress and make things as relaxing and fun as possible in Danny's company.

Lysander's cool fingertips stroked down the nape of his neck, and Lysander searched his face with those ink-black eyes.

"I should get back," he said reluctantly.

Danny tightened his arm briefly around Lysander and stooped to kiss him. He wasn't surprised when Lysander slid his fingers back to tangle in Danny's hair and opened his mouth to the kiss, taking refuge in the contact before heading back to reality.

When he pushed against Danny's arm, Danny let him go at once.

"I'll be about," Danny said, hooking his thumbs into his belt to keep from touching. "You know where to find me."

Lysander brushed his fingers down Danny's cheek. "Best behaviour, remember."

Danny widened his eyes, trying to look as virtuous as possible, and sketched a cross over his heart with one finger. "Scout's honour."

Lysander smiled, to Danny's satisfaction, as he headed back out the door.

Chapter Eighteen

LYSANDER'S DAY HAD gone from bad to shit.

First the alarm, then the confirmation had come through: a gate had been opened.

The Met's team had reached the coordinates of the power surge in less than fifteen minutes, and what they found confirmed Lysander's worst fear. The site was a stretch of open wasteland with nothing that could provide such a massive burst of power.

Several buildings had been demolished there months earlier, and the grounds were fenced off from the public. There were no CCTV cameras within the grounds, and the ones on the streets outside only provided a handful of angles.

Someone had opened a gate to a demolition site on purpose. Whether anyone had come through was a different question.

The Met agreed that a rogue time traveller could be considered a serious threat and had assigned a number of officers to search through all available CCTV footage, covering the fifteen minutes between the power spike and their arrival at the site.

Jacob had cursed explosively while Ben listened, stone-faced, as the information came in.

Lysander felt sick to his stomach, but the TRI was his responsibility and panicking would help no one. He'd requested updates as and when they became available. He brought in some of the senior staff members to update them on the developments and confirm the lockdown would stand until further notice.

The only brief respite he had was checking in with Danny. Going over to see him didn't count as hiding out. More like finding an oasis of calm when his professional world seemed to be falling apart.

Somehow, Danny seemed to realise how serious things were, without being told any details. He hadn't pushed for answers. Instead, he gave Lysander a safe place to eat and take a moment to catch his breath.

It gave Lysander a second wind as he headed back into the breach.

Forty-five minutes after he returned from Danny's, the Met were back in touch.

One of the officers had tagged a suspect in the footage they sent through to Lysander—a young white man in unusual clothing, behaving erratically, less than two hundred metres from the fence, four minutes after the gate had connected.

Unfortunately, the camera had been at a distance. The grainy footage meant they could barely make out the man's features, but he was small and seemed to be bald. He was walking back and forth, staring around him. A megapod bus shuttled by on the road, and the man turned to watch it, then bolted out of camera range.

"That's it?" Ben made a face. "He could just be a junkie or a drunk."

Lysander watched the fragment of footage again. "I don't think so."

"You see it too?" Jacob was studying the clip as intently.

Ben glanced between them. "What am I missing?"

Lysander scaled up the video. "Watch his face."

Ben squinted at it. "Yeah...and?"

Lysander played it again. "I think he was trying to get his bearings."

"Every time he turns around, he focusses on something different," Jacob agreed, reaching out to pause the footage. "There's purpose there. As if he's trying to get his bearings. He's not staggering around aimlessly."

Ben went very quiet and still.

"Ben?" Jacob nudged him. "You okay?"

"I feel like I'm the only one surprised by this." Ben had his right fist clasped in his left hand. "You're both sitting there, acting like you expected this. It's not like it's ever happened before."

That Ben knew of. He didn't know about Mack, after all.

"It's possible they could have been sent by us in the future." Lysander hoped like hell that he was right. "It matches some of our mission parameters—isolated location, avoiding attention, set destination."

"Not the key parameters." Jacob met Lysander's eyes through the projection. "There's only one jumper."

"Not TRI, then," Lysander had to agree.

"The ones who took my dad's stuff," Ben finally said, his voice tight as he struggled to get the words out. "That's who you think it is. They still had some of it, didn't they?"

Jacob hesitated too long, and Ben's expression tensed.

"We can't be sure of that," Jacob said.

Ben pushed off from the chair, walked over to the window, and stared out, his arms folded tightly over his chest.

Jacob glanced at Lysander. "Do the Met have a plan?"

Lysander skimmed the message from the Met superintendent. "They're trying to track his movements from other cameras, and they sent someone to the transport depot to see if any footage can be pulled from the passing megapod."

"And what do we do until then?" Ben demanded. "Jacob, you said you'd caught the people responsible for what happened to Dad. They must have had some of the tech hidden away. This must be them!"

Lysander could see the effort it was taking Jacob to keep himself in check.

"It's possible," Lysander offered, "that someone else managed to create a functioning gate the same way your dad did. It doesn't mean it's your father's technology."

Ben bared his teeth. "That's bullshit, and you know it. Building a gate with an identical energy signature? That's impossible." He turned on Jacob. "Tell me."

Jacob rubbed his eyes with one hand. "I don't know what you think I can tell—"

"Jacob." Ben took a step towards him. "I know you were protecting me back then, but Christ! This is bigger than us now. Someone out there could be using my dad's stuff. Don't you think I have a right to know about it?"

"You know how many NDAs were slapped all over your dad's case," Jacob said quietly. "If I could tell you anything, you know I would."

Ben stared at him, then turned to Lysander. "Do you know?"

"I got a redacted version of events." It wasn't completely a lie, even if it was partially untrue now. "If it's been restricted, you know there has to be a good reason for it."

Ben clenched and unclenched his fists by his sides. "You don't trust me with it?"

"Ben—" Jacob held up a hand.

"No, that's it, isn't it?" Ben shook his head. "You think I'll do something stupid. I help Qas do one illegal jump years back, and you think I'll do what? Go back to stop whoever did this? That's why I can't see the..." He stared at Jacob. "Is that why I can't access any information on Mack? Is he something to do with all of this?"

Lysander's heart jolted sharply. "What could Mackenzie have to do with any of this?" he asked, hoping he didn't sound as tense as he felt. "You've said it yourself he's hardly technically proficient. Are you saying he's some kind of criminal mastermind who managed to build a temporal gate?"

Ben turned away, running a hand over his face. "You know I'm going to find out what you're keeping from me, sooner or later."

Lysander shot a glance at Jacob, who looked even grimmer than usual.

"We know, Ben," Jacob said. "When I can tell you everything, you know I will."

"But not today."

"Not today," Jacob agreed. "Not when we have a rogue time traveller loose in London. Once we find him and we get some answers, maybe then I can tell you what you need to know."

Ben turned back to him. "And if we don't?"

"Don't?"

"Find him? Get some answers?"

Jacob and Lysander exchanged glances.

"We'll cross that bridge when we come to it," Lysander replied. "Right now, containment and damage control has to be the priority." He got up from his chair. "I know this is frustrating for you, Ben, but you know the laws restricting us."

Ben leaned against the window. "Fine." He folded his arms again, silent for several seconds. "This energy signature—does it match an older gate or a new one?"

"Would it make a difference?" Jacob asked, frowning. "I thought you said all the gates had the same signature."

"Practically, yes, but it varies slightly depending on the age of the design and whether the power source is electricity or a battery core. I could probably tell you which kind of gate they used from the signature." Ben glanced between them. "It might help you find the guy. Some of the older ones would leave trace radiation residue on people who used them."

Jacob rubbed his jaw, and Lysander knew why he was hesitating. Only one file had the matching signature: the Sanders file. When Jacob opened his Leaf, he showed Ben a fragment of data, too complex for Lysander to identify.

Ben came closer, staring at it.

"Anything jumping out?" Lysander prompted.

Ben's lips were moving as he skimmed over the data, his eyebrows drawing together.

"Ben?" Jacob reached out to touch his arm. "You still with us?"

Ben blinked at him. "What?"

"Do you see anything useful?"

Ben's eyes darted back to the screen. "It's an older gate. If the police down south can get hold of a Geiger counter, they may be able to pick up his trail from where he was last sighted." He sank to his seat, a pensive expression on his face as Jacob drew back the screen and started drafting a message.

"Something wrong?" Lysander asked, watching him carefully. After the anger, the sudden calm was unsettling to say the least.

A brief shadow of a smile crossed Ben's face. "Sentimental bollocks," he said. "I remember Dad's old gates. He always said the first ones were about as much use as a fart in a bottle."

Lysander half smiled at that. "He didn't think much of his own work?"

"His own worst critic," Ben said and glanced at Jacob. "They'll need to hurry. If there's any residue, it's a trace amount, and it's already been hours."

It was close to midnight by the time the police team confirmed a trace had been found, and they'd tracked it for several blocks beyond the last sighting before it went cold. It gave them a set of streets to cross-check in the CCTV, which meant they were more likely to get a clearer image of the man now.

Lysander felt like he was sitting on a knife-edge.

He wanted—needed—a moment to catch his breath. Usually, he would retreat to his office, but with Ben alternating between pacing and slouching in one of the chairs and Jacob disappearing off to his own office now and then to reach out to his contacts, he had no chance.

"You should go and get some rest," he suggested to Ben.

Ben frowned at him. "And if news comes in?"

"I'll let you know." He could see the doubt in Ben's eyes. "This isn't one of our restricted files. If I know anything, I'll let you know."

Ben unfolded from the chair. "What about you?"

"Me?"

"Getting some rest," Ben said. "You look knackered."

Lysander laughed wearily. "You're not the first to say so." He glanced towards the couch at the far end of the office. "If it gets to that stage, I've got somewhere to put my head down."

"Better than nothing, eh?" Ben knuckled at one eye. "I'll hit H-block."

As soon as the door closed behind him, Lysander sank in his chair, pressing one hand to his eyes. Ben wasn't wrong. He was exhausted, but he didn't have time to rest, not until they knew how things would play out.

The lockdown would continue until they got their mysterious jumper in custody.

His door buzzed a split second before it opened.

Lysander dropped his hand from his eyes, unsurprised to see Jacob back again. "Any updates?"

"They have a couple of people still working through the footage," Jacob replied, "but the timing worked out well for the bastard. He went by a school as the kids were coming out. It'll take them a while to pick him out of the crowd."

"No chance for facial recognition?"

Jacob shook his head. "Not until we get a decent angle on his face."

"Right." Lysander picked up his glass of water, unsurprised when it trembled in his hand. "How the hell did you deal with this when you were investigating Sanders's disappearance?"

Jacob took the opposite seat. "We tracked the evidence. It was all we could do when we had no idea time travel existed." One side of his mouth curled up, a rare expression. "You've no idea how confusing it is to have a dead body with DNA matching a newborn. We thought we were in the twilight zone or something."

"Sounds frustrating."

Jacob looked at the projection over Lysander's desk. "This is nothing. Twelve hours? Wait until you hit twenty-four or several days. You should get some rest. It'll take a while for them to get through the footage."

"I'd prefer to wait for it."

Jacob studied him. "And what good are you going to be to anyone if you're keeling over from lack of sleep?" He leaned forward, bracing his arm on the desk. "Trust me. I'm speaking from experience."

Lysander hesitated, glancing at the projection. "I don't know..."

"There's bugger all you can do right now," Jacob said with his familiar bluntness. "The grounds are on lockdown, so no one will be coming in or out. The Met are on the trail of our man, and if they pin him down, we won't be able to do anything until they transport him up here." He sighed. "All you'll be doing is staring at a screen in the hopes it makes you feel useful, and I can tell you it won't."

"Are you going to rest?"

"I've been on this ride before. I know when to take the chance to catch a kip, and if I don't, Kit'll come over from H-block and drag me there by my ears." Jacob laughed tiredly. "Anyway, it's not like you won't be on-site if we have any breakthroughs overnight."

Lysander reluctantly had to agree. "I have a room in H-block too. I guess it wouldn't hurt to use it for once." He got up from behind his desk. "Do they have any idea on timeline?"

"How long's a piece of string?" Jacob shook his head. "Could be minutes. Could be days."

It was tempting to stretch out on his couch and wait it out, but Lysander knew Jacob was right. If he exhausted himself in the first day of a major incident, it would throw him off for days to come.

"Back here first thing, then?"

"Sounds like a good idea." Jacob got up. "Have a big breakfast. It'll probably be a long day."

Lysander nodded, then ushered Jacob out of his office. He glanced back at the desk with the screens still running and forced himself to lift down his jacket and head for the elevator.

It was pitch-dark when he stepped outside, the air bitterly cold, and the path to H-block glittered with fresh frost. Lysander shoved his hands deep in his pockets and walked rapidly to the other building.

The front desk was deserted and the halls empty, so no one saw him get out of the elevator a level early or approach Danny's door. A bad idea on so many levels, but he was exhausted and even ten minutes in Danny's company earlier had helped.

He touched the buzzer.

No one answered.

Of course he didn't.

Danny, like any sane person, was probably asleep.

Lysander turned to head back to the elevator, halfway there when Danny's door opened. Light cut across the hall, and he turned around to see Danny squinting out at him, mussed and sleepy.

Neither of them said anything; then Danny opened his door wider in invitation. Lysander sagged with relief and made his way back down the hall. Together, they went into Danny's apartment.

Chapter Nineteen

A STORM ROARED outside, waking Danny. Hail pelted against the windows, the sky dark beyond the glass. There was something to be said for waking up in a warm bed and listening to the wonders of nature when you didn't have to go out in it. Another person in the bed beside you was an added bonus.

Danny glanced at his clock. The glowing digits showed six thirty.

No surprise that Lysander was still asleep.

He'd shown up at Danny's door the previous night, well after midnight, ashen with deep shadows under his eyes. He'd barely said anything except to thank Danny for letting him stay, and all but collapsed into the bed once he'd shed his suit.

Danny had slipped back under the covers on the other side of the bed and found himself facing Lysander's bare back, the skin prickled with goosebumps and his shoulders rigid.

Danny snapped the lights off and slipped a little closer. "Cold?"

"Mm."

It was invitation enough, and he spooned against Lysander's back, letting Lysander steal some of his warmth. When he brushed his hand against Lysander's side, he was relieved when Lysander's hand covered his to pull Danny's arm around his middle.

Danny had kissed his shoulder and closed his eyes, too sleepy to stay awake any longer.

Now, Lysander was still tucked against Danny's side, his braid a dark snake curling over his throat. He didn't snore, but every few seconds, he gave a quiet squeak. Danny tried not to smile. It sounded like some animal in a cutesy animated film.

He lay there for a little longer, listening to the wind outside and the sleepy squeaks of Lysander within. All things considered, if Lysander felt he could safely rest in Danny's bed, Danny was happy to oblige him. It was a hell of a compliment to be trusted like that, and he wasn't about to break that trust.

Lysander stirred, rolling from his side to his front. The covers slipped down off his back, and he grumbled drowsily, groping for them to pull them back up, then buried his face in the pillows and went back to sleep.

No one that attractive had any right to turn into such an adorable wee grump when sleepy.

Danny left him to get some more rest and padded off to the bathroom. By the time he'd showered and made a start on breakfast, it had turned seven.

Coffee steamed gently in the pot and the bacon and eggs sizzling in the pan when Lysander emerged from the bedroom. Danny glanced over. Lysander had already dressed, although his shirt was still undone and his fingers were deftly rebraiding his hair.

Danny waved the spatula cheerfully. "Good timing! Park yourself and I'll dish up."

"I'm never going to go hungry with you around, am I?" Lysander murmured with a small smile.

"It's a guarantee," Danny replied. "D'you fancy scrambled or poached or both?" He paused, considering it. "Or neither?"

"Poached if there's toast." Lysander sat down. "Scrambled if there's none."

"What kind of kitchen do you think I'm running?" Danny held up the well-stacked toast rack. "Bacon too?"

"Mm."

By the time Danny carried the plates over, the toast rack balanced on the rims, Lysander had filled two mugs with the strong black coffee and wrapped his hands around one of them.

Pale as a ghost, with shadows under his eyes, he didn't look his perky best, but Danny knew better than to ask how things were going.

"Thank you."

"It's no bother." Danny smiled. "You're saving me from eating it all."

Lysander met his eyes. "You know what I mean. You didn't need to let me in last night."

Danny added some sugar to his coffee. "And you didn't need to come here, but you did, so I'd say we're even." He nudged the toast rack towards Lysander. "I'm guessing you're going to need all the energy you can get."

Lysander took two slices and set them down on his plate. "Seems that way."

It didn't feel like the time to make light conversation. If Lysander was exhausted and shaken up enough to come to a man he'd only known a few weeks for support, something earth-shattering had to be happening. He probably didn't have the brain space for chat.

So they ate in silence, and Danny fetched fresh toast and refilled the coffee pot. When Lysander set his fork down and sat back, something in the air had shifted.

"I feel like I'm infringing on your hospitality," Lysander said.

Danny slouched in his chair, his mug of coffee warm between his hands. "You're not exactly hard work, y'know." He cocked his head and gave Lysander a smirk. "I like making food. I like people eating my food. I like sexy half-naked men in my bed. What part of that's infringing?"

Lysander hid one of those rare small smiles behind a curled finger. "Flattery, Mr. Ferguson?"

Danny flashed a grin. "Maybe I just like it when I make you call me Mister."

Lysander shook his head, clearly amused. It faded quickly. "I need to get back."

"Figured." Danny put his mug down. "No coding for me today?"

"Not today."

"Fair enough." Danny hesitated. Another day stuck in the flat with only his worries to occupy him didn't sound like fun. "I know there's some lockdown bullshit going on, but can I head down to the gym or walk in the grounds? I need to do something instead of just sitting on my hands."

Lysander blinked, surprised. "Oh. Yes. I'll arrange something."

Danny had already formulated his own theories about what was going on, but since Lysander couldn't tell him anything, he leaned closer, resting one arm on the edge of the table. "So I'll be safe from them, then?"

"Them?" Lysander's brow wrinkled.

Danny widened his eyes. "The plague zombies who've escaped from history…" He blinked in feigned stupidity. "Isn't that the reason for the lockdown?"

Lysander gaped at him, then dissolved into helpless laughter. "No. No zombies."

"Hm. You're not saying that for nondisclosure reasons?"

Lysander pressed his hand to his chest. "I promise you there are no zombies."

"Bah." Danny snorted. "Then it's a hell of a lot less interesting. It would've been good cardio, being chased around the compound by someone after my brains."

"Hardly an aperitif for a keen zombie," Lysander said dryly.

"Hey!" Danny mock glared at him. "I bet you were going to leave me to sit all day again anyway." He immediately felt guilty when Lysander winced. Of course the last thing he would be worried about was Danny's entertainment.

"I'm sorry." Lysander sighed, rubbing his forehead. "There's been so much going on I forgot you were in solitary over here."

Danny couldn't help himself. He sighed dramatically. "Told you this place is like a prison."

To his pleasure and relief, Lysander actually smirked at him as he got up from the table. "Maybe because you've been bad, *Mister Ferguson*."

Danny pushed his chair back and motioned for Lysander to come closer, grinning at him. "Best behaviour," he reminded him, tugging the bottom of Lysander's shirt to pull him to stand between Danny's knees. Danny fastened up the row of buttons, his knuckles skimming Lysander's chest. "Scout's honour, remember?"

Lysander smiled down at him and caught one of his hands. "Were you ever a Boy Scout?"

"Er...is it compulsory?"

"For Scout's honour to apply, I'd say so." Lysander slid his other hand into Danny's hair and leaned down to kiss him quickly. "Thank you," he murmured against his lips.

Danny claimed another kiss before Lysander could draw back, then shrugged. "I got some cuddles. Like I said, I'm easy pleased."

Lysander stepped back, still smiling. "I'll remember that."

"You know where I'll be if you need company or whatever." Danny relaxed back in the chair. "Mostly because I'm imprisoned in my cell."

Lysander started laughing again. "You are so full of shit."

Danny spread his hands and sketched a quick bow. "Known for it." He looked back up at Lysander, more seriously. "But still, the offer stands."

Lysander picked up his jacket and drew it on. "I know." He walked over to the door, paused, and glanced back. "I'll send word over once I know what the situation is. Hopefully, you should be able to get outside in a couple of hours."

In fact, Sabine swung by only an hour later to grant his limited freedom with the proviso that if he spoke to any member of staff, he and they were not permitted to discuss the ongoing situation.

"Including you?"

From her pained grimace, he suspected Lysander had been very specific. "Well, I am a member of staff."

He smiled wryly at her. "Fair enough. I won't ask anyone else about the alien invasion or whatever."

"Pardon?" She looked baffled.

He grinned ruefully. "Never mind. Entertaining myself with the possibilities." He grabbed up his holdall. "Are you headed back across?"

"For now," she said. "Do you want to share the elevator down?"

As the lift descended, he couldn't help noticing the change from his first day. Then, she'd been smiling and chatty. Now, she was as tense as Lysander, which meant she either knew everything or had been told nothing.

Either way, he hated seeing them both like that, and as much as he wanted to know, he kept his mouth shut.

It was an easy enough rule to keep when he headed down to the gym and pool for a couple of hours. There were a few other people in, but no one spent time there for the chat.

At home, he usually spent at least an hour in the gym a night, especially after an intensive day with far too many snacks instead of meals. Habit and routine, but both of those things had been broken in a new place with new challenges and distractions and time travel and everything.

Still, he had the courtesy to shower before he headed to the canteen. No one liked a smelly tablemate, no matter how buff they were.

The change in the atmosphere was palpable. The usual rumble of noise and clatter of dishes seemed muted. People sat in small knots, talking quietly among themselves. He saw a few heads turn his way, then back to their companions. Normally, the canteen felt like any other busy food hall, but not anymore.

Whatever had happened, the ripples were spreading.

To save anyone the awkwardness of trying to avoid the topic, he took his tray of food and sat at an empty table and opened out his Leaf to work on a crossword. He sat, chewing on a piece of mushroom and puzzling over the answers when he heard someone approaching.

"No company today?"

Danny turned in his seat, surprised to see Janos standing there, tray in hand. "Uh. No." He shrugged. "People know they're not meant to tell me what's going on, so I thought I'd make things easier for them."

Janos circled around the table and sat opposite him. "I promise you I will not tell you anything." He said it with a straight face but with a glint in his eye. Danny had the sneaking suspicion he was being teased.

"Aye," he said, prodding another mushroom with his fork. "Who knows who I might be reporting back to?"

Janos chuckled. "Ah. You have not forgotten our first meeting, I see." He turned his plate on his tray by ninety degrees and considered it, then rotated it back halfway. "You have been here some time now. You can see why I might have concern."

"Especially since you've seen things getting out from here before, eh?" Danny said around a mouthful. "I mean, you were here when it all went public, weren't you?"

Janos grimaced. "Yes. It was...not a good time. You understand I would be suspicious."

Danny sketched a cross over his chest. "Cross my heart, I won't breathe a word of your secrets." He paused, considering everything he knew about Janos. It boiled down to Hungarian-born, coder, some kind of tech wizard, and married. Not exactly exciting. "I mean, assuming you have any worth telling."

Janos tore his bread roll in half. "Everyone has some secret." He smeared some butter on the bread and raised his eyes to meet Danny's. "Even you, I think."

Danny inhaled his mouthful of chasseur and started coughing. He thumped himself on the chest, coughing, his eyes watering. "What?" he croaked, groping for his glass of water, and forced some down until he could swallow and breathe normally again.

For someone so stone-faced, Janos seemed to be fighting back a grin. "Ah."

"What 'ah'?" Danny coughed again.

Janos raised his eyebrows. "If you had no secrets, you would not have choked so much on your food."

"Sod off!" Danny huffed indignantly, grateful he could blame his flaming face on the choking fit. "I was *trying* to laugh and inhaled instead."

"I see." The threat of a grin was visible in Janos's eyes now, though it hadn't reached his lips. "You have no secrets. Of course. This is my mistake. You are transparent in all things."

Danny wrinkled his nose at Janos. "Are you always this sarcastic?"

Janos blinked at him as if he couldn't understand. "Never. Just as you have no secrets."

Despite himself, Danny couldn't keep from grinning. "You're a bit of an arse, you know?"

Janos inclined his head graciously. "It is often said." He peered at Danny's screen. "You are doing a word puzzle?"

"Mm." Danny flipped it around. "Are you any good at them?"

"Very," Janos said, expressionless. "That is my secret."

They managed to keep straight faces for a couple of seconds; then both started laughing.

Chapter Twenty

SOME PROGRESS HAD been made.

Not much, but they had a clear shot of their target's face.

Lysander had been to his own room to change before heading to his office where he had a message waiting from the Met. He promptly shared it with Jacob and Ben when they arrived. The facial recognition software was doing its work, which left them with nothing to do but wait for news.

"He doesn't look like much," Ben said, studying the image.

"You mean the same reason we choose agents?" Jacob said. "For their ability to blend in?"

Lysander tuned out their conversation and gazed at the freeze-frame of their potential enemy. It had been captured from a podcam mounted on the first megapod bus passing the site. Thank God for the proximity cameras legally fitted on every megapod.

The illicit jumper was young. Twenties, maybe thirties at the latest. His head was shaved, only just beginning to darken with stubble. Wide dark eyes and a narrow scar curving up from his right eyebrow to his hairline. He seemed surprised, as if he hadn't expected or seen a megapod before.

Like Ben said, he didn't look like much. Regular features. Much shorter than average, but otherwise nothing to make him stand out.

Lysander tapped his thumbnail against his lower lip. The face wasn't holding his interest as much as the clothes. The coat was oversized and shapeless as if made for a larger man, and under it, the shirt—off-white, dirt-smudged—had an open collar. No fasteners, Lysander noticed, and something seemed off about the seams...

"Seen something?" Ben's voice interrupted his train of thought.

"Hm?"

Ben motioned to the image. "Is there something there we haven't noticed?"

"I think I'm too tired for this." Lysander rubbed at one eye with two fingers. "Ben, could you do me a favour and run down for a coffee for me?

I don't think instant is going to cut it, and they know how I like it downstairs."

Ben rolled his eyes. "I'm your trolley dolly now?"

Lysander chuckled ruefully. "I know how busy they get in lockdown, and if I send you, at least my coffee comes back warm and when I need it."

Ben rose and then glanced at Jacob. "You want anything?"

Jacob shook his head. "I had a cup already."

As soon as the door closed, Jacob's eyes fixed on Lysander.

"You spotted something?"

Lysander leaned forward. "It may be nothing," he said. "With Roberts—with your traveller, did you notice anything off about his clothing?"

"Actually, yes." Jacob rubbed his beard, a thoughtful look on his face. "You know when you see vintage clothing in films and reference material, it's usually the high-end or fashionable stuff?"

"He showed up in a fashionable outfit?"

"Pretty much. His coat could have dropped straight off a catwalk. The rest of it might have passed muster, if it hadn't been for the coat." Jacob glanced at the image between them. "You seeing something in his clothes?"

Lysander frowned, tapping his fingertips on the desk. "I'm not sure. It's definitely not contemporary so they aren't trying to blend in, but it— This is crazy, but I don't think it's as modern as it should be. The shape of it, the irregularity of the stitching..." He chewed his lip in thought. "There's something wrong about it all."

"And you know fashion." Jacob frowned, a line cutting between his brows, and he leaned closer to stare at the projection. "You're right. It doesn't make sense."

"Maybe they were trying to go to a different time? You said Robertson and his partner were aiming for an earlier period?"

"Maybe." Jacob rubbed his jaw. He didn't sound convinced. "We're flying blind here. Best we can do is deal with the evidence as it comes in."

By the time Ben got back, another message had come in about a woman who had crossed paths with the missing time traveller. The Met were working on finding her, which meant more useless pacing and waiting until a call came through.

"Mr. O'Donohue." Chief Superintendent Falconer inclined her head in greeting. "An update for you."

"Go ahead." Lysander folded his hands together in his lap to keep them still.

"We've found our witness, a Celia Mendez," Falconer said. "She works in Short Cuts, the salon in the footage. Apparently, she saw our mystery man in a state of some distress outside the shop and went to speak to him."

Lysander sat up a little straighter and saw Jacob do the same. Ben was already tense as a wire beside him. "She spoke to him?"

Falconer nodded. "Briefly. Enough to confirm he was disorientated, but when she asked him where he wanted to go, he became agitated and ran off before she could stop him."

"Damn it," Jacob muttered, sinking back in his chair.

"Did she have any idea of a destination?" Lysander asked. "Or anything else?"

Falconer glanced sideways, no doubt checking the statement. "We have the initial direction, and the footage and facial recognition are already being sifted." She turned back to the screen. "I can tell you we know our man is English now. She said he sounded northern, but it could mean anywhere beyond the midlands."

"I doubt the accent makes much of a difference these days anyway," Jacob said, shaking his head.

Lysander rubbed at his temple, his head throbbing. "What do you think the chances are of finding him?"

Falconer pursed her thin lips. "It's hard to say. It depends on whether he stayed on the public byways. There are more cameras there than anywhere. If he managed to get out of sight, he could probably disappear if he knows what he's doing."

"Do you think he does?"

Lysander glanced at Ben, who'd been silent since the superintendent had called in. "What do you mean?"

"Know what he's doing," Ben said. "Do you think he does? The witness said he seemed distressed..."

Lysander glanced back at Falconer. "Any thoughts?"

"Based on the original footage, I assumed he was moving with a purpose." She frowned thoughtfully. "Until we received the megapod footage, when he ran, it seemed to be in a set direction. After seeing the footage, he looked startled. Alarmed even. I don't think he's as in control as we previously believed."

Jacob's frown deepened. "Which suggests he's not a trained agent."

Lysander frowned, puzzled. "Why would someone come through a gate without preparing for it?"

"Could be a guinea pig." Jacob rubbed his jaw thoughtfully. "Maybe whoever built the gate didn't know it would work and decided this poor bugger would be expendable to test it without safeguards in place."

"Maybe." Ben's voice was flat. "Or maybe he volunteered."

Jacob flinched. "Shit, Ben. Sorry."

Lysander glanced between them. "Excuse me?"

"After." Jacob motioned to the video link.

Lysander turned his attention back to Falconer. "Sorry, Superintendent. You were saying? Something about the chances of finding him?"

"Now, I'd say we have a better chance," she said. "Someone in a state of distress is more likely to draw attention than someone moving with purpose. People sometimes call in to express concern, which means we have eyes on the street as well as the cameras. If he can be found, we'll find him."

Lysander offered his thanks and terminated the link. He looked across his desk. "What did I miss?"

"My mother was a volunteer for one of the first gates." Ben stared at his hands, clenched on his knees. "*Not* a guinea pig." He raised his eyes back to Lysander's. "That doesn't matter now. What happens when they find this guy? What do we do with him?"

Lysander shook his head. "We've never had to deal with something like this before. First things first, we'd need to get him in-house."

Jacob got up and walked over to the window, his hands folded behind his back. One thumb tapped against the other, Lysander noticed. Jacob rarely showed any nervous tics, but given the circumstances, hardly unexpected. "I'm not sure it's a good idea."

And once more, the rug was pulled out from under him, Lysander thought, baffled.

"Excuse me?"

"Bringing him in-house." Jacob stared blankly at his reflection in the window. "What if that's what this is all about?"

Ben gave a sharp bark of a laugh. "What?!"

Jacob turned, his expression grim. "I'm serious." He met Lysander's eyes. "This place is impossible to access and has some of the most controversial tech held on-site, and now, we're just going to bring some random guy in without any security clearance?"

"Some random *time traveller*!" Ben exclaimed in disbelief. "He used a time gate! Where else is he meant to go?"

"We can have him held somewhere else." Jacob's lips were a thin line. "It would be safer."

Ben stared at him, slowly shaking his head. "No."

"Ben."

"No!" Ben shoved himself up from his chair. "We keep everything about time travel inside these walls! It's always been the rule! Time travel is our remit and no one else's. Who else knows how to deal with shit like this?" He swung around urgently to Lysander. "He needs to come here. He— If he used the gate, maybe he knows who took the tech. Maybe he can tell us who it was. Maybe we can find them."

Lysander's heart ached for him. He could see Jacob's concerns, but Ben had a point too, despite his emotional investment. "There *is* more potential for leaks if he's held outside, even if the police are thorough," he murmured. "But if we bring him here, we can dictate the security clearances and protocols."

Ben jerked his head sharply, crushing one hand with the other. "We have the quarantine block," he said quickly. "We can keep him there. Limit his access. Make sure we know what we're dealing with."

Jacob's frown deepened. "And then what? We hold him indefinitely?"

Ben stared at him. "What?"

"This man. We can't put him back where he came from, can we?"

Shit.

Ben's face darkened to red. "No, but—it—" He shook his head, looking young and helpless as a child. "We deal with time travel. No one else does. He needs to be here."

Lysander held up a hand to silence them both. "He has to come here," he said quietly. "I don't like it, but for our own security, it's better to contain him here for the time being. We can't risk the outside world getting hold of him and what he knows."

Jacob's shoulders sagged. "True."

"And," Lysander added, trying to sound optimistic, "he may be able to give us some answers."

"What if he won't?" Ben was picking at one of his nails.

"We can't speculate until we get him here," Lysander said, praying his own discomfort wasn't showing as visibly as theirs. He'd come in for the purpose of streamlining the time travel business, not dealing with rogue time travellers from the future. "Right now, I say we take the chance to catch our breaths. Take a break. Thinking ourselves in circles isn't going to help anyone."

Ben rose at once and hurried out of the room, but Jacob remained by the window.

"You know we have no real choice here," Lysander murmured.

"I get it. I keep remembering the mess. There were so many complications. So many issues to tidy up." He stared out over the rain-lashed grounds. "This isn't going to be a quick fix."

"I didn't think it would be." Lysander rose and went to refill his glass from the pitcher on the countertop. He frowned at the water, then looked over at Jacob. "Ben's mother— I was told it was an accident?"

"Technically, if you count using a faulty gate." He rubbed his brow. "I don't know if I understand it all right. She went through a gate to a set place, but when the gate disconnected, no matter what he tried, Sanders couldn't identify the time. It was hit or miss with the oldest test gates. You could arrive days before or years after and you could never be sure which."

"Like Robertson."

"If Ben was right about him coming through an old-style gate, it's possible our new arrival had the same problem, which is why he's so turned about by everything."

It would make sense, if he'd prepared for one past and stumbled into another.

Lysander glanced towards the door. "Ben isn't— I don't think I've seen him like this before."

Jacob grimaced. "You know how much his father's passing can trigger him." He turned away from the window. "Do you want something to eat? If I'm going down, I can grab you something if you want it."

Lysander hesitated. "If they have a chicken salad. Nothing too heavy. I had a big breakfast."

By the time the afternoon rolled on, he wished he'd gone for something more substantial. Stress apparently burned up a chicken salad in minutes. None of them needed to be sitting in the office together, but, somehow, it felt better not to be waiting for the news alone.

"Why is it taking so long?" Ben asked for the fifth time in as many hours.

"London's a big city." The same answer from Jacob.

Lysander said nothing, walking back and forth behind his desk. Yes, it revealed his discomfort and anxiety, but a man could only sit on his emotions for so long before he had to let them out. Pacing was harmless and at least felt like he was doing *something*.

Rain was torrenting from a black sky when an incoming message chimed.

Lysander sank into his chair and picked up the connection.

Falconer.

"We have him."

Lysander rocked back in the chair as if the strings holding him upright had been severed. "Thank God. Where did you find him?"

"Hiding out under one of the bridges not too far from the last sighting." She frowned at the screen off-camera. "The man seems to be in shock. He's being looked after downstairs, but we'll have transport arranged to bring him your way as soon as possible."

"It would be the best idea," Lysander agreed. "We have the facilities to keep him secure and safe."

"Did you get anything out of him?" Jacob asked. "A name? A point of origin?"

"No point of origin, unfortunately, but we have a name. He calls himself Enoch. He wasn't very coherent when we found him, drenched and shaken and babbling about getting home."

"It couldn't be simple." Lysander sighed. "Did he give any indication how far he came back?"

For a moment, Falconer seemed confused. "Came...back?"

"From the future," Lysander said. "As we mentioned this morning."

Falconer's brow furrowed. "You mentioned time travel, but this man isn't from the future. At best guess, I'd say he's from at least two hundred years ago."

Chapter Twenty-One

IN HINDSIGHT, JOGGING around the compound wasn't the best idea Danny had ever had.

If a morning started with a hail shower, you could guarantee it wouldn't get much better in the afternoon. Halfway around the perimeter, it was pissing down, and when Danny eventually managed to get back to H-block, he squelched his way to the lift, soggy as a drowned rat.

Another member of staff jumped into the lift with him and gave him an amused look. "Been swimming?" she inquired as the lift rose.

"I wish." Danny pushed his hair back to keep it from plastering to his forehead. "At least it would've been warm."

"Have a hot shower!" she called after him when he stepped out on his floor. "We don't want a lockdown cold!"

He could imagine how bad it could get with hundreds of people getting sick at the same time. Plus, freezing his balls off didn't appeal, so a hot shower—or even better, a bath—sounded like the best idea in the world.

After a quick bite to eat as the tub filled, Danny turned down the lights and sank himself neck-deep in steaming water. It was hot enough to turn him lobster-red in seconds, and he sighed, relaxing back, and listened to the rain battering against the windows outside.

For a day spent doing sod all, he'd knackered himself.

The time in the gym had been a sharp reminder why skipping out on so many days of exercise was a no-no. He'd resorted to the run to compensate for abandoning the machines and weights earlier than he should have.

Danny needed his routine for a reason.

If he let himself slide again, he could and probably would slide all the way back to overindulging in his mother's cooking and a few too many pints a week, the return of the pot belly, and an inevitable heart attack at forty-five like his dad.

He sank in the tub until his knees formed little islands and the water lapped at his ears.

The lockdown had given him a kick up the bum, at least. He needed to set a timer to remind him to leave the coding work alone for half an hour or more. Or maybe go in the morning. Get the juices flowing and all that.

Outside, the wind was rising again.

He was still steeping there an hour later—after multiple top-ups to keep himself simmering nicely—when someone buzzed at the door. Danny groaned, so warm and pruney he nearly considered ignoring it.

But then it struck him only one person would come knocking at his door at this time in the evening.

With more effort than he cared to admit, Danny managed to climb out the tub and grabbed the smallest towel he could feasibly sling around his waist. His legs were aching from the run, and while it was a good ache, it meant he did a pretty good cowboy strut all the way to the door.

Unfortunately, it wasn't Lysander waiting for him.

Sabine's eyes widened in surprise. "Oh! Sorry!" Colour flooded her face. "I didn't realise— I could come back."

Danny gripped the towel more securely, suddenly regretting the choice of outfit and feeling a lot more exposed. "I'm out now." He motioned for her to come in. "Give me a minute to put something else on."

"You mean *something* on?" she called after him.

"Semantics," he replied over his shoulder. In his room, he pulled on a T-shirt and a pair of pyjama bottoms, then headed back through to the living room, towelling his hair. "I'm guessing if you're here, there's been a development?" He frowned. "Does O'Donohue want me to come over?"

Sabine shook her head. "He's currently in a meeting with the heads of staff." She held out a memo-slip to him. The slim square of transparent tech shimmered as he took it, holding it carefully by the edges. "There's a message on there from him. Confidential. Needs your right thumbprint to open it."

He jerked his head towards the bedroom. "Mind if I go and watch?"

"I'll wait."

Danny retreated to the bedroom again and shut the door. He tilted the slip up and pressed his thumb to the raised circle on the bottom corner. The memo opened at once, a video from Lysander, who looked worse than he had the night before.

"Danny, things are happening, and you can't be around for them. We still need the coding issue resolved, but, unfortunately, I need you off-site for the time being." He drew a breath and exhaled. "I can't tell you anything more right now, but Sabine has transport details for you, and a room has been booked at the hotel again. Take a notebook if you have to. I don't think they'd be happy if you ruined another set of sheets." He fell silent for a moment, rubbing his forehead with a knuckle. "I don't know how long this mess is going to take to clean up, but I'll let you know when I can."

The video cut out, leaving the memo-slip blank.

"Fuck..." Danny glanced towards the door. If Sabine was waiting for him, it meant leaving immediately, which meant some serious shit had well and truly hit the fan.

Best thing to do would be to make things as simple as possible for everyone.

Five minutes later, he came out of his bedroom, fully dressed and carrying a holdall with enough changes of clothes to last a few days. If worst came to worst, he could always buy supplementary stuff in the city.

He didn't miss the relief on Sabine's face. She must have been expecting some degree of resistance, especially so late in the evening. "You're ready already?"

"Just about." He took the time to grab his toothbrush and drain the bath, then shut down everything he wouldn't need. He hesitated as they headed for the door. "The stuff in the fridge—can someone come in and clear it out? I don't want to be responsible for a biohazard."

Sabine nodded. "It'll be seen to."

Danny checked the living room and made sure everything important had been switched off. "I think that's me, then."

Thankfully, someone had thought ahead and provided one of the small external pods to get them from H-block to the main building and the transport hub. As the rain lashed down the sides of the pod, he studied Sabine.

"Are you stuck here for now?"

She hummed in confirmation as the pod drew into the transport hub. "It could be worse."

Danny glanced back across the grounds at H-block. Every other night, one side of the building lay dark and empty. Now, windows glowed with light on every level. He'd wondered why they needed to keep so much accommodation space available. The question had been answered.

He climbed out of the pod and hastily stepped under the alcove leading to the platform. Sabine accompanied him all the way down the ramp to the waiting shuttle.

"Can you give O'Donohue a message from me?" he asked. "Tell him this isn't a chance for him to skip his lunch again."

Sabine laughed. "I'll make sure he knows." She held out a hand, which he shook. "A pod will be waiting for you on the other end. I hope it won't be too long until we see you again, Mr. Ferguson."

"Maybe not *quite* so much of me next time, aye?"

She smiled. "I don't know. It's not a bad view."

He laughed too, then hefted his holdall onto his shoulder. "Good luck with..." He waved vaguely towards the stairs. "Well, with whatever the fuck is happening."

By the time the shuttle started moving, Sabine was already halfway up the ramp.

Beyond the windows of the shuttle and the pod, the world was wet and black. Water streaked along the glass, too fast to contemplate a drop as it moved.

Danny sank into his seat. He didn't put any music on, lost in thought.

Something serious was going on at the TRI, and so soon after the mysterious coding had appeared as well. Two major issues within so short a space of time couldn't be a coincidence, especially not something bad enough to put the whole agency on lockdown.

He doubted it.

He couldn't do anything to help, not when he was exiled to the city, but then again, he'd been in the city when he had his last breakthrough. Lysander clearly suspected he would continue to work without access to the code. A notebook would work, even if he couldn't guarantee its security. But then again, no less secure than a bed sheet.

It was too late to do anything about it when he finally reached his destination, knackered and still aching from too much exercise. He barely did more than check in then fall straight into bed as soon as he could.

The next day, he headed out into the city with a purpose.

There were plenty of shops nearby and a handful of them carried notebooks.

As a precaution, Danny bought half a dozen and several pens. He could still remember both sides of the bed sheet and how little space he'd had left by the time Lysander came knocking at his door.

He sat at the desk in his room, opened one of the books, and picked up a pen.

An hour later, he still had sod all written down.

He got up and walked in circles around the room. The coding was still dancing across his memory. He'd been staring at it long enough he could probably have recreated reams of it in his sleep.

It wasn't until lunchtime, as he glared at a steak, that he realised the problem: like before, he was concentrating too hard on the little details and overlooking the bigger picture because of it.

The last time...

Danny stared blankly at his steak.

Well, shit.

After lunch, he headed to the nearest off-license and returned with a box of his favourite caffeine shots and a large bottle of whisky. Technically, he would have preferred a cider or six, rather than the inevitable punishment he got from spirits, but time was of the essence.

He returned to his room, sat back at his desk, and lined up three caffeine shots on it. The seal on the whisky cracked as it broke, and the liquid shone gold by the afternoon sunlight as he poured a generous measure.

He opened the fresh new notepad in front of him, laid the pens beside it, and looked at the glass.

The hypothesis might be incorrect. More likely than not, he was about to condemn himself to a caffeine- and alcohol-induced hangover from hell for no good reason.

"I'm going to regret this," he said to himself, then knocked back the glass.

Chapter Twenty-Two

THEIR NEW ARRIVAL had been delivered first thing in the morning.

He'd been through a basic decon to sweep him for historical infections—moot, since he'd been running around London for more than twenty-four hours—then the medical team descended to examine him fully. When they finally finished their checks, the man had all but collapsed into something between sleep and unconsciousness.

After a discussion with the heads of staff, it was agreed any information should be limited until more details became available. Currently, Lysander was backed up by Ben, for his technical knowledge, and Jacob for his familiarity with TRI history and his connections to the police force.

The rest of the TRI staff had been given a summary of the situation, but without specific details about the traveller. Details were difficult to provide when they were so uncertain.

Lysander was exhausted beyond the telling. He'd grabbed a couple of hours of sleep here and there, but nowhere near enough. Now, sitting behind his desk, he was trying to maintain the illusion of calm, but he could feel the mask slipping. At least, he thought bleakly, they were all in the same boat, left shaken as they read the information from the decon and medical teams.

Falconer's estimates, it seemed, were correct.

Either that or the stranger was putting on one hell of a show and had the props to support him.

The clothing came from a different era, the fabric sturdy homespun cloth, and as Lysander had observed, the seams weren't quite right. There were no labels. Images of the clothing had been sent over to the historians for corroboration.

The traveller himself was still in shock.

Though he'd clearly received some kind of sedation to calm him, he was trembling and wide-eyed when the police officers had handed him over to the decon team.

"I don't understand how it could be possible."

Jacob had said it before, and Lysander knew it wouldn't be the last time.

Time travel was complicated in many ways, but in one way, it was simple: you opened a gate, and you went to a different time.

For someone to come from the past was impossible. They didn't have the power or the capacity to build and open a gate, which meant, logically, their visitor had to be from the future. Yet, according to all their data, he had come from the past.

He was small, barely 150 centimetres, and wiry and muscular. The full-body scan showed one leg had been broken and unevenly knitted years earlier, and there were traces of faded cracks on his ribs. Old scars scattered his body, some of which looked like marks from a lash. His hands were thick with calluses, a sign of manual labour. After decon, he still had dirt ingrained in his skin. His teeth showed no signs of any dental work.

Jacob suggested—sounding sceptical as he said it—that maybe he'd been chosen for all of those features.

"You really don't believe he's from the past?"

Jacob scrolled down the projection of the medical report. "It doesn't make *sense*."

Lysander had to agree, but the evidence was compelling. "Is there anything there indicating otherwise? Anything I've overlooked?"

Jacob scanned the text. "The hair thing is weird, but nothing else."

"The hair thing?" Ben prompted.

Jacob scaled up a section of the report. "He's been shaved."

Lysander and Ben exchanged puzzled frowns.

"Yes," Lysander prompted. "And? Didn't they used to do to people to prevent lice?"

"Heads, yes. Whole body? Not so much."

Lysander blinked at him and then leaned forward to pull the report closer. "What do you mean whole body?"

"I mean everywhere. The man is stubble all over, like someone shaved him head to toe."

"So?" Ben snorted impatiently. "Maybe he had really bad lice? Ly— we don't have time—"

"Or maybe he knew about our skin and hair analyses," Jacob interrupted. "His hair was shaved so short we can't get a feasible sample from any part of his body. We can't test it to pinpoint his environmental influences or confirm his origin point."

Lysander's head wouldn't stop thumping. "It's hardly a cause of reasonable doubt."

"If he's a trained agent," Ben snapped, "I'm a monkey's uncle."

"He *can't* be from the past." Jacob said flatly. "He would need access to a gate from then to now, and we know it can't be possible." He paused, frowning. "Unless he doubled back?"

"What?" Ben laughed sharply. "He ended up in the future and then stumbled back to here?"

"Or someone accidentally let him through and then tried to put him back, and it didn't work?"

Ben snorted. "You can't *accidentally* stumble through a gate."

Jacob started to speak, then snapped off his response and ran his hand over his eyes. "Right."

Lysander ran his knuckle along his lower lip, staring at the spread of data projected in front of him. In the middle of it all, they had a new image of their intruder taken by the medical team. He seemed much younger and warier now, his features tense and pale.

If it was impossible, then there could only be one explanation: he was from the future.

The evidence, though...

Either an impossible traveller from the past or a perfectly selected actor from the future and no way to know which one.

Lysander noticed both Ben and Jacob staring at him expectantly. "What?"

"That's what we want to know," Ben said. He seemed as tense as their new visitor. "Where do we go with this?"

Lysander shut down the screens. "If you'll give me fifteen minutes, I'd like to have some time to think."

"We don't have time—"

"Ben." Jacob touched Ben's shoulder. "We can spare fifteen minutes." He met Lysander's eyes, and Lysander could see the sympathy there. He'd been in Lysander's seat before. He knew how it felt. "We'll be in the canteen."

As soon as the door closed behind them, Lysander pressed his head into his hands, his elbows propped on the desk. It was a terrible feeling, to be pushed into a bottomless deep end and expected to swim. He took several gulping breaths, trying to ignore the sick feeling in his stomach.

Past or future.

They had to know.

He tried to gather himself. Air. It would help.

The storm of the day before had blown itself out, leaving the sky clear with brushes of wispy cloud scattered low on the horizon and the sun high overhead. Even so, it was still bitterly cold, the smell of frost still on the air, as he stepped out onto the rooftop garden.

Sometimes, he missed the freshness of the cold of home.

A path wound its way around the roof, so he followed it as he went over the possibilities of what they could and would do.

He'd just started on his second circuit when his personal Leaf chirped in his breast pocket. The screen showed a message from Danny.

Got a book!

Lysander stared at the message, wishing he had the energy to smile. *Good*, he replied, wishing he could steal another night in Danny's bed, no questions, no demands. Danny made things easy, if only for a little while, and, God, he needed it right now.

Another chirp, this time an image of a half-empty bottle of whisky and two open caffeine pods.

"Oh no..."

Another image: a thumbs up.

How drunk are you?

A wee totty wee bit.

Lysander pressed his forefinger and thumb to his eyelids. He could see the logic behind it, but all things considered, Danny using a caffeine and alcohol cocktail to stimulate his brain had the potential to end very badly.

Lysander sent a quick message: *You don't need to.*

It's science. Channeling the hypnosis.

A pause.

Fuck. Challenging the hypothesis. Stupid Leaf.

Well, it was too late to stop him now, but Lysander made himself feel better by reminding Danny to drink plenty of water and not forget his meals.

I had cow. Cow with gravy. Good stuff.

Lysander smiled, but it didn't last. He glanced over his shoulder towards the door. Technically, Danny needed to be around for the corrupted coding, but with everything going on, he knew it would be more secure to bring the coding issue back in-house.

He just had to pay Danny for his troubles and send him home and—

Lysander blinked as a thought occurred to him.

Their new arrival had been babbling about getting home.

If he came from the past, as he appeared to have, then it narrowed the courses of action down to confirming whether it had been directly or via some other point in time along the way. If his origin was directly from history, once he was relieved of all possible information about his temporal jump, they could send him back to his correct timeline. If he was from the future...

Lysander walked back towards the doors.

Identification first. Once they knew his origins, then they could work out the ways to deal with him.

He explained this course of action to Jacob and Ben when they returned to join him in the office.

"He's not about to tell us, is he?" Ben said, shaking his head. "You saw the state of him when they brought him in. I'm amazed he hasn't gone catatonic already."

Jacob thoughtfully ran a finger across his chin. "We go in gently. I've done plenty of interrogations before with victims and perpetrators. Either he is who he appears to be, or he'll give something away about his real origins."

Something in Ben's expression made Lysander inquire, "You think it's a bad idea?"

"I'm thinking in context," Ben replied, glancing over at him. "Let's say he *is* from history, two hundred odd years or whatever." He shot an apologetic smile at Jacob. "No offence, Jacob, but you're not exactly the face of a historical authority figure in England from the eighteenth century. Maybe I should do it?"

"But then, that could be a tell itself," Jacob pointed out. He leaned back in his chair, gazing into middle distance. "I'll need to prepare the questions beforehand. It's going to take some careful wording."

Lysander shot a glanced at the footage from the medical bay. "Well, I think you have some time. He's out for the count now."

"Do we have historians free?" Ben asked. "If they can gauge an era from his clothing, they could come up with targeted questions."

"Great minds think alike," Jacob agreed. "Has wardrobe narrowed it down?"

Lysander touched the console, calling up the connection to the prop team. It took several seconds before anyone picked up the call. Finally, a video link opened.

"Mr. O'Donohue!" The grey-haired woman on the other end stared at him in astonishment. "I—you don't normally call directly."

"Exceptional circumstances," he said mildly, fishing his memory for her name. "Rhiannon, isn't it?"

She glanced over her shoulder. "I'm guessing this is about those pictures?"

"Has your team been able to place them in a particular timeline?"

"It's tricky without access to the original articles," Rhiannon said, scratching her jaw. "We'd be able to tell better with examination of the fabric and stitching. Based on the pictures, our best guess would be mid-to-late eighteenth century. Maybe early nineteenth."

Almost exactly as Falconer had estimated.

"Explain."

Rhiannon launched into a detailed description: the cut of the collar, the line of the shirt, the shape and size of the coat, the quality of the shoes. There were a lot of details, each one annotated with a reason why it could knock plus or minus several decades off their estimated time frame. In conclusion, they couldn't narrow it down any further, not unless they were given access to the clothing itself.

Lysander saw Jacob nod through the projected video. He probably had someone in mind to help with putting together the questions. At least one element was safely out of Lysander's hands. Jacob knew the historians and agents better than anyone. He would be the right person to make the choice.

"I'll see about getting the clothing to you as soon as it has been cleared by decon," Lysander said once Rhiannon finished speaking. "It may be later today, or possibly tomorrow."

She lit up with delight. The wardrobe department's experts always did like to lay hands on historical artefacts, but rarely got the chance when historians could claim them first. "I'll look forward to it. Marked for my attention?"

"Of course." He closed the link and glanced at Jacob. "Do you have people who can work within that time frame?"

"At least a dozen." Jacob unfolded from the seat. "You mind if I...?" He jerked his thumb towards the door.

"The sooner the better."

As soon as he left, Lysander focussed on Ben.

The younger man had slouched in his chair, his mouth pressed to his fist, a distant look on his face. He must have noticed the silence because he blinked and turned to meet Lysander's eyes. "What if he is from history? Do you really think we could send him back? After all he's seen, people would think he's mad."

"If we can, I think we have to try," Lysander murmured. "He has his own place and his own timeline to follow. If there's a chance we can get him back to it, we need to."

Ben frowned down at his hands. "And what if we can't?"

"Get him back?"

"It's not like we can send someone back into the future."

Lysander had the horrible feeling of standing on the edge of a precipice and swaying, not knowing whether he would fall or keep his footing. He wondered if this was how Jacob felt, wondered if these were the questions they had dealt with back in the day.

"We need solid facts before we can start speculating about possible courses of action." He hoped he sounded more confident than he felt. "Until then, head to security and go over the details of the surge. There might be something else in there to give us a clue where and when this man came from."

Ben got up stiffly. He pressed his hand against the back of the chair. "Jacob thinks this is something to do with my dad, doesn't he? Or something the thieves stole?"

"I don't know," Lysander said. "I never know what he's thinking." Ben hummed doubtfully, and Lysander smiled tiredly. "You've known him longer than I have. Do you think he'd tell me anything if he thought it would compromise the security of the agency?"

"Point," Ben agreed as he rubbed at his face. "I was looking forward to working on my new gate designs. Now, rogue time travellers and code training and weird kids who might or might not be secretly connected to my dad..."

Lysander sympathised and wished he could say something to make things easier, but right now, he had nothing left to give. The best he could do was offer, "Well, we're all stuck in the same boat now."

Chapter Twenty-Three

"FUUUUUUUCK..."

Morning had come in the shape of a bright, clear day.

Nice, if you didn't have a hangover from hell and hadn't left the curtains open and gotten lasered in the eyes by the sun.

Danny pulled the blankets up over his head.

It didn't help much, not when they were all fusty and stinking of sweat. He rolled over to the far side of the bed and dropped onto the shadowy side, pulling the blanket with him. The floor was bloody cold and gave him a sharp nudge towards wide awake when his bare arse hit it.

He managed—feebly—to scoot the blanket under his bum and groped up on the bedside cabinet for the bottle of water he'd put there. Forward planning, there. Unfortunately, he hadn't thought far enough ahead to include some paracetamol or any kind of hangover-reducing pills, but water never hurt.

The room spun around him as he finished the bottle of water. Unfortunately, a body had needs, especially a body full of booze and caffeine and, now, a litre of water. He stottered across to the bathroom and, for once, parked himself on the loo seat. It was easier than trying to keep his feet. Plus it meant he could lean sideways and rest his thumping head against the nice cool tiles.

He only closed his eyes for a minute.

At least it felt like a minute.

His bum had gone numb and ached when he jolted awake again. Christ. Definitely no a great start to the day.

By the time he'd dashed some water on his face and knocked back some painkillers, he felt a little more human. Food always helped, even if it sounded stomach-churning, so he ordered some room service and—thankfully—remembered to put on some pants before he opened the door.

Danny picked at the full English while leafing through his work from the night before. Ha. Work. A professional liar couldn't have made that sound true.

He'd hoped the cocktail would give him the same kick as the night at the club, but apparently not. There were a handful of potentially useful notes, but most of it was a load of bullshit and an unexpectedly recognisable portrait of Lysander scribbled all over two pages.

Danny squinted at it. It was made up of tiny squiggles of code. He'd probably started working on the code and then got distracted, and, of course, he knew why. When he got hammered on spirits, it sometimes went straight for his knob, leaving him randy as fuck with nowhere to go. At least he hadn't jizzed all over the pages, because that would have taken some explaining.

"Sod," he muttered, throwing the book back onto the bed.

If getting completely wrecked hadn't solved anything, then he had to get back to the old-fashioned and sober way, which couldn't happen when it felt like someone was thumping a hammer against the inside of his head.

It took ages to get himself in any state to do anything, and getting under the shower felt like a small victory, although the heat made his head spin all over again. He padded back out into the main room and switched on to one of the news channels as he sat on the end of the bed to wait for the world to stabilise.

He was towelling at his head when the newscaster's voice penetrated the fog around his brain.

"...according to eyewitnesses, the man was taken into custody and allegedly transported to the Temporal Research Institution..."

Danny lowered the towel from his head. "Eh?"

The scrolling headline made his mouth drop open.

Mystery History Man Captured In London.

He sat, slack-jawed, as the news washed over him. A suspected time traveller arrested in London and taken to the TRI with the news breaking in the early hours of the morning. Police denying all and any of the story and being pissy about it. The TRI not responding to any inquiries.

"Shit..." Danny breathed.

No wonder Lysander had been so tense.

Danny glanced over at his Leaf, lying on the bedside table. It would be easy enough to drop a message to check in and see how things were going, but then if it had hit the news, Lysander would be swamped already.

He rubbed at his jaw as he turned his attention back to the screen.

Everything had gone tits up three days ago, but the story had only just broken. It was possible they hadn't picked him up for a few days, but Danny wondered if maybe he'd been exiled from the TRI because they were expecting a delivery of one captive time traveller, and he couldn't be around for it. It meant a gap of at least twenty-four hours before the story broke.

Something felt off about all of it.

They were talking about eyewitnesses, but if a rogue time traveller had been running around, they would have tried to keep it quiet. He couldn't see a bunch of police officers talking out loud—in front of witnesses no less—about sending someone off to one of the most top-secret facilities in the country.

A leak, then?

Jesus, Lysander was probably having kittens about it. Bad enough the TRI were getting thrown into the spotlight, but for having a rogue time traveller was even worse. A bit of bollocksed coding was probably at the bottom of his list of things to worry about.

The newscaster moved on to the next item. Danny swore under his breath and scrambled up the bed to grab his Leaf to see if there was anything he was missing from the story. It turned out all the news outlets were running with the same limited information. All they knew was the time traveller was a young man, and according to someone who had spoken to him, he sounded as if he came from England.

Danny was still working his way through the articles when the Leaf chirped in his hand. He brushed away all the news pages and opened up the messages. To his surprise and relief, the message had come from Lysander. The contents, however, were not what he expected.

I guess you've seen the news. If you want to return to London now, it would be understandable.

Danny stared at it.

Sod off. You paid me to do a job. I haven't finished it yet.

This isn't going to blow over overnight. You don't need to be involved.

Danny snorted. *I get it, but I swear to God if you take me off the code when I've got so far with it, I'm going to storm the gates and kick your arse from here to kingdom come. You don't set me a puzzle to solve, then take if off me when I'm nearly done!*

A few minutes later, a video call connected.

Danny opened it at once and couldn't help swearing. Lysander looked like death warmed up. He hadn't shaved, his face grey with dark rings around his eyes that made him look like a skinny panda.

"Compliments all the way, huh?" Lysander managed a brittle smile.

"Sod compliments," Danny said. "You look worse than I feel and that's saying something." He frowned, taking in the creases in Lysander's clothes and his tangled hair. "Have you had any sleep?"

"Mm. A little." Lysander sighed. "There's a lot going on."

"I'll say. What do you need me to do? If you want me out of your hair for now, I can go back to London, but if there's any way I can be useful up here, I'll do it."

Lysander fell silent for a moment, and when he spoke, he gazed out of frame. "I think— I'd like you to stick around." One side of his mouth twitched. "I don't have anything for you to do, but I—" He turned back to the camera. "I'd like to know you're around."

Danny's heart felt like it stopped for a second. "Yeah?"

"I miss my waiter." Lysander laughed self-consciously, as if he'd said too much. "I have to go. I'll let you know if and when you can get back out here to finish the coding."

He terminated the call before Danny could say anything else, and Danny couldn't help being a little bit relieved Lysander didn't see him go beet red.

He put the Leaf down and glanced back at the news. The TRI story was still the primary scrolling topic, which meant more pressure on Lysander and his people. Danny knew he couldn't be much use, but he had his notebooks, and if it would take at least a little bit of the pressure off Lysander, then he'd get it done.

First things first: the hangover.

He'd worked hungover before, but only in the right mindset and when he hadn't picked the wrong cheap drink as his wingman. This time, work-brain had been buried somewhere under all the whisky and the thumping headache.

There was one sure-fire way to start pushing it back, but it meant getting upright and out to a bigger and better shop for a strip of the best hangover tablets money could buy.

He headed to the bathroom, turned the shower on at full power, and dragged the heat as low as it would go. He could feel the chill from three feet away and whimpered, then leaned forward and shoved his head under the stream.

It was cold enough that he yelped between clenched teeth and his hands skidded on the wet wall as he tried to keep his balance. Unsuccessfully, as it turned out, but pitching full length and half-naked into an ice-cold torrent of water did amazing things to get a man moving. He shot out of the tub like a scalded cat, cursing the air blue.

Technically, it helped.

At least, it put the stinker of a headache into perspective when his teeth were clattering and his skin had turned white with cold, all prickled in goosebumps.

Phase two was some fresh air.

The notebooks went with him, and he nipped into one of the bigger grocery shops half a mile away from the hotel. Thank Christ they had a better selection than the wee local, and he gratefully knocked back a couple of pills. He could swear they were made of some kind of magic because they started to clear his head within minutes.

He forced himself from a gentle walk into a cautious trot, and when his head didn't feel like it was about to fall off his shoulders, he managed to get up to a steady jog. With his headphones in and the music down low, he lost himself for an hour.

Something about the rhythm of running brought things into focus. The rest of the world dropped away for a bit, and his mind could fix on other things. By the time he reached the canal, flushed and sweating like a pig, the headache had been reduced to a dull throb, and he knew exactly what some of those notes from the night before meant.

He drew to a halt, staring blankly at the horizon.

"Well shit," he said, surprised. "I'm a genius."

Chapter Twenty-Four

IT HAD TURNED into a full-blown three-ringed circus.

The PR team was running interference, Fana was fielding more calls than she knew what to do with, the police were denying responsibility for any leak, and all Lysander wanted to do was kick everyone out of his office and sleep for more than an hour.

"You're sure you're ready for this?"

Jacob had a sheaf of papers in his hand. The historians had recommended it, instead of depending on high-tech equipment. Something less alarming than digital projections and floating screens. "I have the bud in, if you have questions to add."

Lysander retreated and watched as Jacob stepped into the pod.

The rogue traveller had been settled in the quarantine building, and instead of panicking him with the internal pod system again, Jacob was going over to see him.

"I don't like this," Ben murmured. "Shouldn't one of us go with him?"

"Call this the first run." Lysander watched the pod shuttle into the dark tunnel towards the quarantine unit. "Jacob did this professionally. If he can't get answers, then we can consider other options."

Ben hummed uncertainly and followed Lysander back to the elevator.

They had a communication room waiting for them with a direct video link to the quarantine room where they'd housed they intruder. It looked like a standard hotel room with a bed and a bathroom, basic home comforts for a modern person.

Whoever he was, their rogue traveller was playing his role well.

Once he'd slept, he slunk around the room in the afternoon light, exploring every part of it. When the electric lights came on, he cowered in the corner for an hour, babbling something like prayers. He didn't use the bathroom, relieving himself in the trash can in the bedroom instead. When given a tray of food, he stared at it and then wolfed it down using his hands. He shied away from anyone who approached him and, when night fell, curled on the floor beside the bed, wrapped in the blanket.

Now, he was sitting on the edge of the bed like a lost child.

He didn't move until the door opened.

Enoch scrambled to his feet. "Might I go…" he began and then trailed off, backing up. His eyes were wide as he stared up at Jacob. Jacob could be imposing at the best of times, but someone head and shoulders taller than the young man had to be a shock.

"Shit," Ben whispered.

Jacob either didn't notice or—more likely—chose to ignore the young man's expression. "I'm Jacob Ofori." He approached the table and sat down with a smile. "They tell me your name is Enoch?"

Enoch nodded, still staring at him.

"Do you have a family name?"

Another nod. "B-Baker." Enoch rolled his eyes towards the door, as if trying to work out his chances of escape. He was rigid with tension.

"Jacob's scaring him," Ben said, gesturing to the screen. "Look at him. The poor bastard's about to piss himself. You need to send someone less intimidating—"

"Just wait."

Jacob casually shed his coat and loosened his tie. When he relaxed back in the chair, Enoch watched him warily. "I'm not here to punish you, Mr. Baker. I'm not an enemy. I only want to know where you come from so we can get you home."

Enoch's lips trembled. "Right true?"

"Right true." Jacob had pitched his voice low and gentle. "If you can tell us where you come from, we can get you back there."

Lysander wasn't surprised when Enoch wrapped his arms across his middle, shrinking back. "Fairhurst."

Ben had a screen open and searched for it. "Shit. It's not on any maps. Jacob, we need specifics."

"And where is that?" Jacob asked gently.

Enoch looked confused. "England?"

"Do you know the county? The parish?"

Enoch shook his head, visibly distraught.

Jacob held up his hand soothingly. "All's well, Enoch. All's well." He leafed through the papers in his hands. "Can you tell me how you came to be here?"

"A-a coach but...but no wheels," Enoch stammered. "The folk fetched me by the brig and telt me to go in it."

"Jesus," Ben murmured.

"Before the coach," Jacob said in the same gentle, patient tone. Lysander could see why he'd been so effective as a police officer—calm and unrelenting. "You were in a field before you went into the city. Do you remember the field? There were fences about it?"

Enoch shivered. "It were all mashed."

"How did you get there?"

Enoch recoiled in his seat, shaking his head. He covered his face with his hands, and muffled prayers leaked out between his fingers.

"Ly..." Ben looked at Lysander. "This isn't working. He's too scared."

Lysander had to agree, watching as Enoch rocked on his seat. Jacob pursed his lips and then glanced at the camera.

"Let's give him some time," Lysander decided. "We can find someone less imposing."

Jacob said he would let Enoch have some more rest and then withdrew, leaving orders with one of the quarantine team to get the poor man a mug of warmed milk to calm his nerves.

It was another ten minutes before Enoch uncovered his face, but he seemed less fearful as he reached for the drink. He sat there, sipping it carefully, the mug shaking between his hands.

Jacob was back in Lysander's office by then. "If he's an actor, he's one of the best I've seen," he admitted, watching the feed. "I hate to say it, but I think Ben's right. I don't know if it's race or height or authority, but he's too scared of me to give me the answers we need."

Lysander watched as Enoch went to the bed and gingerly climbed up onto it as if afraid of sinking into the softness of the mattress. "He needs someone who isn't a threat," he murmured. "Someone who knows the questions we need to ask." He glanced at Ben. "Are you still up for it?"

Ben looked startled. "You think I could do it?"

"You *did* suggest it."

"I didn't think you'd let me!" Ben glanced towards the screen, chewing his lip. "I'm not— It's not— I'm not exactly a professional at interrogating." He turned back to Lysander. "What if he can tell I don't know what I'm doing?"

"That's the point," Lysander said. "You're around the same age as him. Same ethnicity. Going in uncertain will be a point in your favour;

it'll give you something in common, and he might see you as a safe person to talk to. Or an easier person to play."

Ben darted a glance at Jacob, then back. "I—it—what am I meant to ask?"

Jacob held out the bundle of papers. "Your script."

"Jacob!" Ben protested. "You're not meant to encourage him! This isn't in my job description!"

"This isn't any of our jobs," Lysander said quietly. "Ben, you know how tightly this information needs to be restricted now. We can't risk it being leaked any more than it already has."

"Well, what about you?"

Jacob snorted. "I thought you didn't want to intimidate him."

"Which would have been my reason." Lysander shot a wry smile at Jacob and turned back to Ben. "Ben, please. I'm asking you to do this. We need answers, and we need them as soon as possible."

Ben opened and shut his mouth, but no sound came out. He got up and walked in a circle, fiddling with his watch. "Do you think I can do it?"

"You're one of the most personable people here," Jacob said. "If you can't get him talking, no one can."

Ben stared down at his hands, then back at Lysander. "Ly, if I cock this up—"

"You won't." Lysander smiled tiredly. "I know you, Ben. You'll do your best. You always do."

"Do my best at what I know," Ben huffed, shifting anxiously from one foot to the other. "We don't know how he's going to react to me."

Jacob gave a strained laugh. "Well, it can't be worse than how he reacted to me."

Fifteen minutes and a brief coaching session later and Ben was dispatched to the quarantine building.

"Do you think this is a good idea?" Jacob inquired.

"No," Lysander admitted, watching Enoch sitting on his bed, "but right now, we don't have time to wait for a better one."

Jacob sighed and ran his hand over his face. "Press conference impending?"

Lysander shook his head. "Statement. Press conferences will come when we have something significant to say and can answer their questions."

There was a long silence, and then Jacob quietly asked, "Do you think this has anything to do with the code issue?"

Lysander hoped his expression didn't give anything away. "Do you?"

"I have no clue," Jacob admitted. "But I'm always suspicious of coincidences, especially when it comes to this place. Could have been the opening move, couldn't it? A distraction to keep your attention, and now this is the main event?"

Lysander had been wondering the same thing. The TRI had plenty of vultures circling all the time—governments who didn't like the results of the research, independent historians who begrudged the restricted access, and who knew what else. A security prank wasn't good to begin with. But then the rogue time traveller added another layer of trouble, and on top of that, someone had leaked the story and forced the TRI into the spotlight.

"To what end?" he asked. He'd been puzzling over it for days now, but so far it had done nothing more than made his life a lot more complicated, forced a lockdown, and given the PR team an inconvenient amount of work to deal with.

"I couldn't tell you." Jacob met his eyes. "But you can't deny it's dodgy."

There were so many little connections: Mack Robertson's arrival, the code's appearance, a gate with the same energy signature as Tom Sanders's old gates, the schematics for those old gates still missing since Sanders's death. Maybe it was all connected. Maybe it all came back to Jacob's imprisoned criminal.

"It's difficult to prove," Lysander said.

"True, but at least if you can solve the code issue, we'll know whether there's definitely a connection to dig into."

"Danny," Lysander said. "You think I should bring Danny back in?"

"One problem solved is better than none."

Lysander frowned. "People will wonder about external agents being allowed in and out of lockdown." He rubbed his head, trying to ignore the haziness that had started creeping in on the edge of his vision. God, he needed a good night's sleep. "We have Baker in custody. The campus is secure. I guess we could terminate the lockdown with conditional NDAs to ensure no one talks to the press."

"Keeping everyone closed up isn't going to make any difference now," Jacob agreed.

"Later." Lysander pointed to the screen where Enoch had scrambled off the bed when the door of his room opened.

Ben was standing nervously in the doorway. "Um. Hello."

Enoch looked like a deer in the headlights, shifting from one foot to the other. "Where's t'other one? The big dark one?"

"Jacob? Oh. Um." Ben shuffled the papers in his hands. "He's busy. He— I'm here instead."

Enoch visibly relaxed. "Aye?"

"Atta boy," Jacob murmured. "He's not so afraid of someone like him."

Ben smiled, but it could have been in response to either man. He held up the papers. "I've got some questions for you, if you don't mind?" He smiled hesitantly. "I'd like to help you get home."

Enoch watched him for a moment and then approached cautiously.

Ben went and sat at the table and waited for Enoch to join him. The young man was skittish as a frightened cat, but he reluctantly sat. He pulled one bare foot up onto the seat and hugged his knee.

"More relaxed," Lysander observed.

"Mm."

Ben laid out the papers in front of him. "I'm Ben," he said. "Ben Sanders."

"Enoch Baker." Enoch was watching Ben intently, his eyes wide and unblinking.

Ben stared at the pages. He seemed unusually nervous, Lysander thought, his face flushed and his hands shaking. When he spoke, his voice shook. "Can you tell me how you got here?"

"Not the coach with no wheels?"

"No," Ben agreed. "Before the flat building bit."

Enoch wrapped both arms around his upraised knee. "You'll think I'm mad," he whispered it, barely loud enough for Lysander to hear.

Ben was quiet for a second; then—to Lysander's surprise—he flipped open a Leaf screen. Enoch slammed back in his chair, staring, his face cast in pale blue by a shimmering projection extending up to the ceiling. Ben played a video file of a roaring waterfall and then shut the screen down, leaving the room darker for it.

"I won't think you're mad," he said softly. "I'll believe you."

Enoch stared at him and licked his lower lip. "A door. There were a door," he whispered, "It were made of light." His eyes darted up to the place where the projection had been, and he pointed towards the bud under Ben's finger. "Is—is it witchcraft?"

"Science, made by men, nothing more," Ben said. He pressed the bud, opening up a smaller screen. "It's made of light and pictures."

Enoch reached out to poke at it, like a child trying to touch a candle flame. "It has numbers 'pon it," he said, pushing his finger through the clock.

"It shows you the hour." Ben squinted at it and blinked in surprise. "Coming up on noon already." Enoch's face creased up. Probably confusion, Lysander guessed. It was nothing like a watch after all. Ben shut the screen down and tucked his bud away. "Don't worry. It doesn't matter just now."

"Right enough," Enoch said, still frowning.

"I do have some more questions, though." Ben spoke too quickly, anxious no doubt, and leaned forward on the table. "Enoch, tell me about the door."

Enoch hugged his knee more tightly. "We seed it and thought it were a trick. Matthew, he bade me not to go by it. He swore it were a gateway to...to Hell. I-I said he were addle-yedded." He laughed, short and sharp. "I said I'd look to see..." He was rocking again. "I would I'd listened."

"Did you go through the doorway?"

"It were cold," he whispered. "Cold and wind like winter." He propped his chin on top of his knee, his hands clenched so tight the knuckles were visibly white.

Lysander tapped his fingers on the desk. "He's very good, if he's acting."

"Convincing, isn't he?" Jacob agreed. "Ben, you need to find out where he started."

"Enoch," Ben began, but Enoch gave a strangled gasp. "Shit!" Ben lunged off the chair and got around the table in time to catch Enoch as the young man slumped sideways off the chair. "Meds!" Ben roared. "Now!"

Exhaustion mired Lysander's thoughts as he stared at the footage and Jacob barked out commands through the comms. Ben had Enoch on his back on the floor. He'd checked his pulse and was performing CPR, muttering urgently under his breath, too low to make out the words.

After what felt like an eternity, Enoch gasped, his eyes flying open, his breath a rasping wheeze, but he managed to grasp at one of Ben's arms, clinging to him like a lifeline.

Ben, visibly shaking, slid his arm under Enoch's shoulder, steadying him on the cold floor. "All right." His voice trembled. "You're all right. I've got you." He sounded hysterical, fighting down the panic. "You're fine. It's all fine. It's all over. You're okay now."

Enoch squinted up at him, his face half lost in shadow. "Aye...all fine." His head lolled against Ben's arm.

The med team swept in, and Ben was pushed to one side as they surrounded the prone Enoch. Ben crawled out of their way, still staring.

It had all taken less than a minute.

Lysander looked blankly at Jacob. "What happened?"

Jacob hadn't moved, staring at the footage, his expression one of horrified comprehension as Ben anxiously paced back and forth while the med team worked on Enoch.

"Jacob?"

Jacob took an unsteady breath. "We've hit his crossover point."

Lysander knew he was too tired. Very little made sense anymore. "What?"

"He's from the past, but also from the future."

"How can you know that?"

Jacob rubbed at his eyes. He was tired too, but awake enough to see something Lysander couldn't. "You can't cross your own timeline. Tom Sanders experimented with it when he started out, and it nearly killed him. The original person in the timeline is the one who gets the blowback. The same thing happened with Mack Robertson when he went back. If they hadn't put him on a ventilator at birth, we wouldn't be in this mess."

Lysander stared at him, then back at the young man who had inexplicably collapsed. On the back of Jacob's theory, there could be a reason for it. "When you said he'd come from the future," he said cautiously, "what you mean is that he came from five minutes ago?"

Jacob nodded. "Someone must've realised their mistake when Enoch came through unexpectedly and punted him back through as quickly as he could."

"Because Enoch's still alive?" Lysander guessed.

"So far." Jacob looked grimly back at him. "If I'm right, some bastard is out there playing with a temporal gate right now and doesn't care who gets in the way."

Lysander sagged in his chair. "Fuck."

Chapter Twenty-Five

IT WAS BLOODY difficult to try to construct a three-dimensional coding model when you were working with half a dozen notebooks and a rapidly drying-out packet of pens.

Danny tossed the last of the blue pens into the bin.

The pages of the notebooks were packed with text in six different colours. He'd scribbled down as much as he could, taking the vague ideas he'd had while pished and refining them with the epiphanies he'd had while jogging. He'd stopped to eat in the periods when his hand cramped up. He'd even remembered to sleep when his eyes crossed, and he couldn't focus anymore.

At least he'd gotten it all down in writing, he thought, as he closed the last of the books up. All the thoughts pulled out of his head were now organised and ready to be used, whenever he was allowed back to the TRI and the code.

Unfortunately, the TRI still took prime place in the news, which meant he probably wasn't getting back any time soon. They still got a mention in every big bulletin. Two days of the same discussions and limited number of facts being trotted out. Once, they'd managed to catch some hairdresser who claimed to have met the time traveller, and Danny had no doubt she'd be well paid for her chat.

The only major development had been a neutral statement issued by the director of the TRI to the evening news the night before, indicating the TRI was currently working with the Met to identify a young man, who appeared to be lost and disorientated. It could not be confirmed whether said young man was, in fact, a time traveller. Standard and straightforward, but Danny could feel Lysander's frustration fizzing underneath it.

More than once during the day, Danny had considered sending messages of condolence or a line to remind Lysander his waiter would appreciate it if he remembered to eat. Of course it was selfish—but also tempting. And more than once, he'd gotten as far as typing in a message and then deleting it.

It made it more of a surprise when a message came through at four o'clock in the afternoon.

A pod will be waiting outside at six o'clock. Be ready.

Danny blinked at it. *Where am I going?*

Trust me.

Well, that went without saying. *Best behaviour.*

Two hours later, he hopped into the pod outside the hotel, the notebooks securely closed up in his satchel. Even if he had no idea where he was going, he'd spruced himself up, had a shower, and generally made himself more presentable.

There was something exciting about going on a mystery journey. Danny watched the city skimming by and couldn't hazard a guess where he was headed. It definitely wasn't the TRI, since they were heading in the wrong direction.

After half an hour, the pod drew to a stop.

Danny stepped out, frowning in confusion. It looked like an old-fashioned housing scheme with a cluster of a dozen squat blocks of flats around a modest park. None of the flats were above four storeys. A path wound down the middle, and as far as Danny could see, it was all completely residential.

He sent a message to Lysander, but got no reply, so he approached a passing grey-haired woman walking her dog.

"Excuse me." He flashed a hopeful smile at her. "I'm here to see Lysander O'Donohue."

She studied him and then pointed down the path. "The block on the left at the far end."

He thanked her and hurried off down the path. An elderly man at the door was wheeling his shopping cart in. He didn't seem surprised when Danny hurried over to help him. "You'll be looking for Mr. O'Donohue, too?"

Too?

"Yes. He's in this block, right?"

The old man snorted. "Nah. Two blocks down."

The third resident he passed tried to send him off in the opposite direction. 'Too' started to make sense. Lysander was the director of the TRI. The press were probably trying to find him at home, and Danny had shown up, bright-eyed and bushy-tailed with no sense of direction.

Messages weren't enough, so he chimed through and waited.

Twenty seconds later, Lysander finally picked up—audio only, no visual.

"Yeah?" Lysander sounded half-asleep.

"Your silver army is trying to keep me at bay," Danny said. "I got your pod, but I have no idea where I'm meant to go from here."

Lysander caught a small, almost silent breath and then uttered the faintest "Oh shit."

"You forgot?"

"No!" Lysander exclaimed. "Sorry. I meant to send you the address, but I must have fallen asleep. I'll send it now. Make your way up."

It turned out the pod had stopped outside the right door, and Danny laughed quietly. He could see the old woman and her dog farther down the block. Trust Lysander to have a fleet of old biddies watching his back. He buzzed in and headed up to the third floor, hunting down Lysander's flat number.

Lysander opened the door as soon as Danny touched the buzzer.

Danny had considered making some gobby remark about him being a lazy bastard, but the second he saw Lysander's face, he squashed the idea. The poor bugger looked knackered, with deep bags under his eyes. He hadn't shaved properly for days, his hair half-undone, and his clothes were creased all over.

Still, he smiled in welcome and started in surprise when Danny stepped across the threshold and caught him in a bear hug. He only tensed for a second, then wrapped his arms around Danny's waist and held on as tightly.

"What's this for?" he murmured close to Danny's neck.

"You needed it," Danny replied, then loosened his arms and let Lysander step back. "You all right?"

Lysander shrugged and scratched at his brow. "I've had better days." He motioned for Danny to come in. "Sorry. I needed to sit down for a few minutes when I got in. I must have fallen asleep."

Danny waved his words away. "It's no bother."

He stepped farther into the flat and glanced around, whistling through his teeth.

The area hadn't seemed like Lysander's kind of place, but the flat suited him just right: open and spacious with warm ambient lighting. The external walls were almost all window. At the right-hand side, a gap in the floor-to-ceiling bookshelves revealed a bed. The middle of the flat was given over to a huge curved couch, a dining area and the kitchen, and, to the far left, the bathroom.

Lysander glanced to the kitchen. "I wanted to surprise you with dinner."

Danny stared at him, astonished, then took a step closer to Lysander so he could lean down and kiss him. Lysander caught his arm, holding him there, and reached up to curl his fingers in Danny's hair.

When they broke apart, Danny searched his face and nuzzled the tip of his nose. "That bad, eh?"

Lysander jerked his chin down once, tightly.

It didn't take a genius to realise talking about the shit, its impact on the fan, and everything else in between was a bad idea. Lysander had come home for a break. His inviting Danny over was both flattering and breathtaking.

Danny pushed all thoughts of TRI or coding to one side and gave Lysander's arse a firm squeeze through his trousers. "You said something about dinner?"

Lysander visibly relaxed. "Mm." He drew back. "Feel free to have a look around."

Danny laughed as he slid the satchel off his shoulder. "You sure it's a good idea? I might find out all your dirty secrets."

Lysander glanced back over his shoulder as he walked to the kitchen. "My dirtiest secret right now is you." He waved a hand towards the door. "Leave your jacket by the door. Shoes, too, if you want."

Danny gratefully toed off his boots and put them on the rack beside all of Lysander's shoes. He propped the satchel beside the rack and glanced at the door, unsurprised to see the number of security features Lysander had in place. The notebooks weren't about to go anywhere.

"You sure you don't mind me poking about?"

Lysander had rolled up his sleeves and made a start on chopping some vegetables. "I invited you over, so you're welcome." He smiled. "Or do you need orders?"

"You sent me on a magical mystery tour," Danny corrected, padding across the hardwood floor to the bookshelves. They were packed with books but also lined with framed photographs. "For all I knew, you might have been trading me to the Russians for caviar or something."

Lysander chuckled. "You place a high value on yourself, *Mister Ferguson*."

Danny grinned at the bookshelves. So Lysander was in that kind of mood as well? All the better. "Seems to be good enough for you, doesn't it?"

"A man can be cheap once in a while."

Danny laughed and picked up one of the picture frames. The grey-haired couple in the photograph were unmistakably related to Lysander. "Grandparents?" He held up the frame. Lysander nodded, and Danny looked back at it. The man had to be the Iranian grandfather. He'd passed on his impressively thick head of hair, bone structure, and dark eyes. The grandmother's smile was familiar too.

Scattered between landscape shots from a dozen countries were more photographs of people who had to be family members. One of those photographs caught his eye, and he took the frame down to look at it.

Unlike the other landscape photographs, this one had a shaggy-haired young man standing in front of a spectacular ruined city. He had a backpack on his back and was beaming, though the expression disappeared beneath a straggly beard and under the shadow of an impressively crooked broken nose.

"Who's the nose?" Danny inquired. "Your brother?

Lysander started laughing. "No."

Danny glanced at him, puzzled. "Cousin?"

"Me."

Danny blinked and studied the photograph again. All right, if you knocked maybe twenty-five years off and squished the nose into the right place and taught him about grooming. "This? This is you? With the..." He couldn't pick where to start. The youth in the picture was the antithesis of the stylish man he knew.

"After I turned eighteen, I took a year off," Lysander said warmly. "My voyage of self-discovery."

"I guess the discovery included a brush?"

Lysander chuckled. "And a razor, and the concept of less is more. But in my defence, I'd never had facial hair before, and I wanted to show it off."

"Fair enough," Danny conceded, then frowned at the picture, unable to tear his eyes off one very prominent feature.

"If you're wondering about the nose," Lysander said as he stirred up the vegetables in the pan, "I'll give you some advice— Don't pick a fight with an Iranian trucker."

"I wasn't—it—"

Lysander raised his eyebrows in amusement. "'Who's the nose?'" He echoed Danny's own words.

Danny winced. "Right. Aye. It's...impressive."

"A mess," Lysander said. "The words are a mess."

Since it clearly wasn't a sore point, Danny laughed. "A couple more degrees and it'd be horizontal," he agreed. He paused, frowning, as Lysander's words caught up with him. "What do you mean, picking fights with truckers?"

Lysander gave him an innocent look. "I can't spill all my stories in one go."

"No fair." Danny wandered across the room to perch on one of the stools by the kitchen island. He flicked a fragment of onion at Lysander, who caught it deftly. "First I find out you used to dress like a hobo? What next? Tattoos? A motorbike?"

Lysander added a dash of spice to the pot. "Yes."

Danny opened and shut his mouth. He frowned again. "Are you winding me up?"

Lysander only raised his eyebrows and smiled slightly.

Danny managed to button his lip for about five minutes, then exploded, "Oh, come on! A man can only take so much mystery!"

It was both a relief and pleasure when Lysander burst out laughing. "A fender bender in Iran."

"Eh?"

"Your first question." Lysander reached up and tapped his nose. "I didn't react well when someone—"

"A trucker?"

"A trucker wrecked my bike."

"Bike?" Danny's eyes were wide as saucers. "As in...motorbike?"

"Not much of one, but I'd saved for it and paid for it. He stopped suddenly. I ran into the back of him, and then he backed up over it, then tried to act like it was my fault." One side of his mouth turned up. "He didn't think I spoke Farsi."

"How does that change your nose?"

Lysander grinned, and suddenly Danny could see the young man in the picture frame. "When you tell a man he's as good a liar as he is a driver, he might not like it."

Danny gaped at him. "You're insane, aren't you?"

Lysander laughed as he fetched plates from one of the shelves. "Some people can't handle the truth. I gave the son of a bitch a kick, but he'd gotten a lucky shot. My parents went nuts when they saw it." He started serving up the food. "I thought it was impressive. Gave me a bad-boy edge."

Danny eyed him in amused disbelief. "A tattooed biker thug with a nose broken by a trucker? No one would believe me if I told them."

"That's the best part," Lysander agreed cheerfully.

"So what happened?" Danny folded his arms on the counter. "I mean, no offence, but you're not exactly...bad-boy material right now."

"Apparently, being able to breathe through your nose is useful."

"Ah."

Lysander grimaced. "Mm. Some of the internal damage was pretty bad, so they had to reconstruct it." He waved towards his nose. "Not exactly my bad-boy look, but it's been useful."

"Useful?" Danny echoed.

Lysander shrugged with a wry smile. "It's amazing how people react to someone aesthetically pleasing. They get distracted and sometimes speak out of turn. Sometimes, they're intimidated. Sometimes, they underestimate you because of your face. Like I said. Useful."

Danny hummed in understanding. "And you always look good."

"Deliberately so," Lysander replied and slid one of the plates across the table to him. "All the better to keep them on their toes."

Danny smirked at him. "So I've uncovered your big secret, eh?"

Lysander laughed, coming around the island to perch on the stool beside him. "Hardly a secret." He offered Danny a fork. "After all, it's my face. It's right in front of them."

"Hiding in plain sight." Danny nudged him. "Thanks, by the way."

"For what?"

Danny glanced around the room and then tapped his fork on the edge of his plate. "All this. You didn't need to."

"And if I wanted to?"

Danny's grin made his cheeks ache, and he leaned over and planted a firm kiss on Lysander's perfectly straight and symmetrical nose. "Then good for both of us." He took the proffered fork and sank it into the steaming plate of food. "You get bonus points for feeding me."

"Is it possible I've discovered your weakness?" Lysander feigned shock.

Danny narrowed his eyes. "No."

"What if I told you there's a chocolate fondant and ice cream for dessert?"

"...bugger."

Chapter Twenty-Six

IT WAS RAINING again.

Lysander liked the rain when he was settled comfortably indoors. It definitely didn't hurt when he was lounging on his couch with a good-looking man and didn't have to think about work and the chaos awaiting him for the next twelve hours.

Fortunately, the lockdown was lifted in time for him to get to his quarterly medical, although he'd originally planned to go straight back to the TRI after the procedure. When Jacob heard that, he told Lysander in no uncertain terms to go home, get some rest, and not come back until the next morning. Lysander didn't know when Jacob had claimed the authority, but since the world had become a little blurred, he'd conceded.

It wasn't as if he'd have been any use to anyone, frazzled and exhausted, with no technical skills to speak of. The medical team was taking care of the half-sedated Enoch, so he couldn't ask him any more questions. An eighteen-hour furlough to rest, clean himself up, and breathe was exactly what Lysander needed.

Danny shifted beside him on the couch to peer back at the windows. "Lovely."

Lysander drew his attention from the movie playing in front of them. "It's not like you're going out in it."

For all his intellect and witty comebacks, a surprised Danny managed to be even more adorable. It took him a second, as if he was figuring out what Lysander meant, and then he beamed. "Aye?"

"If you want to stay?"

Danny answered in his usual direct way when he leaned in and kissed Lysander. Lysander smiled against his lips, bracing one arm on the back of the couch for balance. He stroked his other hand through Danny's rumpled hair again and curled his fingers enough to pull.

"Is that a yes?" Lysander murmured close to Danny's lips when they broke apart.

"Do I get cuddles?"

Lysander couldn't help laughing. "I *do* owe you one night with them."

Danny's face lit up, and he reached out to pull Lysander closer, but Lysander clenched his fingers just hard enough, and Danny arched his neck with a soft hiss.

"You're going to behave," Lysander murmured, watching Danny's face carefully. It was selfish to want to have a moment of control, to have *something* in his life not spinning wildly out of his hands, but if anyone would understand, it would be Danny.

Danny's tongue darted out to wet his lower lip. "Aye."

Lysander sighed softly with relief. He brushed his lips over Danny's again. "I want you to stay very still; do you understand?" Danny's eyes were dark, his face warmly flushed. He twitched his chin down as much as Lysander's grip would allow. "Good."

Lysander pressed his lips to Danny's throat, to the rapid throb of his pulse point. He bared his teeth and nibbled his way down Danny's neck, keeping his touch light, teasing, until he reached the curve of neck and shoulder where the skin was barely covered by Danny's shirt.

When Lysander closed his mouth over the bare skin and drew on it hard enough to leave a mark, Danny hissed out a profanity, his body twitching against Lysander's. Lysander examined it by the low light, a dark rosette on Danny's skin. He laved his tongue over it, as if to seal it.

"So you don't forget."

"It'll show," Danny said hoarsely.

"And you'll have to come up with a convincing excuse," Lysander replied, nuzzling the length of Danny's throat. "Tripped. Fell. Landed on a mouth-shaped rock."

Danny snorted, then caught his breath when Lysander closed his teeth gently on Danny's windpipe. All it would take was a little pressure to steal his breath, but it wasn't the time or place for those kinds of games, not tonight.

Lysander drew away to look at Danny. "I'm going to let go of your hair, but it doesn't mean the rules are changing. You're going to stay still for me." He loosened his grip on Danny's hair and then began undoing the fastenings of Danny's shirt. It was a beautiful fit on him, but the moment Lysander had seen it, he wanted nothing more than to get it off.

Danny had pressed his hands down onto the couch, and though Lysander kept his eyes fixed on Danny's face as he slowly, slowly unfastened the shirt, he could feel the couch shifting as Danny kneaded at it with his clenched fists.

"You're being very quiet," Lysander murmured once the shirt had fallen open from collar to navel.

"I'm behaving," Danny said, his voice a little breathless. "S'what you asked for."

"Mm." Lysander smiled, his heartbeat picking up. Danny had a few inches in breadth and height on him and definitely much more physical strength, yet he'd happily submitted all over again. Lysander spread one hand on Danny's bared chest and laughed when Danny jolted. "Still too cold?"

"As usual," Danny grumbled good-naturedly. "You have bloody awful circulation."

"So I've been told." Lysander leaned down and exhaled a warm breath on the poor cold-touched skin. He raised his eyes to Danny. "Better?"

Danny licked at the corner of his mouth. "A bit."

"Only a bit?" Lysander braced one arm on Danny's thigh and brushed his lips over the same spot. "How about now?"

"Getting warmer." Danny was watching him like a hawk, and when Lysander darted his tongue across one nipple, Danny drew a breath between his teeth. "Like that, aye."

Lysander rubbed his cheek against Danny's chest, then closed his lips over Danny's nipple and tugged it between his teeth. Danny made a low, hungry sound, which sent a shiver right through Lysander. He trailed his mouth across to nip at the other small nipple and, at the same time, let the hand resting between Danny's legs brush along the seam of his pants.

"Fuck..." Danny groaned.

"Danny," Lysander murmured, hoping his voice sounded more steady than it did to his own ears. "I'm going to suck you off."

Danny's eyes popped wide open. "You what?"

Lysander laughed a little breathlessly. God, the expression on Danny's face, the delight and the desire made his stomach flip. "Mm." He pressed another kiss to Danny's chest, below his sternum. "But if you move, if you hurry me, if you try to touch me without my permission, I'll stop."

"Right..." Danny's breath caught sharply. "Right. Behave."

"Exactly."

Lysander pushed himself up and claimed a quick kiss, then got off the couch and sank onto his knees between Danny's spread legs. He slid both hands along Danny's taut thighs, from knee to hip, then up to tug Danny's shirt wide open. He ran his fingertips along the waistband of Danny's pants, wondering how far he could tease the other man before it was too much.

Danny fixed his eyes on Lysander's face. Lysander couldn't help pausing to admire the colour in his cheeks and the way his lips were parted and the tip of his tongue pressed against his teeth.

"Making me wait, eh?" Danny sounded strained.

"Mm." Lysander pressed one palm against the front of Danny's pants, and with his other hand, flicked the fastening loose. He wasn't surprised to feel Danny's cock already hard against his hand as he slowly undid Danny's pants, then laughed—unsurprised—to see Danny was going commando when his erection strained out of his half-open zipper. "Keen."

"And without a drink in me and all." Danny shifted his hips to nudge his pants down a little, sliding closer to the edge of the couch. Comfort, Lysander figured, since he didn't move any further.

He'd obeyed every instruction. Lysander was startled at the rush of want surging through him, having someone who would listen and obey and not question him. And such obedience definitely deserved a reward. He kept his eyes locked with Danny's as he dipped down and took Danny's cock in his mouth.

Danny made a stifled sound, cut off but hungry. It was a *good* sound, and Lysander wrapped his tongue around Danny's cock, sinking down over him, dragging up, trailing down and raking his teeth lightly up until Danny made that delicious sound again. His hips were twitching, but tension tightened his thighs as he tried not to move.

Lysander raised his head and smiled lazily. He had his hands braced on Danny's thighs and now hooked his fingers to scratch from inner thigh to knee, hard enough to leave marks, even through Danny's pants. As he drew his hands back up, he cupped Danny's balls with one, squeezing as he caught his cock with the other, stroking once, twice, hard and firm. Smiling, he returned to his task, teasing his tongue along the slick head of Danny's cock. Stroked, squeezed, and stroked again, until Danny's breathing staggered, and then, when his breath hitched hard, Lysander took a breath of his own and swallowed.

"Shit..." Danny whispered. "Lysander..."

Lysander lifted his head to look at him. God, he looked so hot and desperate, and he still hadn't moved. Lysander smiled and rubbed his cheek the length of Danny's cock, his eyes half-closed. "You can move now," he murmured, "but only your hips."

Then he took Danny's cock in his mouth again. Danny's hips jerked, thrusting his cock deeper, and Lysander kneaded at Danny's thighs. It only took a few strokes before the familiar pulse on his tongue, and he tilted his head to see Danny watching—dazed and wide-eyed—as he came all over Lysander's face.

"Shit..."

Lysander laughed, brushing some of the cum from his cheek with the tip of his finger. He studied it and then licked it clean. "I hope not." He rose on his knees, bracing his hands on either side of Danny's. "You should clean me up. It's your mess after all."

Danny stared at him so hungrily his heart beat a little faster. "Can I move then?"

"Ye—"

Danny caught Lysander's face between his hands, kissing him, his hands trembling. Lysander basked in the dizzying rush of giddiness knowing he was the cause. Danny drew back, then pulled up his own shirt and tenderly wiped Lysander's face clean, his other hand cradling Lysander's head beneath his braid.

"You ruined your shirt," Lysander murmured between swipes of the shirt and scattering kisses.

"It'll wash," Danny replied. He shrugged it off and tossed it aside. He leaned closer to kiss Lysander again, his tongue teasing against Lysander's. He nibbled Lysander's lower lip, soothing the bite with a lick before plunging his tongue back between Lysander's lips, kissing him greedily.

Lysander leaned up into him, wondering if it would be too much to climb onto his lap and grind on him. It was tempting, knowing how big Danny's eyes would get, but it wasn't as much fun without some audience participation, and Danny had been good enough to get a treat.

"Danny," he murmured, nuzzling his way along Danny's cheek. "You've earned a reward."

Danny's grin spread against Lysander's own cheek. "Aye? Like what?"

"Mm." He nipped Danny's earlobe between his teeth and tugged. "What would you like?" Danny went unusually quiet. Lysander drew back to look at him. "What is it?"

Danny cocked his head thoughtfully. "How about I get to return the favour?"

Always had to be surprising, didn't he?

"It's meant to be a reward for you," Lysander murmured.

Danny gazed back at him, dark-eyed and earnest. "But would you like it?"

Lysander hesitated. Yeah, they had already slept together, but no matter how much time went by, the first time completely uncovering himself in front of a lover made him freeze like a rabbit in the headlights. It was infuriating and frustrating but it *wouldn't* go away, no matter how much time passed or who he had in his bed.

He flinched in surprise when Danny touched his cheek.

"It's all right," Danny said with a small smile. "I don't want to toot my own horn to tell you you'd be missing out on a treat, but it's only a suggestion." He tucked a finger over the curve of Lysander's ear, smoothing a loosened strand of hair. "I can always go for more chocolate pudding."

Lysander stared at him, then dropped his head forward to rest on Danny's shoulder. The first time always felt the same, but after, once he'd risked the step and taken the plunge, things could get so much better. He moved one hand to brace it on Danny's thigh and pushed himself to his feet between Danny's splayed legs.

"I don't want to be blamed when you complain about putting weight on," he said as lightly as he could, reaching for the fastening of his pants.

Danny looked up at him. "You don't have to—" he began, then trailed off as Lysander twisted open the buttons. Danny's tongue darted out, wetting his lips again. "You sure?"

In response, Lysander shoved his pants down before he could change his mind, stepping out of one leg, then the other, before kicking them aside. His heart pounded painfully, the blood rushing in his ears, drowning out anything Danny might have said, as he reached up to undo the buttons of his shirt.

He swore under his breath. His hands were shaking with the self-consciousness, but also the lust that had been boiling up from the moment Danny had stared at him like he'd set the stars in the sky himself.

"Danny," he said, knowing he wouldn't be able to do it himself. "My shirt. Same as the first time."

Danny sat bolt upright on the couch, reaching for the shirt at once. "Folded or balled, when I'm done?"

Lysander couldn't stop the small smile. "Planning ahead?"

"Working out how much concentration I'll need," Danny replied, working the buttons open with impressive speed. He flashed his brilliant smile up at Lysander. "I get distracted when you're in front of me with not much on."

The shirt was already crumpled beyond salvation. "Toss it," Lysander said. "It'll need to be washed and pressed anyway."

Danny had the last buttons undone in seconds and sat back expectantly. Lysander obligingly shrugged and let it drop off his shoulders, though his hands were still shaking and, now, he was as bare as he'd ever been in front of Danny. It was crazy. He had biked alone through the wilderness in distant lands and had never been afraid, but pulling his shorts off for the first time...

He'd always faced things head-on—and this? This wasn't meant to be difficult.

He hooked his thumbs into the waistband of his shorts and pushed them down enough to free his cock, trying to ignore the blood throbbing in his ears. With one hand, he brought himself erect to save Danny any confusion.

Danny grinned up at him, mischief all over his face. "I wish mine came up that quick."

Lysander reached down and reproachfully tugged his earlobe. "As I recall," he said, "it did."

Danny gave him a sheepish smile, tilting his head into Lysander's touch. "Aye, true enough." He slid a little closer, brushing one hand up Lysander's thigh, which raised a rash of goosebumps, and Lysander had to take a breath. "How d'you fancy it?"

Lysander loosened his grip on Danny's ear and stroked his fingertips over Danny's crown instead. "You said you had a horn to toot. Show me what you've got."

For a split second, pure panic crossed Danny's face, and then he looked at Lysander's cock with the same studious concentration he applied to his work. When he reached out and caught Lysander by the hips, he didn't hesitate. "If you want me to stop, grab my ear."

Lysander swallowed hard, as Danny lowered his head and wrapped his mouth around Lysander's cock. Lysander combed his fingers through Danny's hair, closing his eyes and taking a shaky breath. Danny's mouth was warm, and he was taking his time.

It took Lysander a few giddy seconds to realise what Danny was doing—trying something out, gauging the reaction, and working on from it. Always so analytical. He moved from mouth, to mouth and hand, never straying under Lysander's shorts, but stroking against them, and when he tightened his grip at a particular angle, press-rubbing with his thumb, Lysander hissed and clenched his fingers in Danny's hair.

Danny raised his eyes, wide and innocent, which looked ridiculously hot when he still had the head of Lysander's cock in his mouth. He darted his tongue over and over, but his hand, Christ, his hand tightened, dragging slowly up and down. Lysander bared his teeth, his breathing coming hard. He clutched at Danny's shoulder with his free hand, and Danny shifted his hand to find the same particular angle, grinding slowly, sending heat surging through Lysander's veins.

When Danny moved his head and took Lysander in his mouth again, he dragged his teeth up slowly, and Lysander tossed his head back, a keening sound catching in his throat. His nerves were on fire. He couldn't stop himself thrusting against Danny's mouth.

Danny lifted his head back. "Wait," he said hoarsely, then wrapped his hand around Lysander's cock.

No, Lysander wanted to protest, the mouth was good. But Danny, God, he knew what he was doing. Hot and tight and firm and squeezing enough to make Lysander curse out loud. Tight strokes, smooth rhythm, top stroke to bottom, release, other hand, and a lick between, a flick of heat and, Christ, tightening his grip again and then relaxing and tight again.

"Fuck..." Lysander gasped out, his hips jerking against Danny's hands. His head fell forward. Too much coming too fast. The first stroking pressure right there and wet and Danny's mouth and teeth and Christ! Hand again, again, again. He clutched at Danny's shoulder, other fingers in Danny's hair, and shuddered as the pleasure hit him like a wave.

Danny's hands were at his hips again, holding him steady. "Fuck me," Danny breathed, staring up at him.

Lysander drew an unsteady breath and laughed. "Not right now."

Danny snorted and wrapped his arms around Lysander's waist, pulling him down to sit on Danny's thigh. "You know what I mean," he said, stroking one hand up Lysander's side, and it really didn't help when Lysander's skin was still thrumming. "You look fucking gorgeous when you come."

"Red-faced and sweaty?" Lysander said with a self-conscious smile as he reached down and slipped his cock back inside his shorts.

Danny leaned up to kiss him. "Uninhibited." He nuzzled the tip of Lysander's nose. "Like you don't have a care in the world." His smile turned into that familiar playful grin. "Doesn't hurt when I know I made it happen."

Lysander prodded him in the middle of his chest. "Your horn is definitely worthy of the toot."

Danny's lips twitched. "Is that what we're calling it now?"

Lysander burst out laughing and drew Danny closer to kiss him again. "If you ever call it that, I think I may have to disown you," he warned, smiling, then covered his mouth to stifle a yawn.

"Oh, I see how it is." Danny feigned indignation. "You get off, and now you want to roll over and sleep?"

Lysander twisted his fingers into Danny's hair again and tilted his head back. Danny met his gaze with a glint in his eyes. "I believe you mentioned cuddling?" He inclined his head towards the bed, half-hidden beyond the bookcases. "I hear its siren song."

Danny beamed at him. "If I didn't think you'd ding me around the lughole, I'd carry you through."

Lysander couldn't keep himself from laughing. "I think I can walk." He pressed his hand to Danny's shoulder and pushed to his feet.

"I don't know," Danny said, gazing up at him. "How about fireman's lift with your arse in the air? Always a sexy look."

Lysander laughed and held out his hand. "You coming?"

"Again?"

"Danny..." Lysander groaned.

Danny grinned and grabbed Lysander's hand. Lysander hauled him to his feet, taking the chance to steal another kiss. He was tired, true, but he felt more relaxed than he had in a long time. Tomorrow, it would all come crashing back in on him, but right now, he had a sweet, good-looking man beside him and a welcoming bed waiting for them. What else could he really want?

Chapter Twenty-Seven

AN ELBOW IN the ribs was one way to wake up.

Danny grunted and squinted around the darkened room. A clock glowed on the bedside table. Five twenty. The curtains didn't keep out all the light, so he could make out the shape of Lysander sitting up close beside him. In the silence, Lysander's breathing seemed much louder.

"You all right?"

Lysander started. Probably hadn't noticed he'd whacked Danny in the ribs. "Yeah. Yeah, sorry." He exhaled. "Just a dream."

Danny groped out and found his arm, tugging. "Get back here."

Lysander lay down beside him, his chest pressing to Danny's side, his heart thundering. Whatever he'd been dreaming, it had left him shaken. Danny stroked his hand down Lysander's back, wondering how he could help.

"Work or life?" he finally asked.

"Hm?"

"The dream."

Lysander sighed warmly against Danny's chest. "A bit of both." He traced his fingers in a figure eight on Danny's skin. "You should go back to sleep."

"You going to?" From Lysander's silence, he guessed no. Well, going back to sleep would be rude. "Nah. I'm awake now." Danny covered Lysander's hand on his chest and gave it a squeeze. "I'll take more of the cuddling, though. I like a good cuddle."

Lysander laughed quietly, a soft, warm puff of air. "I noticed." He lay quietly for a while, still tracing patterns into Danny's skin. A few times, it sounded like he was taking a breath to say something and then stopped. Fifteen minutes went by before he finally said, "You're coming back into the TRI today."

Danny peered at him in the darkness. "Eh?"

Lysander sounded tired. "You've seen the news, I'm guessing."

"Oh, aye. Rogue time traveller or something."

Lysander hesitated before confiding, "It's true."

Danny winced. "Aye?"

"Mm." Another sigh. "It's—complicated right now. I can't tell you anything else yet, but Jacob and I both suspect the corrupted coding is linked to it."

"So I solve the coding, and you find your guilty party?"

"If it's not tied to this situation, at least we'll be able to mark off a suspect." Lysander rubbed his cheek against Danny's shoulder and curled one leg over Danny's. "I planned to tell you last night, but I—it's all been crazy at work. I needed a break."

Danny grimaced. "No wonder." He ran his hand down Lysander's back again. "A real random time traveller, eh?"

"Mm."

Danny considered his options. He could press for information, but he'd be at the TRI soon, and he could go full interrogation mode there. Now, they could both to take a breather before everything went mad again. "I used to want to do it, y'know."

"Hm?"

"Time travel." Danny knocked his chin gently against Lysander's crown. "Meet da Vinci and get him to do me a drawing. See if Cleopatra was as smart as she sounds. Go to the Colosseum in its heyday. Listen to Mozart." He grinned at the ceiling. "Can you imagine the people you could meet?"

Lysander shifted against him. "As much as I'd like to go back, I wouldn't be allowed to."

Danny frowned. "How come?"

He could feel Lysander's small smile against his chest. "Well, let's just say some parts of me aren't exactly historically accurate."

Danny snickered. "All right. Apart from your...nose." He gave Lysander a squeeze. "If you *could* go, where would be your first choice?"

Lysander hummed for a moment. "Persepolis. I'd love to see the city in all its glory. You?"

"It changes every five minutes," Danny admitted. "I mean, I know I'd probably be limited to places where I could blend in, but if I could go anywhere, I'd love to see how they built the pyramids."

Lysander's shoulders shook as he stifled a laugh. "Really? The pyramids? They already know how they were built."

Danny huffed and gave Lysander's braid a playful tug. "I like mathematical engineering. Those things are fucking amazing! Do you even know how much science they must have worked out to get them all so accurately placed in relation to the constellations?"

Lysander was laughing openly now. "I keep forgetting that's always your first love—numbers and codes and science."

Danny shrugged. "It makes sense to me." He pressed his arm against Lysander's back and smiled when Lysander shifted to sprawl halfway over him. "You, I'm still figuring out."

Lysander folded his arms on Danny's chest, propping his chin on them, and one of his legs settled snugly between Danny's. "I like to keep you guessing."

"Aye, I noticed." Danny spread both hands on Lysander's back, stroking them lazily up and down. "First, it's the boss of the TRI, then it's the Persian, then the dancing, then the biker getting into fistfights with truckers. I'm trying to guess if you're going to come out as the Pope next."

Lysander's laughter vibrated through his chest. "You'll have to wait and see." He reached down between their bodies to adjust himself, then shifted and pressed his hand into the pillow beside Danny's head. Somehow, he found Danny's lips with his own in the dark. As his tongue darted against Danny's, he started to rock his hips, dragging his thigh against Danny's cock.

Danny drew a sharp breath, sliding one hand down to squeeze Lysander's arse through his shorts. "Bit early, isn't it?"

Lysander smiled against his lips. "No such thing."

Danny spread his thighs a little wider to give Lysander more room. It would have taken a much stronger man to resist, especially with Lysander's mouth on his and the way he rocked himself sensuously against Danny's thigh.

In the dark, with nothing to distract him from the heat of Lysander's body and lips and his breathing, Danny was hard in no time. He caught Lysander's arse with both hands, encouraging, demanding, as he tore his lips away from Lysander's and scattered heated kisses along one cheek and down to his throat.

Lysander's breaths gusted against his ear, his free hand sinking into Danny's hair again, sliding under his head to guide him, guide his mouth, and when Danny nipped sharply at the base of his throat, he felt more than heard Lysander gasp.

Turnabout, he thought giddily and sucked sharply on Lysander's skin. Lysander twisted his fingers tight in Danny's hair, and his hips stuttered against Danny. Danny could only squeeze his arse in response, pulling Lysander flush against his own body, grinding his cock against Lysander's thigh.

Neither of them spoke. God, it was erotic and fucking intense. Breathing in sync, holding on to each other, moving together. Harder. Faster. Breathing rapid. Sweat on their skin. Sweat on Danny's tongue. Mouths meeting again. Lysander rocked harder, shuddering. Close, Danny thought. Same as the first time. Harder. Sharper. He found Lysander's ear, whispered, "Come for me."

The sound Lysander made, his body going taut and tense and shivering…

Danny caught his thigh, pulled it harder against his cock, jerking his hips. A slim hand suddenly there too, catching him, squeezing, and Lysander's breath in his ear, a low, hungry growl, "Your turn."

Danny bucked up against him, his breath escaping in an explosive gasp as he came in Lysander's hand.

Lysander sprawled down over him again. "Mm." He stroked Danny's cock lazily. "Morning."

Danny laughed, only a little breathlessly. "You dirty bugger." He patted Lysander's arse gently. "I think I might have left fingerprints."

Lysander nuzzled at his throat and chuckled. "Well, it's not as if anyone's going to see them." He pressed a kiss under Danny's jaw. "Thank you."

"For what?"

Lysander paused, and when he spoke, Danny could see why. "For coming."

Danny burst out laughing and skelped his arse. "Right first time. Dirty, dirty bugger."

Lysander shook with silent laughter too. "I didn't mean it that way, then I realised how it was going to sound."

"Aye, right." Danny smiled as Lysander slid down to rest by his side. "And you've left me a right mess, you know. My shirt and now me."

Lysander traced his cum-slick fingers from Danny's belly all the way up his chest, up his throat, and brushed them across Danny's lips. "You talk a lot of bullshit," he murmured, though his words hitched when Danny sucked on his fingers one by one, licking them clean.

Danny never had the chance to find out where the finger-licking goodness might go because somewhere in the dark, something started beeping. Lysander groaned and rolled away from him, calling out for light. The lights all came on at once, fading to a bearable brightness.

"You'd think," Lysander said from the side of the bed as he turned off the alarm, "they'd come up with an alarm with a verbal command."

Danny snickered, sitting up in the middle of the bed and stretching. "They did, then too many people told it to piss off and were late, so they brushed it under the carpet and pretended it never happened." He pulled his knees up and propped his arms on them. "Work soon, then?"

"Mm." Lysander walked across the room, then paused to peel off his shorts and drop them in a laundry hamper by the bookshelves, giving Danny a lovely view of his firm little bum. "I'll grab the shower first. You can get some more sleep if you want. Or some breakfast."

Danny flopped dramatically on the bed, arms outstretched, and gazed up at the ceiling. "I'll be here then." He sighed mournfully. "Naked and neglected."

"Your argument doesn't really stand when you're already covered in cum," Lysander said, and Danny heard the smile in his voice.

Danny blew a raspberry and then rolled to the side of the bed. He got up and stretched again until his hips and shoulders popped.

All things considered, it seemed a bit pointless putting any clothes on until he'd showered. He gave himself a quick wipe down with tissues from a box by the bed and wandered through to the kitchen. By the time Lysander emerged from the bathroom in a bathrobe, combing his half-dried hair, Danny had two pans sizzling on the hob.

"I guess I should have expected this," Lysander said ruefully. "After all, you haven't fed me for days."

Danny waved a spatula. "I was hungry anyway. Fancy some?"

Lysander smiled. "I could eat. Let me dress and I'll join you." He paused on the way across the room. "Danny."

"Aye?"

"Try not to sizzle your sausage, okay?"

Danny snorted. "Thanks for your concern."

When Lysander joined him at the breakfast bar five minutes later, he looked like his usual self in beautifully tailored trousers and a blood-red shirt with his hair pinned up in a knot at the back of his head. In the name of good manners, Danny spread his stained shirt on the stool before sitting down but still had to snicker at the contrast.

"I feel like a lowly lackey," he said as he poured his coffee.

"A lowly naked lackey," Lysander agreed with a laugh. "You could have put your pants back on."

"Could have." Danny grinned at him. "Breakfast and a show instead."

While they ate, Lysander laid out the plans for the day. Danny would return to his hotel by pod and get some unstained—*your fault, you dirty bugger*—clothes. He would be picked up from there an hour later and returned to the TRI, where he'd be brought up to date. The amount of information he would receive depended on any new developments in the past eighteen hours.

"Will there be any?"

Lysander piled some scrambled egg onto a wedge of toast. "God knows." He glanced at Danny. "You're going to have to play ignorant until you're given the information."

"You weren't meant to tell me anything?"

Lysander studied his plate. "I also wasn't meant to fuck you, but here we are."

Danny put his fork down and gave Lysander's thigh a warm squeeze. "Top secret," he said with a playful wink. "For your eyes only."

Lysander met his gaze, then let his eyes drop downwards. "I'd hope so."

Danny laughed and poured him another coffee.

Chapter Twenty-Eight

THINGS HADN'T IMPROVED during Lysander's eighteen-hour absence.

The security team hadn't been able to pinpoint any corresponding power surges, either locally or globally, which undercut Jacob's theory: if Enoch's second gate had opened simultaneously with his collapse, then surely, there would have been a matching power surge.

So far, they had found no sign of one, but as Jacob pointed out, just because they couldn't find it didn't mean it hadn't happened. After all, they used dampeners in-house, but they didn't know whether they expelled bursts of power when the gates opened at the other end.

Enoch remained on bed rest. According to the medical team, he had suffered a cardiac event, but they couldn't isolate a cause, which had convinced Jacob his theory was right. Enoch had a little more colour in his face, but otherwise didn't look much better than he had when Lysander left.

Ben had stayed with Enoch, going as far as having a camp bed set up in his room in case their unfortunate visitor collapsed again. Lysander thought it unnecessary, but when the medical team was present, Enoch had clung onto Ben's arm. If it reassured him and prevented another heart attack, they would allow it. Ben had agreed at once. Seeing the man practically drop dead in front of him must have been a shock.

"So what you're telling me is we're no further forward?"

"No further back, either," Jacob said. He was sitting on the opposite side of Lysander's desk, tired but alert. Once, he must have been used to that life.

He knew how to deal with it, Lysander thought, while the rest of us pushed too far and didn't know when to stop.

"Enoch may be able to provide some answers today."

"We can hope." Lysander tapped his fingertip on the desk. "Danny will be on his way in soon."

Jacob sat up a little straighter. "How much do you think he needs to know?"

How much indeed? Lysander rubbed his jaw. It would have been so much easier to explain everything, but the TRI could never be fully transparent. Still, there were certain things Danny knew already and would need to be told, on the record. "He already knows about the corruption in the code, and with all the news coverage, he probably suspects the time traveller element."

"So, we tell him we need to see if there's a tangible link."

Lysander nodded, inordinately grateful he and Jacob were singing from the same song sheet. "Sounds good. Did I miss any updates from the Met yesterday?"

"They're still working on finding the leak. Whoever did it wasn't after money; they posted in anonymous letters to several media outlets."

"Letters?" Lysander raised his eyebrows. "A little old-fashioned, isn't it?"

"Harder to trace than digital," Jacob pointed out. "Until it reaches the sorting offices, there's no mark put on it, and with fewer sorting offices, it could have crossed several counties before anyone got anywhere near it."

Lysander restrained himself from pressing his fingertips to his forehead. Back for less than an hour and he could feel the promise of a headache building. "When did it arrive?"

"In the Friday mail delivery."

Enoch had been found on Wednesday night, which meant it had to have been dispatched on Thursday. At least it cleared all TRI staff of any suspicion, with lockdown as a convenient alibi. Even if the internal staff had been in contact with their families, they didn't know the details about the lockdown, and certainly none of the details in the letter.

"What are the chances of them tracing the sender?"

"Unlikely," Jacob said. "They were damned careful. All typed, no signature, no DNA trace or any prints anywhere on the envelope except from mail and press in-house staff."

"Great." Lysander rubbed at his eyes. "We'll see where the cold trail leads, then. What about the agents in prep? I can't imagine they're enjoying the delay."

Jacob grimaced. "Well, they understand the necessity and kind of expect the backlog. We've scheduled an extra jump per day for the next few days to clear it. It'll mean some tight deadlines, and we may have a busier quarantine block than usual for a couple of days, but it'll get us back on track."

Lysander glanced at the screen showing one particular room in the quarantine block. Enoch was a tiny lump in the broad bed, flanked on all sides by machines monitoring his vitals. Meanwhile, on the far side of the room, Ben had a dozen projections flung up around him at his worktable.

"We need to tell him why Danny is really here," Lysander said.

Jacob winced. "I don't think he's going to be happy to know we kept something this significant from him."

That, Lysander felt, was an understatement.

"I'll talk to him privately," he said. "He might take it better."

Sometimes, he could be very wrong.

"Are you fucking kidding me?"

"Ben..."

Ben stalked back and forth across the room. "You keep on telling me you trust me and then, oh wait, here's something else we didn't trust you to know, even though we trust you *so* much!" He stumbled, and Lysander started to rise, but Ben shot a blazing glare at him. "Oh, don't try and help me now, not when you've been lying to me and keeping me in the dark for months! Years, even!"

Lysander sank in his seat. Ben rarely lost his temper, which showed how stressed and exhausted he really was. Better to let him vent and let it all out, then they could maybe have a conversation about the details.

"And Jacob knew all this, didn't he?" Lysander didn't reply at once. Ben threw up his hands and stormed across to the window. He smacked one fist against the glass and pressed his brow to the pane, staring outside. "Jesus. When I came back, I thought things had changed around here, but it's still the same—all manipulating and covering shit up." He pressed his brow hard against the glass. "I do one thing wrong to save my friend and this is the thanks I get?"

"Ben—" Lysander murmured, raising his hand.

"Don't!" Ben whirled on him, eyes blazing. "Don't you *try* to tell me this isn't personal. The coding is *mine*. If we have a problem with it, I'm the one who fixes it, not some random guy you bring in from the outside!"

"This isn't a matter of fixing—"

"Fine! Finding the problem and sorting it out!" Ben braced his hands on the back of the chair, his face white as bone. "I get not telling me about things tied to my dad and what happened to him, but this isn't about him! This is my department! These are the problems I can deal with! You just needed to tell me and adjust my security access, and it would have been dealt with!"

Lysander sat quietly, letting him rage until he finally sagged into the chair. He had to be using up what energy reserves he had left, watching the TRI getting dragged through the dirt, sitting in with Enoch for days, seeing so many secrets unravelling in front of him.

"I needed discretion," Lysander said as gently as he could. "I wanted to tell you, but you..." He offered Ben a brief, tired smile. "Well, you're known for voicing your concerns loudly. I didn't want to risk scaring off the perpetrator."

Ben pushed his fingers through his hair. "Right." His eyes were bloodshot and underscored with shadow. "You were happy enough to use me before."

"But not this time."

Ben glared silently at a point beyond Lysander, and then he turned his head. "When I saw him in his study room, working on coding I didn't give to him—you had him on this problem of yours?"

"You can understand why I needed discretion," Lysander said. "If someone within the TRI is working against us, for whatever reason, I figured it best to keep it to myself until I knew if we had something to worry about."

"Yourself and Danny." Ben made a sound of disgust. "I thought he was too good to be true. Nice to see I wasn't wrong about him being here under false pretences." He considered Lysander. "Are you telling me this because I'm going to be working with him now? Officially?"

Lysander shook his head. "Danny can handle it. I need you to pinpoint a possible source for Enoch."

For a moment, Ben looked like he wanted to argue. "Okay." He sounded reluctant. "I know he's good, so if you think he can handle it, I'll trust you."

Lysander hoped his relief wasn't too visible. Ben *did* know the coding, but if anyone in the TRI could correctly identify and locate a potential external gate, he was the one to do it. With the progress Danny had already made in the decoding, it would take too long for Ben to catch up. Better to assign them tasks where they could be of the most use.

"He's already made significant breakthroughs," he said. "He's found the date the corrupt code was first added to the system and is trying to unravel it all to find the perpetrator."

Ben seemed startled. "He must be good."

Lysander inclined his head. "I think the word you're looking for is 'stubborn.' He's seen a challenge, and he's determined to solve it."

"Fair enough." Ben braced his hands on his knees, a frown furrowing his brow. "Is it all right if I work from the med bay? Enoch's still unsettled by everything, so if I can be around to keep him company..."

"Whatever makes things easier for him," Lysander agreed at once. "It's not his fault he got caught up in this mess. I'll come by and speak to him later, since you'll be occupied. You're sure you'll be able to work in there?"

Ben smiled wryly. "He's asleep half the time. It's like babysitting a really good baby." He got up. "I'll head over now." He added with a tinge of bitterness, "Unless there's anything else you're not telling me."

Lysander gave him a look. "If there is, it's my job."

Ben made an abortive gesture of dismissal, then turned and walked out the room. Lysander sank in his chair, running both hands over his face.

The conversation with Ben turned out to be the most difficult part of the morning. Danny made things so much simpler. He came in, played convincingly ignorant and shocked about the revelations, and immediately agreed to work as effectively as he could to finish the job at hand.

When he tilted his head to listen to Jacob, it made his collar shift, baring the ruddy bruise Lysander had left on his neck. It had almost been enough to crack Lysander's stern expression. Danny knew it as well.

As Jacob led him out of the room, he glanced back and shot a wink at Lysander.

It came as no surprise at all when a lunchbox was delivered to Lysander's office an hour later.

"Some things haven't changed, then?" Fana said, as she set it on his desk.

Lysander managed a drawn smile. "We have to take the little consistencies where we can."

By mid-afternoon, there were no new developments, apart from the medical team chiming to confirm Enoch could manage a visitor.

Lysander wasn't surprised when the head of the medical team jumped to attention when he emerged from the pod at the medical bay. With Ben preoccupied with finding the source of the gate and Jacob too intimidating, Lysander took on the mantle. The fewer people who knew the details and crossed paths with their young visitor, the better.

"For security purposes," he murmured as he passed the man, "I need your staff out of the room."

"Sir," Doctor Calvin acknowledged. He hesitated. "I thought Jacob and Ben were dealing with him directly."

Lysander gazed at him. "Indeed. Your staff?"

Calvin hastily ordered his team out of Enoch's room, though Ben remained, working at the table at the far end of the room but close enough for Enoch to see him in case he needed reassurance.

Ben glanced up from his screens. "Already?"

"The sooner the better," Lysander replied. "Don't let us distract you." He approached the bed, where Enoch sat up among the pillows. He still seemed weak, but no longer as terrified as he had. Up close, he seemed smaller, wiry and slight. His stubbled brows drew down over his deep-set eyes, and his lips were cracked and dry. "Good afternoon, Mr. Baker."

Enoch stared up at him, clutching the edge of his covers. "S-sir."

Ben called over, "You need not fear him, Enoch. He's a kind man."

He chose to adjust his speech pattern to speak to their guest, Lysander noticed as he drew up one of the chairs by the bed and sat with a smile.

"My name is Lysander," he said as gently as he could. "This is my building."

If anything, it made Enoch's eyes grow wider. His voice was faint when he asked, "You're master of this house?"

Lysander smiled. "You could say so, yes. I hope you don't find it too uncomfortable."

Enoch's knuckles were white on the edge of the quilt. "It's very grand, sir. Very clean."

Lysander hesitated and then patted one of his hands comfortingly. "You are welcome here as long as is necessary. We will try to get you home as soon as we can, but until then, you are welcome."

Enoch's hand trembled under Lysander's. "Thank you, sir."

Lysander opened up his Leaf. "Now, if you can, I would like you to help me. We need to arrange transport to get you home." He opened out the list of questions put together by the historians. "Is that all right?"

Enoch nodded, licking his dry lips.

The questions were all straightforward, but Lysander remembered how anxious the young man had become when Jacob had pressed him for answers. "You said you come from Fairhurst. Is it a big town?"

"Small," Enoch replied. "A few houses on the high street."

Well, that explained why it hadn't appeared on any maps. He made a note. Next question would give them the option of searching parish records. "Did you have a local church?"

"The chapel over by. It were St. Marys afore."

It didn't help much for a location, but it was something. "Now, this might sound strange, but can you tell me what month and year you were in?"

"It were coming up on t'harvest." He eyed Lysander, puzzled. "I never pay mind to the year." He shrugged uncertainly. "They all pass, by and by."

Lysander sighed in frustration. "They do," he agreed. "What about the king or queen? Do you know who ruled the country?"

The young man glanced in Ben's direction, a disbelieving look on his face. No wonder. It must have seemed like a strange kind of question. Ben must have gestured for him to reply. "King George, my mam said."

Lysander wished he could swear aloud. "Do you know which one?"

Panic crossed his face. "There's more'n one?"

Lysander held up a hand soothingly. "Not at the same time, but if we know which of the kings were there, we will be able to find which year you were in."

"Mam only said King George." Enoch tugged spasmodically at the covers. "I would I could tell you more."

Lysander reached out to pat his hand again. It seemed to calm him. "It's all right. You can only tell us what you know. We can't ask for more." He squeezed Enoch's thin hand. "It all helps."

The rest of the questions were equally useless and only confirmed that the young man was an uneducated farm labourer who had barely strayed beyond the boundaries of his own village. He was illiterate, though clearly bright and quick to offer answers where he thought they might help.

Unfortunately, most of them were about the harvest days and feast days long since lost to the records. Geographically, he could only be sure about the nearest 'big town,' Wigan, and the local river, the Douglas, where he saw all the boats going by.

Lysander checked the information against old records, drawing up composites of a historic and a modern map. There was indeed a River Douglas winding its way through Lancashire, including Wigan, and it used to be one of the transport links for traders. He opened a page about the history of the river, then smiled.

"Did you ever see the canal?"

Enoch frowned in confusion. "The canal?"

"Like a river, with locks and gates to move the boats up and down?"

"On the Douglas?" Enoch smiled eagerly. "It were all made with gates and bridges."

"No," Lysander said, feeling a rush of hope. "They built the canal close to the river. It's like a straighter and more direct river. Did you ever see it?"

Enoch stared at him as if he had grown a second head. "Men building a river?" His expression suggested Lysander was crazy.

Lysander sagged with relief in the chair. It wasn't as specific as he'd hoped, but it had narrowed their search field based on the area where the Douglas had been canalised. It also gave them a timescale between the canalisation and the cutting of the Leeds and Liverpool Canal.

Even if Enoch came from an isolated rural area, he would have noticed the decline in the number of boats on the Douglas. If he lived on a certain part of the Douglas, he couldn't have missed it as the new canal ran alongside the river.

Of course, Enoch had no idea, but right now, it was the best lead they had to narrow down the search—to help them find the church and hopefully the church records with the registers of births and christenings to tighten their timeline.

Lysander shut the Leaf down. "Thank you, Enoch. You've been very helpful." He rose. "You should rest now."

Enoch sank gratefully back against the pillows.

Ben glanced up as Lysander headed towards the door. "Anything useful?"

Lysander glanced over his shoulder at the bed. Enoch's eyes were already closed, and he looked like he'd already fallen asleep. "He's from Fairhurst in the area formerly called Leylandshire, probably within walking distance of the River Douglas and a few days journey from Wigan. Date-wise, definitely somewhere between the 1740s and the 1770s."

Ben gaped at Lysander when he turned to face him. "How the hell did you figure all that out?"

Lysander patted him on the shoulder. "Because, sometimes, you're not the only genius in the room."

Chapter Twenty-Nine

DANNY WAS PRETTY sure his eyes had gone beyond crossed and had swivelled around backwards.

When he returned to the TRI, he'd come armed with his colourful notebooks. The minute he got back to his workroom, he started building the model he'd sketched out on paper.

Thank Christ for good digital software which let him juggle projections, pushing and pulling blocks of text, moving lines here and code there, and building it up around him until the room glowed on all sides. There were layers of colours, and they wove together like a…huge colourful three-dimensional projection thingy.

He finished the latest page of the third book, then smushed the heels of his hands against his eyes. It didn't help much, not when it felt like he had a mesh of rainbow imprinted on his retinas, but it let his eyes rest for a few seconds and gave him a breather to think.

The tension across the whole compound had hit him like a brick wall. They had new security measures in place and had adjusted the settings for his workroom, limiting access to the people who knew everything— from the sounds of it—which meant only Lysander, Jacob, and Ben.

He'd seen a few other staff about, between his arrival and getting from Lysander's office to his workroom, but the chatty and relatively informal atmosphere he'd grown used to had vanished.

While Lysander and Jacob had filled him in, it was nothing more than Lysander had already told him: rogue time traveller, code possibly linked, answers please. He wondered if the TRI staff knew any more than he did. Probably. If so, it would explain why they were being quieter than usual around him.

He dropped his hands from his eyes and sat on the floor in the middle of the glowing web of code. The next page of the book awaited him.

He managed to get through another four pages before a chime notified him that the door was about to open. A shaft of light split the room down the middle, brilliantly bright, even with the code rainbow glowing all around.

"Jesus!"

Danny squinted at the silhouette framed in the door. It sounded like Ben. "Danny, actually." He got up off the floor as Ben came into the room and closed the door behind him.

"Funny man." Ben snorted, shaking his head. He walked into the middle of the code, turning on the spot. "Jesus…" he said again, more softly, "This is what you've been doing all this time?"

Danny winced as his shoulders twinged. "Aye. A bit." He self-consciously rubbed the back of his neck. "Sorry about not telling you, but Lysander asked me to keep it to myself."

"Yeah, I heard." Ben was still staring around at the code. "If I'd known you were this good, I'd've made the training harder." He turned around to face Danny. "They told me to let you get on with it, but I had to come and see how you were doing."

"It's—" Danny shook his head. "See, half of me is loving every second because this coding is so bloody beautiful. The other half wants to beat my head off a brick wall because every time I think I've got it, I find something else to pick apart."

One side of Ben's mouth curled up. "Sounds about right for coding." He waved around the room. "I've never seen it done on this scale before, though."

"Me either," Danny admitted, "but it's only because I've never really been able to get my hands on this level of projection software without restrictions or a time limit." He reached out to the contrast control and lowered the brightness a little. "I mean, technically, I'm improvising some of the techniques, but, so far, it all seems to be working."

"It definitely looks that way," Ben agreed. "Fancy giving me the tour of what you've found?"

Danny shrugged. "You'll probably see right through it all anyway," he said, crouching down to retrieve his notebooks from the floor.

Ben looked at them, amused. "How retro."

Danny made a face as Ben took one of the books and started leafing through it. "It's not like I had access in a hotel in the city." He noticed Ben was staring at him. "What?"

"You did this in the hotel?" He tapped the book. "Without access to any of the code?"

"Aye." Danny fanned out the other five notepads. "I'd nearly run out of space as well."

Ben seemed dazed as he studied the book, turning page after page. "Ly knew what he was doing," he murmured. "Christ, at this rate..." He glanced at Danny. "Do you think you can solve it? The source of the problem?"

"Give me a few more days, and I think I might." He cocked his head. "You were saying something? At this rate...?"

Ben blinked. "Oh. Yes." His mouth twitched halfway to a smile. "Sorry. Yes. If you can code like this, there may end up being a job here for you."

Danny thought he might be staring. He knew he should say something or blink or at least not gape like a bloody goldfish. "Aye?" he managed hoarsely.

Ben offered him the book back. "I'd say so."

Danny hugged the books to his chest, trying to find some words instead of just screaming like an overexcited moron. It must have shown all over his face, because Ben smiled and knocked him on the shoulder.

"We need good coders," he said. "From what I'm seeing here, you're definitely high up there."

"Cheers."

Well, it was a word, even with only a syllable.

"You okay?" Ben grinned. "You look a bit stunned."

"I could kiss you right now," Danny said honestly.

Ben held up both hands. "You can admire the merchandise, but no touching."

Danny snickered. "Aye, you have that non-existent love interest. Don't want to make anyone jealous, do we?"

Ben rolled his eyes, but a bit too dramatically. "I only said it to shut Mel up. It's impossible to have any secrets in this place."

Danny thought of the way Lysander's hair felt between his fingers and the sensation of breath on his lips. "Aye..." Damn it, he needed to remember to focus. Not on hair or cock or breath or anything else. It was Lysander or work. Not both at the same time. Or, he did have one thing he really wanted to ask. "So...about this time traveller..."

Ben looked startled. "What does that have to do with anything?"

"Nothing," Danny said. "But you've seen him, haven't you?"

"Oh! Yes." Ben said with a laugh. "Sorry. It's been a long week."

"Lysander said the same," Danny said. "Too much to do and not much sleep and what have you."

"I don't know what I can tell you," Ben said apologetically. "It's all restricted at the moment. Young. English. Short. In shock at the moment." He shrugged. "We're still working on stuff and can't really say more."

"Guessed as much, but no harm in asking, eh?"

"Pretty much." Ben glanced around the room again, the projections glowing on all sides. "I should let you get back to this." He smiled at Danny. "I'll see about putting in a word for you with Ly, see if we can't get something sorted for you."

He was grinning like a Cheshire cat, his cheeks aching. "You don't have to."

Ben headed towards the door. "Still going to," he said over his shoulder. "I need someone around here who can keep up with me."

As soon as the door shut behind Ben, Danny pressed his forehead to the cover of his book and did a wee jig on the spot. A job at the TRI! Ben! One of the top people in the TRI saying he'd get a job for Danny! Working with time travel! Jesus! Aye, it would mean moving north again, but time travel! His parents would be thrilled to bits as well. There would be visits and everything.

He lowered the book and stared around.

All right, so he'd impressed Ben with what he'd gotten down so far.

If he wanted to definitely get a job here, he'd have to prove he could do more, better and faster than they expected. The coding in the notebook had to be done first, and then, once the model was in place, he could really dig in.

The next time he turned his attention away from the code—from the sixth book, at bloody last—was when the door chimed. It didn't open, which meant someone without authorisation would be waiting outside. He closed down the model and flipped the notebook shut, then went over and opened the door.

Leon groaned in dismay. "Bugger."

Danny squinted at him. "Eh?"

"O'Donohue called down to coding to get one of us to check you weren't being a workaholic," Leon said. "I bet Mel a twenty you'd've gone for the night."

"Night?" Danny glanced at his watch. It was coming up on nine. "Oh. Shit."

Leon grinned at him. "It's easy to lose track of time, like." He jerked his head towards the lift. "O'Donohue'll want you to take a break."

Danny glanced over his shoulder. The last book needed to be finished, but he had to admit his eyes were dry and aching, and he had the beginning of a king-size thumping headache.

"Aye," he agreed, stepping out of the room and closing the door. "I think he'd throttle me if I worked myself into an early grave."

Leon wandered along beside him. "So it's true you're a spy, then?"

Danny looked at him in surprise. "You what?"

Leon's dark eyes were dancing. "The 'I'm here for training' bollocks. Got you in for some special job, they said. So, spy?"

Danny snorted. "If I say no, will you believe me?"

"It's not as fun," Leon replied, skimming his palm over the lift sensor. The doors opened at once. The building had to be quiet for it to be waiting. "Private contractor doesn't sound as good. Cyber spy sounds all mysterious and exciting."

Danny laughed. "Maybe I should get a sexy outfit. Sexy glasses too."

Leon sniggered as the lift descended. "Mel'd be made up, if you're as buff as Sabine says."

Danny groaned, clapping a hand over his eyes. "She told everyone?"

"Only one or two people," Leon said cheerfully. "But you know how we enjoy the chat around here."

"I remember." The lift came to a stop, and the doors opened. "You heading to H-block?"

Leon made a face. "Nah. Getting off home. I'm on the late again tomorrow, and I like my own bed better." He looked Danny up and down. "Want me to see if I can find a tight shirt and some braces so you can make Mel's head explode?"

Danny feigned indignation. "I'm not some piece of meat."

Leon's grin widened. "Shouldn't have answered your door in a towel then, should you?" He clapped Danny on the back. "Go and get some kip."

It sounded magic.

Danny could feel himself reeling as he wandered towards H-block. Food first, though. He hadn't had a chance to restock his fridge in the flat, what with the covert missions and secret code, so he stopped in at the canteen and grabbed enough to tide him over until morning. He considered sending an invite to Lysander, but given how tense things were, it probably wasn't a good idea, so he shelved it.

And then, once fed and watered, he fell face-first onto the bed with no intention of moving until morning.

Chapter Thirty

"AND WE HAD a primary on the afternoon jump. Both agents returned safely and clear in all screenings."

With all the unusual occurrences, Lysander was grateful for the chance to take a brief respite in the standard operation updates from Sabine.

On a normal day, he would have read all of the daily summaries himself, but there was no time, not when he felt like he was dancing on a bed of nails, trying not to cut himself. Sabine, thankfully, had stepped into the breach, covering all his standard tasks, and providing a condensed report to keep him in the loop.

"No problems on any of the jumps?"

She shook her head. "We've never had this many consecutive primaries in a week, let alone a month."

It was uncommon. With history being unpredictable, all agents were given three potential pickup sites over three twenty-four-hour periods. If an agent missed the primary rendezvous, then they still had two more chances to get home.

Lysander winced. "Please don't jinx us. We have enough going on already."

"Are you sure there isn't anything else I can do?" Sabine asked.

He shook his head and immediately regretted it, pressing cool fingers to his temples. "I don't know if there's anything else *I* can do right now. I feel like I'm juggling every department and doing nothing at the same time."

Sabine closed down her screens. "Delegate. I could take on supervision of Ferguson and the coding issue, so you can focus on Baker."

He'd been skirting the decision for days, not out of possessiveness. But...

But they didn't have much time, especially when Danny had almost finished his job. It was selfishness, pure and simple. As soon as Danny resolved the coding issue, he would return to London, and they would probably never see each other again. It was stupid and sentimental and taking up his already limited time.

"Yes," he said. "It would take some of the pressure off."

Sabine smiled. "Is there anything I should know?"

God, he was tired. Again. "Know?"

"About how to handle him?"

Thank Christ for thirty years of honing a polite and inexpressive mask. He leaned back in his chair and gazed at a point on the wall, as if considering his answer and not the way Danny's cock fitted nicely against his palm.

"Generally, he's good at working on his own," he finally replied. "I'd recommend keeping one eye on him because he tends to lose track of time when he gets caught up in a task. If he acts up or is being stubborn, tell him he's still working under my orders, through you. It should keep him on track."

"What about the coding problem? Do we have any idea beyond basic tampering?"

"Far from basic." Lysander opened up a screen showing Danny's workroom only a few hours earlier. Danny was barely visible in the middle of the illuminated lines of colourful code. Sabine stared at it in astonishment. "Don't underestimate him. The man is a genius, even if he doesn't act like it."

"Last time I saw something like that... he works like Ben, doesn't he?"

"Which is why Danny is still on this and Ben is working on the Baker case."

Sabine leaned forward, scaling up the footage and watching Danny. He was walking in meandering circles, a notepad open in his hand. But every so often, he tucked the notepad under his arm, and he'd shuffle pieces of code together like a deck of cards, redistributing them, staring at them, and moving them again.

"How does he do it?" Sabine asked, shaking her head. "He doesn't look like he's concentrating."

"The same way an artist paints a masterpiece," Lysander said with a small smile. He had no right to feel proud of Danny, but he couldn't help himself. Danny *was* brilliant, but he cast up so much bluster and show, very few people actually noticed. "I don't think it's something you can learn. Pure skill, nothing more, nothing less."

"So, in this case, let him get on with it but don't let him forget the necessities?"

"Exactly," Lysander agreed gratefully. "A daily update, if there's anything new or any information he and you agree is relevant. Otherwise, let him continue until there is something to report."

"And if there's a breakthrough, I bring it straight to you?"

"If there's a breakthrough, it'll either mean the code is nothing or it'll be huge," he agreed, "So I want to know as soon as possible. We need to tighten our scope, and the sooner the better."

"Do you want to be the one to tell him, or will I?"

"I'll see to it for tomorrow." Lysander motioned towards the door. "You should go and get some rest while you can. If you're going to be Danny-wrangling, you'll need all your energy."

"I could say the same for you." She got up. "Are you planning on getting some sleep tonight?"

"I have a few things to check on before I can rest." He smiled. "Between you and Fana, I'm amazed I haven't been tucked up with a warm milk and a lullaby."

She snorted. "It's called concern for your well-being. It's what good employees do."

He laughed. "I'll be fine. Have a good night."

As soon as she left, he turned his attention to the remaining outstanding tasks.

Despite the late hour, there were still a dozen historians in the conference suite, sifting through data. Thankfully, many church records were indexed on digital archives, which made the searching easier.

Lysander chimed into the room, and Dieter Schmidt, one of their oldest and most experienced historians, picked up the call. He'd been with the TRI since its inception, and despite getting an early retirement package a couple of years earlier, he'd volunteered to come in and help. Some links weren't easily broken.

"Evening, Ly."

"Dieter." Lysander said. "How's it going in there?"

Dieter glanced around the room. "Well, we've managed to strike off a couple of years. We've also got people doing general searches on a wider scale for Bakers in the area, in case we can't find him, but we can find family ties."

"I'm waiting for updates from the archives in the area about analogue records they haven't put online yet," Lysander said. "There shouldn't be many, but if there are, we can request copies of the volumes as required."

"And anything that isn't digitised is probably fucked beyond recognition anyway."

Lysander smiled wryly. For all the years he'd known him, Dieter had never been able to keep his tongue in check. "Make sure your team gets enough rest," he advised. "We don't want to miss the information because we're all exhausted."

Dieter closed the call.

Lysander turned his attention to the med bay and Enoch. Only the top of Enoch's dark head could be seen on the white pillows, his body a lump under the blankets. From his vitals, he appeared to be peacefully asleep.

Enoch had been a surprise to Lysander, so alert and quick to answer all the questions. Lysander didn't know what he had expected. More awe and terror, maybe. Enoch seemed to be taking it all in stride. Still, given all of the drugs they'd pumped him with to keep him alive and stable, he'd probably have coped with anything. It wasn't as if they had any scale to measure it against.

For once, Ben wasn't in the room, which relieved Lysander. As much as it might help Enoch, it wouldn't end well if Ben burned himself out by trying to do too much.

Checking in with the security team's late shift took less time. No, there were no updates and, so far, no hint of where the mysterious gate might be. No, they were really sorry they couldn't give him better news.

Next port of call was chiming to Ofori in his briefing room, which served as his contact point for his former colleagues and Falconer's people from the Met. Unsurprisingly, there were no developments there, although they had managed to pinpoint the sorting office—London-based, as expected—and were working back to the post offices and pickup points where the letters could have been collected from.

"It's more than we expected," Jacob admitted. "But given the number of sites we're checking, it may be impossible to pinpoint it."

"It's still worth a try," Lysander murmured, even if it was a needle in a mountain-sized haystack situation.

"I had a hunch you might think so. As soon as we have a list of sites, we'll see about the possibility of getting CCTV footage from them." He reached out of frame for a moment, then leaned back in. "I know we don't know anything set yet about Baker, but I've managed to get hold of Temple."

"Temple?"

"My ex-DC. She's the superintendent now. She's going to have her people look into Harper's visitor logs for us and see if he's made contact with anyone on the outside."

"Our gate builder, for example?"

"The way I see it," Jacob said, "someone has built a gate, and since he's the only one who had his hands on the plans, it would make sense he's behind it."

"Let me know if there's any new information."

As soon as Jacob terminated the link, Lysander exhaled.

If someone in the present had a gate outside the TRI, then Jacob's theory was a logical leap. If Harper had the plans, surely he would have had someone to use them. Something had been bothering Lysander about all of it, though. Something about the energy surge when Enoch arrived and the lack of one when he collapsed. If Jacob was right, it made things simpler, but it didn't make *sense*.

Lysander propped his elbows on the desk and rested his head in his hands, far too tired again. A decent night of rest had helped, but it was nowhere near enough. He just needed to get to H-block, and then he could sleep. It was tempting to go and curl up beside Danny again, but no. Not now, when they both needed all the rest they could get.

The door chimed, and he groaned inwardly before pushing to his feet and heading over.

"Ben?"

Ben raised a hand in greeting. He looked about as tired as Lysander felt. "All right?"

"Not really. You?"

"Getting nowhere," Ben admitted. "You got a minute?"

Lysander stepped back, motioning for him to come in, then retreated to sit behind his desk. "Something up?"

Ben hesitated and then stood behind the chair opposite Lysander, leaning on the back. "I wanted to apologise."

Lysander blinked at him, surprised. "For what?"

Ben shrugged with a tired half-smile. "For being a top-grade arse the last few days. I've been acting like an idiot all because you were doing your job."

Lysander sighed fondly, waving for him to sit. "You don't have to apologise. It's been a tense situation for everyone, and to find out all the things we'd been obliged to keep from you must have been the last straw."

"Doesn't mean I should have started yelling and blaming you. I'm a grown man, not kid." Ben rumpled his hair and smiled wryly at Lysander. "Can I play the tragic childhood card now? It seems like a fitting time for it."

"As long as Jacob and I can also play the exhausted, overworked, and confused cards."

Ben laughed, slouching back on the chair. "Yeah, we're all in a mess, aren't we?" He shook his head. "Only a few months ago, I thought the most exciting thing I'd be working on was the design for the timers. I'd've had it all worked out for Christmas."

"Don't even mention it," Lysander said with a groan. "I haven't thought beyond the end of this month."

"I was looking forward to my lonely dinner-for-one..." Ben twisted his expression into something appropriately wide-eyed and tragic.

"And I know you're talking bullshit." Lysander snorted. "If you'd pull your head out of your ass, you know Mariam would invite you round for dinner with the whole family."

Ben's expression tightened. "Don't start."

Lysander sighed. "Ben, she did everything she could."

For the past few years, Ben's relationship with Mariam Ashraf had been frayed. While she'd been his foster mother after his father's disappearance, she had also shut down the search for Tom Sanders seven years earlier when the trail went cold. It was the right call. Everyone agreed. Everyone except Ben.

Ben stared down at his hands. "Yeah. I just—it's—" He raised his eyes back to Lysander. "I see her and I remember. I—I don't want to be angry with her, but when I see her..." He shrugged. "It's stupid, I know."

"Believe me," Lysander murmured, "I get it."

Ben scratched his fingers through his hair. "Yeah." He cocked his head. "What about you? Heading back to the snow?"

Lysander hesitated before shaking his head. Christmas had always been a tricky holiday in his family. His father's side were traditional with Mass and church, but his mother's side didn't celebrate it beyond demanding a huge meal and the extended family altogether. Sometimes, it felt like adding a flame to gasoline when both his grandmothers were in the same room.

Lysander had hated it for as long as he could remember.

"If this mess doesn't blow over, at least I'll have an excuse," he said.

Ben rocked his head back against the back of the chair. "Yeah." He closed his eyes for a second and exhaled slowly. "It's definitely not how I saw things going this year." He sat up again, straighter, and ran a hand over his face. "Have there been any developments I need to know about?"

"Nothing solid. All the teams are working flat out, but it's probably going to take days at least, if not more."

Ben nodded. "I checked in on Danny. He's tearing through the coding stuff, isn't he?"

Lysander had to smile. "If he could use caffeine as fuel, I don't think he'd sleep."

"Not like we don't have other people who do the same around here," Ben said with a pointed look. He got up off the seat and stretched his arms over his head until his back crackled. "Speaking of, he said you've not been sleeping well. Nice of him to worry, isn't it?"

Lysander felt like he'd been pulled into slow motion. "What?"

Ben blinked at him. "Danny," he repeated. "He said you've not been sleeping well." He considered it and laughed. "Mind you, we could say the same for everyone working on this case."

Lysander felt ill. Danny had always been discreet, but if he'd been telling people about Lysander's sleeping habits, then speculation would lead to revelation, and the last thing either of them needed right now was their reputations being ripped to pieces. "I guess." He unfolded from his chair. "Speaking of which, I think I need to call it a night."

"Same." Ben glanced in the direction of the quarantine block. "I'd better get back."

"You don't need to stay in with him." It felt like speaking by rote now. "The med team are there."

Emotion flared on Ben's face. "I want to," he said. "I was there when—he almost died on my watch. I want to keep him company as long as he needs me there."

Lysander knew he couldn't win against that particular argument. Or if he even cared about it right now. His thoughts were in H-block, and as soon as Ben left, he closed down his systems and made his way out into the night. It was bitterly cold, and he'd left his jacket, but he wanted—needed—to speak to Danny, to find out what the hell he'd been saying to people.

By the time he got to Danny's apartment, his shivers were subsiding, though it took three buzzes before Danny opened the door. He must have been asleep, his face pink and creased down one side and his hair standing in all directions.

"Evening." He smiled sleepily, opening the door wider.

Lysander rubbed his hands together as he walked into the room, the warmth of it making the skin on his face tingle. "What have you been saying to Ben?"

Danny meandered over once he'd closed the door. "About what?"

Lysander stared blankly at him, too tired and drained to really draw on anger. "Did you tell him you'd been sleeping with me?"

Danny blinked as if Lysander had slapped him around the face. "What? No! What did he say?"

"He said you'd been talking about how badly I'd been sleeping."

Danny stared at him, then approached cautiously, as if Lysander might bolt. "You daft bugger," he said, his voice thickened with sleepiness. "It's called a sweeping generalisation. All of you lot have been working your arses off and forgetting the fundamentals."

There was the weird slow motion again. God, he was tired, too tired, and he was screwing up and turning on the wrong people, and Danny was right. He *had* been sleeping badly, and he was exhausted.

"I'm sorry." He rubbed at his head. "Sorry. I hadn't— I didn't listen to what he actually said."

Danny reached out and took his other hand. "It's— Jesus fuck, you're freezing!"

To Lysander's astonishment, Danny pulled Lysander's hand up and pressed it to the middle of his warm bare chest, then grabbed Lysander's other wrist to do the same with his other hand. He rubbed the backs of Lysander's hands, and Lysander felt the thump of Danny's heart against his palms.

"I'm tired," he confessed in a whisper. "I'm so fucking tired, and it won't stop."

"I know." Danny squeezed Lysander's hands. "Come on. My bed'll still be warm. I'll help you get some sleep."

Lysander knew he should step back and walk away, but when Danny took him by the hand and led him towards the bedroom, he followed unresisting.

Chapter Thirty-One

THE EMPTY SPOT on the other side of the bed still felt warm when Danny woke up.

He squinted around at the clock, unsurprised that it wasn't quite six yet. Lysander was an early bird, but not necessarily by choice. A thin line of light sliced down one of the walls through the gap between the door and the frame, which said he hadn't left the flat yet.

The bed was snug, but Danny hated the idea of leaving Lysander sitting on his own.

He shoved back the covers and poked his feet about under the bed until he found his slippers. The floors weren't too cold, but he could never say no to a pair of T. rex—shaped slippers. They gave him a certain something, even if it also screamed immature arsewipe.

When he shuffled through into the main room, Lysander didn't turn. He was sitting at the table, his hands wrapped around a mug, his head bowed over it. Still knackered, obviously.

"Y'should come back to bed for a bit," Danny murmured, stopping behind his chair and giving Lysander's shoulders a squeeze. "You can sleep a bit more."

"I wouldn't be able to get back to sleep."

Danny had guessed that would be the answer and started kneading at the tense knots down Lysander's neck and shoulders. "Cuddling, then? I give a mean cuddle."

Lysander nearly laughed, but it cut off before it could escape. "You do." He turned the mug between his hands, and his breathing hitched as Danny pressed at a particularly tight spot. "You don't need to."

"Eh." Danny bent down and dropped a kiss on top of his head. "I like pawing at you."

He got a quiet laugh. "I'd noticed." Lysander leaned back into Danny's touch. "You didn't wait to be asked."

"Because you're a stubborn son of a bitch who doesn't know when to ask for help," Danny said and then bit his tongue. Diplomacy had never been one of his strong points.

"Maybe a little," Lysander agreed, and Danny felt like he could breathe again.

"Maybe," Danny echoed. He frowned at Lysander's half-untangled braid, all bedraggled and getting in the way of his hands. "You mind if I sort your hair before I get back to the shoulders? It's all over the place."

Lysander waved vaguely, which Danny took as a yes, so he loosened the band and unravelled Lysander's hair. It was warm and soft, and he dragged his fingers through it, untangling it as gently as he could. From the sounds of it, Lysander was enjoying it more than the shoulder rub, so he took his time, drawing his fingers from scalp to the very ends of the blue-black waves.

"Word of warning," Danny murmured, "I'm shit at braiding things, so you're going to have a basic ponytail."

"Leave it down," Lysander murmured, his head rocking forward as Danny eased his fingers up the back of Lysander's neck to rub the base of his skull. He sighed, and Danny leaned forward cautiously to see Lysander's eyes were closed again. Okay. A good start. Danny continued to gently massage his head and neck, and draw his fingers through Lysander's hair until he heard the familiar quiet little squeak of Lysander's snore.

"There you are," Danny said softly, drawing his hands from under Lysander's hair.

It took more effort than Danny wanted to admit to move his lover from the chair to the bed without waking him. Lysander had tucked his legs well under the table, and dragging the chair back and lifting him was a feat of science. Still, Danny managed it and carried Lysander through to the bedroom, setting him down on Danny's side of the bed. It was warmer, and Lysander immediately curled up on his side, drawing the covers around him.

Danny slipped into the other side of the bed, lying with his back to Lysander to make sure he didn't give in to the need to cuddle up behind him again. He drifted back to sleep to the sound of the erratic muffled squeaks from the other side of the bed.

When he woke again, it had grown lighter outside, and an arm had slipped around his waist and a warm body pressed against his back. He smiled drowsily, moving his hand to brush Lysander's forearm.

"You cheated," Lysander murmured against his shoulder.

Danny chuckled. "You were the one who went to sleep on me." He shifted under Lysander's arm to lie on his back and gaze up at Lysander. He had more colour in his cheeks, and his hair was still loose around his shoulders. Danny wanted nothing more than to bury his fingers in it again but restrained himself. "Feel better for it?"

Lysander gave him a stern look. "Not the point."

Danny gave him a sunny grin. "Kind of is." He stroked Lysander's arm again. "You going to stick around for breakfast?"

Lysander glanced at the clock. "I should get back across."

"And not eat and undo all my hard work?" Danny dragged Lysander's hand up and kissed his palm. "It's like you don't give a rat's arse about me at all."

Lysander's expression softened. "You're being presumptuous, *Mister* Ferguson."

"Aye, I am." Danny kissed his fingers. "How about it? Bacon buttie? Or French toast? I can do French toast and all. Or eggs and soldiers."

Lysander smiled, stroking his thumb along Danny's lower lip. "And if I say no, you barricade the door until I eat something?"

"You're already shattered," Danny pointed out. "Why make things worse by not eating?"

"A bacon sandwich would be a good start." He leaned down and kissed Danny. "And then, we both get back to work. Deal?"

Danny couldn't help sinking his fingers into Lysander's hair. "Deal," he agreed, tucking a long strand behind Lysander's ear. "As long as I get a snog before you go."

Lysander laughed and his eyes danced. "You drive a hard bargain," he said as he sat up.

Danny deliberately glanced down his body. "Not that hard."

Lysander smacked him on the thigh, shaking his head with a smile. "Up."

Danny sat up, grinning. "It doesn't do verbal commands either."

Lysander's severe expression would probably have the coders quaking in their boots, but Danny could spot the barely visible telltale twitch at the corner of his mouth. "Breakfast, or I walk out the door, *Mister* Ferguson."

Danny scrambled out of the bed. "Yes, sir, Mr. O'Donohue, sir." He bowed dramatically, which made the twitch turn into a suppressed laugh. "I'll nip to the bog, and then you can have the shower while I throw together a couple of butties."

"How generous," Lysander said, following him through to the main room.

By the time Danny returned from the bathroom, Lysander already had a pot of coffee brewing, and the bread, butter, and bacon were all laid out for Danny. In turn, when Lysander emerged, he found a toasted bacon sandwich waiting for him beside a mug of coffee on the dining table.

"Not a bad way to start the morning, eh?" Danny raised his mug in a salute, but he could see the lines of tension deepening around Lysander's eyes again. "What is it?"

"It's after eight."

"Aye."

"We're into working hours. There are going to be people in the halls."

Danny winced. "Bollocks." He frowned as Lysander wolfed down his sandwich and drank his coffee as quickly as he could. "How about this? If you walk out into the hall and there are people there, you start yelling at me for not being in my workroom in time and tell me I'm a lazy git."

"Danny—"

"And then I stagger out in my PJs and everyone believes it and—"

"Danny, you don't need to do that!"

Danny shrugged. "Would it make things easier for you?" Lysander didn't even have to answer. "Anyway, Ben already thinks I'm a chatty boozer. Being a bit lazy in a morning isn't a big thing."

"Or," Lysander suggested, putting his mug down, "we don't make you look bad. I came down because no one had heard from you or seen you, and we were worried you might be ill. You've been working pretty hard, after all."

Danny was brought up short. "You'd do that?"

"You were offering to do the same thing," Lysander pointed out. "Small white lies."

Danny knew he had a stupid soft grin on his face. "You're taking care of me again."

"Said the man who made me breakfast." Lysander licked a smear of ketchup from his thumb. "Does it sound okay to you?"

Danny frowned again. "What about the security footage from the halls? Doesn't the guy on the desk keep an eye on it? Won't someone have spotted you coming in?"

Lysander snorted. "No. We've never had anything happen in H-block in all of the years I've been here. Anyone on the front desk downstairs is usually there for access. Footage is only checked if something goes amiss." He drained his mug and then considered it. "I do need to warn you there's a change in your work situation from today."

Danny cocked his head. "Ben?" he guessed. "Will I be working with him?"

Lysander shook his head. "Ben will be occupied with our visitor. You're being assigned to Sabine. She'll be your supervisor in the meantime. If anything comes up or you feel there's information I should know about, you bring it to her, and she'll see it gets to me."

Danny wasn't surprised. With everything going as haywire as it had been for the last few days, no wonder Lysander had decided to spread the work around where he could. "And you'll be dealing with him as well?"

"I'll be dealing with anything that needs to be dealt with."

It sounded a lot like working himself to exhaustion. Danny made a note to remember to put in a lunch order for every day for the rest of the week to be on the safe side. Even if Lysander wasn't sleeping as well as he should, at least he'd have a decent meal in him.

"I'll stick with my coding, ta," Danny said. He put his mug down. "You know where to find me if you need a hand getting to sleep."

Lysander rose. "I'll keep it in mind." He glanced towards the door. "Ready for some Oscar-worthy acting?"

Danny grinned at him. "Go on then..."

Lysander opened the door and stepped out into the hall, clearly ready to play up the concerned boss, and then his shoulders sagged. "Oh."

"No one about?" Danny guessed with a laugh.

Lysander looked back over his shoulder. "One less thing to worry about." He raised a hand in farewell. "I'll see you when I see you."

Danny remained where he was sitting, considering the closed door. Lysander hadn't given him any instructions about Sabine, but staying on his best behaviour and making things as simple as possible for everyone sounded like the order of the day.

When Sabine dropped in for her first meeting with him as supervisor, she'd clearly drawn herself up for battle, ready to face a notoriously stubborn contractor. He listened attentively to her instructions about keeping to a schedule to ensure he ate and slept well enough to provide optimum working conditions.

"That sounds all right," he said, when she finished.

Sabine squinted at him suspiciously. "What?"

"Everything you said," he replied. "Sounds fine to me."

She eyed him as if she expected a trap. "You're...okay with it?"

Danny gave her a half-smile. "I'm trying this being cooperative thing. Everyone here has enough on their plate. You don't need me being a pain in the arse to complicate things."

"Oh." She smiled uncertainly. "Well. Good?"

He had to laugh. "Cross my heart, I'm on my best behaviour." He sketched a cross over his chest with his fingertip. "Let me get on with my work and make sure I remember what time of day it is, and you'll have the easiest job in this place."

She relaxed in her seat, the uncertainty giving way to visible relief. "Thank you."

He wasn't surprised and could guess why. "Lysander let you read my HR file, didn't he?"

"I looked it over," she admitted.

"Ah."

While a lot of it could show him as a conceited twat, it was a necessary evil.

He remembered when he started out. He wasn't exactly shy, but being the youngest person on a team of brilliant people made him hesitant. There were those who took his shyness as uncertainty at best, and ignorance at worst. So many of his ideas were getting overlooked, so he'd decided to try confidence for a change. It turned out there was only so much confidence people could take before it became 'obnoxious' and 'cocky.' Still, more often than not, when he put his foot down, he was right, so he'd kept at it, no matter how much it pissed people off.

"I'll put it aside for now." She opened a file on her Leaf to display a rota, scheduling set hours. "This is the timetable we need to work within." She touched a blue pane on it. "I have a meeting scheduled with O'Donohue every day at this point. In the half hour before, we'll go over anything you've found and deem relevant for him to know. If there's nothing, you can let me know in advance."

Danny studied the timetable. It took him a few seconds to work out the colour key, and he whistled under his breath. On top of wrangling him, she also had full responsibility for supervising the temporal agents, their supervisors, and the numerous reports they were generating. "You're keeping yourself busy, aren't you?"

She shrugged, closing down the file, and transferred a copy to him. His Leaf chirped as he received it. "This place can't stop running because of one little complication."

Danny couldn't help admiring such a massive understatement. "Want me to get to work?"

"And if anything urgently needs my attention, ping me."

Sabine's office was—unsurprisingly—on the top floor of the building, several doors along from Lysander's. Danny suspected he'd underestimated the woman's position within the organisation, especially if Lysander trusted her to handle so many parts in his stead.

He was tempted to stick his head into Lysander's office and see how things were going, but Lysander needed everyone to stay focussed, and, now, Danny had a timetable to work within. He popped it open as the lift descended and studied it. All he had to do was divide out his work to fit within the neat little blocks and avoid a bollocking from anyone.

Of course, it didn't go to plan.

He was sitting on the floor some time later, sifting through strings of code. He'd stopped long enough to rub his eyes and stretch when his Leaf wailed so loudly he almost shat himself.

"Jesus!" He scrambled across the room, grabbed at the bud, and flicked it open.

As soon as he did, a video link popped up.

"Already?" Sabine sighed.

"What the fuck was that?" Danny demanded. "Jesus Christ, you could warn a man."

"It's after one. You didn't take your lunch break, and this is the first time the system registered you were resting, to remind you."

Danny blinked stupidly at her. "Oh." He frowned, affronted. "Oh! So when I miss a break, you're going to make me shit myself every time?"

She leaned closer to the camera. "Optimum. Working. Conditions."

"God damn it, Sabine!" he groaned.

"Get a handle on your time management, Mr. Ferguson," she said sweetly. "We don't need to have this conversation again."

He made a face at her and shut down the call. Right. First things first: lunch for him, with a side order for Lysander, then setting an advance alarm for himself, so he could bugger off on lunch on time and not have his bloody Leaf screeching at him.

Still, he had to grin. She reminded him of a younger, less jaded version of Carrigan at work, enough to make him feel at home.

Chapter Thirty-Two

"WE NEED TO come to a decision and soon."

Lysander had his elbow propped on the arm of his chair, supporting his forehead on his fingertips. "I know, but the research team are working as fast as they can."

"Put the research team aside. We need to consider the alternatives. If they haven't found the information now, what are the chances of them finding it at all?"

Lysander had been trying desperately to ignore the decision in the hope they'd be able to return Enoch to where he belonged. "It's only been a week—"

"And what happens when it turns into two? Three? A month? Six?" Jacob's expression was grave. "We both know this might need a permanent solution if we can't find where he came from. How long do we wait before we tell him?"

Lysander shook his head.

Jacob leaned forward in his chair. "Ly," he said gently, "I know this is a shitstorm to be caught in the middle of, and I know we're all exhausted, but we're holding his life in our hands. We can't keep him in there indefinitely. The press are already having a field day with speculation. It'll only be worse if they get the wind of what's happening here."

Lysander closed his eyes for a second, trying to gather himself. "How can I make a decision?" He looked back at Jacob. "How can I tell Enoch his life as he knew it is over, and he's stuck here? How the hell is he meant to survive in a world he knows nothing about? This isn't something anyone can prepare him for."

Something in Jacob's expression caught his attention, something he knew he could have analysed and identified if he wasn't so fucking tired. Everyone expected him to have all the answers and to tell them what to do, and it was taking every bit of will he had not to give way under the pressure.

"We might not have a choice."

Lysander rose and went over to the window to look out over the grounds. His hands were shaking, so he balled them into fists, then took even breaths, counting down from ten. Sometimes it helped. Now, not so much.

Jacob was right, though.

Technically, right now, Enoch could be seen as their captive.

"I'll need to talk to legal," he finally said. "Work out how we do this, if we can't get him home. If we let him out of here and the media find out, he'll be fresh meat." He took an unsteady breath. "I don't know how they'd classify him. Illegal immigrant? Temporal refugee?" He laughed sharply. "No, not immigrant. He's local, after all." He pressed his forehead hard to the glass, letting the ache distract him. "They're going to have to write new laws for all of this."

Jacob's chair scraped on the floor, and he walked closer. "They've done it before, Ly." He sounded so calm, and it grated across Lysander's already raw nerves. He hated feeling out of his depth in his own damned company. "When we went public, it was as bad as this. It gets easier."

"Hard to believe it."

He flinched when Jacob pressed a hand to his shoulder.

"I know." Jacob sighed. "And I know it's shit to hear it coming from someone else, but we've survived it before. We'll survive it again. I could call Mariam. She held the reins when the TRI went public. She may be able to give you some advice."

Lysander lifted his head from the glass. It had been growing more tempting by the day, with every new complication. Everyone knew they were up shit creek just now. No one would judge him for calling in an extra paddle.

"Call her," he said. "Meanwhile, I'll get Fana to call the heads of legal in." They needed to be proactive instead of waiting for the next sucker punch. "I want to talk to Enoch again as well. There has to be more he can tell us now he's back on his feet. Maybe he'll be able to give us something we can use."

Jacob looked doubtful. "I suppose it can't hurt to ask."

Lysander tried to gather his thoughts, then forced himself to say, "I think you should come in with me. I'm not— I know I'm missing things. Too many balls in the air now. You might catch something I don't."

He could see a hint of approval in Jacob's expression. "Now? Or later?"

Lysander opened up the link to Enoch's room, surprised to see the young man out of bed and sitting at the table with Ben, picking suspiciously at the his breakfast. The catering staff had tried to keep it as authentically eighteenth century as possible, but clearly it wasn't authentic enough.

"I'll speak to legal first; then we go in."

The impromptu meeting with legal was every bit as draining and bewildering as Lysander had expected. He laid out the situation, explained what their problems might be, and asked for their views on the legal and moral standpoints.

Words flooded over him: potential human rights issues, residency status, the possibility of historic identity theft if Enoch turned out to be a fraud, and so many more complications and difficulties he hadn't remotely considered. Everyone agreed they were going to have to do some very urgent checks on the latest legislation on residency.

"I doubt this is a circumstance they'll have listed."

"No," Victoria Cheung, the head of the legal department, said. "But it'll give us a foundation to work up to." She waved the rest of her colleagues towards the door. "You should have brought this to us sooner."

Lysander wondered if he looked as drawn as he felt. "I'm well aware, but until we stabilised his health and could confirm whether he came from the past or the future, we had no idea what we'd be dealing with. Now, at least, we know something." He hesitated and then asked, "Are we going to get raked across the coals for keeping him here without legal counsel?"

"Hm." She rapped her violet nails on the edge of the table. "Right now, I would say no. He was given into our care not our custody, and we provided medical treatment and support for him when he took ill. He's still recovering, and you've only been asking the questions you needed to, to try and get him home."

A weight had been lifted off Lysander's shoulders. "That's a relief."

"Still," she continued, "you might want to have a member of the legal team present if you need to ask him more questions. Cover our backs, so to speak."

Lysander swore under his breath. "Do you have someone I could borrow this afternoon?"

Victoria raised her eyebrows. "You think I'm going to let one of the drones deal with this, sweets? If there's information to be had first-hand, I'm going to be there."

"A bit of respect, maybe?" Lysander gave her a feeble attempt at a glare. "I *am* your boss, Vic."

She patted him on the knee. "Only when it comes to paying my salary." She pushed off from the chair and smoothed down her skirt. "Give me an hour to get all the tasks allocated and the research assigned; then I'm all yours."

"I bet you say that to all the directors," he retorted with a brief smile.

"You know it, sweets." She winked as she headed for the door.

She was still smiling as she left, which meant he definitely wasn't as far up shit creek as he'd feared, at least on the legal side of things. When she started frowning, it would be time to worry.

On his return to his office, he found a lunch pack waiting for him.

"Hand-delivered," Fana said. "He said he had five minutes to spare to drop it in. I think Sabine has him on a tight leash."

"I'd expect nothing less," Lysander said and then retreated into his office to take a minute to enjoy the silence and the still-warm dish of curry. He hadn't seen Danny since their breakfast together three days earlier. He didn't have the time or privacy to slip away for some peace. Still, there was something comforting about the food deliveries.

He was only halfway through his meal when Fana chimed through.

"Jacob's arrived. Do you want him to wait?"

Lysander thumbed at his temple, knowing Jacob would only show up uninvited to deliver bad news. "If he doesn't mind me eating while he's here, send him in."

To his surprise, Jacob came in with a middle-aged woman in a police uniform by his side. She smiled politely to Lysander. Lysander lowered his fork and glanced at Jacob in silent inquiry.

"Mr. O'Donohue." Jacob's formality caught Lysander as much by surprise as the woman. "This is Superintendent Abigail Temple. She was my DC during the Sanders case."

Lysander rose, extending a hand. "Superintendent. A pleasure."

She smiled. "Likewise. I'm only sorry these are the circumstances we have to meet under."

Lysander motioned to the vacant chairs across the desk. "Please." He hesitated and picked up his fork. "You don't mind if I...?"

Temple and Jacob exchanged rueful smiles.

"Of course not," she said. "We've both been in a similar position."

Lysander breathed out in relief. "Jacob said you might be interested in assisting us in this case?"

Temple was a cheerful-looking woman, despite the uniform and the severe knot she had her silvering dark hair pulled back in. "If Harper *is* involved with this case, I want to be the first person to know about it." She opened out her Leaf, spread several files across Lysander's desk, and expanded one of them. "Unfortunately, at this moment, it doesn't seem like we have a connection." She flipped the file around to let him see it. "These are Harper's visitor logs for the past year."

Lysander studied them as he ate. "Nothing suspicious at all?"

Temple shook her head. "I'm afraid not. His lawyer has been in half a dozen times in the last few months, but he's been doing the same for the past decade. Business matters and handling finances and the like. His sister, three times this year. A few former colleagues, but no one of significance. No recordings of the visits either."

Lysander's heart sank. "Right."

"That doesn't mean these people don't have contact with friends on the outside," Jacob put in.

"He's right," Temple said. "Harper has been known to use middlemen before, including his former lawyer. Given the circumstances of this case—the fact that Harper had handled outstanding stolen temporal technology, and his current convictions—we've been authorised by my superiors to put him under surveillance."

"We can do that? On a hunch?"

To his surprise, Temple actually laughed. "We try not to call it a hunch, Mr. O'Donohue. We're the police, after all. We have to sound like we know what's going on."

He couldn't help smiling. "Of course. What do we call it? Suspicions?"

"Good enough. We have evidence to suggest Harper has and will eventually use temporal technology, which means right now, he's the only available suspect we have. The best we can do is find proof he's complicit. At worst, we confirm he isn't involved, and then we know to look elsewhere."

Lysander sighed. "I guess it's all we can hope for, isn't it?"

"You'll find it happens a lot in this situation, sir," Temple said sympathetically. "Jacob's probably told you how bad things were when we worked the Sanders investigation. These cases are never easy."

"Can I ask you something?" The question had been bothering Lysander since he'd seen the Sanders file in full.

"Of course."

"You knew this man had the technology and would inevitably use it." Lysander said quietly. "I don't understand why you haven't had him under surveillance from day one. Yes, it would be expensive, I have no doubt, but you have evidence he will commit a crime."

Temple shot another wry look at Jacob. "Ah." She leaned back in her chair and crossed her arms, tapping the end of her nose with a knuckle. "You have your rules about changing the past. We have similar...guidelines in place in the case of Mr. Harper. He doesn't—and can't—know the role he will play in the future. We maintained a degree of surveillance on him, but we can't let him know he's still under our scrutiny. Now, we have the authority to expand it, but it has to be done carefully."

Lysander grimaced. It felt like balancing on a high wire. "I'm surprised, if he's holding on to temporal tech. You'd think it would be a priority."

Jacob rubbed his thumb along his knuckles. "We suspected he only has the gate built after he gets out. Otherwise, his people would have opened the gate and broken him out. He didn't seem like the kind of man who would stay in a cell unless he had no other choice."

Temple nodded in agreement. "Unfortunately, we may have been wrong."

Lysander pushed aside his box. "Enoch?"

"Enoch." Jacob said. "It's possible they're developing it now. Maybe Enoch was a casualty of their trials."

"Or maybe it wasn't Harper at all," Temple added. "He could be innocent, for once."

"Which would mean someone else has got hold of the tech somehow." Lysander laced his fingers over his lap, tapping his thumbs together. "So, right now, is there anything you need us to do, Superintendent?"

"You handle your side of the investigation," Temple said with a quick smile, "and we'll handle ours. If anything needs your attention, I'll keep Jacob up to date."

Lysander rose, abandoning his half-finished lunch. "I'll look forward to it." He held out his hand, which Temple shook. "Jacob, I'll need you to meet me at the quarantine hub in twenty minutes. I have some data to collect, and then we have an appointment with Enoch. Victoria is going to be joining us."

Jacob raised his eyebrows. "Legal counsel?"

"Better safe than sorry," Lysander confirmed as he snatched his jacket off the back of his chair.

Thankfully, the squad of historians had been busy since the morning. They'd put together a new list of questions to narrow down region and year, ranging from local news right up to the US wars of independence.

"There's no guarantee," Dieter warned as he sent the file to Lysander's Leaf. "These are the big events you'd think everyone would hear about, but it's possible he was too isolated for it. If he doesn't remember the year, he might have no fucking clue."

"It's worth a try." Lysander glanced over at the cluttered table. Their teams had been working around the clock. "Truthfully, do you think there's a chance we'll be able to pinpoint him?"

Dieter scratched at his silver-peppered brown hair. "No."

"That simple?"

"Would 'fuck no' be more convincing?" Dieter waved in the direction of the table and the dozens of projections. "We've been through almost every available digitised and analogue archive for the area. If he had a record in any of them, we would have found him already. We've got a dozen volumes left, but we're not holding out much hope now."

It was as Jacob had said: Enoch needed to know he wouldn't be going home, unless he miraculously remembered anything that could help. Lysander knew he was being a coward, pushing back the decision until the last possible second, but the idea of ruining someone's life turned his stomach.

"Let's hope one of us has some luck," he said, hoping he sounded less fraught than he felt.

With five minutes to spare before he needed to be at the hub, he took the elevator back up to the top level and went out into the roof garden, the one place he knew no one would come looking.

It was designed to be peaceful with winding paths between the frost-tipped shrubs and the small, slim evergreens. The gravel crunched underfoot as he walked. The tang of snow whirling in the chilly air around him, clouds thick and grey overhead. When he closed his eyes for a second, he could picture himself home on his mom's porch.

For the first time all day, it was quiet.

A chirp from his Leaf brought him back to reality minutes later.

We're waiting, sweets.

Lysander took a last sharp icy breath and retreated indoors.

He could see the concern on Victoria's face when he stepped out of the elevator, but she knew better than to ask if he was okay in front of someone like Jacob. Professional appearances had to be maintained, even among friends. None of them spoke as they shuttled over to the other building.

We have to do it. It may be an exercise in futility, but we need to be sure we have all possible information before we wreck his life.

"I'll stay back," Jacob murmured as they emerged from the pod. "I don't want to scare the kid again."

Victoria glanced between them. "Throwing people of Iranian, Ghanaian, and Chinese descent at a scared little rural white boy is one hell of a way to introduce him to the future."

"Which is why Ben's been keeping him company," Jacob said. "It not like we had much choice in the matter."

Ben glanced up when they entered, but he didn't seem surprised. Enoch was sitting at the table with him, watching him work, but leapt to his feet as soon as he saw them, his eyes darting warily from one face to the next.

"Good afternoon, Enoch," Lysander murmured. "We've come to ask you a few more questions."

Enoch glanced nervously at Ben, who shut down his screens.

"They mean well," Ben said. He got up and circled the table to stand beside Enoch. "I'll stay here if you want."

"Aye." Enoch's expression immediately brightened. He seemed much better than the last time Lysander had visited, with colour back in his cheeks. He waited until Lysander sat before sitting back down. He shot a look at Victoria, who folded her hands before her and kept her peace.

"You're feeling better?" Lysander asked.

Enoch fidgeted with his hands under the table. "Yes, sir. Thank you, sir. Your people were good to me. Master Sanders, special like."

"I'm glad." Lysander opened up his Leaf. It said a lot for Baker that, this time, he didn't flinch. Days of watching Ben playing with glowing screens must have made it less frightening. "Now, I need you to answer any of these questions for me..."

Enoch licked his lips nervously.

As cooperative as he tried to be, his answers were as unhelpful as before. He'd heard of America, but not about a war. Yes, an army from Scotland went by, and he went to see them with his friends, but he couldn't remember when, because he was only small. Once, he'd seen a man with black skin, "like that 'un," come all the way up from Liverpool on the river.

Lysander slanted a glance at Jacob, standing by the door. His face gave nothing away, but when he noticed Lysander's attention, he shook his head minutely. Lysander turned to Victoria. "Would you like to ask Mr. Baker any questions, Ms. Wu?"

Victoria inclined her head. "Thank you, Mr. O'Donohue." He rose, and she took his place on the seat, smiling warmly at Enoch. "Hello, Enoch. I'm Victoria."

He bowed his head slightly, politely. "Yes, miss."

"I'd like you to answer me truthfully, all right? You don't need to be afraid." He nodded, so she continued gently, "Have you been treated well here?"

"Aye, miss. Very well. There were food and that." Enoch reached up and wrapped his hand around Ben's wrist. Ben gazed down at him with a half-smile. "Master Sanders kept me from being afeared of the magic lights."

"Not magic," Ben murmured, barely audible. "I'm not a witch."

Enoch snorted with a crooked grin. "As you say, Master Sanders," he said seriously. "It int magic and Master Sanders int a witch, though it were warm all night with no fires or candles or aught else."

Victoria actually laughed. "It would be a lot more interesting if he were a witch. Electricity becomes so mundane after a while."

Enoch tugged Ben's wrist once more and released it. "Lectricity. The wall-wires, aye?"

"Yeah."

Victoria smiled. "And you understand why you have been kept in this room?"

"To be sure I don't have the sickness." He glanced up at Lysander. "Until I can go home, aye?"

Lysander couldn't find the words to confirm it.

Whatever else Victoria asked, Lysander couldn't seem to hear her. He could only see the trusting expression on Enoch's face shattering when he was told he would never be going home. He felt unsteady, and it must have shown on his face, because next thing he knew, Jacob had a hand under his elbow and had guided him out into the hall.

"Breathe," he urged, clasping Lysander's shoulder. "Deep breaths. Slowly."

Lysander wanted to snap at him for suggesting something so stupid, but he realised he couldn't speak. He had no air for words. He wasn't breathing properly. He was hyperventilating. Oh God. A panic attack. An honest-to-God panic attack. He stared at Jacob, clutching at his arms, and fought to catch his breath.

Jacob held his arms, drew him down to sit on the floor by the wall, held him steady. Lysander could only clutch at the front of Jacob's coat. He couldn't breathe and he was about to turn a kid's life on its head and they all seemed to think he knew what he was doing and he didn't and he'd spent so long wearing the mask and now it was falling apart.

An arm wrapped around his back. A glass of water pressed into his hand. Supported by a hand with violet nails. Vic? When had Vic come out? Jacob was sitting back. Not touching now. Just Vic. Lysander held on to her arm, sipped the water, and counted the beads on her bracelet over and over until he could breathe again. Vic was close and her perfume was sweet and smothering and her voice was a meaningless hum in his ear.

Eventually, his rasping breaths were the only sound in the hall, and his face was wet, and, God, he felt sick. He hadn't had a panic attack in more than twenty years. His whole body was shivering, his bones as solid as water. Walking was going to be a miracle.

"H-block?" Victoria asked. She wasn't talking to Lysander.

Jacob agreed. "H-block."

Chapter Thirty-Three

SABINE WAS THE first person to be informed, but Danny only realised it in hindsight.

He'd been updating her on some of the patterns he'd noticed in the code when a striking woman came into Sabine's office without waiting for permission. Sabine rose from her chair. "Vic?"

The woman—Vic—glanced at Danny, then back at Sabine. "A word?"

"I'll wait outside," Danny said, rising.

Sabine sat back down, relieved, as he walked out and closed the door behind him. Vic emerged several minutes later, barely glancing at him. Danny watched her go and then went back into Sabine's office.

She was paler than she'd been, but with a grim set to her jaw. "Is there anything in these patterns you'd consider absolutely vital for Lysander to know now?" she asked before he could sit back down.

"Only as part of the grand scheme," he replied, frowning. "I can probably go deeper and find some more links."

"Focus on it for the rest of the day," she said curtly. "I'm afraid I have to cancel the rest of our meeting. There are some other matters requiring my attention."

Danny braced his hands on the back of the chair. She'd already been covering a lot of Lysander's tasks. If more had come up, it meant something big was going on. "Has something happened?"

"Nothing you need to be concerned about," she said after a moment of silence. "Take the rest of this meeting time to have a tea break. Stretch your legs. I don't want you back in your workroom until the allocated time."

He snorted. "As if I could get in." He straightened up from the chair. "Our evening debrief?"

"Cancelled meantime, unless I let you know otherwise." Despite the strictness in her tone, he could see the silent plea in her eyes for cooperation, which made his stomach churn. Something unexpected had happened, and she was worried. "Remember, tea break or exercise. Something to keep you occupied for fifteen minutes."

What with the snow flurrying outside, indoors seemed like the best option, so he headed down to the canteen on the first floor. Though tiny compared to H-block, it did the job when all he needed was a cup of coffee.

A few of the other coders were there, huddled around a table, and glanced up as he approached.

"Did you hear?" Mel asked.

"You're going to have to be a bit more specific," Danny replied, sprawling into one of the chairs. "Did I hear what?"

Guy leaned closer across the table. "O'Donohue's sick."

The expression on Sabine's face suddenly made sense.

"Sick?" Danny echoed. "What do you mean sick?"

Mel shook her head. "We don't know. Someone saw him coming back in from quarantine. He was leaning on Ofori like he could barely stand."

"We think exhaustion," Guy murmured. "He's only been home one night in the last two weeks, and most nights, he stays in his office until late."

Danny felt numb. He remembered the last time he'd seen Lysander, when he coerced him to sleep more than five hours and eat a full meal. He'd been sending lunches, but he had no idea if they were being eaten.

"Where is he now?" he asked.

Mel waved towards the window, in the direction of H-block. "Hopefully resting."

"Hopefully," Danny echoed.

Guy and Mel continued to talk, but Danny couldn't think about anything but Lysander. He couldn't go striding over to see him, not yet, but later, he could swing by. Soup. He could take some of the soup he'd made. It always helped, and everyone knew he took Lysander food, so no one would be surprised.

Everyone Danny overheard spoke with concern, which said a lot about how well-respected Lysander was. They all also agreed that he'd overworked himself. He cared too much about the job. He didn't want anything to go wrong.

If Lysander *was* sick and Sabine had taken over his role, they both needed Danny at the top of his game. He had a job to do first, and they'd both give him a right bollocking if he acted like a soft bastard instead of getting his work done.

He could play the soft bastard card later, when he'd finished the job.

Danny headed back towards his workroom as soon as he could.

To his surprise, there was someone already there, touching the control panels and frowning when the door didn't open.

"Can I help you?"

Mack Robertson whipped around like a startled cat. "Don't sneak up on people!"

Danny raised his eyebrows. "Walking up behind you from the lift is sneaking?" He frowned, studying the boy. "Were you looking for me?"

Mack shifted uneasily from one foot to the other. "There's a lot of stuff going on right now."

"Aye. And you were looking for me?"

Mack hesitated, colour blooming on his cheeks. "Uh..."

Danny folded his arms over his chest. "That's what you're going with?"

"I thought I could help?" Mack tried to smile. "I mean, I know they took me off coding, but maybe I can help you since everyone else is busy? I mean, doing historical stuff isn't going to help much now, is it?"

Danny sighed, unfolding his arms. It was a generous gesture, but everyone except Mack knew the kid's coding skills were non-existent. "You need to learn to obey your supervisors," he said as gently as he could. "If they took you off coding, they did it for a reason."

Mack's lips pressed into a line. "Right. Okay. Thanks."

Danny watched the younger man slouch off. He'd been there before but had no right to undercut the kid's managers, especially not when he had something so confidential to work on. He swiped his palm over the control panel and retreated into his workroom.

Sabine had given him enough to keep him busy, digging into the underwritten patterns in the code, so he made that his focus.

They weren't part of the original coding but also didn't appear to be part of the corrupted code, which seemed impossible. The patterns had only appeared after the initial amendments, so there was definitely some connection. Some kind of subroutine, perhaps.

He rubbed his eyes and studied the data again.

Something seemed very familiar about the structure, but he couldn't put his finger on why.

He was lying on his back on the floor, sifting through the glowing web of light, letters, and numbers spread above him, when his Leaf chirped with his five-minute warning. He'd missed Sabine's deadlines twice on their first day working together, and both times, the cacophony had nearly deafened him. Now, he made sure to stick to her schedule and couldn't help feeling a little Pavlovian.

Keeping regular hours definitely helped. He'd started sleeping better, and the headache that had been plaguing him for days had receded. He'd even made some minor breakthroughs in the code he should have noticed days earlier.

Before he headed back to H-block, he stopped in at the deserted canteen. Most of the people working during the day finished at least an hour before he did and the evening shift wouldn't need to eat yet.

While he couldn't be certain of her preferences, he put through an order to be delivered up to Sabine, including rich slices of cheesecake and lemon meringue pie. On the off-chance she was on a diet, he added some fresh fruit for good measure and a note: "Dear Kettle. From Pot."

That done, he headed outside where thick soft flakes of snow were settling in drifts across the grounds. If it kept up much longer, the path would vanish completely under a sheet of white.

Danny trudged through the snow, considering his options. Technically, he could order food to be taken up to Lysander, but habit—instinct—was to provide food and comfort when the person you cared about was ill. He'd learned it at his mother's knee, visiting sick relatives and proudly carrying boxes of chocolate crispy squares he'd made himself while his mum brought soup and casseroles. Every new birth meant a biweekly run to his aunts' homes with a stack of fresh meals to go in the freezer.

He was still humming and hawing over it when he reached the lobby and kicked the snow off his boots.

The woman at the reception desk looked up from her screens. "Evening, Danny."

"It's Beth, isn't it?"

She grinned at him. "Well-remembered. What can I do for you? Forgot your pass?"

Danny feigned shock. "Nah. I've got some nibbles to drop into O'Donohue, but I'm not sure which flat is his."

The proverbial light bulb went on over her head. "Oh *you're* the lunch boy?" She touched the console out of his line of sight and hesitated. "Is he expecting you?"

"Well, would I be going if he wasn't?" Danny lied amiably. "It's only snack delivery. I've heard he might need something filling."

Seemed like she'd heard too. "Top floor. Number eight."

He winked at her. "Thanks."

He stopped off in his own flat to fill a plastic box with soup from the giant pan he'd made the previous night because he'd always loved coming in from the cold to thick warm sweet potato soup. The fact that half the pan ended up in the box for Lysander was irrelevant.

He stacked another box with generously cut slices of bread, and piled them into a bag before heading back out into the hall to the lift.

Danny's flat was only one level below Lysander's, and while the layout of the hall matched, there were fewer doors, which suggested fewer but bigger flats. It looked like the big cheeses got first dibs on the top floor, with the lower levels reserved for the rest of the staff.

He only hesitated when he reached the door. If Lysander was sick enough to take time to rest, then it might be best to leave him be instead of disturbing—and maybe waking—him.

Danny was about to turn around and go back down when the door opened.

Lysander stood there, wrapped in a dressing gown, his face pale and deep shadows under his eyes. His eyes somehow were darker than usual, and he swayed on the spot.

"I brought soup," Danny said stupidly, holding up the bag.

Lysander's face broke into a tired smile. "Beth called and mentioned nibbles." He opened the door a little wider. "Come on in."

Well, that explained why Lysander had opened. He must have heard the lift doors ding when it arrived.

"I don't need to stay," Danny said, hesitating on the threshold. "I came to make sure you had something to eat." Lysander just stared at him and raised his eyebrows. Danny made a face at him. "Well, I'm not spoon-feeding you, you lazy bam."

Lysander's flat was open-plan and as big as Danny had expected with wide living room windows with a view out over the countryside. The snow fell more heavily now, dancing in whorls in the wind.

Lysander padded over to the dining table near the kitchen and picked up a half-finished cup of pale green liquid, which he tipped down the kitchen sink. Tea, Danny supposed, as he followed and set the boxes on the counter.

"I'm guessing everyone's heard now," Lysander murmured, rinsing the mug out.

"That you're not well? Yeah." Danny held out the box. "You hungry?"

"This rings a bell." The familiar spark of humour glinted in Lysander's eyes as he returned and sat at the table. "Soup would be good, thanks."

Danny raked through the cupboards to find the bowls and plates, then filled a bowl generously with the thick, rich soup. While it was warming, he raided the fridge and buttered a couple of slices of bread, which he set down in front of Lysander.

"You want to ask."

Danny fidgeted with the butter knife. "They were guessing exhaustion downstairs. You've not been sleeping again, have you?"

Lysander sighed. "Not as well as I'd like." He laughed self-consciously. "They gave me something to help this afternoon. I think I've been out cold for a few hours."

"You could've said something."

Lysander looked up at him. "You have enough to think about."

Danny couldn't help reaching out and running his fingers along Lysander's cheek. "And you don't?" When Lysander tilted his head, resting his cheek against Danny's palm, his eyes closed, Danny could see every line of fatigue on his face. He drew his thumb down Lysander's temple, then pulled back, startled, when the microwave beeped. "Oh! Right! Soup!"

When Danny returned to the table, the hot bowl balanced carefully on his fingertips, Lysander had drawn himself up again. He smiled as Danny sat on the opposite side of the table.

"You could have some soup as well."

Danny wrinkled his nose. "Kind of defeats the purpose of bringing it for you if I eat it."

"Even if it's inhospitable for a host to eat while his guest doesn't?" Lysander stirred the soup. "It goes against every bit of my cultural conditioning." There was a hint of mirth around his lips. "I might not be able to eat from the shame of it."

For the first time, Danny could actually tell Lysander was playing him, and it felt weird. "You're not subtle when you're tired," he snorted, but he went and put half a bowl of soup into the microwave for himself.

Lysander was swirling a piece of bread in his own soup when Danny sat down with his bowl. "I get the feeling you're humouring me." He glanced towards Danny's half-empty bowl.

"Fuss, fuss, fuss." Danny sighed melodramatically. "There's no pleasing some people."

They exchanged smiles across the table, and Lysander subsided into silence, dipping bread into his soup and slowly working his way through the bowl, his coordination shot. Danny could see how much concentration it took him to navigate the spoon. Probably a combination of straight-up exhaustion and whatever relaxants the doctors had provided.

"Danny." Lysander set the spoon down.

"Mm?"

"Can I ask a favour?"

Danny gulped down his mouthful of bread. "Aye. What do you need?"

Lysander wiped some breadcrumbs off his fingers. "It's—when I'm wound up, sometimes a hot bath helps." He hesitated then admitted, "I'm not 100 per cent right now. I can't guarantee I wouldn't fall asleep in the tub."

Danny could see the unasked question and the amount of trust it carried. It made his heart thump harder. "I can sit with you if you like," he offered. "Make sure you don't go and do a Titanic."

Lysander smiled gratefully. "The press would have a field day if I did that." He pushed the almost-empty bowl back. "Is now okay? Do you have somewhere you need to be?"

Danny picked up both their bowls to take them to the kitchen. "According to Sabine, my very strict schedule has me marked for 'downtime.'" He poured the dregs of the soup down the sink and rinsed the bowls before popping them in the dishwasher. "I'm not exactly busy." When Lysander's chair scraped on the floor, he turned, raising one finger. "And you stay put. I'll go and run the bath."

Lysander subsided onto the chair. "I don't need to be babied."

"No," Danny agreed, walking over to the table, "but sometimes, you need someone to remind you to sit on your arse and rest, which clearly you haven't been doing in the last fortnight." He leaned down and kissed the end of Lysander's nose. "So this time, you're on your best behaviour and doing as you're told, and I'm running a bath, understood?"

Lysander's lips twitched. "Look at you, *Mister* Ferguson. So forceful."

Danny couldn't help grinning at him. "Don't get used to it. I'm a pushover."

Lysander snorted aloud, one finger curling over his lips to hide the smile. "Sure."

Danny laughed and glanced around. "Bathroom?"

Lysander pointed, and Danny headed towards it. The bathroom was about as big as his own, but while his bath and shower were on the inside wall, Lysander's bathroom had a tub close to the west-facing windows, which had to be one hell of a view on summer evenings.

He left the bath running—with a generous dash of some fancy bath oil—and fetched some fresh towels to stack them by the tub. He then checked the water for temperature as it rose up the sides. When he called Lysander through, he blinked at the other man. Lysander had used Danny's absence to pin all his hair up on top of his head. It should have looked daft, but instead, he managed to make it regal.

He paused when he reached the door, and Danny could take a wild guess why.

"You want me to wait outside while you get in?" he asked, stepping aside to let Lysander into the room.

To his surprise, Lysander pulled him down to kiss him.

"You," Lysander murmured against his lips when they broke the kiss, "pay too much attention."

Danny ran a hand the length of Lysander's back. "Well, yeah. S'why you hired me. On my CV and everything." He squeezed him around the middle. "Want me outside?"

Lysander shook his head. "It's not anything you haven't seen before." He drew back and unfastened his dressing gown as he walked to the bathtub. He had a loose top and long pyjama bottoms on underneath it. Somehow, they made him seem smaller and more vulnerable.

Danny closed the door and followed him, picking the dressing gown off the floor and accepting the top as Lysander removed it. When Lysander loosened the tie of his pyjama bottoms and let them drop, Danny offered him a hand as Lysander lifted out one foot, then the other.

"This isn't necessary." Lysander didn't meet Danny's eyes, and his grip on Danny's hand tightened.

"You were wobbling all over the place," Danny retorted, giving his fingers a squeeze. "I'm not going to be found with your body after you dunt your head on the tub when you fall over."

That earned a wan smile. Lysander pulled his hand back and climbed into the tub, sinking into the steaming water. Danny ducked to grab the pyjamas and draped the whole lot on the heated towel rail.

"All right?" he inquired as he wandered over to the tub.

"Yeah." Lysander had propped his arms on his knees, which were jutting up like small islands, and his eyes were fixed on the swirls of oil on the surface of the water around them. "Thanks for this."

"Aye, it's really torture for me, this." Danny sighed mournfully, kneeling down on a folded towel beside the tub. "My man all wet and naked and asking for me. Christ, I don't know how I'll survive this."

For a second, there was silence only broken by the ripple of the water against the sides of the tub.

"Your man?" Lysander slanted a look at him.

Danny stared at him, mortified. "Shit. Did— I said it out loud, didn't I?" It was one thing to have the thought, but throwing it out there? Jesus. It was as bad as accidentally 'I love you'-ing someone.

Lysander was smiling, only a little but enough. "A little." He raised one dripping hand to brush along Danny's arm on the edge of the tub. "You're blushing."

Danny ducked his face behind his arm. "Mm." He peered over his wrist. "Sorry."

"Why sorry?" Lysander's normally cool fingertips were warm on Danny's forearm. "Three dates and a couple of overnights count."

Danny blinked owlishly at him. "Aye?"

Lysander prodded the middle of his forehead gently. "For someone with such attention to detail, you missed that?"

Danny knelt up. "I thought we were just having a bit of fun."

Lysander smiled, leaning back in the tub and stretching out his legs. The oil on the surface made his skin shimmer, rippled with light and shadow. "It can be both." He sank down until the water lapped around his neck and his head rested against the end of the tub. "Until you go back to London."

Danny folded both arms on the edge of the tub and propped his chin on them. "Yeah. Sounds good." Then, because he could never keep his mouth shut for long, he added, "As long as you don't try and drop dead from exhaustion before then, because that would get right on my tits."

Lysander had his eyes closed, but he laughed. "Noted."

A few minutes went by in silence, and Lysander sank a little farther in the tub. Danny unfolded one arm enough to flick some water at Lysander's face.

Lysander cracked one eye open. "Must you?"

"Making sure you're not dead," Danny said, wide-eyed.

Lysander considered him blearily and then dashed a handful of water in Danny's face.

Chapter Thirty-Four

DANNY HAD LEFT by the time Lysander got up the next morning.

He'd stayed through the night, though. Lysander hadn't asked, and Danny hadn't offered, but it felt right and comfortable when Danny sprawled out on the bed beside him. He'd been so patient, helping Lysander out the bathtub when he struggled to keep his feet and getting him dry and back into his pyjamas.

Lysander wished he could have blamed the relaxants he'd been given, but he knew he had to take responsibility for his own actions. He'd been careless and reckless with his health, working himself to breaking point, and now, everyone knew it.

He sat up in the empty bed and ran his hand over the space where Danny had slept beside him.

Danny was much sweeter than Lysander had anticipated. He also made a pretty good comfort blanket. Lysander couldn't remember the last time he'd slept so well.

Even so, when he saw his reflection in the mirror, he still had rings under his eyes, his cheeks painfully sunken, which never looked good. A little weight loss and he turned from streamlined to gaunt. He tidied himself up, dressed sharply to compensate for what he lacked in colour and energy, and settled for twisting his hair into a complicated arrangement of loops in a knot on the back of his head.

If he wasn't 100 per cent physically, he damned well wanted to look the best he could.

When he reached for the door of his apartment, he paused and took a slow breath.

People were going to see him differently now. There would be stares, murmurs. True, most of them would be out of concern, but it didn't make it feel any more comfortable. He had to ignore them and get to his office, and then, he could focus on work.

Thankfully, he only ran into a few people as he made his way from the top level of H-block to the top level of the main building. There were a few good mornings, but no one pressed their luck to ask how he was. Definitely a good thing since he didn't know what he would say.

Fana glanced up from her desk when he arrived. She didn't have to say anything, but one of her perfectly sculpted eyebrows arched inquiringly.

"I'm much better, thanks." He smiled wanly. "I hope I didn't miss too much."

"Sabine and I handled it." She laughed. "See? We can be useful. Also, Jacob called up. He has Mariam Ashraf to see you when you're available."

God, that conversation felt like a lifetime ago. "Let them know to come up."

"Of course." She motioned towards the door of his office. "Also, Ben came to see you. I thought you wouldn't mind if he waited inside."

Ben had to be one of the easiest people to start with.

Lysander stepped into his office, startled when Ben jumped to his feet. Of the pair of them, anyone would think Ben was the one who had collapsed from exhaustion. He looked like hell, his face ashen, his clothes—the same ones from the day before—rumpled and stained.

"You're okay?" Ben took an abortive half step forward and then retreated back. "Shit. Sorry. Dumb question." He raked his fingers through his hair, leaving it standing in every direction. "You—when you went out the room with Jacob, you looked like you were about to keel over, and then Jacob said you weren't well, and I didn't know what—"

He'd barely stopped to breathe, and Lysander held up a hand to calm him.

"Maybe we both sit down?" he suggested.

Ben sank into the seat, pulling his legs up again, and wrapped his hands around his crossed ankles. His eyes were fixed on Lysander as if he could read what had happened in the lines of his face. "Sorry. Sorry. It's just—you're *never* ill."

Lysander shifted on his chair, trying to make himself comfortable. "There's a lot going on," he finally said. "The proverbial straw had to land at some point." He pressed his fingertips to the edge of the desk. "Some rest and time to get my head straight helped."

"Right." Ben shook his head. "It—this—I didn't expect it. Not you."

Lysander remembered the suffocating panic in the hall of the quarantine wing, Jacob's hands the only thing keeping him from falling, his vision fading around the edges. "You're not the only one." He watched as the tips of his fingers whitened against the edge of the desk.

Ben laughed unsteadily. "I'm the one who's meant to be all melodramatic and over the top." Lysander glanced over at him. Ben was staring at his own white-knuckled fingers. "But no, you had to go and swoon all over Jacob."

Lysander smiled wanly. "Well, if you're going to swoon on someone, there are worse people than the one person in this facility who never panics." He sat up a little straighter. "It's been a lot to deal with."

"You always have a lot to deal with," Ben pointed out.

"I think I moved up a level," Lysander admitted ruefully. "You can expect hacking and corrupted code in any job with computers, but this whole..." He waved vaguely. "The situation with Enoch is something I never saw coming. It's not something you can have a contingency for."

Ben rubbed at his earlobe. "I s'pose I always saw you as the plan man. You always seemed to find a way around everything." He raised his eyes to Lysander. "Look at how you got the top job."

Lysander laughed. "Long-term planning is easier, and I had time. This time..." He sighed. "This is an emergency situation, and a solution is needed as soon as possible. Not exactly the best circumstances to come up with a plan."

"Mm." Ben rumpled his hair again. "But at least you're feeling a bit better, yeah?"

"A lot better," Lysander murmured, and it wasn't entirely a lie. "You don't need to worry. I have no doubt I'll have Sabine and Fana coming down on me like the wrath of God if I don't start taking better care of myself."

Ben smiled as he got up, but it didn't look as convincing as usual. "And your lunch boy."

"And him." Lysander watched Ben as he walked to the door. "Ben, are you all right?"

Ben turned to him. "You're the one going over like a skittle, and you're asking me?" He forced another smile. "Just worried about my silly bugger of a boss, that's all."

Lysander chuckled. "What are we like?"

Ben opened the door and stopped dead in his tracks. It took Lysander a moment to realise why. Ben's voice sounded oddly childlike and bewildered when he asked, "What are you doing here?"

Beyond him, a woman spoke. "Jacob and Lysander called me in for some advice."

Lysander groaned inwardly, rising from his seat. "Mariam has experience dealing with the fallout of a major incident," he said quickly, hurrying over.

Ben stood rigid in the doorway, staring down at the woman. The contrast between them was marked—Ben, pale and gangly and unkempt, and Mariam, small and round and dark, with her purple hijab tucked neatly around her face. "So?"

"We thought she might be able to help, especially with the media."

Ben jerked his chin stiffly. "Yeah. Right. Fair enough." He stepped out of the room, pushing by her and all but running for the hall.

Mariam flinched as if he'd slapped her. She never really aged, but her features seemed to crumble as she watched him go.

"You should try to talk to him," Jacob suggested quietly from behind her. "You know he's too stubborn to make the first move."

"Like his dad." Mariam looked between Jacob and Lysander. "If you can spare me for a couple of minutes?"

"Take as long as you need," Lysander said. She bustled off after Ben, and Lysander waved Jacob through into his office. "Should have thought about that."

Jacob sank into one of the chairs. "They were bound to run into each other eventually. We can't keep them apart forever." He ran his hand over his eyes. "On that note, we need to get Ben out of the med bay. He can't stay in there any longer."

Lysander tried to ignore the way his heart picked up a beat. "Why? Is Enoch sick? Is Ben at risk?"

Jacob shook his head. "When you were talking to Enoch yesterday, I kept an eye on Ben. I think he's gone and got a soft spot for our little time traveller. The last thing we need is him getting a crush. It would make things more complicated, especially if Enoch ends up sticking around."

Lysander had the strangest feeling of the world going at a different speed from him. "Ben has a crush on Enoch? Are you joking?" He laughed uncertainly. "If this is meant to put things into a different perspective, I'm not sure it's the right tone."

"I'm serious," Jacob said quietly.

Lysander propped his elbows on the table and buried his face in his hands. "Oh, fuck me." It was inappropriate as hell in front of a colleague, but then, he'd had a complete breakdown in front of the man the day before. Lysander tried to remember how to breathe again. Another complication in a mangled train wreck of epic proportions.

"I'll deal with it," Jacob said.

Lysander lowered his hands. "What?"

"Ben. I'll make it seem like he's being moved for other reasons. You don't need to worry about it." Jacob's expression had lost some of the usual sharpness. "I thought you'd want to know before I did anything." Lysander's confusion must have been apparent because Jacob smiled, deepening lines around his eyes and mouth. "You've got enough to worry about. I can interrupt the unrequited puppy love. It's a little below your pay grade."

It was one way to take the sting out of usurping Lysander's role, but Lysander didn't mind. There were much bigger things to be dealt with, and if Jacob could relocate Ben without causing a fuss, then all the better. "Self-delegating, huh?"

"Something like that." He glanced back at the door, then leaned closer to the desk. "I've also had word from Temple about their investigation."

"Any news?"

"Nothing yet." Jacob grimaced. "Abby says they're not holding out much hope. No contacts. No shifts in Harper's finances. No major changes appearing on any of their standard checks. If he *is* the one behind all of this, he's definitely learned a lot about subtlety in the last twenty years."

"Not so much before?"

"Sent someone to spy on me with a digi-lens, then tried to blackmail me into cooperating with him to clear him from any involvement in the case."

"Really? Blackmailing you?" Lysander wondered if Harper had ever tried speaking to Jacob. Integrity poured off him. "This man doesn't sound like the brightest." He studied Jacob. "Since he's locked up, I figure you didn't bend to blackmail."

"Ha!" Jacob looked amused. "I quit the force and recorded his blackmail attempt. Temple nicked him five minutes later."

Lysander stared at him in surprise. Well, it definitely explained why Jacob had gone from high-profile police detective who'd discovered time travel to little more than an investigation supervisor within the TRI. "I didn't know."

Jacob chuckled. "Well, he wasn't about to tell anyone, and I don't enjoy regaling people with it."

"Though I bet you enjoyed the look on his face."

They shared a rueful smile, and both looked over as the door opened again.

Mariam Ashraf came in, her expression tense and unhappy. "Sorry, Lysander."

Lysander guessed it hadn't gone well. "He wasn't in the mood for talking?"

Mariam shook her head. "Later," she demurred. "We've got bigger things to worry about. It must be bad if you've called me in."

Several years earlier, she had elected to take an early retirement package after the birth of her first grandchild. The TRI had swallowed up her time with her kids, she'd said. She didn't want it to do the same for her grandchildren. The only exception was if the TRI had no one else to turn to. Lysander had stood by her condition and, until now, nothing had merited her attention.

"I expect Jacob's filled you in on what's been happening?"

"After some security clearance updates, yes," she said as she sat down. "Sounds like you're having quite a time."

"You still have a gift with the understatement." Lysander took his own seat and folded his hands on the desk in front of him. They weren't shaking yet, but with the tension in his back and the sick feeling sitting in his stomach, it was only a matter of time. "Jacob said you might be able to offer some guidance when it comes to dealing with a situation like this, when the wolves are at the gates. After all, you dealt with the transition from private to public for the whole TRI."

Mariam grimaced. "Yes. Not fun, as I'm sure you've guessed. Jacob acted as my main liaison with the police force at the time, and with the loss of Tom and taking care of Ben, it was a bit of a nightmare."

"What would you recommend in this situation?"

"I hate to say it, but this is a simpler scenario," she replied bluntly. "Everyone knows time travel exists. Everyone knows there has to be a degree of confidentiality. However, thanks to your anonymous leak, everyone also knows about Enoch's existence."

"And the Met have had no luck finding the source either," Lysander said, shaking his head. It still made no sense. Most people went to the press with a story for the money. Something felt off about the biggest story of the year being dropped in anonymously to not one but five different networks.

"Could be some anti-authoritarian type," Jacob said. "If they saw the police hauling Enoch in and overheard TRI, it could have been done because they wanted to stick it to the authorities."

"It doesn't matter now anyway," Mariam said. "What matters is how you move forward. You can't cover it up, not when he's been seen in public and spoken to. Depending on what happens to him, either way, you're going to have to acknowledge his presence."

Lysander nodded. "I guessed that would be the case." He sat back a little. "The problem I'm foreseeing is that if the world knows he exists, they'll want a piece of him."

"You're not wrong there," Jacob murmured.

Mariam studied Lysander. "He's not the only one who's going to be in the spotlight. Time travel has been mundane for two decades now, but this? This is new and exciting. You can tell from the coverage for the last fortnight." She hesitated and then inquired, "Are you going to nominate a spokesperson or do it yourself?" Lysander tapped his chest, and Mariam's expression clouded. "Well, I need to warn you. This isn't going to be pleasant for you."

"I've dealt with unpleasantness before."

She gave him a pitying look. "They harassed my family until we had to go into protective custody. They dug up any stories they could from my past, my husband's past. They speculated. They spread rumours. They dragged us through the dirt to try and provoke us until we took preventative legal action."

"Kit, too," Jacob added.

Lysander glanced at him, surprised. "Kit? But he's just an engineer."

"They knew he worked in the TRI." Jacob shrugged. "They targeted anyone who worked here. Mariam got the worst of it, but this hit everyone involved. Kit had people staking out his flat, harassing him in the street. You name it."

Lysander's heart jumped to his throat. God, if they went for his family, if they started to dig, his private business would be all over the press. "What could they hope to achieve?"

"A story. Any story." She folded and unfolded her arms. "I know you've come to me for advice, but the best I can give you is don't be the public face of this. If they know your face and your name, they'll come after you as much as they'll come after this boy."

"Who then?" He shook his head. "I'm the director. If I don't take point on this—whoever does will be the target. What right do I have to throw someone under the bus in my place? What right do I have to put Enoch out there? He didn't ask for this. I did."

"There's another option," Jacob said.

Lysander frowned at him. "There is?"

"You assign a spokesman who has already been scrutinised by them and has nothing left to uncover." Jacob gave him a wry smile. "They already ran the story about me being caught shagging a member of the TRI when I was investigating them. The best they'll be able to do now is confirm I'm still shagging him and that we take holidays to sunny climes once a year."

Lysander stared at him. "I can't ask you to take that bullet for me."

"You don't need to ask," Jacob replied. "I'm offering. I know what it's like to be dragged into the limelight. I've dealt with it plenty of times. One more time can't hurt."

"Jacob—"

Jacob leaned forward. "Lysander, I know you well enough to know you're a very private person. Hell, it's pretty much about all I know about you. Yeah, I get it, you're the director, and you feel accountable for all this bullshit, but you've always told us the TRI and the Supervisory Board are in this together." He laughed quietly. "Christ, you've beaten us over the head with it like a big stick."

Lysander had the grace to nod. "Well, it was the only way anyone would listen."

"Consider this my big stick moment, then," Jacob said. "We can't let you be the spokesperson. You've driven yourself to the point of exhaustion already, and I'm not about to sit back and let you walk into a situation where you'll be under more pressure and scrutiny."

"I can handle it." Lysander knew he didn't sound convincing.

"I know you probably could," Jacob replied. "But here's the thing—you don't have to take it all on yourself. I'll be the spokesperson on your behalf. I'm one of the leads on the investigating team on Enoch's case, and I'm the one liaising with the Met. Plus I know how to dodge trick questions like a professional."

"He's not wrong," Mariam said. "It was like tap dancing on a landslide, being confronted with this one back in the day."

Jacob seemed flattered. "Thank you."

She wrinkled her nose at him. "It's not a good thing."

"Not if you're hiding something," he agreed. He returned his attention to Lysander. "Consider it this way—I get to have fun terrorising the press again, and you have the time and energy to focus on Enoch instead of being chased by the paparazzi."

Lysander wanted to argue, but Jacob's reasoning was solid. Not just that his previous experience and his private business were already common knowledge, but Lysander had been trying to do it all. He had a bad habit of trying to ensure everything was done to his standards by handling everything himself. But right now, it felt like the landslide had swamped him and Jacob had thrown him a lifeline.

It must have shown on his face because Jacob smiled.

"I'm guessing it's a yes?"

"Conditionally," Lysander said. "Before any press conferences, we need to sit down with the legal teams and work out exactly what needs to be said and done. God knows we're about to step into a legal minefield if we can't get Enoch home."

"Didn't expect anything less," Jacob said. "You're the one who decides what does and doesn't get said." He glanced at Mariam. "How did you do it back in the day?"

"Committee," she said. "You need to be as well-informed as it's possible to be. Delegation is vital to make sure you know everything."

Lysander inclined his head. "Why do I feel this is a conspiracy to make me do less?"

"Call a spade a spade. This is an intervention by people who have been through this shit before." Jacob shrugged. "We know what it did to us and everyone round about us."

"You'll also need to get some tighter NDAs in place," Mariam added. "Anyone who works here will be considered a source, so if someone is willing to risk selling Enoch's story, they need to know they'll be out on their ear and sued to within an inch of their life."

Lysander nodded grimly. With a leak already out in the world, people would want the full story. "Our staff now are pretty solid, but I don't doubt there are one or two who wouldn't mind a pricy backhander."

"The anonymity clauses in place on their contracts will help," Mariam said. "We had to deal with a firestorm when we went public. We lost a good forty per cent of our staff when the press came crashing in. At least, this time, this place is inaccessible, and the staff can come and go without being harassed."

Lysander looked at the woman with admiration. "I don't know how you handled it."

She laughed quietly. "Because I didn't have a choice. I was accountable for well over 100 people. Tom thought I could handle the responsibility, so I did what I had to."

Lysander could appreciate that. Life and lemons. "So, we have our spokesperson, the legal team are currently working out where we stand, our security team are trying to identify a source..." He tapped a fingertip on the arm of his chair and forced himself to breathe slowly, evenly. "That leaves one issue. Enoch Baker."

"You know the decision needs to be made," Jacob said.

Lysander nodded, trying to ignore the sick feeling in the pit of his stomach. "If—when—we tell him, my concern is how he'll deal with it. There's the loss of his whole life, but he'll also have to deal with the modern world."

"People are adaptable," Mariam murmured. "They learn and adjust."

"To something this extreme?" Lysander raised his eyebrows. "He comes from a time before electricity or modern science or space travel." His hands were shaking again, so he folded them in his lap, hidden by the desk. "I don't know how he'll cope. It's nothing we've ever seen before. We can't know how it'll turn out."

Mariam and Jacob exchanged a loaded glance.

"Actually," Jacob said, turning back to Lysander, "that isn't 100 per cent true."

Lysander felt the world shifting again. "What?"

Mariam met his eyes, her expression calm. "He's not the first."

Of course. Of *course*, when they had a mole corrupting their code and some stranger had access to a gate and his whole steady reliable world was turning on its head, shocking news would keep on coming.

Lysander closed his fingers tightly together. "Excuse me?"

Mariam frowned for a moment, as if deciding what to say. "You've read about the way the original gates were operated, I expect."

Lysander inclined his head in agreement. Energy stored up over several weeks, then used for an hour-long jump. The gates were kept open during the jumps with a minimising lock to restrict access until the agents returned. "I was told you used a secure locking mechanism to prevent unauthorised access."

"Only after a point." She hesitated again. "A few years before we went public, there was an...incident. Despite the life-scans and the usual checks, someone got through the net. This person disabled the team member guarding the gate and came through before anyone could stop them. They were injured, and Tom—"

The blood rushing in his ears drowned her words. The room suddenly seemed far away, and Lysander struggled to catch his breath. A hand on his arm. He turned, startled. Jacob crouched beside the chair, his grip firm and warm. An anchor. Lysander clutched at his arm, too, trying to remember how to breathe.

"This isn't something you need to worry about," Jacob said, holding Lysander's eyes. "The person in question has been living and working in the modern world for years now. No one knows any different. The few people who do know aren't about to breathe a word of it."

Lysander shook his head. Words took effort. "You covered this up?"

"I made the decision," Jacob said. "When the TRI went public, this individual offered to step forward, but after all they'd been through and how well they had assimilated, it seemed like an unnecessary cruelty to make them into a living museum artefact, no matter how interesting some people would find it."

Lysander laughed shakily in disbelief. "So simple, huh?" He looked over at Mariam. "Who?"

She glanced down at her hands, then back up. "It's not my place to say. We've told them you're being informed of their existence. Whether they let you know is their decision."

Lysander stared blankly down at Jacob's hand on his wrist. "You're telling me this, knowing the laws and rules governing this place? I should report it—"

"You know you don't want to," Jacob said quietly. "Enoch's future has been bothering you so much already, you wouldn't want to upset anyone else's life. Anyway, if you wanted to, you couldn't. You don't know who it is. All you have is our word."

Lysander drew his hand back from Jacob's and folded his fingers together in his lap to keep them from trembling. "So why tell me?"

"So you understand you're not the only one who has had to face this decision," Mariam said. She was standing on the other side of the desk. He hadn't even noticed her get up. "So you understand that telling Enoch this is his life now isn't the end of the world. So you know it's possible for him to be happy and settled."

"The only difference being that the world knows about Enoch." Jacob remained crouched beside Lysander's chair. "He can survive and thrive here, but it all depends on how you choose to play this."

Lysander's laugh sounded shrill in his ears. "No pressure."

Jacob straightened up and squeezed Lysander's shoulder. "That's why we're here; we can help."

Lysander glanced between them. Even if they were hiding another rogue time traveller—and even if they weren't—he needed to know he was going in the right direction. They were the best people he could have as a sounding board.

"So how do we do this?"

Chapter Thirty-Five

"IT'S A TRAP."

Sabine walked in a circle around the room, examining the dozens of scattered projections of code. "What makes you think so?"

"Because the corrupted code hasn't been fiddled with in weeks, but this—" He motioned to the obfuscated subroutines he'd found underlying the code. "—seems to be updating a little each day. Not much. I didn't notice it at first, and it's not doing anything to the code or to the system, but it feels like it's been put in by our saboteur as a safeguard."

Sabine looked at him sharply. "To do what?"

"Best guess? To stop us finding the person responsible."

She stared at him. "They're that good?"

Danny pointedly turned his head left, then right, reminding her of the hours and days of work glowing all around them. "They're good enough to keep me on my toes, and that hasn't happened before." He touched the control to shut down all the projections.

"So if it's a trap, how is it sprung?"

Danny meandered in a circle. The thought had been bothering him for hours, days even. "I've got a feeling if I tried to start removing the code, we'd find out what it does."

"If you were to guess?"

"Best case scenario, it unravels and removes the corrupted code without leaving a trace." He scratched his head. "Worst case, it's pretty much a nuclear bomb to wipe the whole system completely."

She sat on the edge of the desk, one arm folded over her belly, her hand cupping the elbow of her other arm. She ran her thumb along her lower lip, staring into the distance. "Why would someone put a corrupt code in only to erase it on risk of discovery?"

Danny shrugged, sinking into his chair. "Especially a useless code which only seems to exist to be the bane of my life and a complete pain in the arse. I'm starting to wonder if they did it to see if they could."

"They?"

Danny waved a hand vaguely. "General they-ness." He frowned pensively. "Like someone who tries to get into your workroom."

Sabine tensed. "Someone's been trying to access your machines?"

Danny considered it. "I don't know. The other day, when I got back, Mack Robertson was hanging around. He said he wanted to help and be useful, but I know he can't code."

Sabine pressed her lips together, clearly worried. "I know there have been suspicions about him."

"Skulking about like a...skulker doesn't really help his case, does it?" Danny shook his head. "He's crap at coding, but whoever did the code is brilliant and definitely smart enough to cover up how clever they are."

"And the last day he still had access was the last time the code was adjusted..." Sabine tapped her knuckle against her chin and then shook her head with a tired laugh. "God, I feel like I'm jumping at shadows. I'm sure something would have come up in his background checks if he had any technical skills."

"Aye." Danny sighed. "It'd be much easier if it was him, though, wouldn't it?"

"Mm. We've been keeping eyes on him anyway, but if he's trying to access machines again, I think we'll need to keep a tighter rein. I'll get his super to sit with him. Keep him busy until this mess is sorted out." She lifted herself up to sit on the desk, her feet dangling. "You should know people have been speculating that this is all a distraction."

Danny snorted, tucking his hands behind his head. "Distracting who from what? The only people who knew about this until the time travel kid showed up were me and Lysander and whoever wrote it." He frowned at the ceiling and sat up. "Is there any reason someone would want to distract Lysander?"

"You mean aside from drawing his attention and then opening an illegal gate?"

Danny propped his arms on his thighs, thinking. Whoever had written the code had spent a lot of time on it and especially on hiding it. Distractions weren't usually hidden away and only found by sheer luck. No one would put so much work into building such a complex labour-intensive code if there wasn't a reason for it.

Anyway, Lysander hadn't been distracted by it. Aye, he'd brought Danny up to be his eyes and work out where it came from, but as distractions went, it was a bit of a shit one.

He chewed on his thumbnail.

The code had to be some kind of trap, but if they knew which kind, then they might be able to narrow down what bastard had written it. Or bitch. Or both. Hell, there might be a team.

"I think," he said pensively, "we should trigger it."

Sabine made a sound of surprise. "What about 'nuclear bomb to wipe out the whole system'?"

He raised his eyes to meet hers. "D'you think anyone would mind if we nuked one computer unit to try it out?"

"That depends. What do you propose?"

"Load a backup of the current system onto a disconnected server," he replied. "If we air gap it, it can't affect the main servers, and we'll see exactly how it works without any of the risk to the system."

She pushed off from the desk. "What do you think it'll do? Honestly?"

Danny considered it.

The code had been well hidden in such a way that only someone who knew their way around the system would find it. That meant it had to be a staff member, and unless they'd been very shifty, Danny hadn't met who would take the golden goose and wring its neck.

But...

But, but, but...

The IDD had only been involved in the past six months and the code had only been found because of their monitoring. It would never have been found six months earlier or at all without the monitoring.

Someone wanted the code to be found.

Someone had placed safeguards to hide their identity, because they knew it *would* be found. It wasn't a precaution *in case*. It was a precaution *because* they expected it to be found and probably expected someone to try to remove the code.

But why?

He shook his head.

And yet, he couldn't help feeling a piece of the puzzle was missing, so tangible he could almost grasp it.

"I don't think they want to wreck the system," he finally said. "My best guess is even if it doesn't clear the corrupted code out of the system, I think it'll wipe any digital fingerprints our culprit might have left behind. If we can confirm what it does without bollocksing the whole system, it might help point us in the right direction."

Sabine paced back and forth. "All right," she said, turning to face him. "I'll let Lysander know what we're planning. If he gives us the go ahead, then we start preparing for it this afternoon." She checked the time on her Leaf. "You go and have something to eat. I've got a couple of meetings with the supervisors; then I'll see Lysander."

Only one table in the canteen was occupied when Danny got there, and since he didn't fancy sitting alone with only his thoughts for company, he took his food over and gave the sole occupant a friendly grin.

"All right, Janos? Mind if I sit with you?"

Janos looked up from his Leaf and shrugged. "If you want to."

Danny sat down. "I hate flying solo."

Janos's lips twitched. "And I am the only option? Very sad."

Danny made a face at him. "You know I didn't mean it like that." He gestured to Janos's Leaf. "Reading anything interesting?"

"Only some legal paperwork for my husband." Janos closed the image down. "I hear you are very busy?"

"Which version did you hear?" Danny inquired ruefully. "Some people seem to think I'm a spy."

"Are you?" Janos's expression gave nothing away, and Danny glowered at him, affronted. Only then did Janos chuckle. "No. No, I think you are not a spy. Your face shows all your thoughts."

"You were still the first one to ask," Danny said around a mouthful of bangers and mash, waving his fork in Janos's direction. "Thought I was suspicious."

"And now I learn you are one of us from a different company." Janos sighed, sounding convincingly disappointed. "Not interesting." He picked up his cup of coffee and studied it for a few moments. "Your company, they have jobs available?"

Danny gulped down his food. "You're thinking of moving?" He couldn't keep the incredulity out of his voice. "But this place has *time travel.*"

Janos smiled slightly, but it didn't quite reach his eyes. "I know this." He shrugged. "Sometimes a change is good. London is bigger." He turned his cup between his hands, warming his palms. "Your place might be a good place to start."

Danny scratched the end of his nose with the tip of his thumb. "I could drop Carrigan—my boss—a line and see if we have any openings, if you want."

Janos seemed distracted. "It would be kind, yes."

Danny dug into his food, unsure what he could say. Janos was in a world of his own, and it seemed rude to butt in, so eating quietly seemed like the best idea. At least Danny wasn't sitting on his tod like a sad loner.

"You okay?" Danny finally had to ask, when he'd run out of sausage, potatoes, and bread to mop up the last of the gravy.

Janos blinked as if he'd forgotten he had company. "What?"

"You're off in a daze. Is everything okay?"

Janos gave him another of those tight lip twitches. "I am remembering the last time we had so much attention in the news shows. We all had a very bad time. I worry this time might be bad as well." He inclined his head. "Old worries, that is all."

"I don't think you're the only one," Danny said sympathetically. "Everyone's stretched thin at the minute. Speaking of..." He pushed his chair back. "I need to get his high and mightiness some lunch. I think the shock would kill him if I didn't."

Janos cocked his head, looking up at Danny. "Do you feed all of your bosses?"

Danny snorted as he gathered his dishes and cutlery together on his tray. "Only the ones who let me see tech I'd give my left bollock to play with."

That earned a genuine smile. "Only your left?"

Danny nodded solemnly. "It's my favourite."

Janos actually laughed aloud. "You are such a strange man. Don't change."

"I'll try my best." Danny paused, considering his tray, then plucked up a plate with a wedge of cake he'd planned to have later. "Here."

"Now you feed me too?"

Danny shrugged with a smile. "Humour me? It's how I look after people."

Some of the tension in Janos's face seemed to ease, and he took the offered cake. "Thank you."

Danny waved in farewell as he headed back to the counter and picked out a lunch for Lysander—a Caesar salad with a muffin for after. He hadn't seen his lover since the previous morning, when he slipped out without waking him, but lunch had become a habit.

With five minutes to spare before he had to be back in his workroom, Danny took the lift up to the top floor and stuck his head around the door of the reception room. Fana had just finished a call and ran her hand over her face. She looked as knackered as Lysander and Sabine, and no small wonder.

"Knock, knock." Danny tapped the door frame. "Is the boss about?"

Fana gestured to his office. "And in a meeting. Lunch delivery?"

He wandered across the room and set the box down on the empty space she always left for him on the corner of her desk. "Of course." He glanced at Lysander's door and then crouched beside the desk. "Has he been in there all day already?"

"Same as yesterday," Fana said quietly. "People coming and going all day with calls in between." She frowned with a sigh. "I don't think anything's going to change for some time."

Danny grimaced. "No. Probably not." He propped his elbow on the edge of the desk. "Do I need to start bringing you lunches as well?"

She smiled at him. "Sabine told me you have already started feeding her. At this rate, you'll be feeding the whole top floor." She patted his hand. "You save your energy and your clever little brain. I make time to eat and drink, don't you worry."

He pushed himself to his feet. "I think I missed my calling as a waiter."

She laughed. "It's appreciated." Another call rang in, and she rolled her eyes. "I'll be sure he gets his lunch," she added, before touching her earbud. "Temporal Research Institution, director's office."

Danny withdrew and headed down to his workroom to continue tugging at the strands of coding. Trying to tease out the source felt like trying to find a needle in a haystack made of pins. Still, he couldn't really do anything else until Sabine gave him the go ahead for their plan.

Another two hours passed before she appeared in the doorway.

Danny pushed aside the projections. "Well?"

"We're good to go," she replied, smiling. "Lysander agrees it'll help to see what it does. He has people setting up a server for the purpose and copying the system backup overnight. It should be ready to run tomorrow morning."

Danny grinned, relieved. "It'll take another factor out of the equation once we know what it does."

Still, it puzzled him, mulling on what the results could mean. If it nuked the system, then it was a simple case of sabotage, but if it turned out to be innocuous and did nothing but delete the code, it would mean more questions.

"Tomorrow'll be a busy day." Sabine gestured towards the door. "Until we do the test, we should hold off on any more experimentation. It'll be better to continue once we know the parameters we're working within."

"An evening off?" He feigned shock. "Are you sick? Am I sick? Are we going to die?"

She gave him a look she could only have learned from Lysander. "If you don't stop talking, it's a possibility."

Danny held up his hands in surrender, grinning at her. "I'll behave."

She snorted. "That'd be a first." She checked her Leaf. "Meet me back here at seven tomorrow morning. If we can get it out of the way before the day gets started, I think it would be better for everyone."

He cocked his head. "Why? Is something happening tomorrow?"

"You're telling me you wouldn't like it out of the way?"

He could tell she was avoiding the question, and, sometimes, he chose to accept a subtle hint. "Aye, fair enough. I wouldn't mind having some of my questions answered."

"So, tomorrow, seven o'clock."

"Seven o'clock," he confirmed, thumbing his Leaf screen out to change his alarm.

Chapter Thirty-Six

LYSANDER COULDN'T REMEMBER the last time he'd felt so sick with trepidation.

The past couple of days had passed in a blur, but it was done. The Board had been gathered and the situation explained. The historians' data had been distributed. He'd made his case and explained the decision that had been forced on him.

Now, standing in the corridor of the medical bay, Lysander wished he could be anywhere else.

The historians had confirmed what he'd been fearing for days: identifying Enoch's point of origin had proved impossible, since his birth records were either missing or destroyed. They couldn't narrow down the years and or even the village where he lived. People had suggested they simply put him back somewhere around his time frame, but it meant risking his arrival in a timeline where he already existed. He would be as good as dead.

So, Lysander found himself staring numbly at the door of Enoch's room.

It wasn't every day you shattered a man's hopes and ruined his life.

The conversation with Jacob and Mariam had helped a little. There was some comfort in knowing someone had survived the transition from past to future, even if it might be a purely fictional figure created to reassure him.

Still, it didn't make facing Enoch any easier.

Jacob had offered to come with him, but for the sake of Enoch's privacy, it felt better to do it alone.

Lysander took a calming breath and held his hand over the scanner. It registered his details and the door slid open. Enoch was sitting at the table, poking carefully at a projection with a frown, his feet drawn up on the seat. He pushed his finger clean through it, then turned his hand, watching the play of light on his skin.

"Mr. Baker."

Enoch turned with a quick, nervous smile and scrambled off the chair. "I were looking is all. I dint break it."

"It's all right," Lysander assured him. "It's only light. You couldn't break it." He stepped into the room, and the door slid silently closed behind him. "Do you feel well today?"

Enoch nodded, twisting his hands in front of him. "I were wondering if I done wrong. Ben—that is, Mr. Sanders—he says he's not to come back for a bit."

Lysander tried to smile as reassuringly as he could as he approached the young man. "It's not your doing. We have some work Ben needs to do, so we had to ask him to focus on it for a short time." He gestured to the table. "Please, sit down."

Enoch folded back into the chair, pulled his legs back up, and propped his bare feet on the edge, his bony fingers curled over his knees.

Lysander sat opposite him and rested his forearms on the table, lacing his fingers together. "I'm afraid I have to bring you some bad news."

Enoch's lips compressed into a thin line, and his knuckles whitened over his knees.

"I—we—" Lysander looked down at his hands and then forced himself to take another steadying breath and meet Enoch's eyes. "Our people have not been able to find a way to get you home. We— I'm sorry, but there's no way for you to go back."

Enoch stared at him, wide-eyed. "But you said—"

Lysander wet painfully dry lips. "I thought it would be possible, but since we don't know exactly where you came from, we can't arrange the transport to get you back."

Enoch pressed his face into his hands, shivering, and from the sound of his sharp, gulping breaths, he was crying.

Lysander felt like he'd been punched in the gut. "I'm sorry," he said again, knowing how useless and hollow it sounded. He rose from the chair and circled around the table to cautiously lay his hand on Enoch's shoulder. "I—we'll do everything to make you a home here. If you need anything—if we can help in any way, we will."

For a long while, the only sound was Enoch's hoarse breathing. Lysander could feel the tremors running through him.

Finally, the young man knuckled at his eyes and scrubbed at his face with his sleeves. He lowered his hands and looked up at Lysander. "What am I to do?" he asked plaintively.

"We can find something for you," Lysander promised, squeezing Enoch's shoulder. Despite his thinness, the muscles under Lysander's hand were solid. The man definitely wasn't as frail as he looked. "We need a little time to work out the legal ramifications." Enoch looked lost. "The laws for people living now are different. We need to know how best we can help you."

Enoch looked shaken and dazed. Lost for some way to help, Lysander called through to the team, requesting a cup of warm milk for Enoch and tea for himself, something warming and calming and a brief distraction from them both feeling completely overwhelmed.

"If you have any questions—" he began as they waited.

Enoch stared blankly at the table top, hugging his knees against his chest. He seemed smaller and younger than before. His eyes were dry, Lysander noticed distantly. Smudged with shadow and bloodshot, but dry now.

Lysander's tea had gone cold, barely half drunk, when Enoch finally spoke.

"You said I cannit go home."

"No." Lysander's throat almost stifled the words. "Not the place you knew as home."

Enoch had both hands wrapped around his mug, his eyes fixed on it. "Can I know where I am? Ben—Master Sanders said he'd tell me when he were allowed."

Lysander put his mug down and wrapped his fingers around the warm china. "I'm going to tell you something strange." Enoch nodded nervously. "You were from a year in the 1700s. You're now in the year 2065."

Enoch gaped at him in disbelief. "For true?"

"The doorway of light you came through," Lysander explained gently, "was a doorway between your time and this time."

"Magic..."

"Science," Lysander corrected gently. "Machines made by man." He tried to smile. "When you're well enough, I can take you to see the machines."

Enoch sat back sharply in his seat. "You brung me here?"

Lysander shook his head at once. "No, not us. Someone stole the plans for our machines many years ago. We think they made the doorway that brought you here. They tried to send you back, but it didn't work as they hoped."

Enoch looked more confused and lost. "No one sent me. I come through the door, and it were all light and noise. There weren't no one there to send me."

"It's complicated" was all Lysander could think to say. He turned his cup again. "We're close to finding one of the people who might be responsible for all of this. A few days, maybe less. Once we find them, we'll be able to explain everything for you."

"But I still cannit go home?"

Lysander shook his head. "We don't think it will be possible." Even if they found the culprit's gate, there was no guarantee it would provide accurate dates. They'd encountered that very problem in the hunt for Tom Sanders.

"But you'll catch the one what done it?"

"We hope so." Lysander pushed his cup aside. "Is there anything I can do for you, Enoch? Anything I can get for you now?"

Enoch stared into his mug of milk. "Ben. He—he helps. He says—he tells me all's well and—" His lip trembled. "It's not all well."

Lysander reached over the table to gently squeeze his hand. It didn't matter if Ben had a crush on the man. Enoch needed someone he considered safe and a friend, someone to reassure him and let him know he would be all right. "I'll see to it right away."

"Thank you, sir." It was like a blow how pitiably grateful Enoch looked.

Lysander knew he should stay a little longer to explain how things would move forward, but Enoch wanted to see Ben, and sometimes, a man could be a coward. As soon as Lysander stepped into the hall, he touched one of the comm consoles to connect to Ben, who was still working with the security team. The screen connected at once.

"All right, Ly?" Ben cocked his head. "You okay?"

Lysander didn't try to lie. "I need you to meet me down in the quarantine hub as soon as possible. Drop what you're doing."

Ben glanced over his shoulder. "I think this lot can manage well enough. I'll be down in five."

Ten minutes later, Lysander was still waiting in the quarantine transport hub directly below the main building. He'd tried sitting on the narrow bench by the wall, but he couldn't stay still, thoughts racing. He'd paced back and forth across the hub three times before the elevator doors opened.

"What's going on?" Ben asked as he emerged.

Lysander glanced in the direction of the pod tunnels leading to the quarantine building. "I broke the news to Enoch that he won't be going home."

Ben winced. "Shit. How did he take it?"

"Upset. Naturally." Lysander rubbed his forehead with his fingertips. "He's asked for you, and, right now, I think he needs all the reassurance he can get."

"Yeah, of course." Ben's brow creased in concern. "Is there anything you need me to explain? Or is it hand-holding? Or can I take a couple of beers in and see if getting smashed helps?"

Lysander walked in a circle, trying to gather his thoughts. Statistics, numbers, and reports were easy. Dealing with distressed people face-to-face always shook him up. Angry was simpler. Anger could be channelled, but he'd never been able to handle grief.

"We're working on his legal status," he finally said. "As soon as we're able to, we'll get him out of quarantine and start integrating. You—" He didn't know what he wanted to say.

"I'll show him some of the world now with the Leaf," Ben suggested. "It might let him see it's not all bad."

Lysander clenched and unclenched his hands by his sides. "Thanks."

Ben gazed at him. "You're doing everything you can."

"And what if it's not enough?" Lysander asked. "What if it's too much for him? What if—" Babbling out all his worst fears wasn't going to help anyone, especially Ben. "Sorry. I'm— It's a lot to figure out."

To his surprise, Ben reached out and squeezed his shoulder. "He's smart and he's curious. He'll be fine. Whatever happens, it isn't on you."

Lysander appreciated the kind sentiment, but it felt like a Band-Aid on a gaping wound—a generous gesture but ultimately not much use.

Still, he forced a quick smile. "I guess we'll see." He watched Ben heading for the waiting pod, then retreated to the elevator up to the ground level and changed over to the public elevator to the top floor.

By the time he reached his office and opened up the video link to the med bay, Ben was already in Enoch's room, sitting at the table while Enoch wandered in circles in the room. Enoch looked as lost as Lysander was feeling, and Lysander couldn't blame him.

He had an audio option, but the thought of hearing Enoch's voice breaking again, the tremor and the disbelief, would be too much. He tried to focus his attention on reading through the latest updates from Victoria and her team, though his eyes kept slipping sideways to the video link.

He'd been struggling through the legalese when a sudden movement caught in the corner of his eye. He turned to see Enoch fold over, clutching his belly. Ben rose instantly and had him by the arm. Lysander switched the sound on.

"Come on. We'll go to the bathroom. You need to experience the joys of hugging the porcelain express." Enoch gagged pitifully, and Ben slid an arm around his waist to support him. "Lean on me. I'll get you there."

The bathroom in every suite in the quarantine block was a blackout zone, for the privacy of the agents. No cameras and no sound, but there were motion detectors to monitor unexpected lack of motion from living bodies in case of collapse.

When they didn't emerge after five minutes, Lysander patched in to Ben's earbud, worried.

"Ben?"

It took a few seconds before Ben replied, "Not a great time!"

"Do you need medical?"

"Just some puking," Ben demurred. He sounded a little shaken. "I think it's all got to him. He's going to need some clean-up. Can you get some soup and crackers sent down in about fifteen minutes?"

Lysander couldn't help feeling secretly relieved he wasn't the one dealing with it. "Sure. You take care of him."

"Right." Ben hissed through his teeth. "Jesus…maybe make it half an hour? I think he's going to need to lie down when he's done."

"You're sure you don't need medical?"

"Yeah. Yeah, I'll let you know."

Lysander closed the link, put in the request to the catering team, and tried to focus on his work. Twenty minutes later, Ben and Enoch re-emerged from the bathroom. Enoch was leaning heavily on Ben, stumbling his way across the room. Ben guided him to the bed and helped him lie down, pressing one hand to Enoch's forehead, then brushing back his damp hair.

"You should rest now, all right?" Enoch's eyes were closed, but he managed a frail smile. "It's all right," Ben murmured, and now that he knew to look for it, Lysander could see what Jacob must have noticed. "You'll be fine."

Lysander closed down the video connection. If Enoch needed comfort from Ben, Ben's crush didn't matter right now. Enoch's well-being had to be the priority.

Lysander forced his attention back to the legal information arriving in fragments on his screens. Victoria's team was working like crazy to find a solution. If they had something in time for the press conference, it would be all to the good. If not...

Well, if not, they could still say they were working on it.

As Jacob had pointed out over and over, Lysander held all the cards. He had the information, and he could choose how much of that information to release at any given time. They had another meeting scheduled for six o'clock with a dozen of the heads of staff plus Jacob and Mariam to thrash out the body of the press release.

It was another long day in a series of increasingly long days.

The meeting took longer than expected with debate over Enoch's status, whether he should be revealed to the public or put into the equivalent of witness protection, and arguments over his right to decide given his ignorance of the scope of the media. Lysander let them talk as heatedly as they needed to. He listened, considering their arguments, many of which aligned with his own views.

The simple fact was that Enoch needed to be protected, as the victim in the situation. If it meant offering him anonymity and somewhere to learn to live in the modern world, then so be it. They would limit any information known about him until his status was resolved and he decided what he wanted to do with the life ahead of him.

Eventually, they whittled down Jacob's formal statement to a basic summary of the situation. Until they were sure that someone outside the TRI was using a gate in the present, their mystery gate would remain unmentioned. It would serve no purpose to cause undue concern or panic over conjecture. Conjecture had no place in a factual news briefing. They weren't giving out Enoch's name, although they had agreed to provide a few details about his origins.

As the room cleared, Lysander sank back in his chair, aching from holding himself upright and attentive for the whole meeting.

"Could have been worse," Jacob said as he pulled on his jacket.

"Mm." Lysander passed a hand over his eyes. "Someone could have given Anders and Dionne knives."

Jacob snorted in amusement. "To be honest, it would have been more entertaining. She might be a head and half shorter than him, but she looked like she'd bite him given the chance."

Lysander parted his fingers to squint at Jacob. "You're right." Dionne had a lot of rage packed into her four-foot-ten frame. He exhaled and rolled his shoulders. "I think I'm ready to call it a night. Tomorrow's going to be a nightmare."

"We're lucky it's a Sunday," Jacob observed. "The media storm won't really strike until Monday morning." He motioned towards the door. "You should get a good night's rest while you can. Knock yourself out if you need to. We need everyone top of their game for Monday."

Lysander rose. Jacob had no idea about Danny and Sabine's experiment. He had enough to focus on, and Lysander didn't want to burden anyone else with it. "I'll see you here tomorrow. Eight thirty?"

"Plenty of time for last-minute adjustments," Jacob agreed. "Night, Ly."

As soon as the room cleared, Lysander propped his elbows on the table and rested his face in his hands. Tomorrow, they would be a step closer to identifying the person behind the code tampering, and they would also have a rising media storm. More than anything, he wanted to slip into Danny's room and take some little comfort, but Danny's work tomorrow was far more critical than his own. It would be wrong to selfishly distract him from it all.

He had enough pills left from the medical team to stop his whirling brain for a while. He just needed to get back to his room, eat, have a bath, and then sleep like the dead. Simple enough, as long as insomnia didn't rear its ugly head again.

He pulled on his jacket over his suit and headed down through the deserted building. It was already pitch-dark outside, the snow glittering, frozen over with a shimmering layer of ice and crisp underfoot. Most of the windows in H-block were dark already. The meeting had gone on much longer than intended.

Lysander's eyes were already drooping closed with fatigue when he finally stepped out of the elevator on his corridor, but he couldn't miss the bag hanging from the handle. Danny had left him a refrigerated box with a note: *In case you missed dinner.*

Lysander smiled, opening the box as he walked into his apartment. Danny must have been entertaining himself. There was a plate inside the box with a thick slice of home-made pie and a mountain of different vegetables still fresh and bright with colour.

As the food heated in the microwave, Lysander thumbed open his Leaf and sent a note of thanks and good luck for the next morning.

In return, he got a tiny thumbs up.

Lysander laughed quietly, wondering at the way Danny made things seem better without even trying.

Chapter Thirty-Seven

IT WAS FREEZE-your-bollocks-off weather when Danny stepped out of H-block.

The pre-dawn frost had gilded the already rock-hard snow. Despite the salt down on the path to the main building, walking across in the dark felt like a cross between nocturnal ice skating and doing a crap impression of a penguin.

When he got there, he found Sabine waiting for him in the lobby, bundled up in a massive coat any polar explorer would have been proud of and a bright pink woolly hat with a huge purple pompom. "Pleasant walk?" she asked innocently as he knocked salt and ice off his boots by the door.

He made a face at her. "I bet you arrived early so you could watch me go arse over tit."

"And I was disappointed," she replied with a mournful sigh.

Danny yanked his hat off, then frowned, peering beyond her as the light over one of the restricted elevators illuminated. "I thought we were the only loonies up and about this early."

Sabine turned as the elevator came to a halt and the door opened. "Ben?"

He seemed as surprised to see them as they were to see him and looked about as tired as well, whey-faced with bags under his eyes. He was also carrying a couple of packs under his arm. "What are you two doing here so early?"

"Lysander wanted some tests done before the press conference kicks off," Sabine replied. Danny shot a look at her. He hadn't heard anything about any press conference, but it all fitted with her implications of a busy day. "What about you?"

"Mostly watching our guest," Ben replied, with a careful glance directed at Danny. "While he's sleeping, I'm nipping upstairs. I thought of a way for security to expand some of our search parameters."

Sabine glanced at the packs under his arm. "And they need battery cores?"

Ben looked down as if he'd forgotten they were there. "Oh. Right. Yeah. No." He shifted them against his side. "They're for my research gate. Thought I could push through the updates on the other gates to make sure we have a consistent power source. You know, in case anyone accuses us of doing it all. Christ knows whether it'll be useful."

"Feels like everyone's trying anything now," Danny said ruefully.

Ben glanced at him. "You're not wrong. What about you? It's early to be coding?"

Danny hesitated, unsure how much he could say, and thankfully Sabine took over. "We're going to remove the corrupted code to see if it has any effect on anything."

Ben frowned. "Bit risky, isn't it?"

"Which is why our little genius here has been given an air-gapped server to play with." She gave Danny a quick smile.

"Good idea." Ben tugged at his earlobe thoughtfully. "Mind if I tag along?"

"You sure you shouldn't get a kip?" Danny asked, frowning. "You look like you're about to keel over."

Ben waved a hand. "I'm fine."

"Don't you have your expanded search parameters...?" Sabine inquired.

"It'll take all of five minutes, and the outline needs to be given to the whole team. I'm not going to explain it multiple times." He rubbed at one eye and hastily dropped his hand. "I won't be in your way. I'm curious about this code."

Danny and Sabine exchanged glances. "If you don't mind, I don't see why not," she replied.

Danny tried to hide his grin. Demonstrating his skills for Ben Sanders sounded like a much better way to spend the morning. "Go on, then. Maybe you'll spot something I don't when we start removing it."

Ben's expression brightened as they headed for the lift. "Give me ten minutes to drop off the battery cores in the lab; then I'll join you." He frowned as the doors closed. "Actually, where will you be? I'm assuming the server won't be in Danny's workroom."

"Fifth floor, room seventeen," Sabine replied with a smile. "Can't have you getting lost."

When they got out of the lift, Ben continued up a couple of levels.

"Is it me," Danny said to Sabine as they headed towards room seventeen, "or does he look like shit?"

Sabine nodded, her pompom bobbing precariously. "He doesn't look like he slept much."

"Peely-wally too," Danny said, frowning. "Do you think he's coming down with something?"

"As long as he keeps it to himself." Sabine skimmed her hand over the security panel and typed a complicated code in. The door slid open, and the coolness of the room made Danny grateful he hadn't bothered to take his jacket off. "My God, it's cold!"

"Servers can run hot," Danny said as he tucked his hat and gloves into his pocket. "This one, probably not so much since it's not being used by anyone but us, but they're taking all precautions, just in case."

The only objects in the room were the server and the workstation connected to it, plus a chair for each of them.

As the computer powered up, Danny settled into the seat and rubbed his hands together. "You know, there's only one small flaw with our otherwise brilliant plan here."

"Oh?"

"Mm. If the person who set up the server is our culprit, they might have rigged it." He looked up at Sabine with a sunny grin. "We might be blown to kingdom come."

She narrowed her eyes like a pissed-off cat. "And you tell me this after I commute for an hour to get here in time?" He started laughing, and she smacked him on the arm. "You think I'm an amateur? I told them we were trialling updates. No one else knows what we're doing."

He chuckled. "Sorry. I forgot you're the professional here."

"Damn right." She folded her arms sternly, but her twitching lips gave her away. "You get set up. I'm going to run up to my office and make sure I didn't miss anything in the meeting last night."

Danny studied the screen, then expanded the projections up across the wall. "Does this place have cameras?"

"Yes. Why?"

Danny glanced over his shoulder. "In case anything happens too fast for me to catch it all. If we can track the whole thing on camera, then at least I can go back through it if it does fry the computer and take all the data with it."

"I'll set it up. Don't wander off."

In the end, Ben got back to the room before Sabine. He looked worse than he had fifteen minutes earlier. Danny nudged the second seat towards him.

"You look like you should be tucked up with a bowl of chicken soup or something."

Ben smiled wanly. "You should see the other guy." He sat down, pressed his fists to his thighs, and took a few slow breaths.

Danny eyed him. "Ben, seriously..."

"I'm okay," Ben insisted, looking anything but. "Need to be here. All hands on deck." He tried to sit up straighter, but it was too much, and he hunched over again, pressing one hand to his stomach. He must have noticed Danny's doubtful expression. "Stomach ache. Nothing serious."

Both of them turned in their chairs when the door opened again.

"Sabine, are you his boss?" Danny asked, jerking his thumb towards Ben.

"Not technically, no. Why?"

"Someone needs to send him to bed without any supper."

Ben made a face. "Sod off." He looked up at the projection on the wall. "So what are we doing? You said you were going to remove the corrupted code?"

Danny darted his hands over the console. "There's an obfuscated subroutine running underneath the corrupted code," he explained. "It doesn't look like it's linked to the code itself, but the fact that it showed up on the same day makes me suspicious, and I want to see what happens if I try and remove the more visible part."

"Obfuscated subroutine?" Ben gaped at him.

"Mm." Danny shot a grin at him. "I've got a copy in my workroom if you want to see it later. It's pretty clever. I almost missed it."

"How did you find it?"

"Luck. Too little sleep. Too much sleep. Dreaming this fucking code until I could write it backwards on my pillows in drool." Danny shrugged. "Call me a digital archaeologist. I keep on poking around until I find something shiny."

Ben turned in the chair to look up at Sabine. "Where did they dig this guy up?"

"Don't ask me," Sabine replied. "I only supervise him."

Danny grinned at the wall of projections. "Everyone needs a hobby. I made mine my living."

It took him a few minutes to get the system set up and ready to go. Neither of his companions were talking as they watched him, until he glanced at them, fingers hovering over the glowing keys.

"Shall we?"

Sabine looked nervous but eager. "Let's do it."

He'd decided to start with the most recent additions to the main code, which seemed to be the simplest parts. They definitely hadn't been woven as deeply into the system's coding, which meant they were easier to dismantle.

Nothing happened.

He let out a breath he hadn't even realised he was holding in a frustrated huff. "Right."

"Anything?" Sabine asked.

He shook his head, reaching out to try again when there was a painful groan from alongside him. He turned, startled, to see Ben double over, both fists pressed against his stomach. He'd gone white as a sheet, his whole body shuddering, and then he heaved and threw up all over the floor.

"Shit!" Danny grabbed for his shoulder to keep him from falling. "Sabine! Bucket!"

The trouble with being in a server room was a distinct lack of bucket. Sabine raced out of the room as Danny tried his best to hold Ben steady. Ben clutched at his stomach with a groan.

"D'you want medical?" Danny asked, his arm around Ben's shaking shoulders.

Ben waved a hand dismissively, then gagged and doubled over again. Strings of vomit were trailing from his pale lips.

Danny turned with relief when Sabine rushed back in, a bucket—which was probably pointless now—and a tumbler of water in her hands. Ben grabbed the proffered bucket and ducked his face over it.

Danny risked a quick glance up at the code all over the walls. Or the unravelling mess formerly known as beautifully manipulated code.

"Oh bollocks..."

"What is it?" Sabine demanded. She had a hand on Ben's shoulder and looked almost as pale as him.

"Whatever was meant to happen did," Danny said, waving towards the array of projections. At least they'd planned in advance and had the cameras recording everything. A puking Ben hadn't been one of the factors in his equation for missing what happened. He glanced back at Ben. "You okay in there?"

Ben gratefully accepted the glass of water from Sabine. He sipped at it cautiously, as if he expected to bring the water straight back up, but the worst seemed to be over. Danny could see colour returning to Ben's face. "Ugh. Not good."

Danny snorted. "Understatement." He looked Ben up and down. "Told you you should be home in bed."

Ben wrinkled his nose and took another cautious sip. "Might do that." He winced when his stomach growled. "Sorry. Your tests. I got in the way."

"Never mind the tests," Sabine said, patting his shoulder. "The important thing is you're all right."

Danny tried to look on the bright side. They had the footage, and whatever it had been designed to do, it was apparently doing. "Worst comes to worst, we can prep another server overnight and run it again tomorrow." He heard the gurgle from Ben's belly again. "How about we get you to the canteen and get some crackers or toast or something into you, then get you home?"

He wasn't surprised when Ben didn't argue and got unsteadily to his feet. Danny slipped a hand under Ben's arm to support him when his legs shook and the colour drained from his face again, then darted a look at Sabine.

"I'll see if the cleaners are about," she said.

It took ten minutes for them to get down to the canteen. Danny kept a firm grip on Ben in case he stumbled. It was only luck that Ben hadn't thrown up all over himself, even managing to avoid splattering his trousers.

"You sure you don't want to stay in H-block?"

Ben shook his head. "Not if it's contagious," he said hoarsely.

"Point." Danny helped him to a seat, then ducked into the canteen kitchen to scrub his hands in the handbasin. By the time he returned with some plain toast and a cup of peppermint tea, Ben looked a little brighter.

"Maybe something you ate?" Danny suggested, watching him with concern as he nibbled the toast.

"Mm." It took him some time, and, eventually, he pushed away the plate, half-eaten. "No more."

"Better than nothing." Danny offered a hand to pull him up. "D'you have a pod with you?"

"In the transport bay." Ben leaned on his arm. "I'll set the destination and sleep all the way home." He paused and looked back at the kitchen. "Can you steal me a basin? I'm not paying for a full service and clean of my pod if I relapse."

"Ugh. Aye. Not the best plan." Danny ducked back into the kitchen and grabbed the nearest available basin-shaped vessel. It turned out to be a large soup pan, deep enough fit a grown man's head. "And look," Danny said, waving it. "It's got convenient handles."

Ben smiled wanly. "That'll have to do."

It took another fifteen minutes to get Ben's bag and coat and get him out of the building, down into the transport hub, and safely into the shuttle. "You sure you don't need company all the way over? What if you pass out on the shuttle?"

"I'll be fine," Ben assured him. "I'm feeling better." He squeezed Danny's arm. "Can you do me a favour?"

"Of course."

Ben smiled faintly at him. "I know Lysander's going to be stressed out of his mind the next few days. Tell him I'm sorry, yeah?"

"I think he'll understand," Danny snorted, "especially since you puked all over the place."

"Still..."

"I will." Danny stepped back. "Now sod off and get some rest, all right?"

He waited on the platform until the shuttle disappeared into the tunnel, then headed back up to the room to rejoin Sabine. Thankfully, she'd found some cleaner somewhere, and while he could still smell a faint lingering scent of vomit in the air, the mess was cleared up.

"How is he?"

"Going home to rest," Danny replied. He looked up at the projections, which were still unravelling like a badly knitted jumper. "Please tell me you got the cameras on."

"Three, all focussed on the projections," she replied. "It's a good thing you thought to ask for them."

Danny sat back down to watch the code. "I don't think Lysander'd be pleased if we had to delay, especially with the press conference you mentioned." He didn't look back at her, but he heard her sigh. "They're making a formal statement, then?"

"It's reached that point," she agreed. "If we can have this out of the way, it would give them less things to worry about."

Danny had suspected as much based on their conversation the previous day. "If you have stuff you need to get done, this doesn't look like it's going to be as immediate and nuclear as I expected."

"So something's happening?"

Sometimes, Danny wondered what life must be like for people who didn't see coding the same way he did. When he looked at the projections, he could see the strands of corrupted code unravelling from the main code, but to Sabine, it probably looked like a mess of letters and numbers and symbols she didn't understand. Probably like a non-musician seeing a mess of dots and lines where a professional saw music.

"It looks like we were right about it deleting the code," he said, pointing at the changing sections of the code. "I can't see any damage so far, but it's going slower than I expected. I'll keep an eye on it in case it has any nasty surprises in store."

"How long do you think it'll take?"

Danny could only wave one hand vaguely. "Maybe minutes, maybe hours. Could even be days. Since I don't know what the end result is meant to be, I can't really predict anything."

"I'll drop by in an hour or two, then." She paused by the door. "If there's anything you think I should know, I'll have my Leaf to hand."

Once she left, Danny pulled the second chair around in front of him, propped his feet up on it, and made himself comfortable. With a little classical music on in the background, he settled down to watch the code unfurling.

Chapter Thirty-Eight

THE PRESS CONFERENCE was being broadcast from a studio in the city centre.

Every staff member in the TRI knew about it. Lysander suspected the majority of them would be watching it because everyone wanted to bear witness to a seismic shift in their landscape. The new NDAs had been issued the day before. Everyone knew things were about to change.

For once, his office was a refuge.

All meetings had been cancelled during the press conference, and the phone lines—internal and external—had been shut off for the duration. It was quiet with no demands for instructions or advice about a thousand and one little problems magnified in the wake of Enoch's arrival.

Lysander wrapped one hand around his cup of tea, letting the warmth seep through his skin, as Jacob walked onto the podium. The speech, a carefully constructed tissue of information and omissions, gave enough information without providing too much detail.

Jacob had been right to volunteer as the spokesman. Without any visible effort, he exuded confidence and calm. His deep, melodious voice had a note of authority that made people pay attention. He explained what they knew, underlined what they didn't, and detailed what they intended to do in the forthcoming days.

Lysander set one elbow on the arm of the chair, his chin resting against his knuckles as he watched. Somehow, without seeming evasive, Jacob managed to avoid the trickier questions about what they were going to do with their visitor and whether the press would get access to this historic figure. He did it all so smoothly, indicating that until the new arrival was settled and understood his circumstances, no decisions could or would be made.

Jacob knew what he was doing, and it showed. As Lysander watched, he knew he would have been out of his depth if he had tried to do it himself. Meetings with heads of states or diplomatic envoys were a walk in the park compared to an on-the-spot Q&A session with the press.

Lysander's tea had long since gone cold, and Jacob was still taking questions when Fana chimed through.

"Yes?"

She sounded hesitant. "Mr. Nagy would like to see you, sir. He says it's better now while everyone is occupied."

Lysander sighed and pushed away his cup, knowing he'd probably used up the last of his alone time. "Send him in."

Janos Nagy stepped into the room and closed the door behind him. He was one of many long-term coders in the TRI who Lysander could recognise on sight, a tall, broad-shouldered man, a few years older than Lysander, with the gravest expression Lysander had ever seen. They had crossed paths a few times but never really spoken to each other. Nagy didn't seem like the chatty kind.

"You are not busy?"

Lysander indicated to the chair opposite him. "Only watching the press conference."

Nagy's eyes darted to the screen. "Jacob was a good choice."

"But I don't think you've come here to discuss Jacob."

Nagy sat and folded his hands together. He had a prosthetic left arm, but Lysander had never deemed it necessary to ask what had happened. A man's body was his own business after all. Nagy looked nervous, which was unsettling on the face of a man who always seemed stoic. "I hear we are keeping the young man from the gate?"

"Unfortunately, we have no choice." Lysander tried to keep his voice even. "We can't find his origin point or timeline, so there's no way he can be put back."

Nagy licked his lips, his face unusually pale. "I can help with him."

"No offence, Mr. Nagy, but I don't see how a coding expert can help..." Lysander trailed off, staring at the impossibility sitting across the desk from him. The realisation felt like being hit by a bucket of ice water. "You're the one Mariam and Jacob told me about?"

Nagy nodded, and now that he knew to look, Lysander could see the stark fear in his eyes. "I know I could be in trouble." Despite the calmness of his voice, Lysander heard the tremor, and Janos's hands were clenched so tightly around one another that his knuckles were bone-white. "I know this. But this boy, he needs all the help you can give him. I can help you to help him."

"When?" Lysander felt like someone else was speaking for him. "When were you from?"

Nagy met his eyes. "Nineteen forty-three."

It was crazy. Crazy and impossible. Janos Nagy had been on the TRI staff for more than twenty years, and for most of those years, he'd been one of their primary technical staff and coders. The idea that he came from a time well before computers and had been born before Lysander's grandparents, was too big a thought to wrap his head around.

"Right." He tried to find words, but none were coming. "Right."

They sat in silence for several minutes.

"Maybe this is not a good time." Nagy shifted self-consciously on the seat.

Lysander shocked himself by laughing. "I don't think I've got any good times scheduled for the next month." It came out sharpened on the edge of weeks of exhaustion and frustration. He passed a hand over his eyes. "Sorry. It's...yeah...it's not great right now."

Nagy rubbed his hands slowly together. "I'll make a list for you to help the boy. Things to make the change easier for him. Things you might not think about."

"You—" It felt nuts saying it. "You're from two hundred years after him."

"Yes," Nagy agreed, "but before electricity in all places and toilets inside of houses and walls of glass. There are many things I feared when I came. If my list can be used to help him, then it would be better for him." He smiled tentatively. "I would not want it to be difficult."

Lysander stared at him numbly. Sure. Why not? Get advice from the man born a century ago about how to help a man born two centuries earlier. Totally normal thing to do. He realised he was staring at Nagy and forced himself to look away.

"I never realised," he said. "I mean, that you weren't born in this era."

Janos laughed, a little sadly. "No. I don't make a big show of it. I live here now. I have my husband and my home." He fell silent for so long Lysander glanced over to see Janos staring at his wedding ring. Janos raised his eyes. "If I am to be arrested, please tell me, so I can talk with my husband and we can... It is better so we know what is to happen."

Arrested.

Another life—two lives—could so easily be ruined.

Technically, Lysander had obligations under the laws of the TRI, but when he had no evidence and nothing but Nagy's own admission—which could easily be denied and the media were already having a field day—there wasn't any point of adding gas to an already towering inferno.

"Make your list, help where you can, and we'll say that's the end of it."

Relief flooded Nagy's face. "Truly?"

Lysander blew out an exhausted breath. "I have enough to deal with right now, Mr. Nagy. Maybe I'll look at your case in the future and we'll have a talk, but, right now, this current situation has to take priority, not some twenty-year-old incident I knew nothing about."

Nagy got up. "Thank you, Mr. O'Donohue."

Lysander waved Nagy towards the door with one hand, rubbing his brow with the other. The press conference had finished, and he wished he had the energy to go back through it and pick apart the questions, but he already had too much to do. The **PR** team could work on the questions and bring any issues to him.

He buzzed through to Fana. "Any update on Danny and Sabine's project?"

"Sabine's back in her office, if you want me to call her through."

Lysander frowned. With all the preparation and rewriting of the speech for the press conference, he hadn't had the time to check in on them. "I'll take a walk."

Sabine's office was only half a dozen doors away from his own, and she glanced up in surprise when he walked in. She looked as tired as he felt, which came as no surprise when she'd been in since before the crack of dawn. "Morning."

"I thought you and Danny would be busy?"

She gave him a tired smile. "He's still working. He told me to go and keep myself busy. I think he wanted to concentrate, and I was distracting him."

Lysander braced his hand on the back of the chair on his side of her desk. "It worked, then?"

"It's doing something," she confirmed. "He's not sure what it is yet, but he's going through it with a fine-tooth comb. It didn't exactly go smoothly, though."

"Oh?"

"Mm." She leaned back in her seat to gaze up at him. "Ben wanted to help out, but it seems he had a bout of food poisoning or something."

Lysander remembered Enoch gagging and doubling over and being helped off to a bathroom by Ben. "Was he sick?"

Sabine grimaced. "Several times. Danny managed to persuade him to go home and get some rest." She noticed his expression. "What is it?"

"He was in with Enoch yesterday," he replied, his heart sinking. "Enoch had a stomach upset as well. If Ben's been infected with whatever Enoch has, it could be some kind of historic virus."

Sabine's face fell. "Shit."

There were protocols and things Lysander knew had to be done in the face of a potential epidemic, but his brain was fried because he had just spoken to someone who lived during the Great Wars, and, God, it was taking up what little space he had left to think.

Thank God for Sabine.

"I'll get the cleaners to take any trace to medical, in case there's a contagion and they can identify it," she said, already darting her fingers across her Leaf. "I'll buzz Ben as well, see if we can't keep him confined to his own home until we can send a med team over."

Lysander nodded. "Good. You—" His heart jumped sharply. "Danny and you were both there? Do you think there's any chance of contamination?"

Sabine stared at him in dismay. "Double-shit..." She checked her Leaf screen, and the colour drained from her face as she keyed in an urgent note. "I'll let Danny know to stay put, and I'll stay in here until they check for infection."

"Only a precaution," he tried to sound reassuring. "Nothing to worry about. I'll get them to put a rush on it."

"If they don't have a sample..."

"I'll talk to them." Lysander retreated towards the door. "I'll keep you updated."

Sabine tried to smile, but it faltered. "I'll keep a bucket nearby in case."

Out in the hall, he braced a hand against the wall and tried to focus on breathing. He couldn't go to pieces again, not now when he had so much to do. His chest tightened painfully and the world narrowed around him, save the distant tap-tap of shoes on polished floor.

"Lysander?"

He blinked, forcing his head up. Fana had appeared in front of him, and he was still leaning against the wall.

"What can I do?" she asked quietly, slipping her arm through his and walking him back towards their office.

"Sabine and Danny may have been infected with something Enoch brought with him." It was if he was reading by rote. "Sabine has contacted medical. We need a rush put on it."

"I'll see to it," Fana assured him. "But you should know the calls have started. All media-related contact is being relayed to PR. Jacob is on his way back in and sent word ahead that we may need a lockdown for the next few days."

Lysander wished he didn't feel like he'd been cut away from his own body. Everything was spiralling out of control, and he needed to claw some of it back. "Once we know if Ben's contagious, we decide on the lockdown. Not before."

"Does he know?"

"Sabine said she would buzz him." He sank to sit behind his desk. "The meeting with legal..."

"In fifteen minutes, but I can tell them there will be a brief delay?"

"I'll be there." He ran a hand over his face. "Let me have ten minutes undisturbed."

It was the only peace he had for the rest of the day.

The legal meeting turned out to be a torrent of information both completely overwhelming and totally useless. Victoria laid out all the hoops they had to jump through to sort out Enoch's status and how many of those hoops were currently on fire. The larger legal community were now pitching in with arguments, suggestions, theories, and positions.

"We're drowning in it, to be frank," Victoria said, shaking her head. "It's lucky Enoch isn't in any hurry to go anywhere, because this is going to take a lot of time."

"He's a British national by birth, which should count for something."

"It would if we had evidence of birth, which is the sticking point right now." She shook her head. "Semantics are always going to come into play."

Lysander nodded, wishing he were anywhere else. "So we're no further forward?"

"Inching. The legal framework will have to be completely rewritten for...what was it we called him? We found a good term."

One of her aides piped up, "Temporally-displaced persons."

"Sounds official, doesn't it?" Victoria flashed a quick, tired smile at Lysander. "I'm about ready to take a fire extinguisher and a sledgehammer to the burning hoops if we don't get somewhere soon. This is a man's life hanging in the balance after all."

"I guess inching is better than nothing right now."

The team filed out of the conference suite, Victoria waiting until they were alone. "I'm going to be bald with stress by the end of this," she confessed. "All these years learning every new temporal law and now..." She shook her head. "Once all this is done, we're going out and getting fountain-diving pissed again."

"We swore it would only be one time," he reminded her with a rueful smile.

"In this situation," Victoria retorted with a sniff, "I think we deserve it. Drinks and sparklers, and I'm finding some beautiful young specimen and doing a tequila shot off their belly."

"You're such a sophisticated woman."

She flashed a grin at him. "You know it." She braced her hands on the table and shoved herself to her feet. "Back to the grindstone."

He took it as his cue to head back to his own office, where Jacob sat, waiting to give him a summary of the press conference from his side of things.

"Not as bad as it could have been."

"I find that hard to believe."

Jacob laughed. "Well, they didn't pull me down off the podium and hit me with cameras, so I consider it a win. We got the expected questions, and any we didn't prep for, we know to prep for next time. PR let me know they're working through the transcript."

"You pulled it off well."

"Like I said, I've been in this circus before. It's not something you forget." Jacob leaned forward, bracing one arm on the desk. "I had a chat with Fana while you were downstairs. She said Ben got sent home sick. Do you know what's going on there?"

"Possibly a stomach bug from Enoch," Lysander said. The lack of information made things worse with so much up in the air. "We're waiting on the medical results before we know if we need to bring him back in. It might be better if he's isolated at home."

"Jesus..." Jacob sank back in his chair. "It never rains, but it pours."

"Mm." Lysander rubbed at his temple. "I swear some deity is trying to keep us on our toes."

"This is beginning to feel like a theme around here." Jacob gazed at the ceiling. "I miss the days when the worst problem we had was an angry teenager demanding we look for his dad." He laughed ruefully. "Simpler times, eh?"

"All things considered," Lysander admitted, "we've been pretty lucky with how smoothly things have been running until now."

"Ha. It feels like we've had a dam of good luck, and, right now, the pressure of shit behind it is building, and we're about to see a landslide that'll engulf the small village." Jacob lifted one hand to rub at his eyes. "We're the small village in this analogy."

Lysander wanted to smile, but it didn't come. "I figured." He hesitated, then said quietly, "I had a visit this morning. A gentleman who wants to offer advice on how to help with Enoch's transition to the modern world. He thinks his...experience would help."

"Of course he did. Helpful bugger, that one." Jacob smiled. "He's a good one. Smart and far too ready to throw himself on a grenade to help others."

"You know I should report him," Lysander murmured, hating himself for saying it out loud.

"Mm. And I know you won't."

"You sound pretty confident."

Jacob nodded. "Because you're a good man too."

Lysander stared at him, wondering if being a good man was why he felt so wrung out and exhausted and why he cared so damned much about everything that was happening. "I think," he said quietly, looking away from Jacob, "I'd like to be less good and more...anything else right now."

"And that," Jacob said sympathetically, "is the burden of a good man."

Chapter Thirty-Nine

DANNY HAD NEVER possibly maybe had the plague before.

It was amazing how much it concentrated the mind.

All right, maybe *not* the plague, but definitely possibly maybe some illness from a period not too long after the plague. Sabine had let him know and advised him to stay closed up until the medical team could provide confirmation. If Ben's puking was anything to go by, the next twenty-four hours weren't going to be pleasant.

On top of that, if he got sick, he wouldn't be of use to anyone, so the best thing to do was work as hard and fast as he could. He kept his full attention on the puzzle spread over the walls in front of him.

The coding hadn't done anything of things he'd predicted. He'd expected either immediate deletion of the manipulated code or some system-destroying superbug. Instead, all it seemed to do was slowly unravel everything that had been added in by their mysterious coder. It reminded him of his nana when she frogged and rewound her knitting wool, drawing each strand out of the knot one at a time.

He couldn't see any reason for it to go so slowly.

While the program continued to run, he checked every variable he could think of: memory usage, interference with the original system code, transfer speed, the capacity of the computer. The only thing that really jumped out was the memory output. No one looking at it would've guessed it was currently fragmenting a massive piece of code.

It didn't make sense. It could have been wiped in minutes. No one would booby-trap their own corrupted code with a self-delete function that took hours, especially not a process that could be started with a single keystroke. It jarred—the speed of the activation and the slowness of the erasure.

If it had been planting some kind of dirty bomb in the system under the guise of deletion, then might have made sense. But even with the walls plastered with more information than he should feasibly be able to take in, he couldn't see anything out of the ordinary.

Minute by minute, hour by hour, there were no new developments, and, still, it unwound.

Food had been delivered at some point—along with something generously called a potty—and he knew he had looked away from the walls and eaten at some point, but the system had his focus, and it was starting to piss him off how stupid it all was.

It was ridiculous, the whole thing. A code designed to be found but which did nothing, being erased in drips and drabs by another kind of much more invisible code, the only purpose of which seemed to be to delete the first code in slow motion.

Danny pressed the heels of his hands to his eyes. He'd ended up sitting on the floor, his elbows propped on his knees, and was about ready to find a window and toss the computer and server and everything out of it. It was almost done, and part of him vainly held out hope for some kind of booby trap or *something* to make hours of sitting and waiting worth it.

He lowered one hand to see the last of the corrupted code and the traces of the hidden subroutine erase themselves from the mirrored system.

"Fuck!" He kicked the chair in front of him. "Fuckity fuckbuckets!"

With effort, knees stiff from inaction, he got to his feet and stumbled to the console to double-check.

Not a trace. Not a bloody buggering sodding fucking trace of either of them anywhere. No dirty bomb. No clues. No nothing. He dropped into one of the chairs and rested an elbow on the edge of the workstation, pressing his face into his hand.

Positives. Right. There had to be at least one of those. Like… like…like the fact the code wasn't malignant. It hadn't been installed to destroy the system or anything. Which meant…

Which meant what? Experimentation? Distraction? Diversion? Someone bored in the coding department wanting to test their limits? Someone—maybe Mack?—playing with the system because he knew no one suspected him?

The door slid open and he glanced over his shoulder.

Lysander was standing in the doorway, pale with exhaustion.

For the first time in hours, Danny remembered why he'd been stuck with a bowl for a loo behind locked doors. "Is it the plague?" he asked, startled at the raspiness of his voice.

Lysander shook his head as he stepped into the room and shut the door behind him. "You're in the clear."

Danny wiggled one thumb up. "Yay." He waved at the screens. "Got nowhere here." He exhaled and let his head fall forward. "It's not meant to destroy the system. It's deleted the lot, but I'm buggered if I know why."

Cool fingertips touched the back of his neck. "Danny."

Danny lifted his head to look up at Lysander. "Aye?"

"Enough for today." Lysander managed a brittle smile. "You're not sick. There's no virus. They're still doing some checks, but you and Sabine have been cleared."

Danny felt like a grade A muppet. While he'd been burying his head in the code, Lysander had to deal with the news of a possible contagion, as well as juggling the TRI's current series of disasters.

"I'm not," he agreed, turning on the seat to wrap his arm under Lysander's bum and pull him a step closer. "Dinner?"

Lysander slipped his hand to cradle Danny's head. "Your place?"

"Mm." Danny nuzzled his hand. "You can make up some bollocks about coming for an update about this stuff, once I've been fed and watered and pissed in something bigger than a toddler's potty."

"Give me half an hour."

Danny squeezed him around the middle. "I'll be waiting." Lysander tried to step back, and, for once, Danny restrained him, looking indignant. "Got a toll to pay for leaving me cooped up all day."

Lysander looked so tired and confused that Danny regretted it at once. "What?"

Danny pointed to his lips. "Pay the toll."

It earned him a small smile as Lysander leaned down and deliberately kissed him on the forehead. "I don't have any change," he said and stepped back out of Danny's embrace. "I'll be sure to bring some to dinner."

"You'd better." Danny unfolded from his chair and stretched, feeling marginally less useless. Even if his day's work had provided more questions than answers, at least he could cook them a solid meal and feel like he'd done something aside from fannying about and staring at screens all day. "What do you fancy?"

Lysander gazed at him and smiled. "I'll leave it in your hands. I don't think I have the capacity to make another decision tonight." He walked towards the door and paused. "Have you found anything I need to know about tonight?"

Danny made a face. "Sod all."

The slump in Lysander's shoulders spoke of resignation, relief, and fatigue. "Good." He opened the door. "I'll see you in half an hour." As he walked out into the corridor, he straightened up again and seemed convincingly calm and confident if one didn't know the signs.

Danny approached the doorway and watched him walking away.

A relaxing night of no work, good food, and, if they weren't too tired, maybe a quick shag. Given how knackered he felt, it was a pipe dream, but, hey, a man could live in hope.

By the time Lysander showed up at his door, Danny had managed a five-minute shower, a quick tidy up, and he had a big pot of colourful risotto simmering on the hob. As soon as he opened the door, letting the savoury smell wind out into the corridor, he had to smile because Lysander's stomach growled.

"Hello to you too."

Lysander pressed one hand to his stomach. "Sorry. Long day."

"And no waiter?" Danny guessed.

Lysander stepped into the flat. "Fana took it upon herself to play your substitute between all the meetings." He pushed the door closed behind him and hesitated, looking Danny over.

Well, Danny thought, as he stepped forward and wrapped Lysander up in a bear hug, he wasn't known for being a cuddle-monster for no reason. Lysander relaxed into his embrace, curling his arms around Danny's waist and holding on.

"Bad day?" Danny murmured against his ear.

"I thought you might be ill." Lysander's voice was muffled against Danny's shoulder. "I was worried."

Danny lifted a hand to smooth Lysander's hair. "Y'don't need to worry about me, you daftie."

Warm air puffed against his neck, almost but not quite a laugh. "Too late." Lysander took a deep breath and released it, then loosened his arms enough to lean back and look Danny in the eye. "Of course, I'm going to worry about you."

It would have been rude not to kiss him, and they only broke apart when Danny heard a hiss from the stove and the scent in the air changed.

"Shit!" he yelped, racing back across the room and grabbing the pan off the hob. He stirred up the rice and winced at the thick layer clinging to the bottom. It hadn't burned, thank Christ.

Lysander followed, laughing quietly. "Will it survive?"

"Aye." Danny shot a stern glare at him. "No thanks to you being all distracting."

Lysander sat on one of the chairs at the table. "Now you know how I felt today."

Danny waved the spoon at him. "Semantics." He served up a bowl of creamy risotto for each of them. "What about Ben? Did you hear from him?"

Lysander accepted one of the bowls. "He left a message saying he felt better but probably going to sleep through till Tuesday."

Danny was unsurprised. "He looked like shit." He considered the pitcher of water on the table. "I can't wait to go out and get hammered when this is all over."

Lysander's lips twitched. "'This' didn't stop you before."

Danny snorted. "Well, aye, but technically, I considered it an officially sanctioned day out."

Lysander stirred the risotto with his fork. "Vic probably wouldn't mind if you came out with us." He must have noticed the confusion on Danny's face. "Victoria Cheung. She works in legal, and for some reason, everyone thinks she's as terrifying as I am."

"There's two of you?" Danny feigned horror. "One's bad enough." He chewed a mouthful of risotto thoughtfully and couldn't resist inquiring, "Is she fit? You know I have a type."

Lysander, to his surprise, actually burst out laughing. He pressed the back of his fingers to his lips and waved his other hand, shaking his head. "No," he managed to gasp out. "God, no. Yes, she's good-looking, but believe me, you don't want to go there. She would eat you alive and spit out the bones."

Danny eyed him. "And this is the friend you socialise with?"

Lysander nodded, still laughing. It had stripped a mass of tension from his face. "I think I'm giving you a bad impression. You're too nice for her. She doesn't do cuddles or sentiments or home-cooked meals. Definitely not your type."

Danny suspected his cheeks were going red again. He hadn't been called nice very often. "Like you well enough anyway," he said with a sniff and dug into his food.

A foot brushed his under the table, and he raised his eyes to Lysander's face. Lysander smiled as he stirred his risotto again. "I like you too."

By the time the bowls were empty, Lysander kept looking reluctantly towards the door.

"I should go back to my place and get some rest."

Danny collected the bowls and carried them over to the kitchen. "I've got a nice big bed," he reminded Lysander. "Plenty of space. I've got a tub if you fancy a bath or anything."

"Are you asking me to stay?"

Danny smiled down into the sink as he rinsed the dishes under the hot tap. "Nah. I'm saying you'd be welcome if you wanted to, but I'm not about to put any pressure on you by asking." He wasn't surprised when Lysander appeared at his side. He was even less surprised when Lysander drew him around and kissed him. "My hands are wet," he warned.

"I don't think it's going to matter right now." Lysander undid the buttons of Danny's shirt one by one.

Danny gazed at him with amusement. "That's not getting some rest."

"You want me to rest?" Lysander's midnight eyes met his. "Distract me first."

Danny shook his hands dry as best he could and sighed. "It's all work with you, isn't it?" Before Lysander could open his mouth to reply, Danny ducked down and slid both arms under Lysander's arse. He hoisted Lysander up off the ground, making Lysander clutch at him and exclaim in indignation.

"What's this?"

Danny grinned at him as he carried him in the direction of the bedroom. "A very thorough distracting."

Lysander tried his best to feign annoyance, though his hands were kneading at Danny's shoulders. Colour flared across his cheeks. "I didn't say anything about manhandling me."

"Could be worse," Danny said, laughing. "I could have done a fireman's lift like I wanted to before." He paused at the end of the bed, then opened his arms and let Lysander drop to land with a bounce on the mattress.

Lysander leaned back on his elbows and raised his eyebrows in challenge. "Happy now?"

Danny took a moment to admire his lover, reclined there like a king waiting to be paid homage. Lysander gazed up at him between his dark lashes, then pointedly nudged Danny's hip with a foot.

"I'm not a spectator sport."

"I don't know." Danny braced his knee on the edge of the mattress and leaned over him. "I'd buy a ticket." He propped himself over Lysander. "What do you fancy?"

In reply, Lysander resumed unbuttoning Danny's shirt. He spread it open and ran his hand down Danny's belly, and Danny—a wee bit smugly, to be fair—flexed every muscle he could. Lysander's fingers lingered over his still-fuzzy but newly rediscovered six pack. He smiled up at Danny. "You've been busy."

"Sabine's a very strict supervisor," Danny said, struggling to keep his face straight. "You should see the rest."

Lysander pressed the tip of his tongue to his front teeth. "Okay." He pushed a hand against Danny's chest. "Show me what you've got."

Well, Danny never minded taking his clothes off in front of people before. He shoved himself onto his feet. "Professional-like?"

Lysander's eyes gleamed. "If you can."

"You've seen me dancing, right?"

"Mm."

"Then you know this isn't going to end well..."

Lysander laughed. "Indulge me?" He flicked out his Leaf and put on some daft sexy wee tune.

The first few steps went all right. A bit of arse wiggling and shimmying the shirt off his shoulders in time to the music was easy enough. Then the bloody sleeves got caught on his wrists. He flailed his arms to free them, flapping one free at a time.

Lysander didn't help matters, pressing his knuckles to his mouth, his shoulders shaking.

"Shut it," Danny said, laughing as he struggled with his belt. "You asked for sexy naked me. This is as sexy as I get."

Lysander lowered his hand, his lips twitching. "Having trouble?"

Danny snorted. "This isn't as easy as it looks."

Lysander pushed himself towards the edge of the bed. "Come here."

He caught Danny's belt and made fast work of the buckle and fastenings of his trousers. When he met Danny's eyes, his expression nearly stole Danny's breath away. He nuzzled the taut muscles of Danny's belly as he pushed Danny's trousers down over thighs and knees to his ankles, then lipped at Danny's cock, straining against his shorts.

Danny sank his fingers into Lysander's hair. "What do you fancy?" he asked unsteadily.

For a few seconds, Lysander looked up at him, and then he dragged Danny's shorts down and dropped them to his feet. "I want you on your back on the bed." His voice was as uneven as Danny's.

Danny kicked his trousers and shorts off his feet, scrambled onto the bed, and starfished gracelessly across the covers. "Like this?"

To his surprise, Lysander got up and stood there, gazing down at him. It felt like their first night together again, Danny buck-naked and Lysander still fully dressed at the foot of the bed. Danny couldn't help noticing the way he licked his lips.

Danny leaned up on his elbows. "You all right?"

"Do you have lube?" Lysander asked.

"Naturally." Danny rolled over and groped in the bedside cabinet, pulling out a couple of tubes as well as a condom, which he tossed to the foot of the bed. He imitated Lysander's earlier stance and stretched out a leg to poke Lysander's thigh. "I'm feeling a bit exposed here, Mr. Spectator Sport."

The daft sexy music was still playing. Lysander didn't switch it off. From the expression on his face, he didn't notice it. His eyes were fixed on Danny's as he loosened his tie and drew it off, trailing it through his fingers.

"Fuck..." Danny breathed as Lysander slipped each button of his shirt undone. His cufflinks pinged off the floor where he dropped them, and with one smooth shrug, his shirt dropped off his shoulders, slithered down his arms, and fell to the floor.

His trousers followed until he was standing there in nothing but his shorts. Danny's heart was in his mouth, his cock hard and throbbing, but he would have needed to be blind not to see the way Lysander hesitated with his thumbs hooked into the waistband of his shorts.

"Want me sunny side up?" Danny suggested.

Lysander's smile creased new lines around his eyes. "I'm good," he said and pushed his shorts down.

Danny couldn't help giving him a thorough once-over since Lysander was willing to let him. Fuck, he was good-looking, lean without being too thin, dark hair scattered on his arms, torso and thighs, with a fine trail leading down his belly to his cock.

Lysander knelt on the edge of the bed and crawled towards him, grabbing the lube as he came. His eyes met Danny's, and they were gleaming with desire. Danny was still propped up on his elbows, and when Lysander dipped his head to kiss him, Danny craned his neck demandingly.

Lysander laughed and pulled back. "Patience is a virtue."

"Sod that," Danny protested, reaching for Lysander.

Lysander caught his wrist. "Ah, ah." He gently but firmly pinned Danny's hand down by his side, bracing himself over Danny, their bodies so close Danny swore he could feel Lysander's heart beating against his chest. "Best behaviour if you want me to play."

"Oh come on!" Danny groaned, then hissed when Lysander sucked sharply on Danny's throat, enough to send bolts of fire through him and make his hips jerk instinctively. "I had a long day!"

Lysander smiled against his throat. "You're not the only one. Now, let me know if this is okay…"

"Wh—fuck! You git!"

Lysander laughed, removing his bloody cold hand from Danny's cock. "Maybe it needs warming up." He drew his hand up to trace a finger along Danny's lips. "Want to help?"

Danny nibbled his fingertip. "What do I get?"

Lysander brushed his lips against Danny's again, his fingertips caught between them. "A surprise. A restful one."

Danny had already enjoyed plenty of Lysander's surprises, and, hell, a sex one wasn't about to be turned down. He sucked on the tip of Lysander's finger, enjoying the heat in Lysander's eyes as he slowly started to thrust one cool finger and then another into Danny's mouth. They were replaced with a third, then Lysander's thumb. Danny remembered that look when he'd had his mouth around Lysander's cock, and Christ, it made him ache. Maybe he wasn't allowed to touch Lysander but…

Lysander's warm, wet fingers wrapped around his wrist, pinning his arm down again. "You're really not behaving today, are you?"

"I'm sleepy and horny and there's a gorgeous man being all sexy at me and I can't do anything," Danny grumbled mournfully.

Lysander gazed at him and kissed him chastely on the lips. At the same time, those newly warmed, wet fingers wrapped around Danny's cock and stroked a couple of times, the grip enough to make his hips jerk and his head press back against the pillow.

"Fuck a duck!"

Lysander dissolved into helpless laughter, burying his face in Danny's shoulder. "You're such an ass." He propped himself up over Danny and smiled. "Now, I need you to do something for me."

Danny was trying very hard to focus on Lysander and ignore the firmly stroking hand on his cock. "Aye?"

Lysander tightened his grip and stilled his hand. "Close your eyes." Mischief shone in his eyes. "I want to give you your surprise."

Danny hummed suspiciously but closed his eyes. "If this is when you get dressed and run away after taking compromising photos, I'll never speak to you ag-aaaaaaaah!"

Lysander lifted his mouth from Danny's cock. "Too cold?" he inquired innocently.

"Git!" Danny pressed his head against the pillows. "Jesus. You're trying to kill me!"

"But what a way to go, huh?" Lysander sounded amused and pleased. A few seconds later, Lysander stroked his cock from tip to balls, fingers tightening around him, and ran his thumb in a circle around the head. It wasn't as if Danny needed help getting harder, but he wasn't about to complain.

"Maybe a bit tighter?" he suggested, trying to push against Lysander's palm.

"Not yet," he murmured. A rustle, then Danny jolted in surprise when Lysander rolled the condom onto his cock, followed by the snap of the seal on the lube being popped. Jesus! *Definitely* not where he'd seen the evening going.

"What—?"

Lysander was smiling, Danny could hear it in his voice. "Wait..." Lysander caressed Danny's sheathed cock again with firm, long strokes, leaving him slick all over. When Lysander loosened his grip, Danny groaned as his pulse throbbed in his cock.

The bed shifted under him, and Danny's heartbeat picked up when Lysander's knees settled on either side of him.

"Lysander..."

Fingertips pressed to his lips, and the second hand was on his cock, holding him steady. He had a rush of awe and affection when Lysander's arse pressed against him, and his own breath caught when Lysander sank onto his cock. Lysander breathed out hard, and both his hands moved to press to Danny's chest.

"Surprise..."

"Can I...?"

"Open your eyes?" Lysander slid his hands up Danny's chest, bracing himself over him. "Yes."

Danny obeyed and looked up at his lover. A flush had spread across Lysander's face, and he wore a gorgeous shit-eating smile as he slowly rocked his hips down against Danny's, making Danny's breath hitch all over again. "Fuck me..." Danny whispered, clutching at Lysander's thighs.

"Working on it."

Danny laughed raggedly. "Git..."

"Mm." Lysander stooped low enough to bring their lips within touching distance but held himself there, rocking his hips. His erect cock ground against Danny's belly, and he bared his teeth, his hands kneading at Danny's chest.

Danny's words were gone. He slid his palms up Lysander's thighs to his hips, over to his arse. His own hips were moving without thought, and he squeezed Lysander's arse. More. He wanted more. Faster. All of it. Lysander laughed, soft and warm against his lips, and started moving faster.

Danny arched up, hissing through his teeth, trying to catch Lysander's lips, trying to steal his breath and make him feel all fucking amazing. It only made Lysander laugh again and rear up, tossing his head and sinking all the way down on Danny's cock.

Danny stared up at him, dazed and so fucking close already. Blood rushed through him, throbbing down to his cock like it was the centre of the world, and Lysander kept riding him so fucking hard. He rocked his hips up against Lysander's and dragged one of his hands around to catch Lysander's cock. He knew exactly where to touch to make Lysander shudder with pleasure, and he swore to Christ Lysander's heartbeat was thundering as hard as his own and his words were gone and he squeezed Lysander's cock and the sharp, demanding sound Lysander made went straight to Danny's cock and his hips were jerking and hard and Lysander was leaning on his chest, staring at him hungry and demanding. No words, just riding Danny until Danny—no breath, no words, no thoughts—bucked against him, coming hard.

He sagged against the covers, and the hand on Lysander's arse fell away. Not his cock, though. They weren't done yet, not by half.

Lysander sat up over him, smug as a pig in shit, and lazily started rocking his hips again, sending off fresh sparks from Danny's spent cock. Danny groaned, shifting his hand and finding the angle to make Lysander jerk against his palm.

"You are so fucking hot right now..." Danny rasped hoarsely. "Christ, how the fuck do you do that?"

Lysander dragged his fingers against Danny's chest. There'd be marks come morning. "You like this, huh?" He moved more slowly, grinding against Danny's hand. A gorgeous heat flushed his face, strands of his hair clinging to his cheeks. His breath hitched when Danny shifted his grip, and he ducked his head, kneading at Danny's belly. "Fuck."

That word, coming from him, was enough to get Danny going again. He moved his hand, a rhythmic press-grind, until Lysander's breaths hissed between his teeth, and then he gave an explosive gasp and shuddered over him, his fists pressing so hard against Danny's stomach, Danny knew he'd have bruises come morning.

Shakily, Lysander uncurled his fingers and slid his hands up Danny's chest to sprawl over him, clumsily crushing his lips to Danny's. Danny laughed against his lips and brought up his hand from Lysander's arse to smooth his sweat-slicked hair back from his cheeks.

Lysander's lips slid off Danny's, and he buried his face in Danny's throat. "Mm."

"Distracted?" Danny nuzzled his ear.

"Mm."

With a bit of effort, he managed to roll them onto their sides, Lysander already halfway to sleep, arms and legs still all around Danny. Took a bit more effort to get the condom out of the way. They both ended up a mess, covered in spilled cum and sweat, but for once, Danny couldn't find the energy to give a shit. A bit more effort got the covers on top of them instead of under them.

Danny called the lights off.

In the quiet darkness, Lysander sprawled further over him.

"Night," Danny murmured, his eyes already falling closed.

"Mm."

Chapter Forty

LYSANDER JOLTED AWAKE, sitting up when an unfamiliar alarm beeped nearby.

He squinted around, trying to get his bearings in the dark room, but then the warm body stretched out beside him reminded him where he was, especially when Danny muttered a string of profanities and groped for his alarm.

When he dropped back on the pillows, he reached out and pulled Lysander closer and planted a sleepy kiss on his crown. So comfortable and cosy, Lysander had to admit, he really wasn't ready to leave yet.

"What time is it?" he murmured, running a hand against Danny's ribs.

"Seven." Danny yawned, and his body rippled against Lysander's as he stretched. "Sleep well?"

Lysander nodded drowsily. He couldn't recall the last time he'd slept so deeply. "Wore me out." The pleasant ache lingered in his ass and thighs, and past experience told him it would linger. Too many years of playing top for everyone, publicly and privately. It had been far too long since anyone had given him a good fucking. That part was great. The dried cum spotted on his thighs, not so much. He rubbed his chin along Danny's chest. "I'm a mess."

Danny's chest vibrated under him when he laughed. "Not my fault, you lazy bugger. Didn't even get a cuddle before you went to sleep on me." He tugged a strand of Lysander's hair. "Shower's yours if you want it first. You'll have more to clean up than me, this time around."

Reluctantly, Lysander rolled away from Danny to the edge of the bed and pushed back the covers. The chill of the morning air was as effective as a bucket of ice water. He yelped when his feet touched the cold floor, and he grabbed up his scattered clothing as quickly as he could before hurrying to the bathroom.

Thankfully, the shower was wonderfully hot. It eased some of the aches in his limbs, enough to guarantee he wouldn't be waddling when he headed over to the office after breakfast.

When he emerged, braiding back his hair, the smell of coffee and toast washed over him.

"Can't break the habit of a lifetime," Danny called over cheerfully from the kitchen where he was spooning scrambled eggs onto a plate.

Lysander sat and poured a coffee for each of them. "I'm going to get used to this, and when you leave, I'll forget I don't have a waiter anymore."

"I'll send you memos." Danny laughed, carrying over two plates. "Pictures of my gorgeous breakfasts and dinners you don't get to eat anymore." He picked up a piece of toast and started buttering it. "At least I don't have to worry about the puking plague today, eh? It definitely put me off my lunch yesterday."

"Thank God," Lysander agreed fervently. "The last thing we need right now is a historic virus gone wild." He scraped some of the egg onto his toast. "You'll be back on your coding problems as usual."

"And all the new questions it's raising now." Danny sighed. "I don't know what to tell you. It's not there to interfere, and whoever set it up wanted to be able to delete it without any effort."

Lysander frowned. "You're sure?"

"Mm." Danny downed a mouthful of coffee. "I erased one part of the corrupted code and left it alone for maybe thirty seconds when Ben threw up. Next thing I know, the code is already being deleted, and I didn't need to touch it again for the rest of the day." He shook his head. "I can't work out why it took so long. I mean, if they were going to erase it, you'd think they'd want to clear it as fast as possible. But as far as I could tell, it was done to use as little capacity and memory as possible."

"So, no one wanted us to notice it being removed?" Lysander shrugged. "Maybe a fail-safe?"

Danny piled eggs onto his fork. "It doesn't make sense. It looks like they put the code there to be found. Why go to such an effort to hide its removal when you put it there to be found in the first place?"

Lysander frowned. "That is strange." He chewed pensively, then asked, "You're absolutely sure the code doesn't do anything?"

"Definitely. I checked the system twice, and once the subroutine had been triggered and the code unravelled with no trace left behind of it." Danny sighed. "I've got to tell you, riddles and puzzles are all well and good, but only when you can solve them."

Lysander shared the sentiment. Something about it all was tugging at him, something wrong about all of it, but not in the way he'd suspected. He had been expecting sabotage, but now, it had been taken off the table. Now...what?

He was still mulling on it as he finished his breakfast. "Do you think you'll be able to pinpoint a source?" he asked as he helped Danny clear the table. "If it can erase itself so cleanly, how likely do you think it'll be for the culprit to leave fingerprints?"

"I don't know," Danny said honestly. "Whoever did it is *good*. Right now, you know everything I can tell you, and I don't know if there's going to be any more."

"It's more than we knew yesterday," Lysander consoled him, though he couldn't help feeling frustrated. Sabotage was simpler. It meant finding an enemy with intent. Finding someone who seemed to be playing with the system for their own amusement wasn't so straightforward. He touched Danny's back. "Thanks. For last night."

"And you." Danny smirked at him. "For coming."

Lysander arched an eyebrow. "Very mature."

Danny laughed. "I try." He gestured to the door. "You better go and make yourself look badass. I get the feeling you'll need it today."

Lysander gestured to his half-buttoned shirt and rumpled pants. "I guess this doesn't exactly say high-flying professional, does it?"

"Nah. Dirty-stop-out chic." Danny grinned at him. "Looks good on you, mind."

"And on that note..." Lysander snatched up his jacket, stepped into his shoes, and headed for the door.

"Oh! Wait!"

Lysander turned. "Let me guess—there's a toll to leave the apartment too?"

Danny blinked. "No, actually, but I'll remember for next time. Ben asked me to pass on a message yesterday. I forgot what with the plague and the code and all the bullshit."

"A message?"

"He wanted me to tell you he was sorry." Danny gave him a crooked smile. "I told him he couldn't help it if he puked his guts up, but I think he felt bad about skipping out on such a crap day."

Lysander smiled ruefully. "Typical Ben." He raised his hand. "I'll see you when I can, but for now, good luck on the decoding."

"And you on...well...everything else."

Lysander headed out into the hall. He stopped off at his apartment on the next level. Ten minutes later, his crumpled clothes replaced with a diamond-sharp new suit and his braid coiled into a bun on the back of his head, he headed out to face the day.

The press had been busy from the looks of it. PR had left a memo for him with their first meeting scheduled for nine o'clock and second at noon to deal with the expected morning influx. They also had a meeting scheduled with legal based on some of the inquiries coming in to PR, another one with the medical team to discuss Enoch's long-standing injuries and whether they should be treated to bring him to optimum health for his life in the present, and half an hour allocated to speak to the Prime Minister, though *which* Prime Minister wasn't specified and...

He pressed his forefinger and thumb to his eyelids.

When all of this was done with, he needed a holiday.

He ran his hand over his face and settled in his chair to skim through the PR memo before the first meeting of the day. Sabine opened the door and peeked in fifteen minutes later.

"Do you have a minute?"

"Possibly my only one left today," Lysander replied, motioning for her to come in. "Is something up?"

Sabine sat and folded and then unfolded her hands, unusually nervous. "I wanted to let you know you don't need to worry about the footage."

Lysander shook his head, confused. "What footage?"

She glanced at her hands, then back at him. "Danny asked me to record everything in the room yesterday, in case he missed anything. There were three security cameras. Two of them were solely focussed on the code. One of them...wasn't."

For a second, he didn't understand, and then he remembered Danny's arms around his hips and a kiss to the forehead. Lysander closed his eyes. "Shit."

"I stopped the recording at the point when Danny finished with the code," she said quickly. "Cut the rest. Wiped it." She smiled crookedly. "Sorry. I know you probably didn't want anyone to find out."

God no. It would ruin his credibility if people found out he'd been sleeping with a contractor, even if Danny was only on a temporary secondment. Right now, if the press got hold of it, it could ruin him, not to mention the standing of the TRI.

"Not my wisest decision," he said finally. Not wisest, but definitely one of the better ones. At least it was only Sabine. Sabine knew him and had been with him all the way on his rise through the ranks.

She laughed quietly. "With everything that's going on right now, I don't blame you for finding a cute distraction." She got up. "I thought you should know since I'll be giving the footage to Danny this morning. You don't have anything to worry about, and I'll tell him the same."

Knowing Danny, he would have barrelled straight in as soon as he realised they might have been caught on camera.

"Thank you," Lysander said. "Really."

Sabine waved his words away. "I didn't do anything. No one can prove otherwise." She tilted her head towards the door. "Doctor Calvin was waiting outside when I came in. Do you want me to send him through?"

"Please." Lysander brushed aside the memos and offered the doctor a spare smile when he entered. "Our meeting isn't scheduled until later today, doctor."

Calvin hesitated. "This isn't about Mr. Baker." He approached and sat opposite Lysander. "I was concerned about Mr. Sanders's sudden illness yesterday."

"Yes, and you confirmed he was clear of any infection."

Calvin nodded. "Yes, but I wanted to check something about the samples before I raised any concern. I ran some tests overnight based on the small samples we had left." He hesitated. "I don't think Mr. Sanders was ill."

"Food-poisoning, then? Something he ate?"

Calvin shook his head. "I found a considerably high level of salt in the sample. An excessively high amount. If I were to make a guess, Mr. Sanders ingested a large quantity of saline solution—salt water—to make himself vomit."

Lysander stared at him. "What?"

"I think he deliberat—"

"Yes. I heard you." Lysander's head was spinning. "Why do you think he would do something like that? He had no reason to get himself sent..."

The realisation hit him like a truck.

"Mr. O'Donohue?"

Lysander rose from his chair, but his legs were shaking so much they nearly folded under him. "I need you to leave," he said unsteadily. Calvin frowned, puzzled, but retreated from the room. Lysander touched the console on his desk, buzzing through to Jacob's office. "My office. Now."

He stared blankly at the window, praying to God he was wrong.

"What's happened?" Jacob demanded moments later when he opened the door.

Lysander tore his gaze away from the window, feeling sick to the bottom of his stomach. "I know who was behind the corrupted code. And I think I know why."

Chapter Forty-One

"DO YOU KNOW what they want?"

Sabine shook her head as she escorted Danny from his workroom to the lift. "When Lysander is wound up like a coiled spring, you don't stop to ask questions." She stepped into the lift alongside him. "Were you getting anywhere with the footage from yesterday?"

In an hour and a half, he'd watched and rewatched the first fifteen minutes of the footage several times to see what he might have missed. So far, nothing was jumping out, but that didn't mean anything. The code and subroutine had both been buried deep. There wasn't going to be a honking great sign declaring 'I'm the bad guy!'

"I don't think I'm going to get anything out of it," he admitted. "At least not unless our culprit got sloppy."

Sabine grimaced. "And so far, they seem like they're on top of everything." She walked him down the hall to Lysander's office and paused in the reception room. For the first time since he'd arrived, Fana wasn't at her desk. "I'll be in my office if you—or any of them—need me."

Danny nodded, then headed straight to Lysander's office and touched the panel by the door.

A few seconds later, Jacob opened the door. "Come in."

As soon as he saw Lysander's face, Danny knew something must've gone very wrong. Lysander seemed like he'd aged a dozen years, his expression taut and tense.

"What's going on?" Danny asked, glancing between them.

Jacob gestured for him to take the empty seat in front of the desk. He perched on the edge of it himself, looming over Danny. "You've been dealing with this coding mess for a few weeks now. If we could find samples of coding created by a suspect in this case, we need to know if there's any way you could confirm if it was created by the same person."

Danny frowned in confusion. "What?"

"We have a suspect," Jacob said, speaking in the abrupt, clipped tones of a policeman about to charge someone. "We believe they are responsible for manipulating the code. Is there any way you can confirm it?"

Danny darted a glance at Lysander, who was staring blankly at a projection in front of him, his attention a thousand miles away. "Coding—it isn't that simple. Some people do write it in a unique way, but when it works, you don't really change it up too much." Danny returned his attention to Jacob. "I'm not sure I'd be able to pinpoint a single person."

Jacob's face didn't give much away, his cheek twitched and tensed. "Is there a remote chance you could, given samples of the suspect's work?"

It was a very slim possibility, but then it all depended on the person. "I could try," Danny hazarded, "but like I said, I'm not sure."

"Trying will have to be enough."

"Do I get to know who it is?" Danny asked.

Jacob glanced over his shoulder at Lysander, who didn't even notice. He turned back to Danny. "Well, you'll find out soon enough. Ben Sanders."

Danny couldn't stop himself from laughing. "Aye, right." Neither of the other men laughed, and he shook his head in disbelief. "You—Ben? Are you kidding?"

"We have reason to believe he's responsible."

"He can't be." Danny felt like the rug had been yanked out from under him. No wonder Lysander looked grey. Danny had only known Ben a few weeks, but Lysander had known him for years. They'd seemed like good friends when Danny had seen them together. "I mean, why?"

"That's not relevant right now. What's relevant is that you're the one who can confirm whether the corrupted code was his handiwork."

"But surely there are people who've been here longer who would know his work better than—"

"Based on all reports, you're the first person with the skill to rival him." Jacob's expression was deadly serious. "He said as much himself, and we need you now. That's your job from here."

It all felt wrong, the whole world thrown off-kilter. If this was what Lysander had been feeling like for weeks, it felt shite. Danny pushed his fingers through his hair. He was going to be responsible for proving Ben's guilt? Christ, talk about being thrown in the deep end. "I can't make any promises."

"We understand."

Danny glanced at Lysander, who still hadn't said a word. "Can I have a minute with Mr. O'Donohue?" he asked Jacob. "Professional capacity?"

"I don't know if—"

"Yes," Lysander said quietly. "Give us the room, Jacob."

As soon as Jacob closed the door behind him, Danny leaned over the desk. "You going to be okay?"

Lysander finally turned to meet his gaze. His eyes were too bright, and they were bloodshot. Up close, Danny saw the top buttons of Lysander's shirt were undone and his tie had been loosened. Lysander shook his head, his voice brittle. "I don't know."

Fuck protocol and behaving and everything.

Danny was around the desk in four steps and crouched in front of Lysander, offering his embrace. Lysander swayed into him as if he could hardly hold himself up anymore. His fingers dug painfully into Danny's back, his breathing ragged against Danny's throat. Danny didn't know what he could say to make things better or to help or anything. He rubbed his hands up and down Lysander's back, talking some bullshit about it being all right, how they'd get it all sorted out.

When he finally trailed into silence and Lysander's fingers weren't biting so deep, Danny had to ask, "Are you sure it's him?"

Lysander's chin nudged against his shoulder. "All the pieces fit." He exhaled wearily. "He wanted information on the Robertson boy. Didn't have the clearance. Thought he could get more access if we had some problem on the system. Usual protocol."

"And you brought me in instead..." Danny drew back, sitting back on his heels and looking up at his lover. "He would have been pissed if..." A memory surfaced and he groaned. "Shit. He knew, didn't he? The day he came into my room, he saw exactly what I was working on."

Lysander had one hand on Danny's shoulder as if it was the only thing holding him up. "I assumed he was being paranoid about your presence."

"And instead, the bastard knew to stop adding to the code from that day because it had already been found. Shit!" Danny caught Lysander's hand on his shoulder. "This—it makes it make sense." He could see how stunned and dazed Lysander was, how confused. "Remember I couldn't understand why the corrupted code deleted so slowly? What if it gave him a cover for looking through secure files once you upgraded his clearance? If someone asked, he could make some noise about removing it, but he could be doing anything he wanted while it ran in the background."

"Oh..."

Danny knelt up, cradling the back of Lysander's head. "We'll work it all out," he promised. "I'll do everything I can to work this out with you."

A tiny flicker of a smile darted across his lips. "I know." Lysander drew a deeper breath and sat back. "Okay. You saw him last. Did he say where he was going?"

Danny got up off the floor and sat on the edge of the desk, his knee pressing to Lysander's thigh. "Home. He had his pod waiting for him and said he wanted to sleep all the way home." He studied Lysander's face. "And he didn't get there, did he?"

Lysander shook his head. "If he did, he's not answering any comms."

"I think he might have been seeing someone," Danny offered. "I mean, I don't know, but he got a bit wound up when Mel teased him. Maybe he's staying with..." He trailed off at the look on Lysander's face. "You didn't know?"

"I'm starting to realise there's a lot I didn't know about Mr. Sanders." Lysander's voice was clipped.

"Shit." Danny studied his feet. None of it made any sense anyway. If Ben had disappeared before they suspected him of anything, what had made him run? "Why did you think he did it anyway? It's come out of left field, hasn't it?"

"The vomiting. He made himself sick."

Definitely not the action of an innocent man. But it still didn't make sense. Until he'd crossed paths with Danny and Sabine in the lobby, he hadn't had any idea about the tests they were about to run. There was nothing to implicate him anywhere.

Unless...

"There's something in the coding."

"You think so?"

Danny tapped his knuckle against his chin. "There has to be. We surprised him when we told him what we were planning. He seemed shocked when I told him about the subroutine, but I think he was shocked I'd found it." He frowned. "He had some battery cores for gate tests and said something about the security team, but when he heard what we were doing, he insisted on coming, and next thing we knew, he was throwing..." He trailed off at Lysander's expression. "What?"

"Battery cores? You're sure?"

"Aye, but I don't know what that's got to do with the code."

Lysander rose from his chair. "Nothing," he replied, his voice sharp. "But there weren't any tests scheduled using fresh cores."

"Maybe he left them somewhere?" Danny scrambled up off the desk, following Lysander to the door. "Or do you think he took—"

Lysander held up one hand to silence him as he opened the door. "Jacob, I need you to check whether Ben's been accessing vault 26 more than usual."

Jacob's expression mirrored Lysander's which could only mean serious shit was going down. He strode away, leaving Danny standing a few steps behind Lysander.

"What do you need me to do?" Danny asked, touching his shoulder.

Lysander's shoulder rose and fell beneath his hand. "I need you to get back to your room and find whatever spooked Ben so much. He's been sitting on this for months. He wouldn't cut and run unless something implicated him."

Danny nodded at once. "You know where to find me."

Christ, he thought as he stumbled back to the lift, it was a much bigger mess than he'd realised when he signed that piece of paper with all the zeroes. Betrayal, lies, manipulation, and God only knew what else. Even as a spectator on the sidelines, he could recognise a looming disaster when he saw one. Lysander had been standing in the middle of it for days, weeks even.

At least I only have one job.

Okay, yeah, technically, a nightmare of a job since Ben was a genius. It had been tricky enough to identify the main manipulations in the code, but the underlying subroutine was much harder to pick apart. It was meant to be invisible. On the other hand, he'd found it, surprising Ben, which meant Ben had cocked up somewhere, overconfidence making him sloppy.

As Lysander said, he must've left something in there that implicated him.

Danny paused for a coffee from the machine near his workroom. Whatever happened, he needed all the help he could get, starting with a sugared-up double espresso. It buzzed in his bloodstream as he entered his room. He folded his fingers, stretched his arms above his head, and cracked his knuckles.

It was going to be a long day.

Chapter Forty-Two

"THREE UNACCOUNTED FOR."

Lysander pressed his face into his hands. "Since when?"

"July's audit, it looks like," Jacob replied. "I've got the teams checking for the missing cores. It's possible one of the techs moved one to the gates and forgot to log it out. It happens."

"But three?" Lysander lowered his hands. It was taking all the self-control he had not to fall apart. It had been close, hours earlier, but Jacob had helped him through it. "It can't be coincidence."

Jacob sank into the seat opposite him. "He'll be able to power a gate now. I never thought—" He rubbed at his eyes. "I knew he was still holding out some hope for his dad, but this... I never thought he'd be so reckless."

Lysander tilted his head back against the back of his chair, gazing up at the ceiling. There were patterns in the tiles, and he let his eyes follow them until he didn't feel like retreating to the smallest corner of the room and sitting there until no one noticed him anymore.

"He started a rebellion at eighteen," he murmured, tracing a curling spiral with his eyes. "That's not someone who will ever sit quietly and wait for something to happen. And after we called off the search for his dad..."

"I'm starting to suspect those couple of years he took off weren't to take a holiday," Jacob murmured.

Lysander had to agree.

When Ben was barely twenty, he'd been under strict supervision within the TRI because of bending and breaking temporal laws. Six months after they terminated the search for his father, he took off for nearly three years. He said he'd taken time to grieve and work out what he wanted to do with himself. Now, it was beginning to look a lot like bullshit.

Lysander drew a breath and released it slowly. "Any word from Temple's people?"

"Not yet." Jacob sounded as spent as Lysander. "Last I heard, the house was empty, but if they find anything..."

"I've had security checking all the files relating to Robertson," Lysander said. "None of them have been accessed by anyone but people with clearance, so at least we know he didn't find out enough to do some real damage."

Jacob winced. "When damage might involve saving his father's life, I wonder if he'd consider it as evening the balance." He tugged at his beard, frowning. "I'm surprised he ran, though. If he put all of this in place to get the information about Robertson, why would he leave without getting anything?"

"The code. He knew we'd find out he'd set it up." Lysander wished he had more energy to put into thinking, but it felt like the time he'd been on a merry-go-round too many times when he was six, his whole world still spinning around him. "It's not as if you showed him the file about his father."

Jacob's expression didn't so much change as collapse. "Oh *fuck*."

Lysander's heart sank. "What?"

"I showed him the raw file we had for the energy signature from Sanders's disappearance. I don't think he knew the date it happened, but if he realised, then he knows his dad was attacked by time travellers."

Lysander shook his head. "Surely, it wouldn't have any information..." He reached for his comm and buzzed down to Danny's Leaf. "Danny? Do you have a second?"

"Aye?"

"We're sending you a piece of data." He made a gesture to Jacob, who opened up his own Leaf. "I need you to identify anything significant you see in it right away."

Danny sounded puzzled. "All right. Do I need to know what it is?"

"No. It's on its way."

Five minutes later, his Leaf chirped, and he opened Danny's notes. Mutely, he turned the file around to show Jacob: it had the exact date and time of Mackenzie Robertson's arrival on the day Ben lost his father. No wonder Ben had stared so much when he saw it.

"Shit..."

Ben was smart. He had to be, to have pulled the wool over everyone's eyes for so long. He would have put together the few facts he had. The only saving grace was that he didn't know what role Robertson played in the whole affair.

There were times when a man needed a cup of Earl Grey.

Lysander took his time spooning loose leaf into the teapot as the kettle boiled, the routine of it calming. When everything else was falling apart, it helped, though his hands were still shivering more than he would have liked.

When he returned to his desk, carrying his cup and saucer, he could feel Jacob's eyes on him.

"We need to figure out how to play this," Jacob murmured. "Mariam should be on her way in now, and Temple and Danny know. Downstairs will need to be updated as soon as possible, but do we let the media know?"

Lysander stared blankly into his tea. What did they really have to tell? They had been betrayed, sure, and Ben was missing in action, but they didn't have any more information. Did he have the battery cores? Did he intend to use them? Did he have any plans involving Robertson? Was there more going on than the code alone?

"Lysander?"

Lysander held up a hand, as if it could ward off the questions and his spinning on the edge of chaos, not knowing how to stop. "A minute. Please."

Jacob sat back at once.

While Lysander made a game effort to drink his rapidly cooling tea, Jacob opened up the medical bay feed. Enoch was sitting on the floor at the end of his bed, poking at a Leaf screen. He seemed fascinated by it, moving his finger up and down to scroll between a catalogue of images.

"Someone needs to tell him his friend isn't coming back," Jacob murmured. "Do you want me to do it?"

Lysander cradled his cup between his palms. "I need to speak to Vic." He took an unsteady breath. "The Enoch issue is bad enough, but now we've got the legal ramifications of— We need to know how this is going to impact on us."

Jacob got up from his chair. "Want me to send her up?"

She arrived less than ten minutes later and stopped dead in the doorway. "Earl Grey? Already? What got worse?"

He tried to laugh, but failed. "Everything."

He explained, haltingly at first; then the dam burst with all the pent-up grief and shock and frustration pouring out of him. He felt wrung out when he finally trailed into silence, so damn tired of every damned thing.

Victoria pulled the other chair around to sit beside him and gave his knee a consoling squeeze. "I wish I could give you some helpful advice, but until we know exactly how far this goes, we don't know if we're dealing with corporate issues alone or something bigger."

"Bigger..." Lysander echoed. "The battery cores?"

She nodded. "If he's building illegal gates, no matter what his intentions are with them, then it's out of our hands. At the very least, there would be a tribunal, but it could go bigger. Especially given the Baker situation."

"It's all for his dad."

Victoria gave him a patient look. "Big picture, sweets. He's stolen expensive equipment from an internationally funded scientific organisation. He's tampered with the system controlling their mainframe. He's done it all through deception and manipulation. Take your friendship and his dad out of the equation. You know how this would play out."

She was right. He was too close to it all. He'd always held himself distant as he worked his way up. You could do what had to be done, when you kept people at arm's length. The trouble was he couldn't keep doing it. He liked people. He gave a damn. He cared.

What a mistake that had turned out to be.

As much as he wanted to think of Ben as a friend, he had to put on his director hat and deal with it professionally.

"We're working on finding evidence of tampering with the system." He struggled to keep his voice calm. "Jacob is liaising with Superintendent Temple. She sent a team to Ben's home and has issued an APW to locate him."

"It's a start." She pushed herself up to sit on his desk, her legs dangling. "When he's found, the question becomes what do we do with him? We both know he's inextricably linked to the TRI, both by blood and years of experience. We have the option of defending him as one of our own with our team who know the temporal laws inside out and backwards."

That was the question.

There was a lot of loyalty to the Sanders name within the TRI, which made him think protecting Ben would be the best move, but Ben's betrayal went beyond manipulating the code. He had deceived them all to steal technology, which wasn't just a slap-on-the-wrist offence.

"We wait."

Victoria made a dubious sound, wrinkling her nose. "We need to get ahead of this."

"And if it turns out he's been doing far worse, do you want the job of defending him?" Lysander said grimly. "We wait, find out how bad it is, then work out a game plan. He might be given access to advice, but he's not getting the full support from your team. He screwed us over, so he can deal with it."

She looked surprised. "I haven't seen you this ruthless in a while."

He folded his hands together so tightly it hurt. "I haven't been double-crossed by someone I considered a friend in a while."

"And you'd throw him to the wolves, knowing how it would reflect on the TRI?"

He hated himself for knowing it was necessary. "Consider it a deterrent. We've had so many contracts and rules and NDAs in place, most people wouldn't dare to move against us. Ben always got special treatment because of his status. Everyone—inside and out—needs to know those things aren't going to protect anyone anymore."

Vic knocked her calf against his leg. "There's the director I know and love." She offered her hand, and he took it, squeezing her fingers.

"This feels crap."

She nodded sympathetically. "Being screwed over usually does."

Lysander turned his head when his Leaf chimed, and swore under his breath.

"Meeting?"

"Teleconference with some politicians," he confirmed. "Unfortunately, it's been on the books for over a month, so I can't cancel."

She leaned down and refastened the top buttons of his collar and straightened his tie. "Can't have you looking like you aren't ready for it."

"Good enough?"

She examined him critically. "Can't help the sacks under your eyes, but they'll know what's been going and won't be surprised you look tired." She slid off the desk and smoothed her skirt. "Keep me in the loop, okay? We need to start planning as soon as we know where we stand."

"I will," he promised, getting up to see her to the door. "Can you keep this between us for now? Until we know what's going on?"

She smiled. "You know it."

All things considered, the teleconference was a welcome breather from everything else.

There had been a debate raging for months regarding the publication of a summary report covering a decade's worth of research into the Napoleonic era, taking into account the perspectives and positions of all the countries that had been involved.

The issue was maintaining complete neutrality in the report. The agents and supervisors who had provided the data had been even-handed. The politicians and their so-called experts were the ones causing the problems.

On any other day, the topic would have been politically challenging, but compared to rogue time travellers and double agents and God only knew what else, it felt like a walk in the park. He knew the topic inside out and backwards and had ensured he stayed up to date on any developments in the talks.

As always, the representatives from the French and British governments were butting heads. Shared political history always caused friction, but when the history books in each country differed so drastically—propaganda and self-adulation took priority over fact in the contemporary accounts—getting them to agree to the release of research was difficult.

Three months earlier, the Spanish representatives had nearly withdrawn in frustration, but Lysander had managed to persuade them to stay with help from the Austrian representative. If they withdrew, he'd argued, then there would be less chance of neutrality and accuracy. The Polish representative had played go-between a few times as well, and eventually, they'd managed to keep the Spanish at the table.

The only people who hadn't caused any problems were the Russian delegates, who seemed to be amused by the British and French sides verbally re-enacting the whole incident across a conference table. Lysander was sure they were enjoying the Russian equivalent of popcorn whenever anything blew up.

Now, with an iron hand in a velvet glove, speaking politely and calmly, and using their grievances to gently turn their opinion, Lysander managed to steer the conversation in the direction it needed to go. With some people, it took their national pride to nudge them, with others, they wanted to be proved right, and Lysander had known each of the delegates long enough to know which would work.

It was amazing how much you could get done if you knew the right buttons to push.

By the time he terminated the call, he almost felt like himself again. There was something to be said for verbally herding a group of politicians. A decision still hadn't been made, but he was pleased he'd been able to steer the debate in the most feasible and least damaging direction.

He risked a glance out of the office.

For once, there were no calls or guests or messages. Fana was probably down with PR, dealing with the media scrum, second only to Sabine as his eyes and ears.

He took advantage of the brief lull to run to the bathroom and freshen himself up. Victoria had been right when she said he had sacks under his eyes, but at least his eyes weren't as bloodshot as they'd been last time he looked.

It felt like pushing his luck when he walked out into the winter-dusted rooftop garden. He stepped onto the smooth snow, which creaked underfoot as he walked in a slow circuit. The wind had died down, and the afternoon sun eased a little of the bitter chill.

Of course, the peace couldn't last.

He was at the far end of the garden when he heard the door open. He sighed, breath hanging like mist in front of him for a heartbeat.

"Lysander."

Lysander turned reluctantly to face Jacob, who was standing in the doorway with someone a few steps behind him. As Lysander approached them, he recognised Superintendent Temple. He stopped a couple of metres from the door, his heart thundering. If she had come herself instead of calling in with information, it couldn't be good.

"This is unexpected." He hoped he sounded less petulant and more surprised.

"Temple needs to have a word with us," Jacob said. "She says it couldn't wait."

Lysander walked up to the door. "A call would have been enough." He offered his hand to Superintendent Temple. She shook it with her warm grip, though she flinched at the cold he hadn't even noticed. "You didn't need to come all the way out here."

"This wasn't something I felt comfortable broadcasting across the airwaves," she said. "We have secure lines, but sometimes, things slip through the net."

That only made it worse. Dozens of nightmarish scenarios presented themselves in rapid succession, most of them about Ben and many of them specifically his body. It wasn't the first time Ben had done something reckless and dangerous, but this time, it had the potential to be so much worse.

"Of course. Security first," he managed to say. He indicated towards his office. "Please, join me."

Not for the first time that day, he felt the unsettling sense of detachment, as if he was standing to the side of his own body, watching as he led Jacob and Temple to his office. Somehow, he managed to get to his seat and waited until the others were both sitting opposite him.

"You said you had something to tell us." Lysander folded and refolded his hands on the desk, right over left and then left over right.

"Something to show you," Temple corrected, drawing her Leaf out of her breast pocket. "I knew the Sanders house from our original investigation. It's why it took us a little longer to do a thorough search."

Lysander looked at Jacob, wondering what he was missing.

"Safe rooms," Jacob explained. "Tom Sanders protected his work and his family. There were at least three—" His expression shifted suddenly, and he looked at Temple. "The basement?"

Temple's thin lips vanished into a line.

"Sanders's lab," Jacob said for Lysander's benefit. "Shit. Mariam said Ben had sealed it up because he didn't want to see—"

"What was he doing there?" Lysander interrupted. Ben had proved himself a proficient liar. They didn't need confirmation.

Temple opened up a series of images, fanning them out between Jacob and Lysander. "That."

Lysander had been hanging by a thread all day, but now, the thread was fraying. "Is that..."

"A temporal gate." Jacob sounded like he'd been hit with an iron bar. "He built a temporal gate."

"No," Temple corrected, enlarging the images. "He built *two* temporal gates."

Chapter Forty-Three

IT WAS A match!

Danny pressed his hands over his eyes to block out the screens that had filled his vision for hours and flopped back on the floor.

It was a match! At last!

All those days and weeks of sitting with Ben, learning how to code from scratch from the confirmed expert, hadn't been useless. Ben was a bloody great genius, but he had some coding habits that slipped into his work, and now, it was a match!

With effort, Danny rolled onto his side, then crawled to his knees and then hauled himself upright. His arse ached, and circulation slowly prickled back into his newly uncrossed legs. Then, he noticed the increasingly urgent nagging from his bladder. He staggered for the door and out to the nearest bathroom for an Atlantis-levelling piss.

He paused to check himself in the mirror, admiring the way his hair stood on end and his eyes were bright pink. He probably should have taken a break now and then, but with the shit hitting the fan, the sooner the better seemed like a good idea.

As soon as he'd transferred the relevant information onto his Leaf, he made for the lift, heading straight up to Lysander's office. He could hear voices inside, but his news was important, so he knocked once and didn't wait before walking in.

"—know if he actually used them before this incident. Tom did the same..." An older woman in a hijab stopped talking and turned to stare pointedly at Danny.

He blinked at her, recognising her at once. She had aged, but he still remembered the press conference when the TRI went public. He'd watched it so many times to convince himself it was real, and he knew he'd recognise the woman anywhere. "Holy shit..." he breathed. "Mariam Ashraf."

She whirled away from him. "Clearance?" she snapped.

"He's clean," Jacob Ofori said. He was one of four people in the room. Lysander sat behind his desk, and another woman, younger than Jacob but older than Lysander, leaned against the counter by the wall with a mug in her hands. She was tall, stocky, and dark-haired, and the look on her face said she wasn't someone to mess with. "He's the one who found Ben's code."

Ashraf whipped back around, and Danny suddenly felt like to be a microbe on a slide. He hastily held out his Leaf, opened to the matching samples of code from Ben's standard work and the subroutine underlying the corrupted code.

"I found evidence," he mumbled.

On the far side of the room, Lysander gave a sharp bark of laughter that sounded too brittle. Danny tore his attention from Mariam to look towards his lover, who had one elbow on the arm of the chair, his forehead propped on his fingers.

Mariam Ashraf snatched the code samples and sank into one of the vacant chairs.

"It matches," Danny offered, forcing himself to look back at her.

"Is it solid proof he's behind the coding, then?" Jacob asked.

"It's not as if we really need to worry about that now." Lysander finally spoke. He didn't sound like the same man. Danny glanced over at him, but Lysander didn't even seem to notice. "What's a little bit of crooked coding between friends?"

"It's evidence," Jacob replied, sounding as bad as Lysander. "We need evidence."

Lysander glared at Jacob. "We have two fucking gates' worth of evidence."

"Mr. O'Donohue." The other woman set her mug down on the counter. "I know this is a difficult time, but Jacob is right. We need all the possible evidence we can get to build a case. Even if this is a minor crime by comparison, it's connected, and we can't ignore it."

By comparison?

Danny looked at each face, taking in the tension, the anger. The woman seemed to be a voice of authority, and if she was talking about evidence, that had to mean a police intervention. Two fucking gates of evidence, Lysander had said. Danny's heart dropped. Ben had mentioned battery cores, which were used for powering up gates. If the coding issue—which had seemed such a massive problem—was nothing to Lysander now, it could only mean one thing.

"Ben built temporal gates?"

All eyes turned to him.

"Fuck, Danny," Lysander groaned. "Stop paying so much attention."

"How exactly do you know about that?" Mariam demanded suspiciously, rising from her seat.

Danny retreated a step. It was one thing to meet an idol face-to-face. It was another to have her growling at you. He stammered out a couple of syllables, which couldn't remotely achieve the status of words.

"Like Lysander said, he pays attention." Jacob approached Danny. "Listen, no one outside this room knows about it yet, but yes, it seems to be the case. We would appreciate it if you could keep this quiet for now."

Danny stared at him. "Shit."

"Something like that, yes." Jacob squeezed his shoulder. "Good job on finding the proof we needed of the code tampering. It'll help." He glanced towards Mariam. "Mariam'll want to see the rest of your work as well. It used to be her department after all."

Danny made a strangled sound, hoping he was smiling instead of staring like a deer in the headlights. Mariam Ashraf. Looking at his actual work. His sixteen-year-old self would be hyperventilating into a paper bag if he knew what his future had in store.

"Don't break him, Jacob." Lysander sounded amused. "He's still useful."

Danny shot a grateful look over at him, earning a shadow of a smile. "I'll just..." He jerked his thumb over his shoulder. "Scram. Get out of your way." He hesitated as he realised he'd done everything he'd been paid to do, and now, there was nothing left to keep him occupied. "Er. Is there anything you need, since I finished with the code?"

"Discretion," Mariam said. "That's all for now."

Danny backed towards the door, which was bloody daft. It wasn't as if he was in some fancy royal court or in a room full of assassins. So what if some of them were the people who had developed the mind-blowingly amazing tech he'd dreamed about since childhood? He stopped at the door, a thought occurring to him. "Huh."

Development. Something about development. His first day when he got to see Ben's workroom. He had a partially functional gate there as well, but no one thought anything of it. He did a lot of work on new developments too, didn't he?

Danny tapped his knuckle against his chin, frowning. Technically, they knew more of what was going on, but it was still possible it might be a misunderstanding.

"Danny?" Lysander's voice broke through his thoughts.

Danny blinked, focussing on him. "Aye?"

"You look like you're having an epiphany."

Danny laughed self-consciously, aware they were all watching him. "It's—well—the thing is, Ben does development, doesn't he? I mean, he's got a gate he's working on here. If he's built other gates, isn't it like taking his work home with him? It doesn't mean he's up to anything with them, if he only got around to nicking the battery things now."

There was a long moment of silence.

"One of those gates already had a battery core," Mariam finally said. "Superintendent Temple had enough experience with the tech to get specific images for us. We're sending people over to check the functionality, but the latest theft isn't the only one."

"Ah." Danny's heart sank. "Right. So he's an actual arsehole, not a hypothetical one now?"

"You could say that."

"Bugger." He self-consciously shifted from one foot to the other. A wise man would keep his trap shut, but the thoughts were bubbling up, and he couldn't help asking, "D'you think it's why he came back after his time away? I mean, I know he likes working here, but you get all the best stuff in here, and he'd never've been able to access half of it if he didn't come back in."

If they hadn't considered it before, from the dark glances flashing between Lysander and Jacob, they were definitely thinking it now.

"We don't know yet," Jacob said quietly, his expression grim. "Right now, we're just getting a measure of the situation and figuring out exactly what's going on."

Fair enough. Danny wondered if he would look daft if he just bolted for the door. Lysander pissed was bad enough. Lysander, Ofori, *and* Mariam Ashraf spitting tacks was enough to make him find a bomb shelter.

Mariam eyed him and then glanced at Lysander. "You said this man has a good eye for detail."

Lysander nodded. "He managed to outwit Ben."

Mariam glanced over at the policewoman—possibly Temple? "Abby, can you show Mr. Ferguson the images of the basement? He might spot something we've missed."

"I don't know how much help I'll be," Danny hastily said. "I mean, I can try..."

The policewoman opened up a set of photos, and Danny approached to examine. They didn't look like much, a sterile white-walled room with thick ropes of power lines visible along the floor and walls. There were the two gates, similar to the ones he'd seen in the jump and in Ben's workroom, but they seemed more makeshift than the big professional ones down the stair.

He scaled up one of the images, staring at it. The two gates were facing each other with a gap of about two metres between them. It seemed a bit daft to have them so close together, but then, the room wasn't very big.

"Why facing each other?" he asked no one in particular. "You'd think it'd be smarter to have them side by side or something."

"We don't know." Mariam stood beside him. Christ, she was so tiny. He could have picked her up without even trying. "Until we get the techs out there to take them apart, there are a lot of questions we can't answer."

"And only one of them has a battery core?"

She traced a power line leading into one of the gates. "This one seems to be a more old-fashioned gate, closer to Tom's original than the ones used now. It wouldn't be compatible with a battery core."

It was like any gate Danny had seen in-house, but the other gate with the battery core looked like it had been thrown together to do the bare minimum. It wasn't as sleek or streamlined and didn't have the full casing, which suggested it hadn't been finished.

"When did Ben take the first battery core?" he inquired.

"Some time in the last six months," Jacob replied. "Why?"

Danny chewed on his lower lip as he studied the images. "If he already had a gate that worked without a battery core, then why build one with a battery core instead?"

"Stability," Mariam murmured. "There can be fluctuations in energy and power cuts if you're using electricity as a power source. The battery cores are stable sources of energy."

"Right." He scanned through a few of the images for different angles, then cocked his head. "Then why does the old gate have a timer on it?"

Clearly, it was something important because Jacob moved to his other side, and Lysander rose on the far side of the desk.

"A timer?" Mariam sounded mystified.

"To open the gates automatically."

Jacob caught his shoulder, his grip painful. "Where?"

Danny pointed to the small panel concealed in the patchwork of pieces of the gate. "Ben said it was only in development, and it would be a bit pointless putting one on an obsolete gate, wouldn't it?"

"If there's one on the other gate..." Jacob began unsteadily.

"There is." Danny pointed it out. "I mean, the gate looks crap, and you can hardly see it, but he must have put it there for a reason."

Lysander and Jacob swore simultaneously.

"What?" Danny glanced between them.

"Are you sure?" Lysander's voice sounded so different.

"He showed me the one he had on his gate downstairs," Danny explained. "It's not exactly the same, but it's like a similar design."

From their expressions, they could see something he didn't. Danny had no idea what it was, and they seem like they were going to tell him.

"Can you give us some time, Danny?" Lysander said, staring blankly at the image. "We need to discuss this."

Danny nodded at once. "'Course. I'll—if you need anything, I'll be in my flat or the gym."

Lysander didn't even glance at him in acknowledgement. He was ashen, and as Danny closed the door behind him, he saw Lysander sink back into his chair.

Something about the timers was important, but he had no idea what. As he wandered towards the lift, he frowned, mulling on it. According to Ben, the timers could be used to open a temporal gate at a set time without any need for manual intervention, which had to be a good thing.

Unless...

Unless whoever was opening the gates did something they weren't meant to. After all, it would be a perfect alibi, to be in one place and opening a gate somewhere else for somebody to use.

Danny frowned at his reflection in the mirrored wall of the lift as it descended. To be honest, he was more confused by the gates facing each other. It didn't give much leeway for walking through either, so unless someone was trying to go through both of them from one past to another...

The lift had stopped, but Danny kept staring at his reflection. "Oh *fuck*."

Chapter Forty-Four

LYSANDER COULD TASTE blood.

He wasn't surprised. He'd been worrying at his lip, tearing ragged shreds from it from the moment he'd entered the medical bay with Jacob. They had to verify their suspicions, but Lysander didn't trust himself to speak out loud to Enoch. Jacob could— Jacob wasn't— Right now, Jacob had a better handle on his emotions.

Both of them wanted to believe their assumptions were wrong, but the evidence was piling up. It should have been a relief to have an answer to all the riddles of the past few months, but right now, Lysander wished he had remained blissfully ignorant.

The tech team—accompanied by Temple's people—were already working over the basement of the Sanders house. They didn't have much information in yet, but they'd confirmed any computers that had been connected to the gates were gone. Ben had cleaned up after himself, leaving no clue as to whether the gates were functional and had been used.

The only possible proof was sitting right in front of them.

Lysander stood a few paces away from the table where Jacob was speaking—so calmly and pleasantly—to Enoch. Too calm, Lysander thought. He had his arms folded over his chest, his fingers biting into his upper arms, to keep himself from grabbing Enoch and shaking an answer out of him.

It wouldn't help.

It wasn't Enoch's fault he'd stumbled into Ben's plan.

Lysander licked his teeth, metallic and sharp.

"It— I-I telt you afore." Enoch hunched up on the chair, arms wrapped around his legs. "It were all light and noise."

"All right," Jacob murmured, opening up files on the table. "Maybe you caught a glimpse of something? Anything? Maybe somewhere in the light?" He spread the pictures of Ben's hidden laboratory out in front of him. "Does any of this seem familiar?"

Enoch leaned forward, staring at them. His forehead creased in a frown as he pulled one of the images towards him. "I put my hands round my eyes. It were brighter than the sun to look up, but I looked down." He tapped at a pattern of cracks on the concrete floor. "It were like that."

Lysander released a sharp breath.

"Did you stop there?" Jacob's voice was still calm, the tension clear in it.

Enoch shook his head. "I were afeared of being caught and beat. I ran forward and..." He frowned. "It went loud again, then all quiet and darker, and I were in the big mashed place."

Lysander closed his eyes. Proof enough.

"Mr. O'Donohue, sir?"

Lysander forced himself to meet Enoch's eyes. "Yes?"

Enoch licked his lips nervously. "The person who brung me here, is this their place?"

Lysander hesitated, glancing at Jacob, who shrugged. He looked exhausted too. The secret would come out eventually. Of all the people in the TRI, Enoch deserved to know who had fucked him over.

"We believe it is," he said quietly.

Enoch stared at him. "Aye? And you catched him?"

Another deafening silence.

"No," Jacob murmured, "but we're working on it."

Enoch folded his arms on top of his knees, a strange expression on his face, something between relief and grief. "But you cannit send me home?"

Lysander thought of the confirmation from Kit Rafferty and his team at the Sanders house, of the abandoned gates and the missing information. It felt like a rock had settled in the pit of his stomach, knowing Ben was the one behind all of it: the code, the thefts, and now, Enoch's unexpected arrival.

Given how much time Ben had spent with Enoch, Lysander hoped Ben might have left a clue of the poor man's point of origin. It seemed unnecessarily cruel to tear him out of his own timeline as a distraction with no way to get home. But everything they'd found so far said Ben had gone and so had Enoch's point of origin. Even if the team could dismantle the timers on the gates, they were only the control and not the source.

"No." His voice sounded hoarse in his own ears. "I'm sorry, Enoch, but he got rid of anything that might let us get you home."

Enoch stared at him for several seconds, then hid his face in his arms.

"You'll be given all the help you need," Jacob murmured. "You're safe here. You won't be harmed."

"Ben—" Enoch's voice was muffled in his arms. "I would see Ben."

Lysander exchanged a stricken look with Jacob.

"Enoch—" Lysander began and hesitated.

"He did this," Jacob said quietly. "He was the one who brought you here."

Enoch didn't move for several seconds and then raised his head, his eyes wide. "For true?"

Jacob nodded, and Lysander had to reach down to lean on the back of Jacob's chair, his legs in danger of giving way under him.

"It may have been an accident," Jacob said, but his expression belied him.

It had been too carefully planned. Ben needed to create a distraction and an alibi while he planned his second theft and made his escape. The timers on the gates had given him both. His appearance at Lysander's door only moments after Enoch's arrival in London had cemented it. How could he be responsible if he was sitting with Lysander the whole time?

Hindsight was a terrible thing.

No wonder Ben had wanted to be in the medical bay, knowing exactly when the timelines would cross and how it could affect Enoch. No wonder he'd reacted so quickly to resuscitate him. He'd risked the young man's life all in the name of covering his own crimes.

Enoch stared blankly at the scatter of images projected on the table. "Why?"

"We don't—" Jacob began.

"We think he wants to find his missing father," Lysander interrupted. It was pointless to lie to Enoch. He'd had enough lies from Ben. He deserved honesty, a small price for his ruined life. "We didn't expect he would break the law to do it."

Enoch dropped his chin onto his knees. "Aye." He stared at the table again, uncurling one hand to move the projections around.

"As we said"—Jacob propped one arm on the edge of the table—"you're safe here. We'll keep looking for a way to get you home, but until then, you won't lack for anything."

Enoch stiffly unfolded from the chair. "Your pardons." He made his way towards the bathroom and closed the door behind him.

Lysander sagged like a puppet with its strings cut, his shoulders slumping. The effort of holding himself steady and upright was exhausting. "Proof enough?"

Jacob closed down the images one by one. "Yes." When he closed the last one, he pressed his face into his palm. "Fuck."

Lysander couldn't find any words. He reached over and squeezed Jacob's shoulder. If it felt shit for him, he could only imagine how much worse it was for Jacob and Mariam. Both of them had known Ben since childhood and trusted him like their own flesh and blood.

For several seconds, Jacob allowed it, and then he stood. "We should get back to Abby and Mariam. This changes everything."

Lysander glanced towards the bathroom. "I'll join you in a few minutes." He crossed the room and tapped lightly on the bathroom door.

It opened a crack, and Enoch peered out at him. "Mm?"

"I wanted to apologise again," Lysander said, hating how useless it sounded. "For all of this. For not being able to help you more."

"I know." Enoch rubbed at one eye with his fist. "It weren't your doing."

Lysander wished he could believe it. He'd walked blindly into Ben's distractions, too caught up with puzzles and paranoia to stop and think logically. Ben had asked about Robertson a lot, and no one had thought anything of it. None of them had questioned it. If he'd only stopped and listened and considered things more carefully, he might have seen the pattern emerging.

"He's one of my people," he said, "so that makes it my responsibility."

Enoch frowned, shaking his head. "It weren't your doing," he repeated. "It were him." He reached out and gently knocked Lysander on the arm. He pulled his hand back right away, as if he thought he might have misstepped.

Lysander managed a frail smile. "It's kind of you to say so." He glanced over his shoulder, unsurprised to find Jacob waiting for him. "I have to go back upstairs now. There's much to be done." He studied Enoch. "Is there anything I can get for you? Anything you need now?"

Enoch shook his head. "You're being well good to me, sir."

Lysander patted him on the shoulder and turned to leave.

"Sir?" Enoch stepped out the bathroom.

"Yes?" Lysander looked back.

"He said you were good. Master Sanders did." Enoch smiled tentatively. "I don't think he were lying about that, no matter what happened."

Lysander could only force a brittle smile, even if it felt like empty comfort now, words from a man he had trusted and who had betrayed him. He walked back towards Jacob, who closed the door behind them both.

The silence stretched between them until they were in the shuttle across to the main building.

Lysander was leaning against the window, but looked back at Jacob as he sat on one of the seats, staring down at his hands in his lap. In all their years working together, Lysander had never seen him look so defeated, not when they lost agents or when the Board raked him across the coals.

"Are you okay?" Lysander asked quietly.

Jacob didn't move at once. "It's—" He took a deep breath and released it in a shaking sigh. "Ben. It's *Ben*."

"We'll find him."

Jacob stared up at him. "You can't know that."

It was *wrong*.

Lysander had been screwed over before. Even by friends. It hurt like hell when it happened. Right now, he still felt the pain from the twist of an unexpected knife, but Jacob never let anything get to him, and he was sitting there, stooped and old and tired, and it was wrong.

Lysander was tired too, and hurt. But after seeing Enoch realising how he'd been used, after watching Jacob slowly crumbling, being tired and sad helped no one. All his own questions had been answered. He knew what was going on. He knew what he needed to do.

There would be time to grieve and ache later.

Now, he had anger, and anger could fuel him to think harder and get shit done.

"I know it," he said. "Because even if I have to hunt him down myself, I swear to God, that treacherous son of a bitch is going to answer for everything he's done."

Jacob raised his eyebrows. "He's a smart kid, Ly. Smart enough to get one over on all of us."

True. But he'd been hiding in plain sight with no reason to be suspected.

"We know our enemy," Lysander said. "We weren't looking for him before. We underestimated him. Now..." He smiled grimly. "Now, the rules have changed."

Chapter Forty-Five

SOMETIMES, IT WAS a bugger being right.

Danny's suspicions about Ben's involvement in the mysterious time travel saga had been well and truly confirmed. Danny knew this because he'd been hauled out of the gym and ushered back to the top levels of the main building, where Mariam Ashraf, Jacob, and the policewoman were waiting for him in his workroom to grill him about everything he'd seen and worked out.

Lysander had vanished off somewhere, and as far as anyone knew, he was in a meeting. No wonder, if one of their chief members of staff had turned out to be a thieving psycho illegally using time travel as a weapon of mass distraction.

So Danny cooperated with their inquiries and tried not to think how everything was going to shit.

It was one of the more surreal days of his life, standing between rows of colourful code in his favourite gym shorts and an aromatic T-shirt damp with sweat, while Mariam bloody Ashraf threw question after question at him. He'd had a dream like that once, only with less sweat and more gratuitous and mortifying nudity and memory loss.

Jacob didn't saying anything. He was resting against Danny's desk, his arms folded over his chest, watching them. It put Danny unsettlingly in mind of the way apes probably felt when something large and stripy lurked in the bushes.

The policewoman, who had introduced herself as Abby Temple, was walking around the room, examining the miles of code Danny was displaying. Whether she understood it or not, he didn't ask. Mariam's questions needed all of his concentration so he could answer without making a massive tit of himself.

"Not bad," Mariam finally said after what felt like hours.

Danny forced himself not to beam like an idiot. "I only hope it'll be useful."

"It already forced Ben to show his hand," Jacob said, straightening up from the desk. "God knows what else he'd've found out if you hadn't uncovered him."

Temple had settled in Danny's chair. "At least he doesn't know about you-know-who."

"You-know-who?" Danny inquired.

"Need to know only," Jacob demurred.

Something Ben didn't know and probably critical. Danny remembered conversations that felt like a lifetime ago about the fate of Tom Sanders. "Is it the person who took his dad's stuff?" Jacob and Temple exchanged looks, and Danny knew he was on the right line. "He thought if he found the stuff they stole from him, he might be able to find his dad."

"I'm starting to see what Lysander meant about you paying attention," Mariam murmured.

Danny shrugged self-consciously. "I like putting the pieces together." He glanced at Jacob. "You know he won't stop looking. He might not have got the information out of you, but he'll keep looking for it. If he's gone this far already, he's not going to stop."

"No," Mariam agreed. "He won't."

Jacob ran his hand over his face. "Why didn't we see this coming?" He sounded like shite.

"Because we still saw the scared little boy." Mariam crossed the floor and squeezed Jacob's arm. "We didn't want to see how much he was like his dad when it came to finding someone he cares about." She laughed tiredly. "Tom would be so proud. Pissed as hell, but proud anyway."

Danny knew he'd missed out on some critical information, but he didn't have a chance to ask because Jacob's Leaf chirped. Jacob drew it out and flicked up a screen.

"Looks like we're wanted upstairs."

It was the most uncomfortable lift ride Danny had ever taken. One level felt like it took ages, but if he'd hoped getting to Lysander's office would be a respite, the moment he walked in, he knew he was mistaken.

Lysander was seated behind his desk, flanked by Sabine and Fana, his hands folded on his desk. From the lingering perfume in the air, the head of legal had been in as well. Danny glanced at Lysander, who studiously avoided his gaze, then at Sabine, who looked much paler than usual.

"If you've made your decision, we need to get a move on," Temple said, closing the door behind them. "All this delay is only giving him more of a head start."

Lysander unfolded one hand and motioned to the vacant seats. "I called you in here to explain how we're moving forward."

There were only two vacant chairs. Danny remained standing behind one, feeling more out of place than he had ever felt in his life, which was saying something.

"Explain." Jacob stood between Mariam and Temple, once they had sat down.

Lysander inclined his head. "I will be standing down as the head of the TRI, with immediate eff—"

"What the fuck?" Jacob's snarl matched Danny's thoughts. "Everything goes to shit, and you decide it's time to quit?"

Danny looked from him to Lysander and nearly recoiled a step. Lysander's expression was neutral, but the look in his eyes could have frozen lava.

"I'd be careful what you say, Mr. Ofori." Lysander spread his hands on the desk. He inclined his head and smiled like a blade. "If you would let me finish?"

Jacob must have seen what Danny saw in those blazing eyes and made a noncommittal sound, waving one hand for him to continue.

"I will be standing down," Lysander repeated, his voice deceptively calm. Rage radiated off him, and Danny wondered how the hell he held it all in. "This is necessary because Ben's actions will be revealed to the public. We need all eyes looking for him, and if he's to be found, his name and face need to be out there."

"Quitting is a little drastic, isn't it?" Temple sounded surprisingly unsurprised. She shot a look at Jacob as she said it, earning a grimace.

"Quitting is necessary," Lysander replied evenly. "I was the one responsible for Ben, so the world will expect someone to be held accountable. It's better for everyone if I stand down as soon as the announcement is made. A very public show of martyrdom."

"Bullshit," Jacob snorted.

Lysander's thin smile returned. "Indeed. I'm standing down as head of the TRI because as of today, I'm creating a task force with the sole purpose of finding and containing Ben Sanders and preventing anything like this from happening again."

"I'm in," Mariam said quietly.

Lysander met her eyes. Clearly, he'd been expecting that.

"Could I help there?" Danny asked uncertainly. They'd brought him along to the meeting for a reason. If it wasn't to join their new secret club, he didn't know why.

Lysander didn't look at him. Instead, he glanced up at Sabine.

"With Ben's disappearance and all the work you've done in the past few weeks," she said, "we believe it would be better for the TRI if you were given a position in our coding team here. You've proven yourself skilled, trustworthy, and capable, which is something we vitally need right now."

Danny stared at her.

He should have been dancing around the room, whooping, waving his shirt around his head. He'd dreamed about getting a job at the TRI since he was a kid. He was being *offered* the job. He hadn't chased it. He hadn't asked for it. It all felt too good to be true.

Lysander suddenly seemed like the proverbial gift horse.

"Danny?" Jacob prompted.

Danny didn't look away from Lysander. "I'd like a word with Mr. O'Donohue about the terms, if I can have a minute?" He glanced at Sabine. "I mean, he's still the boss now, isn't he?"

Sabine, thank Christ, agreed. "We'll be outside."

They all filed out into the reception, and Danny waited until the door closed before running forward a couple of steps and leaning down, hands braced on the desk. "This isn't a charity case," he hissed. "You didn't need to get me a pity job."

Lysander, who had been studying his hands where they rested on the desk, raised his eyes. "I didn't."

Danny stared at him. "Eh?"

"Like I said, I didn't." Lysander pressed his hands to the arms of his chair and rose smoothly to his feet. He leaned forward over the desk too. "I thought you might be useful for the task force, but Sabine..." He smiled slightly. "She argued you would be more useful here. She made a strong case. She's seen you at work, and she knows exactly what you're capable of."

Danny blinked at him. "Aye?"

"Mm." Lysander inclined his head.

Danny's face split in a grin. "Fuck me! They really want to give me a job?"

Lysander smiled. "And it takes care of an awkward issue."

"What issue?"

Lysander's expression eased, softening the tense lines around his eyes and mouth. "I wouldn't be sleeping with one of my own employees if you hang around." He straightened up and walked around the desk until he stood only an arm's length from Danny. "I know this isn't what we'd expected. I know you wanted to get back to London." He gazed at Danny, offering his small, careful smile. "All I'm asking is that you consider it."

Danny leaned his hip against the desk. "Are you asking for the TRI?"

"For your skills and knowledge? Yes."

"That's not the question."

Lysander moved a step closer. "Then ask the question."

It felt big. So much bigger than getting a job with the TRI. Christ, if someone had told him the TRI would be playing second fiddle to the question he was about to ask, he would have laughed. Still, he wanted to ask it, and he wanted to know.

"If I don't take the job," he finally got the words out, "do you want me to stay?"

Lysander was only inches away now, and when he touched Danny's face, Danny tilted his cheek into Lysander's palm. Lysander smiled, small and shy. "Yes."

Chapter Forty-Six

THE BOARDS WERE filling up with data.

It had been a long time since Lysander took front and centre in an operation, but it had come back to him quickly. Though he'd started out in small departments years before, downsizing to the task force with a dozen members of staff had come as a shock.

Until the weight of the TRI was lifted from him, he hadn't realised how heavy a load it had become. It had been his life for so long that it felt natural, but now he didn't need to juggle a dozen departments anymore. No more balancing diplomacy against fact to prevent an international incident or considering the choice of profit over risk when it came to missions.

It made him suspicious that a potential global manhunt for a genius temporal criminal felt more relaxing than handling standard TRI operations.

He stood in front of a stretch of the wall, examining Ben's communication history. Working with Temple and a group of specialist officers from across the country meant the task force had access to far more information than they otherwise would have been able to get. A temporal criminal was a pain in the ass for everyone, and every officer in the task force wanted to say they were the one to bring him in.

Temple was officially the senior officer in charge. Technically, she held authority over Lysander, though he had created the task force. It was also thanks to her that a set of disused rooms in one of the old police facilities had been reopened as a base of operations.

"You don't need to do this," Lysander had argued when she showed him around. "We can find somewhere nearby."

Temple had raised her eyebrows. "Jacob said you're shit at taking help, even when it's handed to you on a silver platter."

"Of course he did."

Temple snorted. "Pot and kettle, there." She wandered into the centre of the room. "Let me make something clear to you, O'Donohue.

This case started long before you joined the TRI. I've been sitting on it for over twenty years. If you want to play in my sandpit, you're welcome, but you need to know we'll be more effective if we work together." She gestured around the room. "This way, all our information comes together in one place. No chasing each other. No faffing."

It was working too.

"Seeing something?"

Lysander glanced at Jacob. He and Mariam were the only other member of the TRI involved in the manhunt. It felt simpler, as the people who knew Ben best. Jacob still covered a day a week at the TRI to supervise his replacement, but every other day, he worked alongside Lysander and Mariam, going through any fresh data.

"I was wondering about the tech he used." Lysander waved towards the screeds of data from Ben's known Leaf and comms. "Is there any way we can pinpoint where these were located at any given time?"

Jacob came over to examine the data. "It might be possible. What are you thinking?"

"If we can locate his tech, we can pinpoint where he was, correct?"

"Technically, yes."

"Is there any way to identify any other comms in the area at the same time?" Lysander asked. "We know he always had some kind of tech to hand, and if Danny was right about him having a significant other, then they might have been in the same area too."

"Danny didn't sound so sure about this mystery lover."

Lysander glanced at Jacob. "You don't believe it?"

Jacob frowned. If they'd hoped to find anything useful at Ben's home, they'd been sorely mistaken. The whole place had been scrubbed obsessively. After multiple scans, they barely had more than some smudged fingerprints. Anything else carrying trace DNA had been reduced to ashes in the back garden. The few intact fragments they'd found had been identified as scraps of cushion and linens.

"He must've thought there might be some kind of evidence there, something he didn't want us to know," Jacob said. "There was definitely someone involved. My concern is that it might be more than one. I don't want us to get bogged down in this idea of one mystery lover."

"Lover or otherwise, we know *someone* outside the TRI sent the anonymous tip in to the media to keep us busy and distracted. I don't think it was a coincidence. If we can find any of his comms, we might be able to trace any connections he has, and we might be able to find him."

"You don't think Ben doesn't know all the tech tricks in the book?" Mariam Ashraf said. She sat at her own desk, an array of files scattered in front of her. "He'll have bounced his signal around too much. You won't be able to pin him down in any straightforward way."

Jacob folded his arms. "Do you have an alternative?"

"Cryptocurrency. Tricky to track, but I think it's more likely than getting him through his comms."

"You think so?" Lysander said. "Ben never seemed like he knew anything about things like that."

"There's a lot we thought he didn't know." Mariam glanced up from the information she was working through. "Everything here shows he barely touched his bank accounts, so he has to be getting something from somewhere. I know Tom used to dabble when the TRI was running short, back in the day." She paused, riffling through her files. "I saw something somewhere in his will, something about proceeds from his accounts."

"Which Ben would have remembered," Lysander groaned. "Of course."

Jacob rubbed his forehead with the knuckle of his thumb. "It would make sense. He has enough to pay people off to act as brokers. If he needed to, he could probably sell anything he had to through shell corporations in Saipan or God knows where."

"I guess we know where to turn our attention," Lysander said ruefully. "Way to open up the search parameters."

"The trouble with hunting a genius," Mariam said with a tired smile.

"Right. We'll get some of our IT people onto his tech stuff to see if we can't find a connection to his partner, but the currency thing..." Jacob headed over to one of the officers. "Anton, you're going to love this."

The detective inspector looked up with a wince. "Fuck's sake, Jacob. Twenty years, and I still get the shit jobs?" He fanned out a set of screens in front of him. "Let me guess. Any regular, and-or irregular, payments to brokers, or exchanges of anything potentially, possibly, maybe tied to cryptocurrency?"

"And that's why you got promoted."

"Only to become a search monkey again." Anton snorted. He paused, leaning sideways. "You lads expecting anyone?"

Lysander turned, following his line of sight, and blinked.

Of all the people to be standing in the doorway, he hadn't expected to see Enoch Baker.

"Enoch?"

The young man was dressed in modern clothes and looked like he'd put on some weight in the weeks since Lysander had seen him. If not for the close-shaved hair still growing back in and his diminutive height, Lysander could have passed him in the street without recognising him.

Enoch raised a hand in a hesitant wave. "Good morrow, Mr. O'Donohue, sir."

"You can go in." Janos appeared behind him and nudged Enoch forward.

Enoch looked self-conscious as he walked into the room. He looked around, staring at the walls until his eyes settled on a picture of Ben. "They said you are looking for him," he said, still staring at the picture. "I dint know if it were true."

"He wanted to come," Janos murmured. "To see. To help."

Lysander blinked, startled. Janos had said people could adjust to their new circumstances. He was the living evidence after all. It seemed incredible that it had happened in only a handful of weeks since Lysander had left the TRI and Sabine had stepped into his shoes. For God's sake, Lysander was still adjusting to his own circumstances, and he hadn't been ripped out of his life and his own time.

"You're sure you don't need some more time to settle, Enoch?" Jacob asked.

Enoch fidgeted with his hands but didn't turn around. "I dunt like it when someone turns me about." He took a step closer to the wall, still staring at the picture. "I dunt know much, but I would help." He turned to look at them. "You all were good to me. I would help."

Jacob must have read Lysander's questions in his expression. He stepped around Lysander and went to Enoch's side. "Come with me. I'll show you what we're working on."

Lysander waited until they were out of earshot to approach Janos. "You brought him here? Are you sure he's ready?"

Janos watched Jacob and Enoch across the room. "He learns fast," he said quietly. "Some things still scare him, yes, but he is brave." He looked briefly at Lysander. "You were angry when you learned you were betrayed. He was even more betrayed than you."

"But there's still so much he doesn't know about this time and place," Lysander murmured. "I'm worried it might be overwhelming for him."

"It is better to make him sit in a room, learning a little at a time?" Janos shook his head. "He can't sit quietly and do nothing. I think it will help him if he can do something. It will make the change...easier to bear."

Lysander could understand. Anger had pushed him through his shock and grief. It was why he had turned to the task force, to channel weeks and months of frustration and the crescendoing rage at Ben's betrayal into a solution. Enoch was probably experiencing the same fury. A whole life lost because of one man's selfish choice to do what he wanted.

"If it'll help him..."

Janos glanced at Lysander. "It helped for me. Work and people and interaction."

Lysander gazed at him, then smiled. "I'll defer to the expert, then." He patted Janos on the shoulder and walked over to join Jacob and Enoch. "Enoch."

Enoch turned. He looked wary, as if he expected to be sent back to his confinement. "Yes, sir?"

"You're sure you want to help?"

Enoch nodded his head vehemently. "I would help you find him, sir."

Lysander could imagine why. "If we find him, there's still no guarantee we could send you home."

"I know. They all telt me so." Enoch jutted out his jaw. "I still would find him and look him in the eye and tell him what I think on him." He bared his teeth in a feral grin. "I'll give him a bat around the earhole and all."

Lysander laughed in surprise. "I think I might let you." He held out his hand. "Very well, Mr. Baker. Let's help each other find the man who turned our lives on their heads."

Enoch grasped his hand, his grip tight and his palms callused. "Aye, sir."

Chapter Forty-Seven

SOMEONE WAS RATTLING around in the kitchen.

Danny cracked open and eye, squinting sleepily at the clock. Barely eight o'clock, definitely far too early to be up the morning after a party. He groped out with one arm, finding a vacant but still-warm expanse of bed beside him.

"Lysander?"

No one replied, but then the pillow had eaten half his syllables.

It took a couple attempts to roll onto his back. No headache, but everything felt pleasantly fuzzy, and he remembered several big drinks with some of the gang from work. His official final moved-up-from-civilisation housewarming combined with a belated Hogmanay do.

Danny yawned, rubbing at both eyes with the heels of his hands.

It had been a good night. Most of the coding team had showed up. Some of them brought housewarming meals, which was sweet of them but moot since the first things he'd unpacked were all his cookware and kitchen utensils. He hadn't even gotten to the point of making up his bed when his guests arrived, but he had a casserole and curry already cooked for them.

The bed was made now, he thought as he lowered his hands.

He smiled vaguely at the ceiling.

Sometime during the party, someone—probably definitely beginning with *L*—had snuck into his bedroom, made sure the bed was made and left a convenient supply of lube and kinky toys in his bedside cabinet. They'd come in useful after everyone else left. Made the end of the party go out—he sniggered dirtily—with a bang.

"Something funny?"

He peered at the doorway where Lysander was silhouetted against the light. "Nah." He motioned vaguely. "C'mere."

Lysander approached, and as he came closer, the wafting scent of coffee reached Danny. He leaned up on one elbow, reaching out demandingly as Lysander sat just out of arm's reach.

"And here I was, thinking you were pleased to see *me*," Lysander said dryly, handing him one of the mugs.

Danny pushed himself up in the bed, grinning. "It takes a lot to get ahead of coffee in my affections."

Lysander smiled. He looked well rested, which was more comforting than Danny could say. In the weeks since he'd left the TRI, he'd rediscovered his health and a sensible sleeping pattern. "I guess I could bribe you with your one great love," he said thoughtfully. "Threaten an embargo."

Danny made a face over the rim of his mug as he took a mouthful of sugar-laced black coffee. "I can find a coffee shop."

"True." Lysander drew his legs up onto the bed and scooted back against the headboard. "Maybe I'll find something else to bribe you with."

Danny tipped sideways to knock his shoulder against Lysander's. "You could do the thing you did last night again."

Lysander hid a smile in his mug. "That's better than coffee for waking you up?"

Danny reached with his free hand and squeezed Lysander's bare thigh. "I'd have to try it again to be sure. Especially with the wee vibratey thingie."

Lysander looked at him with amusement. "You remember I still have to go home and get a fresh change of clothes before I go to work. I think Jacob would notice if I showed up wearing the same thing two days in a row."

Danny beamed sleepily at him. "Dirty stop-out." He ran his fingers against the warmth of Lysander's inner thigh. "You can be late, can't you? You're the boss. No one to tell you off."

Lysander covered Danny's hand between his thighs, holding it there, and Danny was tempted to whimper until Lysander took pity on him. "That's not the point," he murmured. "But if you're insisting on playing this morning, you're going to do exactly what you're told."

Before Danny could agree or say anything, Lysander pulled Danny's hand against his shorts.

"First," he said as he met Danny's eyes and flashed his small, wicked smile. "You're going to put down your cup of coffee, and then, we're both going to be late."

Danny grinned so widely his cheeks ached. "Yes, sir, Mr. O'Donohue, sir."

All things considered, he thought as he caught Lysander in a kiss, moving back to the north wasn't such a bad thing after all.

Acknowledgements

To the usual suspects, you have dealt with me flailing so beautifully over this one. Beth especially, kudos to you for calmly responding to the e-mails of "OH NO I MADE A TEMPORAL ANOMALY!" and making sure I didn't throw my laptop out the window every single time. Karrie and Marvin, thank you guys for listening to me babble over tea and shortbread. And Elizabetta—thank you for picking up the tangled ball of threads that is my timeline and making it make sense for people who haven't been living with it in their head for five years.

About the Author

C.B. Lewis is small, Scottish, and writes pretty much anywhere, any time. She loves to travel and tends to bring home at least four new plot bunnies from every trip she goes on. She's very excited to continue the adventures of the Out of Time series.

Facebook: www.facebook.com/CB-Lewis-3692937599939573

Goodreads: www.goodreads.com/user/show/41277437-cblewis

Tumblr: www.tumblr.com/blog/cb-lewis

Website: www.cblewis.co.uk

Other books by this author

Time Taken (Out of Time, Book Three)

Coming Soon from C.B Lewis

Out of Time

Out of Time, Book Five

Excerpt

The house was unnaturally quiet.

It looked the same as usual: portraits of a family—mother and baby, father and toddler—on the walls, a scatter of Lego and jigsaw puzzles on the floor, a forgotten coat slung over the bannister at the top of the stairs.

The man walked onwards towards the staircase.

It was too quiet.

All he had to do was call out and break the silence, but he couldn't.

Run and hide.

That was what his dad had told him. He had done what he was told.

The front door was cracked open, a thin slice of pale morning light cutting across the patterned tiles on the hall floor. It stretched on towards the lab, which was impossible. The sun was too high for it to stretch so far.

Something wasn't right.

The stairs creaked underfoot as he made his way down. The tiles in the hall were cold. His clothes were soaked. He didn't remember why. They were wet and he was cold and it was all too quiet.

He saw—did he?—the body. A sheet. A shoe on a foot from under it. He saw it. A glimpse. He walked closer, and the sheet was still there. He reached down and grabbed the sheet to see the face of the one who did it.

There was nothing there. No one. The sheet fell from his numb fingers, vanishing before it hit the floor, and he walked onwards.

The door was open, no longer secret. They had cleaned the bloodstains, but he'd heard them talking quietly when they thought he couldn't hear, and the handprints were back, smeared on the wall. Whose? He didn't know.

Light shone up from the basement. The walls were white where they weren't red. It wasn't silent down there. The electric crackle of power hummed around him as he made his way down. It should all have been bigger. When he was there the first time, it all seemed so much bigger. He remembered the crackle, too, and knew what it meant.

Their secret, something no one had ever known.

He crossed the floor of the laboratory, ignoring the computers and the information all over them. The sound was coming from the next room, and he knew what he was going to see.

The temporal gate connected, blazing with light. The man standing before it, barely more than a silhouette.

"We're running out of time."

The voice was familiar, but it was wrong too, not the voice he remembered. Too many years without. Too many years of his memories being worn away. He couldn't remember it now, not exactly, not the intonation, not the lilt or the accent.

He tried to speak, but his throat was closing up. He reached out towards his father, trying to catch him before he did what he always did. His fingers passed through his father's shoulder as if it was nothing more than a shadow; then his father stepped through the gate. The world turned to blazing white around him, dazzling.

"No!" He ran towards the gate only to collide with solid wall. Wall on all sides. Enclosed. Trapped. He was somewhere safe. Safe and closed and dark and alone until Dad came back for him. The door was sealed and there was no way out, and in the dark he screamed—

Ben Sanders jolted, sitting bolt upright, panting. Iron bands squeezed down around his chest. He turned frantically towards the glowing nightlight on the stool beside his bed. Staring at it, he counted down from thirty until his heartbeat evened out, and he could breathe again. He always kept the lighting low throughout the studio in case the nightlight failed. A shaft of white cracked through the ajar bathroom door. Not dark. Never dark.

His sheets clung to him, soaked with sweat. He pushed them aside and got out of the bed on unsteady legs. It took more effort than he liked to make it to the bathroom. He sank to the floor to sit by the toilet. The porcelain was cold as he propped his elbow on the seat, his fingers sinking into his sweat-matted hair.

Every night, it was getting worse. He knew why. How could he not? With every day that went by, he took another step closer to the day that would ruin his life. Time, time, time. That was what it came down to.

His stomach clenched, and he vomited, acid burning in his throat.

Any day now.

He got up and filled a glass of water at the sink. His reflection seemed more like someone half-dead, pale, with deep shadows beneath his eyes. He needed to rest, but not now. Not with his heart still pounding and the faint echo of his father's voice lingering in his ears.

There was still so much to do.

"AND THIS IS all I will say of the abomination." Enoch pressed one hand to his chest and bowed his head. "Farewell, and God be with ye."

There were several seconds of silence.

"Cut!"

Enoch raised his head, grinning. "It were all right, then?"

"Was," Mack Robertson corrected for the fifteenth time in as many days. He glanced up from his folio, returning Enoch's grin. "And yeah. Brilliant. I've never heard anyone get so angry with a spork before."

Enoch snorted. "Neither fork, nor spoon, and twice as useless." He scrambled off his couch and hurried over to Mack's side. "They liked it?"

Janos Nagy returned from the sink and handed Enoch a cup of water. "They *always* like it." He was some thirty years older than both Mack and Enoch, but he took as much pleasure in the streams as either of them.

"Not all of them." Enoch sat on the arm of Mack's chair, trying to read some of the comments.

"I'll get them all in a file for you," Mack said, looking up. "The live ones as well."

Enoch squeezed his shoulder gratefully. Though he'd been given the best tutors money could hire, he still did poorly with his letters. They became worse when there were a lot of them moving too fast for him to keep up.

Only a few years earlier, he had scarce been able to read at all. He'd had some schooling as a child, but his letters were so poor they thought him thickheaded. He cared naught when he worked the land, but then his life had been turned about when he'd walked through a shining gateway into another time.

Once, he had been a man of the 1750s, working hard to earn a scrap and doing what he had to. Now, thanks to the gateway, he had a grand home in one of the towering buildings of the Temporal Research Institute, dyslexia to confuse his letters, and something called a livestream where thousands of people about the world would listen to what he had to say about strange things from modern life.

"I would that they would let me go back to do another stream from those..." He knocked his knuckles on the back of the chair, trying to recall the word. "The soup-markets?"

"Supermarket," Janos said, sitting down on the empty couch. He was a solemn man, but now his mouth twitched. "You know why they say no."

Enoch frowned at him, shaking his head. "The chicken was monstrous! Did you not see the size on it? I swear I might fit my whole head up its arse!"

"Oh, we know." Mack's eyes were dancing. "Everyone in a three-mile radius heard you yelling about it." He closed down the screens. "Anyway, we can't go back. We're banned. Officially."

"Banned?" Enoch looked between the two men.

"Banished," Mack said gravely. "Forbidden."

"For the chicken?"

Janos leaned forward, propping his forearms on his knees. One arm was false, the other real, but both seemed to work as well as the other. "They say your fans have been causing trouble." His smile was there for true now. "Some of them have been putting chickens on their heads."

Enoch was both flattered and confused. "Why?"

Mack sniggered. "Because you said it. People listen."

It still puzzled Enoch. It was true he was the first man from history to walk in modern times, and people thought him a strange marvel. It was strange to be in a world where people wanted to know his thoughts. They listened to him, and on their account, he was well paid and admired.

Sometimes, scholars came to speak to him, but they wanted to know about dull things, like crops and farming traditions. Waving a ten-pound chicken over his head and crying rage about it in a vast shop was much more fun.

It amazed him that people would pay money for him to talk and so much money at that. Now, he had more than fifty thousand a year, only for talking. No labour, no harvest, no hunting. For only his words, he was worth as much as his former Master.

"About a chicken's arse?"

Janos grinned and Mack laughed. "People like stupid shit." Mack twisted his chair and elbowed Enoch on the hip. "They're calling it 'Noching' when they go and find something you've done and copy it for a video."

Sometimes, Mack made it easy to play the fool with him. "This one," Enoch said, keeping his face solemn as the grave, "should be called Noch's Cocks."

To his delight, Janos snorted aloud.

Enoch stared at Mack instead, wide-eyed and puzzled. "Is something amiss?"

Mack's face twisted up. He wanted to laugh, but Enoch knew Mack was never certain when Enoch was speaking in jest or seriousness. "I...I'm not sure it would be a good idea," he finally said, his voice tight.

Jesu, it was too easy. "Why not?" Enoch widened his eyes. "The words sound akin to one another, and a cock is only a male chicken."

Janos had his fist pressed to his mouth, muffled laughter shaking him. He scarce seemed to notice Mack glowering at him.

"Noooo," Mack eventually said when it was clear Janos would be no help to him. "No. It—there's another meaning..."

Enoch fought a grin. "Aye, and they would not be putting the chickens on their head, I think."

"Ha!" Janos exclaimed, clapping his hands together. "Again! Dieter owes me another twenty."

"Owes..." Mack narrowed his dark eyes down to slits. "Shit, Enoch! Not again! I thought—" He groaned, dropping his head back against the couch. "One of these days, you're not going to catch me out."

"Shame on you," Enoch sighed. "I know cocks well, upon my head or otherwise." Janos made a choked sound. He was a hard man to amuse, some said, but Enoch had never found it so. Enoch pantomimed putting a chicken against the front of his trews. "The security people would like it even less, I think."

Both men burst out laughing, and Mack elbowed him in the thigh. "You're a dick."

"Cock," Enoch corrected, grinning. "Best we dunt give them the idea, eh?"

"I'll say! The chicken-hats are causing enough problems."

Janos raised a finger. "Ah, but he was a farmhand. There are many stories of things lonely farmhands do..."

Enoch had to fight a laugh. So many of the people in the TRI went carefully about him, as if he might break apart if they jested about him. Janos was never like that. He had teased Enoch since the first months after he came through the gate. "I was but a virtuous labourer. I never saw a chicken, and no man can say otherwise."

Mack rubbed at his brow with his knuckles. "Well, this conversation has taken a weird turn."

"You began it," Enoch said cheerfully.

"No!" Mack waved a finger at him. "I'm not taking the blame for you bringing up cocks!"

Enoch pressed his hand to his chest. "I have few enough skills, but bringing up cocks is one of them."

Janos, it seemed, took his meaning where Mack did not. "No one from the world outside would believe the garbage you speak," he said as he rose from the couch. "All this show of chaste little farmhand bullshit..."

Enoch smiled up at him. Janos was a man who favoured men and was married to one. Enoch had never told Janos of his own tastes, but sometimes, when a man was himself before friends, like called out to like. "Best no one tells them, then."

"One day," Mack said, "you're going to say something in the streams, and everyone's going to know what a gutter-minded troll you are."

Also Available from NineStar Press

Connect with NineStar Press

Website: NineStarPress.com

Facebook: NineStarPress

Facebook Reader Group: NineStarNiche

Twitter: @ninestarpress

Tumblr: NineStarPress